UTOPIA PROJECT

THE FRAYED THREADS OF HOPE

BILLY DERING

Printed in the United States of America

First Printing, 2022

Trade Paperback ISBN: 978-1-7354929-3-3
Electronic Book ISBN: 978-1-7354929-2-6

Published by: Pinewald Press, Toms River, New Jersey

Website URL: www.utopiaproject.com
E-Mail: billydering@aol.com

Book cover design: Hampton Lamoureux
Interior book formatting: David Provolo
Editing: Beth Dorward

This book is dedicated to my mother Anne, my brother Chuck, Aunt Ginger (my godmother), Aunt Michelle, Aunt Gail and all of those who passed on too soon. You are all in my thoughts, and have inspired me in your own ways. I love you all.

I want to thank my family, and my wife's family, for all of the love and support throughout my journey in writing this next book in the trilogy, especially my wife Darlene, my father Charles, my children, brother, nieces, nephews, cousins and in-laws. I also want to thank the Manahawkin, NJ Book Club (Eileen, Felicia, Sharon, Christina, Kari & Kathleen), Professor Rosemary Hardie, Jack Germain and many of my co-workers past and present. As I have said before, there are so many more people I should thank individually for their support and assistance, but for fear that I might inadvertently miss someone, I will say thank you to all of you. You know who you are and I will be sure to thank you all personally. I am forever grateful.

Finally, I would be remiss if I didn't also give a big shout out to my extraordinary Utopia Project series team of Hampton Lamoureux (cover), David Provolo (interior formatting), Beth Dorward (editing), Frank Bianchetti (website) and Design 446 (social media). You all do a spectacular job, and have elevated this book beyond what I could have ever expected!

PROLOGUE 1

December 24, 2044
Saturday, Late Afternoon
Near Rutland, Vermont
Two days before the cataclysmic event that would change the world

Evelyn Hyland opened her trembling fingers and stared at the tiny pill. *It would appear I am holding you in the palm of my hand, but it is really the other way around.*

She raised her eyes and peered out the kitchen window of her Vermont home. The postcard scene of snow-covered fields and the Green Mountains beyond always calmed her nerves. Closer by stood her favorite covered bridge. The painted sides were worn to a dull and faded red, but she found the structure beautiful and inspiring. It was a beacon that continued to weather the winters year after year, maybe not unlike herself in many ways. But despite the hardships that came with winter in Vermont, she never regretted retiring in eastern Pittsford, just outside of Rutland.

As she put the pill in her mouth the phone rang.

Her husband, retired United States Army General Chris Hyland, asked, "Who is it?" He ran his hands through his thin, sweaty gray hair as he sat on the couch after his daily jog on the treadmill.

Holding the phone a few inches in front of her face and checking the caller ID, Evelyn's squint eased into a smile. "It's our son." Pushing the pill into her cheek with her tongue and pressing the *Talk* button, she said, "Hello Eric. Where are you?"

"Hi Mom. I'm at a coffee shop near the base. Did Sara leave yet for New Jersey?" General Eric Hyland asked.

"Yes, she left a few hours ago. We are always so sad when she leaves. She is so precious. Hold on a quick second, please." She took a sip of water and swallowed. Again lifting the phone, she continued, "Sorry. I had to take my Levonesex."

"Take your time, I know you need that medication."

"Well, every day my life depends on it so I don't have much choice. And I'm running low. I only have enough to last a week and a half, but the refill order should be here soon."

"You only have enough for a week and a half?" He sounded concerned. "I can call and find out if it was shipped on time. There's still just the one place in New Jersey that manufactures it?"

"Only that one Merck plant as far as I know, but don't worry, hon. The delivery service already notified us that with the snowstorm, it will be delivered Tuesday or Wednesday at the latest," she answered.

He muttered, "That's a problem."

"I will be fine," she assured him. In truth Evelyn was a little worried. The winter had turned harsh and the delivery service was backed up, but there was no need for her son to worry about it too. For a moment there was silence on the phone. Her voice must have revealed her concern. "Eric?" she said.

"Yeah, sorry, Mom."

"You usually call Christmas day, and that isn't until tomorrow. Is something wrong?" She grew serious.

"No, everything is fine. I called today because I won't be able to reach out tomorrow. Some…matters I have to tend to at the base."

Evelyn had to remind herself her son was now 'General' Hyland, having attained the same rank as his father. She understood an Army General's schedule demands, having been married to one for many years. Over the years her husband's schedule had wreaked havoc more than once on their holiday plans. But her son had never missed calling them on Christmas day.

He continued, "I will be home for a time the day after Christmas, so I will reach out to you *Monday night*. I assume you will be there…

Monday night?" He enunciated his final two words.

"Of course we will be here. Where else would we be? Will Sara be available tomorrow, so we can wish her Merry Christmas?"

"Yes, she will call you. But please, make sure you're there *Monday night* for my call. Alright?"

"I hear you, hon. Monday night. I may have just turned 69 years old, but I am not senile yet." Evelyn stood with her hand on her hip.

"Sorry. I just wanted to make sure you remember. I love you guys, and I'll talk to you then. Tell Dad I was asking for him and I have a message for him—just like when we went to Uncle Nick's barbeques, *same old shit*."

"Eric! Don't ask me to pass on expletives to your father," she admonished as she crossed her arm over her kitchen apron, which was spotted with bright colored fruits. "Should I just give him the phone?"

"No!" he snapped and then paused. His tone was relaxed as he continued. "I would love to talk to Dad but I have to go. It's important you pass on what I said—just like when we went to Uncle Nick's barbeques, same old…"

"Stuff?" Evelyn suggested.

After a pause, Eric said, "Stuff, that's fine. Make sure you tell him."

"I will. We love you too and we'll talk to you Monday night." She hung up the phone and sat at the table, lost in thought.

"What's Eric up to?" Chris asked as he picked up the newspaper from the end table.

"Not too much, but he sure didn't seem like himself. He has to work Christmas day, so he was quite insistent we be here Monday night to take his call, and he said it over and over. I usually have to beg him to call us even once a week, and now he wants to talk to us twice in three days?"

"Interesting. What's so special about Monday night?" Chris folded his newspaper over and stared at the front page. Evelyn followed his eyes and read the headline. 'Utopia Project - More Secrets Revealed!'

"I'm not sure. He also told me I had to give you an important message, although I don't see why he was so adamant about it. Just a standard pleasantry really."

Chris's interest seemed to be piqued. "What message?"

"He said 'same old…stuff.' I told him I was not about to pass on any curses. That's not like him."

Laying the newspaper on his lap, Chris seemed perplexed. "Huh," he mumbled. "Strange."

"I know. Actually, I'm sorry, the whole message was, 'just like when we went to Uncle Nick's barbeques, same old…stuff.'"

Getting up from his recliner, Chris did not even notice the newspaper as it fell from his lap to the floor.

"Chris! What's wrong? Are you in medical distress?" Evelyn rose from her chair. She prayed he was not having a heart attack.

"No, no, I'm fine." He waved his hand.

She sighed, thankful her husband was not having the big one. Then again, she would have been quite surprised. Although he was only a year younger than her at 68 years old, Chris was in better physical shape than most 50-year-olds. But why did her husband react the way he did?

Chris said with certainty, "We need to be here Monday night, and we need to prepare ourselves. Something is wrong."

She noticed that despite him being retired for more than five years, her husband's armed forces training and instincts had come back to him in an instant. She just didn't know what was so alarming.

"How do you get that from 'same old stuff'? Sounds quite the opposite, like he's saying it's business as usual."

"No. Anything but, especially with him mentioning Uncle Nick's barbeques out of the blue. He's trying to warn us but can't say anything outright, because the call was probably being monitored. That's why he said it to you and not me. He knew I would have reacted."

Seeing the confused look on his wife's face, Chris clarified. "You know your brother Nick liked to tell tall tales at his parties, and me and Eric were always ready to pull our hair out, so we had our own communication methodology. It kept us amused and allowed us to make comments without saying them outright and insulting anyone. We even practiced this at home a couple of times while we were eating dinner. You never caught on."

"Well, I am still not catching on." She was mildly agitated.

Breaking his laser-beam focus, Chris clarified. "Sorry honey. We communicated by using simple acronyms, which is what I think Eric is doing with those three words."

Evelyn pondered for a second and rocked herself back and forth on the balls of her feet, trying to figure out what he meant. "Acronym? Oh yes. Same old stuff. S, O, and…"

"Oh my word." She stopped rocking.

"S.O.S."

PROLOGUE 2

January 3, 2045
Tuesday, Late evening
New Jersey
Eight days after the event

Kid Carlson drove his red, extended-cab pickup truck through several inches of virgin snow on New Jersey's Garden State Parkway. It struck him that before the destruction the parkway was one of those roads that never slept. Yet here he was, the only vehicle actually moving. The stillness was heavy as it dared him to proceed. All the houses, buildings, and street lights along the way were pitch black. He had never driven on the parkway in total darkness and it was unnerving. But he had to press on.

It was just a few short hours ago that Heidi Leer and Maria Stefano had radioed General Hyland, who was on one of the Utopia Project ships. The general had instructed them to get his mother's life-saving medication from the only place in the world that manufactured it—the Merck Pharmaceutical facility in Rahway, New Jersey. After securing as much Levonesex 212 as they could find, it needed to be rushed to Vermont right away. Kid had left without hesitation. He needed to save Evelyn Hyland before it was too late. It was tragic enough the general had lost his only daughter Sara, but to lose his mother as well? Kid could not let that happen.

Although Kid was prepared to make the trek north alone, most of the group from New Jersey went with him, including Heidi and Maria, but also his best friend Jess Kellen. They also brought along Utopia Project member 801, who was their captive. The only one to stay behind at the marina was Drex, the former attorney turned fisherman.

Kid thought about who *else* wasn't there. While driving a steady 40-miles-per-hour through the snow, tears started rolling down his cheeks. He was still in the throes of grieving for his soulmate Sara, who had perished just three days ago. The all-too-familiar ache was again on a rampage, hollowing out his insides, turning his organs to mush. It was like the ache he felt the last time he saw Sara's father, General Hyland, times one thousand. No, times one million.

The night of the cataclysmic event, after he and Sara had dinner with General Hyland, Kid had felt uneasy. He could not pinpoint any particular reason why, but he just had a bad feeling after leaving the Hyland house. Only now did he realize General Hyland must have already had a plan that last night, and did a good job of hiding it. There was no single word or action Kid could point to that made him uncomfortable, but the accretion of many tiny cues formed a ball that ached somewhere inside of him; a pain he would take in a heartbeat in exchange for what he felt now.

Kid shook his head. He could only imagine how much the general knew, and how much was already in motion, the night of the destruction. Just moments ago, Drex had said in reference to General Hyland, "I hope to one day ask him how he pulled off what he did. How did he do it? And what was his plan after the smoke cleared?" Kid wondered the same and could not have phrased the questions any more concisely.

"Look out!" Jess yelled.

Snapping out of his reverie, Kid jammed the brakes and cut the wheel, but as soon as his eyes took in the scene directly in front of him, he knew it was too late.

I: LIQUIDATION

CHAPTER 1

December 26, 2044
Monday, 6:00 PM (Eastern Standard Time)
Joint Base McGuire-Dix-Lakehurst
(Fort Dix Army Base), New Jersey
The evening of the cataclysmic event that would change the world

At the Hyland house, Christmas came a day late. But that did not stop General Eric Hyland from making a dinner to celebrate the holiday. With the food now on the table, he put his burgundy cloth napkin on his lap and picked up his silverware. He would force himself to eat and make everything appear normal, but it would not be easy. His stomach was already performing circus-like backflips at the thought of what was to come that evening.

His daughter's boyfriend was staring over at a fourth place setting in front of an empty chair.

Amanda's chair.

"Were we expecting someone else?" 21-year-old Kid Carlson asked as he patted down the back of his longer brown hair.

Sara Hyland came up the hallway and returned to the table as her father answered, "No, that space is for Sara's mother. It makes us feel like she is with us during the holidays."

"Oh, I'm sorry…" Kid started.

"Don't be sorry," Sara quickly interjected as she put her hand on his. "It doesn't make us sad. It actually makes us feel a lot better. It's like we're honoring Mom."

The general nodded his head and turned toward his daughter, who put her mobile device on the table. He pointed to it and asked, "Is everything alright?"

"Yeah, that was Karen Stone, calling to ask for advice in dealing with that crazy guy Scott Sherman she had been dating." Sara pursed her lips, which were naturally red and stood out against her lighter color skin. "She broke up with him and now he won't stop stalking her. She's going to tell him tonight to cease and desist. If he doesn't, I told her she needs to file a formal restraining order."

"I'm sure she appreciates your advice, and probably needs it. Karen looks up to you, like the big sister she never had."

The general glanced around the room. Although darkness had fallen, he could see white snow clinging to the branches of a pitch pine outside the window. It seemed to him the slightest bump or breeze would send an avalanche of snow crashing to the ground. The only sounds in the room were the crackling of wood burning in the fireplace and the ticking of the second hand from a clock on the wall.

"Oh, Dad, remember to call Gram tonight. When I called her yesterday, she said they were expecting you to call them *Monday* night."

"I will, after you guys leave." He was relieved his parents remembered. "You are still going to the Casino Pier tonight, right?" he continued as he picked at his turkey dinner without raising his fork to his mouth.

"Yes. But don't worry about us being outside. We're bringing blankets and firewood."

"Always be prepared." He knew his words were an egregious understatement.

He tried not to show it, but the general was relieved beyond measure nothing had changed with her schedule. Before Sara told him a few days ago that she was going to spend the night under the Casino Pier, he had developed multiple ruses to get her over to the coast. Since she was already heading there, he would not have to put any of them in motion. All he had to do was ensure she stayed there until at least 11:00 p.m. Excusing himself from the table, the general stepped into his bedroom to do just that.

As soon as his door was closed, he called the base and ordered military checkpoints be immediately set up at the Tunney-Mathis Bridge to Seaside Heights and on Route 35 heading north in Ortley Beach. Both exit routes from the peninsula would then be covered. Knowing Sara would be at her boyfriend's side all night, the guards were ordered to inform him when Kid Carlson passed through the checkpoint. Especially with a storm forecast for later that evening, if Kid tried to return to the mainland before 11:00 p.m., he and all his friends were to be detained, including Sara. The general lied and said Kid was wanted, and he wanted him trapped on Seaside Peninsula until special reinforcements arrived. With his rank and the urgency in his command, he knew the soldiers would be mobilizing to set up the checkpoints before he even hung up the phone.

The general returned to the table. "I assume you will be out there until around midnight?"

Sara and Kid looked at each other, and since both of their mouths were full, she held up a finger and brought her napkin to her lips. After swallowing, she tucked her wavy, long dark hair behind one of her ears and responded, "Probably."

The general noticed Kid was chewing his turkey slower and cringing, until the general said, "Good."

"Good?" Sara sounded surprised by his reaction.

"Yes. Hold on." The general stood.

He opened a drawer in the China Cabinet and pulled out a jewelry box covered with red rose wrapping paper. He placed it on the table next to her. "This is something special I want you to have. But you can't open it until *exactly* 11:03 p.m. and you have to open it at the beach."

"What is it, Dad?"

Sitting back down across from her, he said, "It's a surprise. All

I will tell you is it was your mother's. It is special and I want you to have it." He was leading his daughter on by invoking the spirit of her deceased mother and knew she would honor his wishes without question.

Staring at the wrapping paper, Sara touched it with her fingertip while saying quietly, "Red roses. Mom's favorite." Her finger stopped moving. "Why do I have to wait until *exactly* 11:03 to open it?"

"It was at that exact moment on December 26 that I proposed to your mother while we sat facing the Atlantic Ocean. It was a running joke between us because I started to propose at 11:00 and babbled for three minutes before finally asking the question. That was in Georgia, but at the same ocean you will be visiting tonight." Another lie.

He wished he could just tell Sara of the cataclysmic event planned for that evening and tell her where to go and what to do, but he could not. With a modern tracking device implanted in the back of his neck, he knew he was under constant surveillance. His words and optical signals were being monitored. Some recent incidences proved how closely the elders were being watched. In the past week alone, three elders had tried to defect from the Utopia Project before the ultimate destruction, and the repercussions were immediate. The tracking device in their necks had been detonated and their brains were blown.

The first defector was the second highest-ranking Russian military operative. The second deserter was an American colonel. The third defector was the most devastating to General Hyland and possibly to the world. The general's long-time friend and fellow elder, American General Van Pelt was found face down in a ravine in Texas. Lying next to him were his wife and his two children, all with bullets in the head. It seems General Van Pelt committed a murder-suicide just before his brain was blasted. What made the loss of General Van Pelt particularly tragic was he was supposed to be General Hyland's partner in a plan to stop the destruction entirely, as one person could not do it alone. Now, General Hyland was just that, alone.

His thoughts turned to the only successful defection he was aware of, but at the time it wasn't really a defection. The project's lead psychologist, Dr. Adele Carmelo, had left before the release of the confidential memo that exposed the top-secret Utopia Project, before the increased security, and before the insertion of a lethal tracking device. He could never imagine her leaking the confidential memo, but the elders had immediately concluded she was guilty. They were relentlessly hunting her, but her head start had allowed her to defy the odds and avoid capture thus far.

"I'll be right back. Let me get the dessert ready." The general said and made for the kitchen.

General Hyland's phone rang while he was cutting the pie on the counter. It was the guard at the Fort Dix gatehouse seeking approval for visitors. It was a group of young adults in a vehicle driven by Brian Mitchell. The general gave his instructions. "Hold them for 15 minutes before letting them through please. We still have to eat dessert here." Catching himself, he said, "Sorry, Tom. I shouldn't mention food when your dinner break isn't for hours yet."

"That's alright, Sir. Enjoy. I will hold them here," Tom Murphy answered. "Sir, do you want to provide advance approval for re-entry later when they return?"

The general paused. He needed to keep his words from conveying the heaviness in his heart. "No…that won't be necessary tonight. Thanks," he said in a low, solemn voice and hung up the phone.

Heading toward the dining room with the pie in hand, the smell of apple wafted in the air. Usually that would have made the general's mouth water, but given the circumstances, even that made him a bit queasy. He stopped at the threshold and tuned into what would probably be the last night of normal conversation for a long, long time, if ever.

He heard Kid ask Sara, "Now that you've had some classes, do you think you're cut out to be a professional actress?"

His daughter was doing very well with her acting classes in college, but tonight it was the general who needed a strong performance. He could have used some pointers since his heartbeat was elevated throughout the entire dinner and he kept wiping away beads of sweat before they ran down his face.

"How do you know I'm not acting right now?" his daughter answered. "Maybe I'm just playing the part of Kid's girlfriend."

The general couldn't help but smile. His daughter could be such a smart-ass, but she always got away with it. And Kid was usually pretty sharp on the retort.

"I'd say you were hard up for good parts, if this was the only gig you could find," Kid said and they both chuckled.

A labored squeak and grind signaled someone was backing up their chair on the hardwood dining room floor. He heard his daughter say, "As far as I'm concerned, this is the best gig around."

Hearing a smooching sound, and with the clock ticking, the general figured it was time to bust up the party.

"At least on this block," his daughter added and started laughing.

As the general walked into the room with dessert, Sara was standing over her boyfriend hugging him. With Kid's face buried in her shoulder, he said, "Your dad is right. You are a military brat! Even if you only moved once."

"A brat for sure," the general agreed as he put the pie on the table.

Kid quickly removed his hands and sat upright. He looked embarrassed and worried. The general just smiled and tried to put him at ease.

Sara was quick to separate, but did not seem concerned about the general catching them in a playful moment. She kissed Kid on the head, tousled his hair and went back to her seat.

Digging into the Dutch Apple Pie, Sara and Kid were soon working on seconds.

The chirp of a horn outside the house made all three stop and turn toward the front door.

"There's your ride," the general said.

Kid checked his watch. "Of all nights, Brian picks the night we're eating together to show up on time."

Sara stood. "Come on Kid, let's clean up real quick before we go."

"Just leave it. I'll get it," the general insisted. "And Sara?"

"Dad?"

Getting to his feet, he looked his daughter in the eye. "Stay alert. A storm is coming in later tonight." Peering down at the table top, he added under his breath, "One hell of a storm."

"We know. Don't worry. Brian has four-wheel drive…most of the time anyway." She slipped on her winter coat.

Her father walked around the table and kissed and hugged her in an unusual display of affection.

She reciprocated with a hug and zipped up her coat.

Sara was trying to wrap a black scarf around her neck, but it got snagged on her necklace. Taking off her American Indian arrowhead shaped locket, she remarked, "I hate taking this off because it is from you Kid, but it always gets caught in my scarf." She opened the gold locket, kissed her finger, and touched the picture of Kid inside. After closing it, she said, "Let me drop this on my dresser and I'm ready to go."

Coming back up the hall from her room, she said, "And Dad, before you even ask—I have the gift box to open at 11:03 p.m., and yes, I will make sure my phone is on at all times." She kissed his cheek as she passed. "Love you."

"Perfect. Love you too." He turned to watch her go.

Kid followed her out and bumped into her as she stopped on the top step. She exhaled and a heavy fog rolled from her lips. She pulled back her hair and put on a hunter-green and black checkered knit hat. Shaking her head, she let her brunette hair flow down the front of her coat. Putting on her thick black winter gloves, she walked down the steps.

Kid turned and waved to the general. "See you later."

"Bye now," he responded and then leaned out the doorway. "And Kid…"

"Yes?" he asked as he turned back.

"Promise me you'll take care of my little girl."

Sara had just reached the sidewalk and called out, "19, and still his little girl!"

Kid made eye contact with the general and said confidently, "I will. I promise."

The general met his gaze, gave a quick head nod, and closed the door to the world, but not fast enough. Like a snap of lightning, he knew he had let his guard down for just that split second of eye contact. His utter despair had shone in his eyes. He had been worried sick and was so concerned with Sara picking up on his apprehension that when she had turned to walk away, his defenses dropped for just a second.

Kid was there to catch it.

CHAPTER 2

December 26, 2044
Monday, 7:00 PM
Joint Base McGuire-Dix-Lakehurst
(Fort Dix Army Base), New Jersey
The evening of the event

General Hyland shook his head, and cursed himself. *What did I reveal? How much did I reveal?*

Cracking the front door open a hair, he watched as Kid hesitated at the top of the steps. *Let it go. Shake it off,* he urged, but his daughter's boyfriend seemed lost in thought. Kid's six-foot frame was unmoving as he stared at the thigh-high snow along the shoveled walkway. *Let it go…*

Kid's trance was broken as a snowball hit him in the chest, while Sara laughed and ran away.

The general exhaled with relief and closed the door as Kid joined the group and the vehicle pulled away. His exhale morphed into a sigh as he dragged his feet to the other side of the room.

Now alone, the general put his laptop computer bag down on the dining room table. The sophisticated tracking device in his neck could pick up sights and sounds, so he had to ensure he was working blind. That way, any monitors would also be blind. Without looking down, and just using his sense of touch, he ensured the walkie-talkie and extra batteries were in the side compartment. With everything in order, he dropped into his chair at the head of the table. He again tormented over how things could have been altered if he had known the Board of Elder's grand plan a little sooner. The 11-member governing board had maintained absolute secrecy with most of the other elders, including him, regarding their cataclysmic plan until it was too late to turn back. He wanted to stop the destruction planned for tonight. He wished he could blow the whistle, but given the explosive device in his neck, the only thing blown would be his brain. The wave had crested and his choices were simple: ride it out and live to fight another day, or try to stand now and die in vain.

While deep in thought, his eyes followed the wall and stopped at a large, dark frame. The dancing flames from the fireplace reflected soft light against Sara's fourth grade school picture. Her brown hair was in two ponytails and she was laughing as she sat against a smoky gray background. That particular picture showed more than her physical appearance. It captured her essence. It always amazed him that without ever knowing her, Sara so closely emulated her mother's personality and free spirit.

With all the effort he could muster, he stood and took slow steps toward the wall. He kissed his fingertips and gently placed them against Sara's cheek in the picture. Being careful to not even whisper the words, he made a promise in his mind. *Don't worry, sweetheart. I'm working on a plan. I'm not going to lose you.*

He pulled out the decorative cross hanging around his neck and let it dangle over the front of his shirt. The cross was his wife's, and he had worn it every day since she died. He walked past a mirror and a glint of light made him stop and turn. What caught his attention was not only the holy pendant, but the ghostly form it hung from. His brown hair had several streaks of gray, visible even with his military buzz cut. A few weeks ago he had noticed the same thing, but at the time, there was only one prominent gray swirl through his otherwise dark hair. With his fiftieth birthday around the corner, he thought he was a step ahead in terms of the telltale signs of age. But in the past few weeks the gray had gained momentum, spreading like poison ivy on his head.

Moving his face closer to the mirror, he noticed the firm lines that had been etched deeper into his face over time. No wonder people thought he was mean. His brown eyes seemed a bit sunken, but he didn't know if that was an illusion caused by the darkness of his eye sockets from being sleep deprived. Standing upright, he could only see from the waist up, but his six-foot frame seemed emaciated. He was usually the perfect weight for his height and had a fairly muscular build, but he had clearly lost some pounds from the tension and stomach unease over the past week. Then again, he didn't know if he could fully trust the reflection. Sara called it a trick mirror because she said it always made her look thinner. He didn't know about that. The image staring back at him, of a man worn from stress and age, seemed spot on. It certainly reflected how he felt.

In the hallway, the general stopped in front of the picture of his wife, Amanda's, tombstone. Behind the frame was the hidden pocket in the wall where he kept his diary, as well as an old-fashioned, oversized skeleton key he knew would one day be used. He wanted to reach into the pocket and read his final diary entry, but he could not. The prior evening, despite sitting with the lights off, he had put a blindfold over his eyes to ensure the tracking device was also completely in the dark. He had written the final entry without the benefit of eyesight, and was sure it was sloppy, but he wrote every word deliberately and carefully. Using his hands and just his sense of touch, he had placed the book back in the wall. That difficult final entry was predicated on Sara's plan to be in Seaside Heights tonight. That had not changed, so there was no reason to touch the diary and take any unnecessary risks. Instead, he just recounted the key points of his final entry in his head.

First, he had to ensure Sara stayed in Seaside until at least 11:00 p.m., and then after the destruction she needed to immediately get his diary. He had covered both of those angles with his gift box ruse. He felt bad about the deceit, telling her she had to open a special gift at exactly 11:03 p.m. at the beach, and leading her to believe there was something sentimental about the time and place. But he chose that time so that immediately after the destruction, a watch with an alarm set for 11:03 p.m. would make her open the box. When she did, she would find the note, which he had also written with a blindfold on. The little strip of paper directed her to his diary and to the instructions therein. He had carefully crafted the wording of the note inside the box so if it was discovered or seen prematurely, it would not be decipherable, except by Sara, and possibly Kid. It said simply, 'Sara, I know what has happened, and that you are scared and confused, but do as I say. Go home immediately and you will find the answers behind the rose.'

His final diary entry, which he tagged in the little black book, directed her to take his laptop computer bag with the walkie-talkie and get away from the Seaside Peninsula. She needed to hide until he made contact with her and guided her from there. He would find a way to get into walkie-talkie range one way or another, but she would already be in range right after the attack if the ships went where he expected them to.

The Board of Elders wanted to set up the new base camp on an island, at least initially, for containment purposes. Three on the eastern seaboard of the United States had made the short list. The board members had not made a final decision and wouldn't until they saw the results of the satellite neutron beam attack, but the general had done everything he could to champion using Long Beach Island in New Jersey. Most importantly, he had sold Elder-2, using Long Beach Island's proximity to McGuire Air Force Base as a carrot. Elder-2, a cold and rigid Russian woman, had said several times her dream was to fly back to her home country and urinate on the remains of the Russian president, who she considered a traitor. With the planes and transports stationed at nearby McGuire, Elder-2 would have no problem fulfilling that dream. Most importantly to the general, Long Beach Island was in walkie-talkie range to communicate with his daughter.

He stared at the wall, with the pocket behind the picture, and thought of the diary one last time. It was special to him. The black book was his gift to Amanda before Sara was born, to record all the milestones in their baby's life. His wife never even got the chance to touch it. The general hoped and prayed his daughter would and everything would go according to plan.

A little over an hour after his dinner with Sara and Kid, the general boarded an M3 Jetlift Transport as he had so many times before. Despite having some standard armaments, including missiles and machine guns, the M3 was primarily commissioned as a high-speed transport. The general saw it as the ultimate commuter vehicle. For years he had taken this same transport to and from the ship each day, despite having his own bedroom on Utopia Project Ship Number One. Only in the past 15 months, with Sara going away to college, did he use his bedroom and stay on the ship a few nights a week.

The M3 ascended and from his window, the general watched McGuire Air Force Base get swallowed by the surrounding snow. His stomach felt no pressure from the rapid liftoff. The equalization technology ensured passengers didn't feel like they were moving, whether they were ascending or descending, accelerating or decelerating. He was thankful for that. With his stomach in tight knots all day any pressure would have been unbearable.

As they continued ascending, he was careful to watch the pilot, noting which controls were used to maneuver the aircraft. This was knowledge he thought would be useful at some point in the near future.

The thruster attached to the wing swiveled up from its perpendicular lift-off position and as soon as it became horizontal, it propelled them forward with great force. He knew they were accelerating even though he couldn't feel it. Within mere seconds they would be traveling at Mach 3.5, topping out around 2,700 miles per hour.

The general never had a full appreciation of the M3's speed until the day Sara had to be rushed to the hospital with appendicitis. He was working on the ships off the coast of Greenland and ordered an immediate transport to take him to the hospital back in Georgia. The M3 Transport had him at Sara's side in less time than if he had driven a car from his house.

A voice came over the intercom. "We are wheels up and on our way. It is currently 2000 hours Eastern Standard Time. With a flight time of approximately 45 minutes, our ETA is 2045 hours," the young pilot indicated for the military officers, who were all elders, in the transport plane.

The general felt a sadness wash over him when he realized that after making this trip thousands of times over the past nearly 20 years, this would be his final commute. He spent the next several minutes reflecting on how it all started. He recalled the chaos that led to the birth of the Utopia Project in January of 2025. The press and social media headlines still looked fresh in his memory and would always hit a nerve—the coverage of Anna Delilah's death, the discovery of the Child Conditioning Program or CCP, and the articles and posts that supported and encouraged the Civil Crisis of 2025. He could see and hear the repeated declarations of victory and of justice being done when the CCP was shut down.

He had been involved in the Utopia Project, the covert continuation of the CCP, from nearly the beginning. In the first year the project went from being in a lab in Georgia, to a secure facility on the southern Greenland coast and then finally to the first of the three Utopia Project ships, which was built in record time. His assignment started in the Georgia lab, right as the project was being relocated to Greenland.

Despite the CCP being shut down, he was always disturbed by the press's relentless fixation on finding Anna Delilah's child, known to the world as the CCP's Baby Doe. One reporter in particular would not let it go, and continued to bring it up every year. Nearly 20 years later, *Washington Post* reporter Lily Black was still writing about the CCP's mysterious Baby Doe...

"We are cleared for landing on ship number one," the pilot announced, breaking the general's reflection.

The general returned to a reality that felt like a nightmare he could not wake from.

CHAPTER 3

December 26, 2044
Monday, 8:45 PM
Atlantic Ocean, Utopia Project Ship Number One
A couple of hours before the event

Arriving right on time, the M3 Transport hovered over the Utopia Project ships. All three enormous ships were now speeding through the Labrador Sea in the Northern Atlantic Ocean, and General Hyland knew they were heading toward the east coast of the United States. The ships were outfitted with state-of-the-art iceberg detection equipment and had advanced turning capability. With their rudder and propulsion systems, they could navigate a tight iceberg field without slowing down a single knot. The ships were already more than a couple hundred miles south of Greenland, where they had been moored for many years.

Outside the window of the M3 the general could see ship number one surrounded by the looming dark ocean. With a seamless vertical descent onto the moving target, they landed with a soft touch on the landing pad. As he departed the aircraft, the general hurried inside the ship. Following the usual protocol, he placed his loose items on a conveyer belt to be screened and stepped through the walk-through security scanner.

"Sir? What is in your front pant pocket?"

Putting his hand in his pants, the general pulled out a gum wrapper and handed it to the security guard. The general could only sigh and endure the invasiveness of the search. They had always had a security checkpoint for all elders who were entering or departing the ships, but in the last week, the security checks had become much more thorough. Even something as small as a gum wrapper would be spotted and flagged.

After his mobile device was scanned, imaged, and returned, he made his way to his room. There he changed into his 'Elder-41' uniform, and headed toward his station in the command center. As he walked past a few rooms, he thought the mood on the ship was somber. He could relate. Or was he projecting?

Before entering the cluster of rooms of the Programming Center, he was approached by Elder-1, who indicated, "We are all systems go. What final targeting adjustments do we anticipate?"

"We are reviewing all of today's tide charts and weather patterns, as well as other necessary data. Final margin confirmations and some necessary adjustments will be made to compensate accordingly, using the up-to-the-minute readings," General Hyland answered.

The neutron beams were supposed to only hit land areas. Margins represented areas where land masses met bodies of water, such as oceans. By adjusting the margins based on high tides and lake water levels, pinpoint adjustments could be made to reduce the land areas to be covered, which would save system capacity and allow for more passes with the beams.

The ability to make these margin adjustments also gave the general his only opportunity to save any lives.

"And the wildlife tracts?" Elder-1 asked.

"We have already tightened up the neutron beam coverage areas for most wildlife tracts, but we will continue fine-tuning there."

"We need to reduce neutron beam coverage areas. All of us on the board are concerned, based on the recent simulations, we will not be able to make at least ten full passes with the beams over their designated coverage zones," Elder-1 said with his cold, steady voice. "To get the desired level of disintegration, as you know, we need at least ten passes."

The general had heard it several times. The lead elders were concerned if the breakdown of carcasses was not accelerated, the earth would be left for too long with an overwhelming stench and an increased risk of disease.

"And in the last simulation, the satellites were overheated after only nine passes," Elder-1 finished.

"Our margin adjustments along shorelines and wildlife tracts will reduce the neutron beam coverage footprint, and will place more areas in the infrared scanning zones," the general noted and had to stop himself from saying more.

They simply did not have the system capacity to cover the entire world multiple times with neutron beams, so for areas such as large bodies of water, protected wildlife tracts and even the sky above such areas, human stragglers would be picked up by the satellite infrared scanning technology. Once a human being was identified by his or her blood temperature and body structure, they would be pinpointed and eliminated by a dedicated neutron blast; one so concentrated that only one strike was necessary to melt a body entirely. This way, boaters, campers in protected wildlife tracts, and even airline passengers would not escape death.

The general almost reminded Elder-1 that, although a smaller draw, the beam blasts used in the infrared scanning zones still utilized system resources and contributed to heating up the satellites. But he chose not to mention it. Making that point may have eliminated Elder-1's desire to make any more margin adjustments, which would destroy any hope the general had that he could manipulate the system and save *some* lives.

"Continue your adjustment process, and do so with great haste. Zero hour is still scheduled for 2300 hours, Eastern Standard Time," Elder-1 said and walked away.

The general's growing disgust for Elder-1 made it increasingly difficult to maintain an emotionless expression. Snapping out of it, he thought of Sara. He prayed her night at the beach was going as planned.

He entered the Programming Center, which was comprised of three interconnected rooms full of computers and system equipment. Everyone appeared tense and focused as they sat at their workstations. As planned, the five elders on the general's team were all checking and adjusting margins.

One of his team members picked up the phone. As required by the computer system protocols, each programmer needed secondary authorization from a member of the Board of Elders for every *fourth* margin adjustment.

The general cursed his own efficiency and security-mindedness. Many years ago he had put such security measures in place to ensure no one person alone could drastically alter the system programming without verification and authorization. These protocols were designed to protect against rogue, or even careless, elders making data entries. In the end the general's controls were facilitating the destruction of the world since neither he nor anyone else could single-handedly stop the cataclysmic event. His system tie-down had become the noose he felt tightening around his own neck.

December 26, 2044
Monday, 10:25 PM
Near Rutland, Vermont
Less than an hour before the event

Cabernet Sauvignon splashed from the top of a full glass as middle-aged Alice Stone slapped her hand hard on the kitchen table.

Really Mom? Come on now! Karen Stone thought.

"You are not meeting that boy at this time of night. Do you hear me?" Alice said as she stood and ripped a napkin from the holder. She pushed a lit candle aside and started sopping up the spill with one hand while holding the baby-blue bathrobe wrapped around her thin frame with the other. "Look at the time. And I have to be at work by 7:00 a.m.," she murmured.

"Boy? Scott Sherman is 18 years old and so am I. Mom, I can take care of myself. Give me some credit for being responsible." Karen crossed her arms and sat back. She lifted one leg over the other, hiding the black, purposely tattered skirt she was wearing.

Karen was trying her hardest not to get agitated. She knew her mother worked hard and was stressed, but she could not see why, at 18 years of age, she still needed permission to go out. She had heard it a hundred times. 'My house, my rules.' Her mother would not understand, but Karen had to go out and deal with Scott Sherman once and for all.

Alice stopped and glanced up, revealing the deep lines and wrinkles on her face. "Responsible? Come on, your hair is purple and look at how you're dressed!"

"I took off the shorter skirt I was wearing. This is the longest one I have, at least that I would wear out. Why do you keep judging people by how they dress?"

Her raised tone accentuated the natural raspiness in Karen's voice. Throughout her life more than one guy had told her how sultry and sexy she sounded. She always took that as a compliment until a male friend said she would be perfect as a 900-line operator. He was joking with his remark, but now she was self-conscious about it.

Alice restarted her circular wiping motion and stared down at the table. Karen could see the gray roots of her mother's regularly dyed brown hair. "Because Karen, that is how the world judges, and society judges. There's nothing 'cool' about being a punk-rocker, or emo, or a goth chick, or whatever they call it these days, with all the wacky hair colors and ridiculous piercings..."

"See, there's a good example right there of me being responsible. My friends have piercings all over their faces." Her voice had a slight edge as she pointed at her head. "Do you see any crazy piercings? No, because I am *responsible* enough to know I might regret it one day."

"Where is your father when you need him," her mother muttered as she continued to wipe the table. The red, soaked napkin was coming apart. "Oh, that's right, he's in Connecticut while I have to deal with everything myself."

Since the divorce 15 years ago, her mother had lived in Vermont, while Karen's dad had stayed in Connecticut. Growing up, Karen used to see her father several times a year. But after she turned 15, it was as if she ceased to exist. She was lucky to even hear from him once a year. Karen tried not to dwell on it, but she felt utterly fatherless.

"You're the one who moved this far away," Karen responded as she uncrossed her legs and put both feet on the floor. Despite her best efforts, she was getting agitated. Even the tangy smell of the wine was annoying her.

With her face turning red, Alice snapped, "Yeah, after he broke me! Don't go there." She seemed to be warning herself more so than Karen. "Anyway, what else would a boy and girl be doing together at this hour of the night?"

"Trust me, we will just be talking."

"Famous last words. No way. You are not going anywhere. I'm not letting you learn the hard way."

Standing up, Karen shouted, "Stop projecting your bad experiences on me! Why do you always do that?" She was tired of paying for her mother's sins.

Throwing the red, disintegrating napkin on the table, Alice yelled with the veins in her neck protruding, "They aren't my 'bad experiences.' They're lessons you should learn from. Love. Romance. Passion. They impair your judgment." She reached for the napkin. "Never mind the alcohol."

Trying to regain self-control, Karen felt herself blush. "Mom, we've had this talk before. I've told you, I'm saving myself…in that way."

"Yeah, so was I," her mother snapped, sounding bitter. "All it takes is one single moment of weakness…"

December 26, 2044
Monday, 10:30 PM
Atlantic Ocean, Utopia Project Ship Number One
Less than an hour before the event

Just 30 minutes before the planned cataclysmic event, General Hyland sat up straight as Elder-1 walked into the room and approached him with a brisk, purposeful stride.

The general was required to make a crucial adjustment to protect the three Utopia Project ships from also being zapped since they were traveling in the ocean, which was part of the secondary infrared scanning zone. Using the anticipated coordinates of the ships in the Atlantic Ocean at 2300 hours EST, and allowing for a large margin of error, the general did a scan of the area he was capturing. He announced, "Sir, only our three vessels are in the 30-mile area to be protected."

"Confirm the coordinates and projections before finalizing," Elder-1 ordered. They contacted Elder-3, and his face appeared in a box in the corner of the over-sized screen.

The general made the necessary entry which eliminated the area the ships would be traversing, plus a 30-mile margin, from the infrared scanning zone. Following secondary verification by Elder-3 due to the size of the area and the importance of this entry, the adjustment was finalized and the general continued his work.

After General Hyland made a few more modifications, he pinged Elder-3 since every fourth adjustment required secondary approval. The elder's scowling face again appeared in the corner of the screen as he reviewed the entries. "Approved. Elder-41. One would hope this is your last call since the moment is just about upon us."

"Yes, Sir," the general said.

With this last approval, the general could now make three more margin adjustments without needing to call again for secondary authorization. He felt despair at only being able to make three minor adjustments. He wanted to enter one big system entry and stop the whole thing, but he could not. The most he could impact was .05 percent of any individual longitude and latitude grid because of the system controls he had put in place some time ago. The last person he would have ever imagined defending against was himself. Like someone smirking with arrogant pride after building a horrific gauntlet, just to find out they would have to run it. *Good job Eric. So efficient in your work.*

An announcement came over the loudspeakers on all three ships advising everyone to stay inside the ships and to not look outside. It concluded with a stern message, "Nobody is permitted outside for any reason! All decks and balconies are off limits to everyone until further notice. Violators, without exception, will be executed."

The words rang in his ears with dark foreboding. It was the final countdown. In just a few minutes, the satellites and neutron beams would destroy all the people on earth. He almost lost his breath at the thought.

General Hyland checked the clock. 10:44 p.m. He still had the three most important margin adjustments to make, but his window of time would be open in one minute. He needed to wait for the final 15 minutes before zero hour because of the activity log review procedure in the Data Center, where all system changes were examined and verified. The Data Center was always at least 15 minutes behind real-time in their review of data logs, usually even longer, but he could not chance it. If they discovered his adjustments before zero hour, they could cancel them. He could not let that happen. This was his one and only chance to save not just some of his loved ones, but humanity itself. He subtly kissed his fingertips, slid them between the buttons of his shirt and touched the cross that hung around his neck.

At 10:45 p.m., he instructed his fellow elders to pull up the system countdown screen. He made sure nobody was turned his way as he pulled his mobile device from his belt holster. Earlier in the day he had adjusted the privacy settings on his device so his call would show up on Sara's phone as a 'private caller,' with no phone number. He had trained her to always answer her phone, and knew she would, but if she knew it was him that hung up on her, she would be in a panic and would keep trying to call him back. Or worse, she might try to race home thinking he was in distress. In the unlikely event his daughter didn't pick up the phone, he would call Kid next.

Moving his hand with the device under the desktop, he dialed Sara.

CHAPTER 4

December 26, 2044
Monday, 10:46 PM
New Jersey coast
Close to zero hour

"Hello? Hello?" Sara put down the phone and looked at her boyfriend. "Nobody there."

Shrugging his shoulders, Kid exhaled heavily as he rested his head against the back door.

"Anyway, it is almost 11:00 p.m.," she noted as she pointed to the jewelry box sitting on her lap.

December 26, 2044
Monday, 10:47 PM
Atlantic Ocean, Utopia Project Ship Number One
Close to zero hour

As soon as Sara answered the call, General Hyland hit the GPS mapping button. He would have been concerned about his unusual activity being revealed when his mobile device was scanned at the security checkpoint upon leaving for the day, but he knew he was not going anywhere. He also wasn't concerned about the visual signals from the tracker in his neck, not at this late stage of the game. They would not be watching him, and even if they did, they wouldn't know what he was looking at or why. Tilting the screen toward his face, the general took just one quick glance. He was relieved to see Sara was still at Seaside Beach, where she was supposed to be. In checking the weather a few minutes before, he had noticed the severe storm was moving in faster than predicted on the New Jersey coast. He was thankful he had ordered the military checkpoints so Sara and Kid could not return to the mainland. To capture her in a margin area, she needed to remain close to the ocean.

Although faint, he had heard his precious daughter's voice answer, "Hello? Hello?" through the phone speaker before she hung up. His heart strings were ripped and he felt pain and torment. He wished he could have raised the phone to his ear and said, 'Sara, I love you, sweetheart,' but now was not the time.

On his computer he outlined a large, rectangular section that extended from the ocean to the middle of the Tunney Mathis Bridge, in case she moved in the next couple of minutes and had to be detained. He knew if they were trying to escape the storm and get away from the coast, they would head for the bridge to the mainland. With a few clicks, he removed that section of the New Jersey shore from both the neutron beam and the secondary infrared scanning zones, which meant that area would remain untouched. The rectangle was more elongated than he had hoped since it had to extend all the way to the bridge. The corridor was so narrow that very few houses or multi-unit dwellings would be spared. But what mattered to him was that Sara would survive. The Utopia Project's thirst for blood would not be sated with that of his daughter.

After glancing over his shoulder, he hit enter. 'Accepted: System Margin Change A-21 Confirmed. Time, 2252.'

He breathed a sigh of relief. *Just don't move too far, honey, just... eight more minutes.* He tensed up. *Eight minutes? I have to move quicker!*

December 26, 2044
Monday, 10:53 PM
Near Rutland, Vermont
Close to zero hour

Folding her arms, Karen Stone said to her mother, "Anyway, I'm not even dating Scott anymore. I broke up with him earlier this month when Sara was up from New Jersey."

Recalling the events of that night, Karen had a quick chill.

In early December, Sara Hyland had come up from New Jersey with her boyfriend Kid Carlson and his friends Jess Kellen, Maria Stephano, Brian Mitchell, and Heidi Leer. Since they were all skiing in Killington, they planned to meet up at the restaurant at the top of K-1, more than 4,000 feet above sea level. Despite her best efforts, Karen was 15 minutes late, per usual. When she saw Sara, they embraced like two long-lost sisters. She had known Sara for just five years, ever since the Hylands had retired in Vermont, but somehow it felt longer. From the day they met, they had connected immediately, like kindred spirits.

Karen introduced Sara and the group to her boyfriend, Scott Sherman, who said nothing to them. He seemed restless and miserable until he saw his brother throwing items into the lodge's large fireplace. Without saying a word, Scott got up and ran over to join his brother Sid.

A little while later when talking with Sara and Kid, they were all startled by a loud pop as glass exploded out of the fireplace. A woman sitting close to the hearth had a shard stuck in her bottom lip and was screaming and waving her arms, like she was trying to fly. As her companion pulled out the sizeable, sickle-shaped piece of glass, blood erupted from her lip like a geyser. She lifted her beige scarf to her lip and within seconds a red rose blossomed.

"What happened over there?" Sara asked.

"I don't know. We should ask Karen's boyfriend." Kid pointed to the Sherman brothers, who were snickering as they stood next to the fireplace.

Karen rolled her eyes and exhaled. *What did they do now?*

Sid's lips were easy for Karen to read. "Did you see that? That was great!"

The manager and three employees came over and threw the Sherman brothers out. As they were departing, it was Sid, not Scott, who waved Karen over. "Come on. We're leaving this shithole."

"This is embarrassing," Karen muttered as she turned away.

"Yo, did you hear me? Come on," Sid yelled. The manager following behind ushered the brothers out.

Karen turned toward Sara, who had an expression of concern.

Scott called out, "Karen! I'll be waiting for you outside."

"I know him. He'll wait out there all night if he has to." Karen started gathering her things. "This is what I get for feeling sorry for the new kid in school. One on one, Scott seemed so sweet at first..."

"We'll go with you." Sara turned to Kid. He nodded without hesitation.

Outside, Kid and Sara stood with her and the Sherman brothers. Karen had her arms folded tightly across her chest. Sid and Scott were high-fiving each other. "The fire was raging! I told you the bottle would explode," Sid said.

Turning to Kid with his arm in the air, Sid was looking for a high-five. "Dude, was that cool or what?"

Kid stood with his arms folded and did not move. He seemed unimpressed to say the least.

The excitement in Sid's face drained away, replaced by contempt and even anger.

As Sid lowered his arm, Karen tensed. Sid was about six-foot-two and outweighed Kid by at least 50 pounds, but it was clear Kid was not backing down.

"Whatever," Sid snapped dismissively and turned toward Scott. "Bro, give me a ride home."

"Sid, I can't. Me and Karen are taking a ride, and she has to be home soon," Scott said timidly.

"Whah, whah. How old are you?" he asked Karen.

Turning to Sara, Sid eyed her up and down. "How about you? Can I get a…ride…with you?"

"Car's full." Kid's voice was firm. He seemed to be tiring of Sid's routine.

"Whatever. Screw you all." Turning around, Sid saw a group of snowmobiles parked next to the lodge. "Hey, Jimmy's here anyway. He's a jackass, but he'll give me a ride." At that, Sid went over and sat on the back of a snowmobile with flames painted on the side.

Before Sara left, she hugged Karen and whispered, "You have my phone number. Call me if you need me. I may be wrong about these guys, but…"

"Honestly, I'm feeling the same way." Karen forced herself to smile as they embraced and rocked back and forth, from foot to foot.

Still whispering, Sara added, "Just follow your gut and trust your instincts, that's all. I worry about you. Listen, call me when you get home tonight. I don't care what time it is."

"What are you, my mother?" Karen quipped.

Holding her tight, Sara whispered, "No, worse. I'm your overbearing big sister. It's like having a mother who's hip to what you're really up to."

Karen laughed and patted Sara's back.

Sara and Kid helped her see the light and that evening Karen broke up with Scott Sherman. He was distraught and kept repeating, "You can't break up with me." As she got out of his car, she froze as he said, "I won't let you." Karen feared this was not the typical high school breakup.

Since that night more than three weeks ago, Scott would not stop following and harassing Karen. He was becoming increasingly desperate in his pleas for reconciliation. She was anxious every time she left the house or picked up the phone.

After talking with Sara earlier in the evening, Karen decided she was going to put Scott on notice that he had two choices: let it go and stop stalking her, or deal with the police and a restraining order. Sara had advised her to speak to Scott over the phone, or in the presence of another person, to be safe. Instead, after Scott begged her yet again, Karen's need for closure trumped her fear. She had agreed to meet him tonight at midnight, albeit in front of a busy 24-hour convenience store and gas station downtown where she knew others would be around. She was dreading it, but she had to be firm and let him know, enough was enough. It all had to end. But her plan was being thwarted by her mother.

She peered up into eyes haunted by pain and fear, and knew her mother was not going to budge. As they stood across from each other at the kitchen table, Karen's feelings were a collage of anger and pity.

Alice exhaled and her tone softened. "Listen, Karen, I love you and worry about you. You are a bright girl with a future, with options and opportunities. You have your whole life and the whole world in front of you. I can't let you make a mistake that will rob you of that."

Karen strained to keep her voice steady. "You mean like you did when you got pregnant with me?"

"Haven't we been through this before?" Staring at her daughter, tears started running down Alice's cheeks.

"Is that all I am? A mistake?" Karen turned to hide her own tears. Now she felt pity for herself, which made her angrier. Her rage turned toward her father, for being so selfish and leaving her alone with a broken woman.

"You're wrong." Alice spoke in a firm voice, but her pained expression belied her answer.

"It's bad enough my absentee-father makes me feel that way," Karen said as she threw her coat across the living room. "But now you too?" She turned and stomped up the hallway. The slam of Karen's bedroom door echoed throughout the house.

Flopping on her bed, Karen wiped at her tears and sniffled as she pulled out her phone. She needed to talk to Sara Hyland.

CHAPTER 5

December 26, 2044
Monday, 10:54 PM
Near Rutland, Vermont
Close to zero hour

"I just can't sleep. I'm worried. Our son never called like he said he would." Evelyn stated as she maintained a brisk pace in her rocking chair.

"I don't know if Eric ever intended to, or if he just wanted us at home," her husband replied while sitting in his leather reclining chair. The footrest was closed tight, and he sat on the edge of the seat, cleaning his snub-nosed 38-caliber Smith and Wesson pistol. Spinning the cylinder and ensuring all five bullets were snug and ready to defend, he flicked his wrist and snapped the cylinder in place.

Evelyn ran her fingers along the arm of her golden oak chair. "But nothing dramatic has happened today either. I had my eyes on the news and I was watching outside. Maybe you picked up all those supplies, and a van, for nothing." She had a nervous smile.

In the past two days, Chris had traveled to many stores, securing non-perishable food and water, another cord of firewood, batteries, a used four-wheel drive van, and a multitude of supplies he thought they may need in a crisis.

"Eve, the day isn't over yet." Chris sat back in his chair and looked at his wristwatch. "Eric went out of his way and took a risk by warning us. He would never do that unless something major was about to happen."

December 26, 2044
Monday, 10:54 PM
Atlantic Ocean, Utopia Project Ship Number One
Close to zero hour

At his computer station on the ship, General Hyland expanded a margin along the border of the Green Mountains in Vermont where his parents lived. He did not have enough time to make a confirmation call to them. *They are home. I told them adamantly to be home tonight.*

"Sir!" Elder-188 called out with urgency.

After the general finished adjusting the settings, he glanced over and snapped, "Not now."

Elder-188 stood and walked over with haste. "But, Sir, Elder-140 just ran out of the room and is heading for the M3 on the deck. Look!" He pointed to a large screen on the wall that was serving as a deck-cam. "Nobody is allowed on deck. We have our orders."

The general checked the clock. The time was 2254. Six minutes to go. He hit the enter key to remove the area in Vermont from both the neutron beam and infrared scanning zones.

"Sir?"

His monitor indicated, 'Accepted: System Margin Change A-22 Confirmed. Time, 2255.'

The general knew the elder was peering over his shoulder at the screen. "That border is too wide. Why are we…" Elder-188 started.

The general turned around. "Get Elder-140 off the deck, now!"

Elder-188 hesitated and seemed conflicted. They all knew the board had ordered that armed guards be stationed on the decks and on the bridges to prevent any last-minute fleeing of elders from the ships.

Fear ran through the general's veins. If anyone caught his adjustments before zero hour, they could be deleted. But he was also the ranking elder. "That is an order!"

Elder-188 relented and after looking back one more time, he sprinted up the hall toward the deck.

The general knew the armed guards on the balconies would follow their strict orders. Using their technologically advanced Medusa smart guns, they would launch a hailstorm of bright bolts at anyone defying orders and running out on deck. He knew what they were in for, as he recalled why the weapon was named, Medusa. It fired bolts which were cut laser beam segments, or plugs, that contained a pinhead sized dose of a powerful neurological agent that instantly froze all the muscles in the body, including the diaphragm, resulting in rapid death.

He glanced at the deck-cam just as bolts from several Medusa firearms hit Elder-140 before he could reach the M3. He was frozen in a full running pose, arms pumping, like the runners portrayed in sneaker advertisements. As he crashed to the deck, his rigid body tumbled like a plastic soldier being rolled across the floor.

Elder-188 had stopped and was waving to the other elder when bolts rained down on him as well. He stood statuesque with his feet shoulder-length apart and his hands straight up in the air, as if giving a sermon on the mountain.

The last M3 lifted off as scheduled. The general knew that within seconds the aircraft would be out of the protected 30-mile area surrounding the ships and the pilot would become just another casualty.

General Hyland hurried to enter the third adjustment, which widened the margin surrounding an island in Europe. A red number popped up on the screen, indicating the area he entered was a change of .06 percent of that grid. 'Secondary Authorization Required.'

"Damn," he muttered. For all three adjustments, he was trying to capture the full .05 percent to save as many people as possible, but his calculation for the third area had been off. He checked the clock. 2257. *Three minutes!*

Without any time to contemplate, he revised the margin border to capture less of the island. The field on the screen indicated .05 percent. *Please tell me you received and decoded my message.* He hit the enter key and watched the screen with growing anxiety. After a couple of seconds passed, he clenched his fists. The system seemed to be frozen or hung up. The general's heart was in his throat.

His monitor display finally refreshed. 'System Margin Change A-23 Confirmed. Time, 2258.' *Only two minutes to spare!* The general exhaled, not realizing he had been holding his breath. His palms had deep indentations from his fingernails.

Looking at the monitor with the deck-cam, he saw Elder-188 still frozen with his hands straight up in the air. He was surprised the elder's body remained upright. But the general knew that unless the seas were rolling to a significant degree, the ship did not bob or roll, at least not enough to be noticeable. He was watching the next time the ship did sway. The shift was so slight the general felt nothing, but it was enough to nudge the pendulum of Elder-188's perfect equilibrium and make him tip backward. The helpless elder could not move to break his fall and his head cracked against the deck.

"Room lockdown. Door is now closed and locked. Remain in your seats!" Elder-2 barked, speaking in English instead of Russian, and enunciating every word as the two armed guards flanking her pulled out their weapons and widened their stance.

Just before zero hour, an announcement blared out of the loudspeaker. "One minute until zero hour. All personnel are to take their positions and do not, we repeat, do not, look outside."

General Hyland knew the protocol. In four separate rooms aboard Utopia Project Ship Number One, the four highest ranking elders prepared to enter separate authorization codes into the computer system. Elder-2 sat at a computer with her back to the rest of the room as she stared at her watch. The general was sitting in the same room and watched helplessly, knowing what was to happen next. As a fail-safe for the most secure levels in the system, a minimum of three of the four highest ranking elders needed to enter an authorization code within a 15 second window of time. When the clock turned to 2259:45, Elder-2 entered her code.

The authorization protocol worked as planned, because in an instant, control over the 48 United States satellites was assumed by the

Utopia Project computer system. Seconds after, the neutron beams sprang to life.

At the precise moment of the cataclysmic event, 2300 hours—11:00 p.m. EST—the general whispered, "This is how our world will end."

The general heard a loud hum and dropped his face into his hands. He knew within the span of a couple of minutes earth's inhabitants would be dead yet her structures would remain intact—the same effect as the primitive neutron bomb, but on a global scale.

All he could do was pray that his margin adjustments saved those who he loved the most.

December 26, 2044
Monday, 11:00 PM
Near Rutland, Vermont
Zero hour

Alice Stone had not moved a step since her daughter had stormed away. "Karen doesn't deserve this," she finally concluded and started walking across the kitchen. "Honey, I'm sorry…"

Suddenly, a bright red light swept through the house. Alice screamed as she fell hard on the linoleum floor. A blood-curdling scream erupted from her throat as a deep hum reverberated around her and inside her. The light around her became blinding and ran from one side of the house to the other several times.

Chris and Evelyn Hyland froze as the world outside burst into a deep, blinding red. Although the window shades were closed, the interior of the house was flooded with a red hue, as if someone had flicked a switch and turned on a brilliant red sun. "Close your eyes!" Chris yelled over the loud hum as he put his hands over his face.

December 26, 2044
Monday, 11:03 PM
Atlantic Ocean, Utopia Project Ship Number One
Moments after the event

Every elder in the room was glued to a monitor watching the event unfold, including General Hyland. The neutron beam barrage was over in mere moments, but secondary beams in the infrared scanning zones still traced through the sky, finding human stragglers and destroying them with pinpoint accuracy. The general knew these beams would continue for no more than a couple of minutes.

As he waited with his fingers on his keyboard, he felt sweat beading on his forehead. The computer system was locked while the satellites were firing, but when the attack results were being compiled, he knew the system security and the activity logging would be temporarily disabled. There would be a small window of opportunity right after the event for system files to be accessed and altered without a trace.

Finally, his screen changed to a detailed, color-coded world map with a notation in the bottom left-hand corner indicating, 'results of event sequence.' An icon showed the results were processing. While others were intently watching their screens, he immediately went to work.

His fingers were quick and efficient as he altered a couple of simple, but vital, computer system files, deleting and changing strings in the many thousands of lines of code. Once these files were altered, they could not be easily corrected or even restored from the data backups. It would take weeks or months for anyone to fix the program, and until they did, the satellites could no longer be accessed remotely by the computers on the ships. The only other copy of the original, working satellite access program resided on the laptop computer sitting safely on the dining room table in General Hyland's house.

Up until six months ago he was allowed to work on the system files on his laptop from home, but he was hearing whispers they were going to tighten the security policies and no longer allow that practice.

The day before they implemented the new policy, he was able to copy his program files to his laptop. At the time, he just wanted his own copy, but he was now thankful for his nearly obsessive need to have multiple backups. Those program files had become critical pieces in his final plan. Over the last week, he had painstakingly memorized all the code changes made in the previous six months for the satellite system program, and then each night he would update the program on his laptop. It was an arduous task, but he was sure the program on his device was fully updated and complete. This would allow his laptop, with a powerful enough antenna, to link directly to the satellite system.

The general finished and saved his changes just in time. Fewer than 20 seconds later the satellite attack result compilation was complete and the system security returned in full force. The screen indicated the neutron beams had made ten full passes. That fact made him queasy, but the Board of Elders would be pleased.

Changing his monitor screen to the world map, the general checked his watch. Now for his next dilemma, the Data Center. In just a couple of minutes, the activity logs in the Data Center would reveal his three last-minute personal margin adjustments. He was ready with his alibi, but he wanted to be there when the adjustments came through on the log. He needed to be ready with a viable explanation, or he would come under suspicion. With any luck, his explanation to the lower-ranking elder reviewer would be sufficient and the adjustments would simply be filed away.

The general swiveled in his chair. "Elder-2?" the general called out as he peered at the elder's back.

Without looking up, Elder-2 asked "What is it Elder-41."

"We may have discrepancies in some of the margin areas."

"Have you contacted the Data Center?"

"We tried, but nobody picked up. We need to get over there right away," the general insisted.

"Elder-41, we are in lockdown until 2315. Nobody may move.

At that time, you can go to the Data Center and check on any discrepancies."

"Yes, Ma'am," the general answered. *Not good!*

"At 2315, Elder-41 may exit," Elder-2 indicated to the guards.

The general turned around to face his monitor and cursed under his breath. He knew post-event computer system procedures, but he was not as knowledgeable with regards to room lockdown procedures. His fingers tapped on the tabletop at a pace he wished the clock would follow.

CHAPTER 6

December 26, 2044
Monday, 11:04 PM
Near Rutland, Vermont
Moments after the event

As the red light disappeared and the hum subsided, Alice's screams continued through the sudden silence, but the timbre of her voice had changed. With the power now out, the room first went black, and then a dim light rose as the candle on the kitchen table continued to burn. Her hands were shaking uncontrollably as she pulled them from behind her head. She turned to examine her lower body and her screams lost all force until the lone sound was her labored breathing. She started to cry as resignation set in with the shock. Her sobs were shallow and weak and her head started sinking toward the floor.

Her eyes went wide and she wailed, "Karen." She stretched out her arms and clawed at the floor. Gaining minimal purchase, she was able to drag her helpless body across the slick, white linoleum. Stopping and panting after making a few feet of progress, she forced out the word, "Help." She was almost at the entrance to the hall. She struggled as she continued dragging her body another few inches using only her hands and arms. Her trembling fingers reached for the molding adorning the entranceway. She willed herself, gritted her teeth and pulled with everything she had. As her head and shoulders lurched forward into the hall, she moaned, "Karen…"

Karen had no idea what had just happened. All she knew was the light in her room had turned red while the house vibrated and her mother screamed. She had closed her eyes and covered her head until the humming stopped.

Raising her mobile device to her ear, she said, "Sara?" Pulling away the device, she saw she had no signal and had lost the call. Sitting still, she thought she heard her mother's voice.

"Mom?" Karen yelled as she popped her head out of her room and stared into the dark hallway. Unable to see, she turned on her mobile device's flashlight.

"Stay there," Alice called back in a low voice.

Shining the flashlight, Karen yelled, "Mom!" Her mother looked awful. "Are you alright?" She leaned forward to sprint up the hall.

Alice raised her hand and yelled, "No! Stop!" Her hand sagged down to the carpet. "Stop."

Karen froze with her hands straight out in front of her. She danced from foot to foot, as if she had to go to the bathroom. She was panic-stricken, and the beam of light in her hand kept shaking. "What's wrong? What happened?" She could see her mother needed help.

"Something very serious," Alice panted. "Some horrible…tragedy."

"But why are you on the floor? You're shaking like crazy. Are you alright? Tell me." Karen thought of calling 911, but the power was out, which meant even the cordless phone was useless. She checked her mobile device, but it still had no signal.

With shallow breaths, Alice uttered, "No, honey. I'm not alright. My time is up on this planet."

Karen felt a wave of queasiness course through her. She started to cry and dropped to her knees. "What are you talking about?" She started crawling up the hall. "How is that possible?"

"Stop!" Alice yelled again. "Please…don't come any closer. I don't want you to see me this way."

"What way?" She continued her slow crawl. Her mother's face was too pale. Something was seriously wrong

"It's bad. Find help for yourself. Go up the road…the nice, older couple."

"The Hylands?"

"Yes." She rested her forehead on the gray carpet. "I don't know what's happened here. It's bad, but fight…survive." She seemed to be fading. "You know I love you Karen."

"I love you, too, but don't you give up on me Mom. I'll get you help. Don't give up," she sobbed as she put the flashlight down on the carpet and brushed the hair off her mother's face.

"No, it's too late for me. Go." A weak cough escaped Alice's lips, followed by a congested wheeze as she struggled to inhale. Her face twitched as she raised the corners of her mouth and said, "This one time, listen to me, honey. Don't look…around this corner. The sight would…haunt you forever."

"I won't, and I should've listened to you more, and I'm sorry for that. So sorry." She winced as blood started running from the corner of her mom's mouth. It was then that it sunk in.

Her mother was dying.

How was that possible? They were talking, and arguing, just a few minutes ago.

Karen cried harder and wiped at the stream of blood, but it smeared on her mother's face. Flustered, she wiped at her own tears with her bloody hand. "I'll be back. I'm going to get you help."

As Alice inhaled, she sounded extremely congested and started gagging. A contorted grin came to her face. "There really…is…a…rattle." She weakly grabbed her daughter's wrist. "Don't let the world darken…your heart. And don't ever let any…man…break you. Not…ever."

"I won't." Karen straightened her body while kneeling. Her mother's face, illuminated by the beam from the flashlight, was downright gory. "I have to get help. I can save you, Mom," she sputtered.

"You already did…save me."

"What do you mean?"

"When you were born. Before you, my life…had gone to shit, and wasn't…worth living anymore."

"Oh, Mom!" She cradled her mother's head and kissed her cheek. Her mother was slipping away and Karen was helpless to stop it.

"Don't ever let any…man…break you," Alice repeated. "Promise me."

"I won't. I promise you," Karen said with the deepest sincerity. She took it to heart.

Alice whispered in a soft but assuring voice. "You were…an accident, but never…a mistake. Never…" and then her breathing stopped.

After sobbing for several minutes, Karen kissed the top of her mother's head and lowered it to the soft, beige carpet. She leaned against the wall to steady herself as she stood. Her cheek rolled against the molding as she stepped forward. She kept rotating her head and the kitchen crept into her field of vision, but she came to a halt. Turning her eyes down, her pursed lips began to tremble. "No!" She pushed back from the doorway and took two steps backward. "I swore I wouldn't look, and I won't." Covering her eyes with her hand, she turned and opened the door to the garage.

December 26, 2044
Monday, 11:15 PM
Atlantic Ocean, Utopia Project Ship Number One
Moments after the event

At exactly 2315, General Hyland stood and marched out the door. He walked at a quick pace up the hall, hoping to get to the Data Center before his adjustments did. As soon as he walked in, he knew he was too late.

Elder-12 and Elder-35 held data sheets in their hands which had already been flagged by the lower-ranking elder reviewer. The two elders looked perplexed and suspicious. The general turned to a nearby data screen and saw the data log was already past the time when he had entered his adjustments. He had lost this race. His alibi had to be all the more convincing and he could not hesitate. He steeled himself and marched forward.

"Sir!" he said as he approached Elder-12. "We must report a potential system irregularity."

Elder-12 turned his eyes up from the data sheets in his hand, and the creases in his face deepened. "Well Elder-41, we would say so. What is the explanation for these?" He showed the general the data log.

"That is what we are here to investigate."

Elder-12 stared at him and the general felt the acute suspicion.

The general continued, "While we were viewing three margin areas a few minutes prior to the event, the three windows we had open on the screen simply disappeared. They may be in our network's cyberspace, but we are hopeful they were simply deleted."

Elder-12 straightened and looked down at the pieces of paper in his hand. "No Elder-41, it appears the system accepted and processed them."

The general was overwhelmed with relief, but could not show it. A second later his hope turned to dismay when Elder-12 picked up the phone to report his finding to Elder-1.

December 26, 2044

Monday, 11:17 PM

Near Rutland, Vermont

Moments after the event

"Really, I'm fine," Evelyn patted her husband's hand with her trembling fingers. Crouched on one knee at the foot of her rocking chair, Chris looked into her eyes. "Well, I'm shaken," she admitted, "but nothing I can't handle."

"It'll be alright. The wave that passed missed us. Otherwise, we would not be here to talk about it."

The eerie calm was shattered by a series of rapid-fire knocks on the front door.

That is the knock of someone in distress, Chris concluded as he ran over to the front door. Signaling for Eve to stay silent and not move, he grabbed his revolver from the end table and stepped across the foyer. "Who is it?" he yelled.

"Help! It's Karen Stone, from up the street." She was in a panic and sounded desperate.

Without hesitation, Chris opened the door, leaving the chain lock engaged. Karen stood hunched over and sobbing, but she appeared to be alone. She looked up and revealed her blood-smeared face.

"Damn!" Chris's eyes opened wide. "Hold on." He pushed the door closed and slid the chain lock off. Re-opening the door, he grabbed Karen's arm and pulled her inside.

Evelyn audibly inhaled at the sight of her. "Oh my! I'll go get some towels. Sit her down!"

Chris led Karen to a kitchen chair. Her feet shuffled along the floor in short awkward steps.

"What happened? Where are you bleeding from?" Chris knelt and put his fingers under her chin and turned her head from side to side. He could not find any open wounds.

"It's not my…" she blurted and stopped. Her lips were trembling as she gazed up at him. "It's not my blood," she gasped through her sobs. "It's my mother's."

Chris grabbed her and hugged her tight. The shoulder of his white sweatshirt was quickly painted a light red as her tears carried the blood from her face.

"Something terrible happened to her, but I don't know what. The world turned red, and our house felt like it was…vibrating," she added.

"I'm afraid it was a neutron beam attack," Chris offered. Although retired, he had kept abreast of the latest military weapons and technology. “But the satellite system belonged to the United States, so I have no idea how it was turned on us, or why the beams missed our houses.”

Bolting to her feet, she stopped crying. “Maybe my mom’s still alive. Will you check? It must be bad, but I only saw her face. She made me promise to leave and not to look at the rest of her. But you could.” Her eyes were pleading with him.

“Where is she now?” Chris got to his feet. If her mother was alive, it wouldn’t be for long if she was bleeding profusely.

“She was on the kitchen floor. The garage is open.” Beginning to double over, she huffed, “I don’t feel so good.” Evelyn had come in with a wet towel and was starting to clean Karen’s face. His wife showed a keen awareness as she led the young girl to the sink just in time to catch the projectile vomit.

With the sound of gagging, Chris quickly grabbed his coat, stuck the revolver in his jacket pocket and headed out the door. Jogging along the snowy road, he glanced over his shoulder. The road was empty and had not been traveled. They lived on a quiet street, but the recent events made quiet seem downright eerie. He turned up the unplowed driveway of Karen’s house and walked into the open garage.

Standing at the door to the house, he took a deep breath and pulled out his pistol. He turned the knob and pushed the door and did not spot anything until it was halfway open. Alice’s motionless fingers and arm were visible on the ground. As he pushed the door further open and stepped into the threshold, he froze. The door continued its forward momentum and came to a gentle stop as it tapped the clothes dryer.

Straight in front of him, Alice’s bloodied face was lit by a mobile device’s flashlight that rested on the carpet. Between that beam and a candle burning on the kitchen table, there was enough light to reveal the rest of Alice’s body. During his military combat days, Chris had seen some gruesome and bloodied bodies, but this one caught him off guard. Maybe his stomach was already unsettled from seeing Karen vomit a few moments ago, but he rushed back into the garage and emptied the contents of his own stomach into a half-full garbage can. Leaning over and wiping his face, he said, "I wasn't ready for that."

Taking a deep breath and closing his eyes for a moment, he turned toward the doorway. Clearing his throat, he stood taller. He needed to assess the situation further, which required him to re-enter the house.

Walking through the door, he stared down at the body on the floor. The problem was it wasn't just a body, it was a neighbor and a friend. He felt his shoulders sag. He was quite sure she was dead, but he crouched down and checked for a pulse as a matter of course. He covered his mouth and raised his eyes.

In front of him lay Alice Stone.

But only half of her.

Although she wore a blue bathrobe, the garment lay flat on the floor from where her body, from the waist down, should've been. A trail of blood, bones, skin, tissue, and innards streaked halfway across the kitchen floor. It looked as if someone had tried to push a huge mound of red gelatin across the floor. "How on earth was she able to drag herself this far?"

Chris swallowed hard as he took in the grotesque sight. At the start of the bloody trail, easy to discern, was a dismembered foot. It lay on its side, ankle bones still attached, with strings of tendons and muscles snaking out along the once white floor. When Alice pulled her seemingly melted body across the kitchen, her foot was left behind, as was the rest of her lower body.

Turning away with a grimace on his face he said flatly, "Karen's mother was right. Thank God the poor girl didn't look."

CHAPTER 7

December 26, 2044
Monday, 11:50 PM
Atlantic Ocean, Utopia Project Ship Number One
Within the hour after the event

An emergency meeting of the 11-member Board of Elders was in progress in a conference room on the floor above, so General Hyland, Elder-41, was called into the meeting to explain his three final margin adjustments. In the center of the conference room table, an enormous globe hologram rotated. The land masses hit by neutron beams were the color gray. The bodies of water and wildlife tracts making up the infrared scanning zones were the color blue. He knew the three bright red dots on the ten-foot tall globe marked the areas he saved. But what struck him most was the entirety of the destruction beyond the red dots. He felt a wave of despair, and at that moment his alibi didn't seem any more rock solid than his stomach.

General Hyland addressed the Board of Elders, and although his stomach was in turmoil, he felt his acting was superb. His controlled outrage was convincing, but not over the top as he explained what had happened with his final three margin adjustments.

The other elders seemed ready to pepper the general with questions, but Elder-35 spoke first and described another computer system anomaly. As he held data logs in his hand, Elder-35 noted, "It appears that at 2303, we had a beam malfunction in an infrared scanning zone. For some reason, the exact same spot was hit four times in succession."

The general could not believe his good fortune. There was at least one legitimate computer system glitch. This would give credibility to his own claim.

"Better four times than none at all," one elder muttered.

Elder-35 held up both of his hands and sounded flustered. "These are not the main beams where one would expect multiple passes! The ones in the infrared scanning zones were programmed to hit each pinpointed area only one time, never twice, let alone four times."

This anomaly immediately gave the general's explanation the credence it needed, and seemed to extinguish any doubt the elders may have had. Soon his three adjustment areas were being referred to as simply, 'the system malfunction areas,' which was a relief.

But Elder-1's next directive stopped him in mid-exhale. "We must inspect all three system malfunction areas immediately since they were left untouched. Any survivors must be eradicated before they leave or spread out!"

The general fought a panic rising inside. He was still surprised at the elders' complete disregard for human life, although he no longer should have been. With an order to eradicate any survivors, Sara and her group were now in grave danger. He hoped she had found his diary and was staying hidden as he had instructed.

"Why do we need to go to any system malfunction areas at all? Can't we just reactivate the beam system and hit them again?" an elder inquired.

The general knew the answer to that question, but remained silent.

"Not possible," said Elder-1. "For some unknown reason, we have lost contact with the satellites."

"Another...system malfunction?"

"We do not understand how we could have lost contact." Elder-1 sounded perturbed. "We are researching that right now, but we can't wait for that to be fixed. It could take days. There is no telling when, or even if, we will be able to communicate with the satellites again."

The elders fell silent, until one finally noted, "Maybe we should have kept an M3 after all. We could have inspected all three areas very quickly."

"No," Elder-2 responded without hesitation. "The board was adamant we not have any M3s available, lest an elder try to escape before or after the attack. We must stick together."

Elder-1 stood and faced the globe hologram. He squinted at a small black crescent sticking out beyond the edge of a red dot. He brushed his finger against the interactive globe and moved the red dot representing Seaside Heights over the Atlantic Ocean. This revealed a full black dot hidden underneath. He tapped the black circle and enlarged the information. "It seems that one of our choices for a base camp, Long Beach Island, is only a few miles away from the malfunction area at…Seaside Heights."

Elder-2, who already had a disposition thanks to the salesmanship of General Hyland, chimed in next. "That makes Long Beach Island the logical choice. It is close enough so that while engaged in the mop-up operation in Seaside Heights, we could begin setting up the new base camp. We should put that to a vote once and for all, so preparations can be made."

"It was the leading contender anyway," Elder-1 noted.

The 11-member Board of Elders proceeded to pass a motion by a formal vote that the base camp would be established on Long Beach Island. This was their first order of formal business after the event.

At first, the general was relieved with the base camp choice. But with the reality unfolding, he was now fearful for Sara and her group. *What if she did not get his diary?* It was then he decided to take a shot at an insurance policy, at least for his daughter. "Sir, would it help our offspring production if we captured any female survivors of child bearing age, if there are any, in the malfunction areas?" he asked Elder-1.

Elder-12 sat up straighter and he scowled as his face reddened, "We are already making adjustments to help boost our numbers."

Being in charge of offspring production, Elder-12 was being held responsible for the lackluster performance in that area compared to estimates. It was known to all that Elder-1 was especially displeased. The general hated to kick Elder-12 when he was down, but he couldn't miss the opportunity. He needed to at least give Sara a fighting chance if she was caught.

"Elder-41, it is not your place to address areas that are not your responsibility," Elder-1 reprimanded.

The general stood at attention. "My apologies."

"That being said, Elder-12, he is quite correct about the offspring production."

Elder-12 stiffened as he shot a glance toward the general and asked, "Even if females were found, wouldn't we be at risk of…corrupting our members by bringing any old-world survivors here?"

"Not if the female survivors were kept confined until they were conditioned," Elder-1 countered. "If there are any female survivors at all, it would help our offspring production, and we should have full confidence in the conditioning methods and practices we spent twenty years perfecting in this project."

"Yes, but the unnecessary risk…" Elder-12 started.

It seemed that Elder-1's patience was being tested. "Any risk factor would be infinitesimal to downright non-existent."

As Elder-12 went to open his mouth, Elder-1 snapped, "Do you doubt that our conditioning regimen would be anything other than 100 percent successful?"

Silence followed until Elder-12 surrendered. "No, Sir. No doubt at all."

"Then so long as they are cooperative, we agree we should capture any production-age female survivors," Elder-1 concluded.

After the meeting ended, the general went outside and took a walk on the deck. He needed to gather himself. In the past several minutes, he had been pummeled by alternating currents of relief and distress.

A half an hour later, while talking to another elder, General Hyland fought to remain expressionless when an announcement came over the speaker system. The voice of Elder-1 closed the address by saying, "Our ETA for Seaside Heights, New Jersey is approximately 1400 hours, Eastern Standard Time."

Checking his watch, the general realized they were about 12 hours away. It was a much longer journey via ship. An M3 would have been there hours ago. He thought of what the announcement did not say; that even though young females would now be captured, any male survivors in the malfunction area would be hunted down and killed by merciless, machine-like forces. The members sent ashore would be incredible physical specimens with technologically superior weapons. He feared for his daughter's boyfriend, Kid, and the rest of their male friends left on the mainland. He could only hope they were in hiding with his beloved daughter.

General Hyland stepped over to the deck rail and watched the sea being effortlessly sliced and parted by the ship. Now alone, a specific conversation from long ago suddenly popped into his mind. It was the day when Eric, like his father before him, was accepted to West Point. After receiving his acceptance letter, 18-year-old Eric had expected congratulations, but was taken aback by the first words out of his father's mouth.

"There will be moments in your career as an officer Eric, when your conviction and unwavering commitment will be tested," General Christopher Hyland had said.

"And I will stand tall and firm," Eric stated. Throughout his entire life, his father had pounded into him that nothing was more important than duty, regardless of the consequences.

"You are committing to a life of duty, sacrifice and the greater good. Commitment to purposes much larger than any single man, woman, or child's life. We know that path, all too well. Remember the sacrifices our family has already made."

"I do recall clearly, Sir," he answered and looked down.

His father did not need to rehash the story again. While the Hyland's were stationed at a United States Army base in South Korea for a brief tour of duty in 2002, two enemy missiles were fired simultaneously at the installation from short range. The ranking leaders, including then Colonel Chris Hyland, had to make a split second decision and they chose to intercept the missile heading for a building full of expensive equipment and armaments first. The second missile's trajectory was the school building on the base and it could not be intercepted in time. 7-year-old Eric was on the playground when the missile hit the school and took the life of his little sister Sara.

"There's not a single day that goes by where I don't think about my little girl," his father lamented.

His words stunned Eric. Up until then, when reflecting on the incident, Chris had always said firmly, "It was tragic, but we did what we had to do and what duty required."

Looking up from the West Point acceptance letter, he saw tears streaming down his father's face. He had never seen his father cry.

It was a moment Eric would never forget as it was the only time his dad ever revealed how much pain and regret he harbored from the missile attack in South Korea. And he knew then, without question, that if his father could do it all over again he would have intercepted the other missile first and saved his little girl.

"I am sorry, Eric. Getting into West Point is one of the greatest achievements of your life." Wiping away his tears and resuming a more rigid stance, his tone steadied. "Listen, I could not be more proud of you. I am sure you will make a top-notch officer."

Although fleeting, he could still see the pain and regret in his father's eyes, so much so that it took him a minute before he even had the courtesy to say, "Thank you, Sir."

Concluding his reflection, he realized how affected he was by that moment with his father. Eric would never make the same mistake. He was doing everything, and would do anything, to save his own little girl; his own Sara. He imagined for just a second how he would feel if he failed. His knees almost buckled and he wished he could give his father a hug at that moment.

CHAPTER 8

December 27, 2044
Tuesday, Afternoon
New Jersey coast, Utopia Project Ship Number One
One day after the event

The day after the cataclysmic event, General Hyland was anxious as the three Utopia Project Ships pulled in side by side, as close to the New Jersey coast as the continental shelf would safely allow. Just as when they were anchored off the coast of southwestern Greenland, he knew the bows would face the shore. They would not risk damaging the large propellers and the propulsion systems at the stern by backing into shallow water. As the general reached the deck, a command blared over the loudspeaker and almost simultaneously each ship dropped anchor.

Each ship had two anchors, one massive anchor chain descended from the hawse pipe at the bow on the port side, and one smaller anchor chain was lowered at the ship's stern on the starboard side. He watched the rear anchor drop into the water, knowing it would keep the stern from drifting and turning with the push of the current toward the shoreline. Similar to the mooring setup in Greenland, the ships were anchored close enough to each other to allow for rope bridges to connect the three ships.

General Eric Hyland stood at the rail and stared toward shore. He was ready to facilitate his own escape. He planned to round up Sara and her friends and then go up to his parent's house in Vermont. They would stop at the Merck Pharmaceutical plant along the way and grab as much of his mother's medication as they could find. His thoughts were interrupted by commotion near the stern.

The general ran over and his heart sank when he learned that a group of survivors had already been spotted at Seaside Beach. He just hoped that Sara was not one of them. With any luck she was hiding out, maybe even back at their house. He tried not to look too hurried as he grabbed a pair of binoculars. As soon as he returned to the deck railing he saw one of their boats already heading to shore. Elder-1, who could never let go of his days as a field commander, was leading the group.

The general raised the binoculars to his eyes and peered at the group of survivors on the beach. "No!" he muttered. To his dismay Sara was there with them. She must not have secured his diary! The group was not even running away. In fact, they were all waving to the members in the boat approaching the shore as if their saviors had arrived. What a colossal mistake. It was not until the boat reached shore the group even seemed suspicious.

An audible, "Damn!" escaped the general's lips as Elder-1 shot Brian.

"Don't fight, don't fight, Sara," he whispered and prayed with desperation. Elder-1 would not follow the plan to capture female survivors if they were uncooperative. He would simply eliminate them. The general was relieved that after Heidi's slight resistance, Sara and her other friends realized their situation was hopeless and they did not struggle as they were put in the boat. Within moments the craft was heading back to the ship. Dropping his hands down, he felt like he had been holding up a heavy concrete block rather than a pair of binoculars.

His mind raced. They would immediately condition any female survivors. For Sara's sake, he had to somehow intervene and fast. He also had to avoid running into his daughter on the ship. Her reaction to seeing him would be involuntary and unstoppable. They would both be revealed and any plan he had would be blown to pieces. He also had to check the member rotation schedules. The rank and file members changed rooms, roommates and sometimes ships, every week to ensure they interacted with new members all the time and did not develop a bond or attachment to any one specific member.

As he started walking on the deck, he stopped in his tracks. He again put the binoculars to his eyes and scanned the shoreline. He could see the four members Elder-1 left on the mainland to search for other survivors, but was concerned about who he didn't see. *Where is Kid?*

For the rest of the afternoon, the general avoided the halls as much as possible and the common areas such as cafeterias and hygiene stations. Through simple inquiries, he learned the captives were all in rooms on the 29th floor, near the bottom of the ship. Their quarters had been quickly converted to containment cells, with the windows being frosted and scanning pads installed to control access.

Sara was alive based on the need for increased offspring production, so they would ensure she was impregnated as soon as possible. The thought stirred great angst within the general, so he pushed his team and his elder superiors to hasten their relocation to Long Beach Island. He wanted them to begin setting up their base camp right away. At that point they would be making frequent trips to the mainland, which would give him the opportunity to take Sara and her friends and escape.

The best the general could do for now was to monitor the closed-circuit camera system on the ship, which his position allowed him access to. That way, he could keep an eye on Sara and make sure she was not being harmed.

After getting the potentially lethal tracking device removed from his neck in the medical suite, the general noticed a long line of elders had formed outside. They all wanted to rid themselves of the rice-sized demon lurking in their body. Between eating dinner and visiting the medical suite, almost all the elders on the ships were preoccupied, so the general made his way down the high security hall to the Programming Center. He sat at his station in front of his monitor and pulled up the video program. He chose the video feed coming from the wall monitors in the containment rooms. One by one, he cycled through each room until he found Sara in room 2912. She was sitting with her head resting in the palms of her hands and her elbows were on her knees. She looked distraught and frightened. He felt like he had been kicked in the stomach. Changing to the video feed to the hallway camera, he swallowed hard as he saw a group of elders walking toward her room.

He kept his eyes glued to the video from the two-way monitor in Sara's room while Elder-1, Elder-12, and Elder-76 were with her. They were doing an evaluation but did not seem to have any intentions of harming or abusing her. He watched and listened for a several moments. He could tell Sara was scared, but she appeared and sounded very much in control despite the dire and stressful circumstances. She was answering Elder-1, who had left and then returned, "Sir, we know there were other survivors, we just do not know how many," she said. Despite the perilous circumstances, he couldn't help but notice that she carried herself like someone much older than the age of 19. He figured that was the result of Sara being the woman of the house for her entire life.

Elder-1 left Sara's room, so the general toggled back to a master list of active video feeds. The list was long, given the abundance of cameras on the ships. Each room had a flat-screen monitor, which was a two-way video and audio communicator in addition to serving as a computer screen. Video was also received from cameras in halls, stairwells, ship decks and outdoor areas.

Over the next hour the general worked feverishly to modify a Test User ID he had created many years ago; one he used to manipulate the video feed and show a still-frame for nights when he wanted privacy in his room. It was highly unlikely that simple modifications of an existing system user would be flagged from the data logs, so he linked specific cameras to this ID and established alerts whereby he would be silently notified of any movement outside of Sara's door.

When he retired for the night to his room at 9:00 p.m., he pulled up the camera program on his monitor. All was currently quiet so he tried to sleep, knowing he would never drift beyond a daydream haze, just like the nights long ago when he slept with Sara's bassinet beside his bed.

In the day following the capture of Sara, Maria, Heidi and a fourth girl he did not know who perished, General Hyland stayed away from common areas. He holed up on the high-security hall or, more often, in his room on the third floor. His living quarters were the size of a typical hotel room but had everything he needed. The standard elder room had a desk, a full bathroom, and a double bed, but for some of his comrades, even a double bed was not big enough. For their own personal sexual activity periods, the elders were permitted to take regular members back to their rooms and some chose to entertain more than one member at a time. The general had never indulged in sexual activity with even one of the members.

That night, while lying in bed in a light sleep, the general was startled by a notification from the video camera system. He had programmed the alerts to flash on his screen as a silent alarm. The clock in the corner of the screen read 3:30 a.m. Grabbing his desk chair and putting his keyboard on his lap, he turned to the screen. Typing a command, the camera view of Sara's dimly lit hallway popped up. His heart rate increased as he used his mouse to focus on a person crouched in front of her door. The person was peering in her window. The general zoomed in a little closer and was shocked as he realized who it was.

Kid? How did he get on the ship? And how did he find her?

He watched as Kid lightly tapped his fingertips against her window. *Don't make any noise!* If the noise was too loud, Sara's monitor would come to life and Kid would be caught. *Does she even know it is him?* He split the screen and also aired the video feed from the monitor inside her room. Sara was pointing and communicating and seemed fully aware it was Kid on the other side of the window.

Kid raised his hand and used his fingers to spell out words on the window. The general followed each letter and jumped up as he put the message together. *Oh no. He's going to try and rescue her tomorrow night.* He felt an ache in his stomach. He watched Kid put his palm up against the glass. On the other half of the screen, he watched as Sara did the same. Even though he was only seeing images on a monitor, he could feel the bond between his daughter and her boyfriend. He knew she cared for Kid, but until that moment, he never realized the depth of their connection. Their palms seemed to meld together, as if transcending the pane of glass that stood in between. The general put his fist against his mouth. Kid was offering her a glimmer of hope, and she seemed ready to grab it without hesitation, while the general was consumed by a wave of dread and despondency.

Turning away from the screen, he whispered, "It'll never succeed, Kid. It'll never succeed."

He knew he had to somehow intervene.

II: SALVATION

CHAPTER 9

January 3, 2045
Tuesday, Afternoon
Near Rutland, Vermont
Eight days after the event

Karen Stone sat with a group of people around the large, brown-stoned fireplace inside the Hyland's Vermont home. After using snowmobiles to case out the town and areas beyond in the week after the destruction, what they had found mostly were fetid, melted bodies. Karen cringed and looked around the room. The number of survivors was alarmingly small. Besides the group in the Hyland house, the only others were the McDermott, Spatz, and Ryan families who were staying in their own homes, but had expressed a willingness to work in cooperation with their neighbors. The one thing the survivors had in common was that all their homes were east of the Hyland's when the destruction occurred. All, except for Karen, whose house was further west. She cursed her misfortune and wished that her house was either hit or missed entirely rather than being cut in half.

Over the past week, Karen had struggled through the grueling stages of the grieving process with the loss of her mother. To help cope, she tried to keep busy and productive. Even now, she got to her feet, lifted a heavy pot of water that was hanging over the fire and poured a cup of tea. She took the steaming mug and walked it over to Evelyn, who was lying in a twin bed that Chris had set up in the living room.

"Oh, thank you, dear," Evelyn said as the cup was placed on a small table next to her.

She patted the bed and took Karen's hand. "Please, sit for a second. Are you feeling alright? You seem tired."

Karen shrugged her shoulders. "I guess I am a bit fatigued, but aren't we all?" In truth, she felt nauseous and was burning up inside.

"True. But do you have a fever? Your face appears flush."

"I don't think so. Anyway," she pulled down the collar of her sweater to expose her reddened neck. "It's not just my face. My whole body is flush. Maybe I'm keeping too warm."

"That's possible, especially since you are always working," Evelyn noted. "But please have Dr. McDermott look at it. His house is just up the road."

"If it doesn't go away in the next few days, I will."

"You really have been such a great help and we can't thank you enough. I don't know what Chris and I would have done without you. He told me you even learned to split wood and spent half a day doing it."

"That's alright Mrs. Hyland. No need to thank me. We all need to pull together here. Frankly, I don't know how I would've gotten through without you and Mr. Hyland after, you know..." She was trying not to burst into tears.

Evelyn rubbed Karen's hands. "It's hard. I know."

"I know you do. I'm grieving for a lost parent, but you lost a child. I just can't imagine."

During the past week, Evelyn and Karen had spent much time talking. They had both broken down when Evelyn, while obviously trying to empathize about inconsolable grief, had shared the story of losing her five-year-old daughter, the original Sara Hyland in the family. She recounted the 2002 tragedy at the United States Army base in South Korea. Evelyn shuddered when describing the sickening image of the fireball that was her daughter Sara's school after a missile found its mark. She said the sight would haunt her forever. Karen had shuddered too because she would also be haunted by the sight that preceded her own tragic loss—the strange red light that startled her right before discovering her mortally wounded mother.

After staring at the ground for several seconds, Evelyn lifted her head and smiled. "You know, I used to see you from time to time, and although I try to never be judgmental, I used to think you were one of those girls who was just a little…lost?"

"I probably was. You should have seen the guys I chose to date."

"I don't know." Evelyn appeared to be in deep in thought. "In the last week, I've been able to really get to know you, and I feel ashamed for any preconceived notions I may have once had. You are a special girl."

Karen blushed and looked down, "Now, Mrs. Hyland…"

"I don't mean to embarrass you, dear. I really just wanted to thank you."

Touching Evelyn's hand, Karen said, "Not necessary, but you're welcome. Anyway, please, drink your tea before it gets cold."

Tim Mahler, a friend and neighbor of the Hylands, no longer wanted to live alone with his foster kids; not with how strange Sid and Scott were acting. And given the widespread death and uncertain world status, he was pleased the assembled group decided it would be best to take up residence together. Tim did not hesitate to offer up his 19th century farmhouse and he was glad the group accepted. Given that his house had six bedrooms, four bathrooms four working fireplaces and a full wrap around porch, it was suitable for such a large group. He purchased the large, white colonial just three years ago, when a mild stroke and a bad hip had led Tim's doctor to give him a one word prescription—retire. Two weeks later his wife died, and he knew it was time. So he sold his thriving carpentry business and purchased a small working farm in Vermont. He kept small herds of cows and pigs whose meat he would never sell. As the animals needed to be slaughtered, he kept enough meat for his own needs and donated the rest to the poor in the area. His farm kept him busy, but compared to his old life, tending to the small farm was more like recreation than work. He wished his foster children felt the same way.

Five months ago, Tim had decided, since he never had children of his own, that he would become a foster parent. He took in two abandoned juvenile delinquents, the Sherman brothers, Sid and Scott. The two brothers, at 18 and 19 years old, were of adult age but were both classified and still in the 10th grade. Despite being 63 years old, more the age of a grandparent than a parent, Tim had wanted to help the boys. He hoped a regimen of school and farm life would get them straightened out after years of getting into trouble and being in and out of juvenile detention centers and foster homes.

At first the brothers worked on the farm, but soon the boys became more work than the farm. In their two months in the local high school, the boys had both been repeatedly suspended for violent and destructive behavior. Their school counselor would no longer even meet with either of the boys without a police officer present. Tim had seen this violent streak in them, having already once been threatened by Sid with a pitchfork. The fire in Sid's eyes was downright disturbing. That was around the time the boys stopped helping with the farm, claiming they were overworked.

When Tim had left the farm to come over to the Hyland house a few hours prior, the Sherman brothers had refused to come. They did not seem concerned about any other survivors, and in some macabre way, they seemed to welcome all of the death and destruction. What was most disconcerting to Tim was not the boys did not want to come, but that when he left, the brothers were both watching him from the front window. They seemed to be sneering with smiles on their faces, and he felt a growing discomfort and sense of dread.

After Tim conveyed his story to the group, Karen shook her head and exhaled. "Let me go and try to talk some sense into those boys. Remember, I used to date Scott."

"Oh no, you're not going over to my house alone." He struggled to stand up.

"Sit tight Tim. I'll go over there with her," said Rusty Davis, a 44-year-old divorced neighbor who lived by himself. Despite all the death they found when they canvassed the area, Rusty still insisted that his ex-wife would be coming next weekend from Middlebury for his visitation with his two kids. Tim didn't want to be the one to burst his bubble with the realistic odds.

"I'll be your wingman. There are plenty of snowmobiles out there," another neighbor, Clarence Moore, added.

Outside, Rusty mounted a snowmobile and Karen jumped on the seat behind him. Clarence mounted another snowmobile and they took off for Tim's farmhouse.

Chris fought to not let the worry show in his face as he walked over to the bed in the living room. Evelyn was running out of the medication needed to sustain her life. He handed her a pill and a cup of water.

"Is this the last one?" she asked.

"No, you still have one left." He did not sound as despondent as he felt.

"No luck finding the UPS truck?"

He sighed. "Not the right one. I found a UPS truck just outside of Rutland this morning. There were a few packages on board, but ours wasn't one of them."

Over the last week, Chris had searched relentlessly for his wife's medicine, which due to the recent snowstorms was scheduled to arrive the day *after* the destruction. He had inspected every last package in the UPS store and warehouse in town, to no avail. Deducing the medicine must have been en route, he had spent several days scouring the roads in Rutland and for many miles in every direction. Besides the one useless UPS truck, all he found was one field after another littered with dead cows and horses.

"We are running out of time," he said resignedly. "I have no choice but to make the trek down to that Merck facility in New Jersey. It's the only place in the world that manufactures your meds, and we are lucky it is on this side of the world."

Chris planned to get his wife set up at Tim's farmhouse by the end of the day and set off for the Merck plant in Rahway, New Jersey at dawn the next morning. Clarence and Marissa Moore, a middle-aged African-American couple who lived next door, had offered to take care of Evelyn while he was gone. He was comforted by having Marissa, who was a registered nurse by trade, staying with his wife. Chris knew she was a caring person, but Marissa also had an excellent professional reputation, and was described as calm and methodical under pressure. The only time he remembered her being anything but was when she told him she could never have kids because of a birth defect with her uterus. She had broken down while telling him and had to walk away, but it was clearly a deep emotional trauma for her.

A little while later, Chris's ears perked up upon hearing the high-pitched rev of an approaching snowmobile. When the engine stopped, the group inside the Hyland house was startled by a voice screaming for help.

CHAPTER 10

January 3, 2045
Tuesday, Afternoon
Near Rutland, Vermont
Eight days after the event

Without hesitation, Chris ran outside to find Clarence slumped in the seat of a snowmobile, cradling his left arm. He was also alone. *Not good*, Chris thought. *Where are Karen and Rusty?*

Marissa ran out and yelled, "Clarence! What's the matter?"

"I've been shot," he said, his voice hoarse.

She put her hands to her mouth and inhaled.

"By who?" Chris asked as he helped him off the snowmobile, but he already knew the answer.

"Was it those boys?" Tim demanded as he approached.

"Yes. They've taken over your farmhouse, and they're obviously armed and dangerous."

"Damn them! They must've broken into my gun cabinet." Tim hesitated. "Where are Karen and Rusty?"

"They took Karen hostage."

Tim did not look so sure. "Was she really taken hostage, or did she join up with them? She dated Scott, at least for a while."

"No, she was definitely taken hostage. She fought them and was screaming at the top of her lungs. But Sid backhanded her across the face, grabbed her by the hair and dragged her in the front door."

Clarence flinched as his wife inspected his arm.

"Jesus. What have they done," Tim said while looking up at the sky.

"And Rusty?" Chris asked.

"Rusty…" Clarence started. He seemed to be dreading what he needed to say. "Rusty is dead. After Karen got off the back of his snowmobile and went to the door, the brothers jumped out and opened fire on him. They spent so many rounds filling him full of holes that when they turned their sights on me, they had to pause to reload. I had a head start, and by the time they started shooting, I was already on the road at full throttle. I drove along the tree line, but they still wound up hitting me in the arm."

Chris and Marissa helped him inside and brought him to the kitchen. Chris retrieved medical supplies, which he had stockpiled after his son's warning call. Like flicking a switch, Marissa's nurse persona took over as she closely examined her husband's injured arm.

After cleaning, butterfly stitching, and dressing his wounds, Marissa breathed a sigh of relief. Dropping her nurse persona, she caressed Clarence's face. "You'll be alright. The bullet chipped away a tiny part of your radius, but it went right through and out the other side of your forearm. Thankfully, there is no major damage."

Chris was relieved. "We got lucky this time," he muttered and then went out to the living room to brief the group about the situation.

James Levy, a 25-year-old junior engineer with Rutland County's largest engineering firm, stood. "I want to go help Karen. Her and her mother were so good to me over the years. I can't tell you how many times they helped me clean my place and prepare food for my dates with Wendy."

Bending down to kiss his wife, James said, "Don't worry, I'll be fine."

Wendy fidgeted and kept twisting her wedding ring, which Chris knew was blessed just a month ago.

After securing weapons, Chris and James were ready to leave.

With Tim struggling to stand up, Chris started, "Maybe you should stay…"

He raised his hand and cut him off. "Oh no. This time, I'm going."

Chris returned an hour and a half later as dusk was falling. He stepped in the front door of his house, followed by Tim and James. Everyone inside was standing and seemed to be anxiously awaiting their return.

Wendy hugged James and said, "We were scared out of our minds!"

Evelyn sat up in bed. "So what happened? Where's Karen?"

"Please take a seat," Chris said. "We'll fill you all in."

When they sat in the living room around the fireplace, Tim started by saying, "I knew something was amiss as soon as I stepped on my porch. Those boys set up a full skeleton in my rocking chair, and put the skull of an infant in its lap."

Chris summarized the search by saying, "The house was empty. The Shermans' grabbed Tim's other two snowmobiles from his barn and took off. All we found was a puddle of blood in the snow in front and…"

"No!" Evelyn blurted out and put her hand over her mouth.

"Hold on, hon, we also found letters on the back of the barn door. We are guessing Karen must have written them to provide a clue as to where they are taking her."

"Written with what?" Wendy asked.

"Blood," James answered.

Wendy looked repulsed, but asked, "What did she write?"

"It's not much to go on," Chris said. "Just, 'K-1'"

"K-1?" Marissa asked. "That's it?"

Wendy proclaimed, "That's enough." The room fell silent, and everyone turned toward her.

She jumped to her feet. "Am I the only one that skis? K-1 is the nickname for Killington Peak, the highest mountain and highest point in the Killington Ski Resort. There is a restaurant up there."

Tim snapped his fingers. "I'm no skier, but I knew that sounded familiar."

Wendy turned to her husband, who appeared to be shrinking. "James, how didn't you remember that? You even skied it once!" she chided.

Chris asked, "Why would they go to Killington Peak?"

Shrugging his shoulders, Tim offered, "Skiing was one of the few non-destructive things the boys liked to do. Even with that, they wound up getting kicked out of a restaurant up there because they blew up something and did some kind of damage."

"We need to get over there now and find Karen," Chris said. He was conflicted, trying to solve two problems at once. "If we can save Karen fast enough, there's time enough for me to get to the pharmaceutical plant in New Jersey and get my wife's medication early tomorrow morning." He sounded frustrated. "I thought for sure I would have found it on a UPS truck by now!"

Wendy looked out the window. "The problem is it is overcast as far as the eye can see, and we can't search around Killington in the dark. We'd wind up killing ourselves, falling down a cliff, or running into something."

"And we can't use any headlights without giving ourselves away," James added.

Tim nodded his head. "I hate to say it, but they're right, Chris. We need to wait until tomorrow morning."

"I can't wait that long," Chris snapped as he stood and started pacing around the living room.

Tim stoked the fire. "Don't worry. We'll handle the Sherman brothers and get Karen back tomorrow. I'll either talk them down, or if not, we have weapons. You take care of your wife's medication."

Exhaling with great force, Chris said, "I don't want to leave you guys, but I don't know if I have a choice." Lost in thought, he continued to pace.

"You can't do that," Evelyn called out in a quiet, but even, tone.

Her husband stopped and turned to her. "Don't worry, I'm going to figure out…"

"Chris," she interrupted. Her voice had an eerie timbre that froze the room.

Tim stopped stoking the fire and turned his head. The room seemed enveloped by the silence and stillness of the moment.

Approaching his wife, Chris sat on the edge of her bed.

"Listen, in all our years, I have never, ever, once given you an order, but this one time…I am. You save Karen and don't stop until you do." Her voice was firm as she took his hand.

Trying to find words, Chris just gazed at his wife. It was true that she had never given him an order, and even her suggestions had always been carefully-crafted to where he somehow wound up adopting them as if they were his own.

"You're down to your last pill," he whispered. "I have no idea how long it will take to find more, and you won't survive without that medication!"

With the same eerie timbre in her voice, she said, "I know."

As Chris grappled with what was unfolding before him, he realized the complete role reversal. He was affected by emotion at the moment while his wife was the calm, methodical one.

"Karen and others could be dead by the time you get back. They need you here, Chris. Karen needs you. Your experience and expertise may save her life. Her life is far more important than mine, and you know that deep inside. Look at what has happened here. There doesn't seem to be many people left, and the young ones like Karen will be our only hope for any kind of future. You have always been guided by doing what is right, supporting what duty calls for, without being swayed by emotion."

"I know, but your perspective changes after you've been retired a while and all those suppressed emotions catch up to you. I don't want to lose another loved one for the sake of mine or someone else's duty."

"It is not just a matter of duty, but of right and wrong. For at least this one last time, you need to be guided accordingly, and do what we both know is right…"

He stared into her eyes, with an incredible level of respect beyond his fear.

Squeezing his hand, she whispered, "You need to save her first."

Chris was speechless. He hugged her tightly and whispered, "I'm sorry."

As she cradled the back of his head with her hand, she whispered, "Don't be, hon. Save her."

After hugging his wife and kissing her forehead lovingly, Chris said, "Rest. Stay in bed."

He stood and called out, "Tim, James, let's meet in the kitchen. You too, Wendy, since you seem to know the ski resort better than anyone. Bring the map and let's get a plan together."

Still holding Evelyn's hand, he turned to her. The strength in her gaze did not waiver. Patting her hand, Chris turned to the others and said with authority, "We'll stay here tonight, and at the first hint of dawn, we are leaving to save Karen."

CHAPTER 11

January 3, 2045
Tuesday, Late Evening
New Jersey coast, Utopia Project Ship Number One
Eight days after the event

Sitting in the Communications Center on ship number one, Elder-51 stared intently at his computer screen. Monitoring a tracking device, he started rising from his chair as the blip continued to move steadily in one direction. Finally, following the standing orders, he reached out to the lead elder, who was now Elder-2, since Elder-1 never returned from his mission on the mainland.

Establishing a video connection, he said, "Ma'am, Elder-51 here. We have an emergent situation. We were to advise if the tracker on the mainland moved beyond five miles. It now has."

Elder-2 jumped out of bed. "Assuming our member is with them, then the enemy is on the move!" She brought her face closer to her flat screen monitor and snapped, "Immediately awaken Elder-3 and conference him in."

General Eric Hyland's monitor suddenly came to life as he lay wide-eyed in bed. The screen was split with the face of the female Russian, Elder-2 on the left and the Chinese male, Elder-3 on the right. Jumping out of bed, the general stood at attention. "Yes?"

"Elder-41, it seems the group of survivors on the mainland is on the move. They are heading north in New Jersey," Elder-2 said.

“How do we know this?”

“One of our members on the mainland is still alive, and we believe he is their captive. But our member has a simple tracking device implanted in his scalp, so within a 50-mile range, we can track his exact location via antenna without need for satellites.”

The general tried not to cringe and show the utter despair he felt at that moment. Just a few hours prior, two of the group of survivors, Heidi Leer and Maria Stefano, had made walkie-talkie contact with him from their hideout at a marina. He had asked them to get his mother’s life-sustaining medication to her, which was why they were likely now on the move. They had said one of the Utopia Project members was with them, but had the general known the member was bugged, he would have told them to get rid of him immediately. The survivors were now sitting ducks.

Elder-2 continued by asking, “Given that you lived here, we assume you have a familiarity with the roads and towns in New Jersey?”

“Yes, of course,” he answered. Elder-2 knew this from the many discussions they had regarding points of interest in New Jersey, when the general was championing Long Beach Island as the most suitable base camp location.

“Then you will join a few other elders in a mission to finally eradicate this group of survivors. Winter gear, weapons, and rations are being loaded into a boat as we speak. Your group will be provided with a handheld signal locator to track our member. The enemy group is heading north but running parallel to the shoreline, so you should take a boat up the coast to close the distance before making landfall. Then you will hunt them down and kill them all.”

The general’s stomach turned sour.

“After completing that mission,” Elder-2 continued, “since you will already be on the mainland and heading north, your team will continue on to the next malfunction area along the border of the Green Mountains in Vermont and eliminate any survivors there as well.”

Elder-3 chimed in, “Including females, given this last fiasco.”

The general was in a state of shock. He had planned to escape as soon as they moved the ships down the coast to Long Beach Island. And then he was going up to Vermont to reunite with his parents. But he was being ordered to leave now, with an entirely hostile team of elders and members, with the mission to kill Kid's group and then go to Vermont and murder the survivors there as well? His heart thumped even harder. Now not only was Kid's group in mortal danger, his parents were as well.

"Understood," he managed to huff while not being able to breathe.

Despite all of his struggles and miracles in executing a plan from the beginning, and in reworking a final blueprint to get to the end, the tattered but still tied remains of his plan had just been obliterated. And in a grotesque twist of fate, he was being ordered to cut the last threads of hope—the ones he himself had purposely left behind in a desperate last-ditch effort to save humanity.

He was stunned as he stood staring at the faces of Elder-2 and Elder-3 on the monitor. He focused on remaining expressionless, but his angst was swelling and he knew his face was turning red. Hopefully it would not be noticeable in the dim light.

Elder-2 continued providing her orders. "You will be accompanied by 15 members and three other Elders: Elder-108, Elder-59, and Elder-44,"

The general was hit with another wave of dread. Elder-44, a Brigadier General in the United States Marines, was aggressive and hostile and had been extensively trained in combat. He was also very bright. The combination made him dangerous and the general wished they had selected some other elder. "That is quite a large force for such a mission," he was able to utter.

"We need an adequate force. The group on the mainland must be…formidable. How is it that such a small group has continued to get the upper hand on our members and elders, given our superiority in terms of training and weapons?" Elder-3 asked.

The general thought of Kid and his group of friends. *If they only knew.*

Within twenty minutes the general was dressed with additional layers to combat the cold. In the frigid air on the starboard-side of the ship, he turned as another elder walked up to the group assembled on the deck. Before they could get in the boat, all members had to be tagged. With a small handheld device, the elder quickly embedded a locator chip under the skin of each of their scalps.

Elder-2 walked over as they were almost finished loading the boat. The general saw her coming and tried to expedite their departure, but he was too late. The new lead elder looked into the boat. "Which three females have you chosen?"

"19, 81 and 269." It had been the general's idea to include some females for the mission.

Turning to an elder standing with her, Elder-2 said, "Update the records accordingly."

Seeming hesitant, Elder-12 asked the lead elder, "Are we sure we should allow them to take three females on this mission?"

"Elder-41's rationale is sound, and makes sense," Elder-2 responded. "The female members are as trained and capable as the males, and since the mission may take several days, their availability for sexual activities would provide a good, and possibly necessary, outlet for the elders and other members."

The general chimed in, "And do not be concerned with any impact on offspring production. We expect the female members to be impregnated by the time we get back."

"Good." Stepping up and reaching into the boat, Elder-2 pulled the hat off the head of female member number 19. "And all tracking devices have been inserted?"

"Yes, Ma'am."

Elder-2 reached out with both hands and rubbed her fingers over 19's scalp until she located the micro-transmitter. She then checked the scalps of a few other team members as the general climbed into the jam-packed boat. Seeming satisfied, Elder-2 motioned with her hand and the davit was engaged to lower the boat to the water.

January 3, 2045
Tuesday, Late Evening
New Jersey
Eight days after the event

In Middlesex County, New Jersey, Kid Carlson jammed the brakes and started to skid in the snow on the Garden State Parkway. Jess had yelled, "Look out," but a car was directly in their path and Kid reacted too late to steer around it. It didn't help the small vehicle was partially camouflaged by a coating of snow. Remembering that his truck had a push bar, and knowing a collision was imminent, Kid turned straight toward the obstruction.

"What are you…" Jess started and was cut off by a loud slam.

The red truck blasted the front end of the small car and sent it helicoptering off to the side of the road. With the truck hardly even slowing down, Kid was relieved the airbags did not deploy. Coming to a gradual stop, he stared at the road ahead. If he did not know any better, he would have thought the destruction happened at midday rather than late at night. A large cluster of awkwardly strewn vehicles created a pileup that blocked the entire northbound side of the parkway. Rather than trying to push through, he crossed the median and drove north in the southbound lanes. He started up the large bridge over the Raritan River on the wrong side of the road and instinctively slowed down, as if a wave of rat-race commuters might be coming over the crest. He knew he was being irrational, so he accelerated.

After getting off the parkway at Exit 135, Kid checked a roadmap and made his way to East Scott Avenue in Rahway. As he pulled through the open gate at the Merck Pharmaceutical campus, he called out, "Wake up! We're here." He watched in the rearview mirror as Heidi Leer rubbed her blue eyes and ran her fingers through her unruly blond hair. "Building 34, right?" he asked.

"Yes. Right there," she said as she pointed to a sign.

Pulling into the parking lot, Kid whistled as he stared up at the five-story structure. "That's a pretty big building."

"Mr. Hyland wasn't kidding when he said it would be hard to find," Heidi noted.

Looking for the silver lining, Kid concluded, "But given the number of buildings on this campus, if he narrowed it down to one building, we should consider that a huge head start."

Driving on the sidewalk, Kid took aim with the push bar on the front of the truck. When he hit the front doors, the tempered glass in the top and bottom cracked. Spider web patterns grew as the metal edging started bending and twisting and the doors burst open. Backing the vehicle up, he grabbed flashlights and a crowbar.

The lobby of Merck Building 34 was chilly, but being out of the winter wind made the conditions bearable. Kid turned on his flashlight and walked over to a directory placard on the wall, which didn't have enough detail to provide any real hints. Walking behind the reception counter, he hunted around and shuffled papers until he located a more detailed directory for the building. The task seemed daunting, and time was not on their side, nor Evelyn Hyland's.

"There are labs and research areas all over, but there are also storerooms listed. Maybe we should check the storerooms first and see if they have any product inventory in there?" he suggested as he studied the directory.

Jess Kellen, Kid's 21-year-old best friend, sounded impatient as he noted, "We could be here all night trying to find this. The building has five stories!"

"It has to be here somewhere."

"There has to be a way of narrowing this down. Do you know what kind of drug it is?" Jess asked.

"No," Kid answered. "All I know is she developed a rare blood disorder and had three heart attacks in two days. Without this medication, her blood almost instantly clots."

"A blood disorder? Let me see that directory," Jess said. "I'm no pharmacist, but with how sick my mother was all the time, I learned more about the types of medications out there than I ever wanted to." He pointed to the floor plan. "Here. Hematology is on the fourth floor. I would start there."

At 3:00 a.m., Kid and Heidi were searching a storage room for specialty medications on the fourth floor. As Kid tried to examine the stock in the first aisle, his eyes kept turning toward a disgusting puddle on the floor. The person looked like they fell backward and simply shattered. He found himself curious as to whether the remains were of a male or female. The repulsive pile of bloody flesh and bones did not seem to offer any clues. Even though he spotted a shoe, it was a white tennis shoe, which didn't help either. His eyebrows rose as he spotted the small loop of a woman's gold bracelet sticking out of a chunky tributary extending from the main mound of remains.

He melded with reality as he heard distant yelling from up the hall.

CHAPTER 12

January 4, 2045
Wee Hours of the Morning
New Jersey
Nine days after the event

On the Garden State Parkway, General Hyland's team traveled in a charter bus. They had secured the empty bus after making landfall in Middletown in Monmouth County, New Jersey. To go further north by sea, they would have had to go around the tip of Sandy Hook, which would have cost them too much time.

The general sat in the first row on the passenger side, behind the door. Looking back, 18 members, including three females, sat in the rows of seats. They all seemed bewildered by the world they were seeing, although they were seeing it in the ghostly illumination of the bus's headlights. At the very back of the group was Elder-59.

Elder-44 stood across the aisle in the first-row behind Elder-108, who was driving. The handheld signal locator had not left Elder-44's hand since Elder-2 had provided it to him on the deck of the ship. This was concerning. Elder-44 seemed intent to lead the mission, which would be problematic since the general did not intend to stick to the original plan. He knew that at some point he would have to assert his higher rank.

"How close are we?" the general asked as they passed Exit 131A for Metropark. The location of the group they were chasing had not changed for a few hours, which meant they had stopped. With the instructions the general had given Heidi over the walkie-talkie about his mother's medication, he knew they had found Merck Building 34. But they were taking too long and were in serious danger.

Elder-44 looked at the signal locator. "Five miles from the target."

"We just need to follow their tracks in the snow," Elder-108 observed.

"That is not foolproof," the general stated.

"It's a shame we couldn't secure an M3 from the Joint Base and head them off," Elder-108 lamented.

The general had forgotten that his fellow elder was a trained pilot and had flown M3 Jetlift Transports before. Fortunately, it was just coming up now. "To secure one would have taken us too far out of our way and would have taken too long. We could not risk losing them," the general responded.

They came upon Exit 135 and Elder-108 slowed down as the tire tracks in front of them veered off. Elder-44 said, "Do not slow down, they are a couple of miles to the east, but we are closing in."

They turned right off the exit and followed the tracks up Westfield Avenue. The general needed to stall. "Turn right here onto Route 27."

"But the tracks go straight." Elder-108 pointed.

Elder-44 jumped to his feet and glared out the window.

"Remember, we lived here," the general noted. "We know where these roads go, and we will be able to sneak up on them by turning right."

It was disconcerting to the general that Elder-108 then looked to Elder-44 for confirmation. Before Elder-44 could respond, the general snapped, "Elder-108, we are wasting time. Let's move!"

At that, the bus turned right onto Route 27. Elder-44 seemed more anxious as he turned his eyes down to the signal locator.

Kid did not recognize the voice as he walked to the doorway of the fourth-floor storage room. He froze and listened intently. The words were loud but carried no excitement or emotion.

801 came sprinting around the corner up the hall yelling, "We

found it." Seeing Kid, he waved his hand, "Jess wants you to come. We found it."

Sprinting up the hall, Kid and Heidi followed 801. After rounding a few corners and nearing the end of a long straightaway, they turned into the Hematology lab area.

Jess held a pill bottle up in his hand. "We had to bust into the locked cabinet back there, but we found it."

Taking the pill bottle, Kid read the label. Levonesex 212. "Thank God!" he uttered as he patted his friend on the shoulder. "You nailed it, Jess. Who would have known you were such an expert in medications."

"Not by choice."

"I hope there's more than one bottle," Kid said.

"A lot more. Over here," Jess said and walked to the back of the room.

Kid followed and then stopped short. "You found the mother lode!" Inside the cabinet were several rows of Levonesex 212 bottles.

"And better still," Jess pointed to the storage case, "this isn't refrigerated."

After finding an empty cardboard box, Kid started packing. In all, he counted 60 bottles, and each one had 90 pills. Evelyn only took one pill each day, so assuming they did not expire, her medication would be covered for almost 15 years. Lifting the box, Kid led them out of the building and back to the truck.

While Kid was placing the box in the vehicle, Jess offered, "I'll drive for a while. You must be ready to collapse."

Kid pulled the keys out of his pocket. "No argument there. After we get back to the parkway, stay on it until we pick up Route 87 in New York, toward Albany."

"Got it." Jess took the keys. "But before we leave I'm going to pull up to those cars parked over there and fill the gas tank and the two 5-gallon gas cans in the back."

"Why don't we just stop when we're closer to empty? There will be more cars scattered on the road on the way up," Maria said.

"Yeah, but they'll be out of gas. I would assume that when the destruction came, people who were driving died, but their cars kept on running," Jess concluded. "That's why they're all over the road and off the road. Or the cars kept bumping into things until they ran out of gas, like the ones we saw on the bridge over to Seaside in New Jersey. Anyway, the cars over there look like they were parked."

Kid plopped in the passenger seat and sounded as drowsy as he felt. "I'm glad someone is still able to think straight."

"They are on the move!" Elder-44 yelled and slapped his hand on the seat.

General Hyland felt a surge of relief inside, like releasing a tightly wound rubber band.

"And we're still more than a mile away. We need to move west, now!" Elder-44 commanded.

The bus was traveling north on U.S. Route 1&9 and a long median of Jersey barriers prevented Elder-108 from turning left and heading west.

"Turn left on Grand Avenue at the next break in the barriers. That was where we were heading anyway to sneak up on them," the general directed, having taken them the long way.

They turned left at the next break in the line of barriers and cut over to East Scott Avenue. The general looked over as they passed the entrance to Merck Building 34.

"They were here. The snow is all chopped up, and there are tire tracks," Elder-108 observed.

"But we're losing them. They are distancing themselves!" Elder-44 scowled, clearly frustrated.

"Damn!" The general sat back. He turned toward to the window so he would not have to continue to grimace and feign anger.

Startled by a change in motion, Kid popped his eyes open as he rested his head against the passenger window. *I must be dreaming, or worse.* Blinking a couple of times, by the light of the full moon he saw the eerie outlines of tombstones sticking out of the snow, trailing off into the darkness. He shook his head and started smacking his own cheek. He turned to see Jess staring at him. He was further chilled as he looked over Jess's shoulder and noticed more rows of tombstones on the other side of the road. "Where are we? Hell?"

"That was a short nap. We're still on the parkway in New Jersey, up around Newark and the Oranges," Jess answered.

With the cobwebs clearing, Kid sat up straight and peered around. He exhaled and dropped his body against the seatback. "I know where we are now. The Holy Sepulchre Cemetery. Not the kind of sight you expect to wake up to."

"Strange," Heidi started. "With the tombstones on both sides, it feels like they ran the highway right through the middle of the cemetery. No wonder people had such a bad impression of New Jersey. If you're not seeing smokestacks on the Turnpike, you're seeing tombstones on the parkway."

"Why are we stopped?" Kid asked.

"We've run into a roadblock." Jess pointed to a multi-car pileup. "I was about to jump out and see if we can push our way past. If not, with the medians and guardrails, we will have to double back and find a way around it."

"I'll go check it out." Kid grabbed a flashlight and opened the truck door. It was still dark at 4:00 a.m., but the night would soon be giving way to dawn. Under an overpass five cars had crashed and created a makeshift wall across the entire north side of the parkway. The cars stretched from the center median to the concrete side wall of the overpass. While searching for the weakest point in the wall of cars he risked taking a peek into a small sedan. Like all the other cars he had seen, the driver's remains were a disgusting puddle spread across the front seat. This one had a large travel coffee mug half buried in the muck.

Kid jumped back in the truck and told Jess to aim for the small sedan resting against the center median. Leading with the truck's push bar, Jess shoved the vehicle out of the way and resumed their trek north on the snow-laden parkway. Kid fell back to sleep and though his eyes were closed, he could still see rows of tombstones rising out of the snow, surrounded by an eerie translucence.

CHAPTER 13

January 4, 2045
Wednesday, Dawn
New York State
Nine days after the event

Kid awoke as Heidi said from the back, "Hey guys, I really need a bathroom stop."

Struggling to open his eyes against the breaking daylight outside, Kid moved enough to conclude that his muscles were stiff all over. He turned and looked in the back seat. 801 was wide awake, Heidi was groggy, and Maria appeared to be sound asleep. "Well Jess, so much for your navigator back there." He pointed to Maria. "I hope we didn't go too far."

With her eyes still closed, Maria murmured, "We just passed the exit for the North Pole."

Jess said, "We're still on Route 87 in New York. We just went through Albany."

Kid stretched his arms. "Now that I'm waking up, I could use a bathroom as well."

"Good timing. We just passed a sign. There's a rest area a few miles up the road."

Kid thought for a moment. "We have to make it quick though. I hope it's not already too late for Grandma Hyland."

A short distance up the road, Jess pulled into the Clifton Park Rest Area in upstate New York. Staring out the window, Kid saw one car parked in front of the building. The lot in the rear had a few tour buses and a cluster of trucks with drivers who had pulled over for a rest that would be much longer and deeper than they had expected.

Jess secured a flashlight and walked toward the Men's Room. "Boys this way. 801?"

801 leaned his head out the truck. "We do not have to use the bathroom."

"Speak for yourself," Jess said as he opened the Men's Room door and turned on the flashlight. As he stepped inside, his words echoed, "*We* sure as hell do."

Kid used the other flashlight to case out the Women's Room as Heidi and Maria stood outside, shivering. Over the years he had conditioned himself to breathe out his mouth when entering the usually foul-smelling rest area bathrooms, and he did so now. Shining the light around the room and creating elongated shadows against the walls, he noted that all the stall doors were open except for one.

He kicked the closed stall door hard with his shoe sole. The door flew open and bounced off the partition wall. Kid held a hand out to keep the door from swinging back. Lifting the beam of light to the area in front of the toilet bowl, he saw a heap of clothes, soaked with blood. Leg bones protruded and jutted out at odd angles from the pair of sweatpants in front of the bowl, like a sack full of carelessly packed pieces of lumber. The arms of a checkered, flannel shirt were draped down each side of the toilet. One sleeve looked full as the bones were stuck inside the shirt cuff and had not fallen to the ground. The other sleeve was pinned under a ribcage.

"Kid?" Heidi called from the door.

Turning his head, he inadvertently allowed a wisp of air to enter his nostrils. Death. The pungent, putrid smell triggered involuntary stomach spasms. "Don't come in!" Kid gasped, his voice sounding nasal.

Against his better judgment, he raised the beam. The light met the eternal darkness of eye sockets. Nestled atop the oval toilet bowl and supported by the shirt draped over the seat, was a skull. The face was angled to perfectly meet his gaze. He stared for a second and then turned away.

Stepping back and removing his hand, the stall door swung back to its closed position. The high-pitched squeal of the hinges echoed around the bathroom, as if admonishing him for disturbing this final resting place.

Walking out of the Women's Room, Kid concluded, "It's a disaster in there. Let's just say that bathroom is out of service. Come on, we'll use the other one."

He opened the Men's Room door and called out, "Jess?"

"I'm here," echoed from within.

Turning to the girls, Kid said, "I'll case out the stalls in there before you go in." He walked into the Men's Room and saw a flashlight on the counter facing the urinals where Jess stood relieving himself. After peeking in the stalls, Kid walked over and stood next to his friend. "Might as well join you."

They heard a knock at the door. Before they could even respond, the door was cracked open just a sliver and Maria asked, "Hey guys, are there any bodies in here?"

"Yes, two. They're frozen solid, standing in front of the urinals," Kid responded and chuckled.

"Let us know when you're done. Heidi really has to go. She's doing the dance out here."

Kid turned to Jess, who shrugged his shoulders.

"Tell her to just come in. It doesn't bother us if it doesn't bother her." Kid's voice echoed throughout the tiled bathroom.

Heidi bolted in and headed for a stall. "Sorry, I would have waited until you guys are out, but I have to go really bad."

"What was wrong with the Women's Room?" Jess asked.

From the stall, Heidi answered. "Kid went in and said it was a disaster in there."

"Gotta love these rest area bathrooms."

Kid turned. "No, it was a literal disaster. Let's just say the bathroom was occupied when the destruction came."

Jess grimaced and zipped up his pants.

In the silence they could hear a crinkling sound coming from the bathroom stall. Jess turned to Kid and whispered, "She found the paper ass-gaskets."

"I heard that," Heidi said. A minute later, her voice echoed throughout the cavernous bathroom as she yelped and declared, "Even with a pile of them this seat is freezing!"

On Route 87, Elder-44 jumped up and fingered his holstered weapon. "They have stopped again. Our distance is under three miles and closing."

The general felt a wave of discomfort. The group ahead of them had no idea that fewer than three miles behind them, a commuter bus full of mostly hostiles was snapping at their tail.

Elder-44 seemed encouraged and energized, like an animal closing in on its prey. He turned to the members sitting in the bus. "Prepare, we are almost upon them. The target is just ahead."

The members moved to the front edge of their seats, ready to engage as they approached the Clifton Park Rest Area.

"We hate to bring this up, but we will need to refuel very soon," Elder-108 noted. "Actually, the fuel light has come on. We just realized what it was. There are many gauges up here."

"We cannot stop now! We are at...two miles and closing," Elder-44 snarled as he watched the signal locator. "Let us get there before the target is on the move again."

General Hyland moved his hand to his weapon. He was prepared for a much different battle than the rest of the bus.

At the rest area Jess smashed the front of a vending machine with a fire extinguisher and started emptying the contents into a plastic bag. As he loaded up potato chips, pretzels and candy bars, Kid yelled from the driver's seat of the truck, "Come on, Jess. We are just waiting on you. We have enough food for a while."

Jess glanced around while heading back to the truck and suddenly stopped in his tracks. As he crouched and squinted, the plastic bag dropped from his hand.

Seeing Jess reacting to something, Kid opened the truck door.

"Turn off the headlights and shut it down! Hurry!" Jess yelled.

Kid was quick to comply and then ran up to Jess's position near the building. In the far distance on Route 87, he could see it. Through the spaces between the trees, the early morning light glinted off the roof of a bus that was motoring up the highway.

"That's a big vehicle coming our way. Friend or foe is the question," Jess said.

"We don't have any more friends, unless Drex decided to take a joyride in a bus. Let's wait in the truck and see if they pass the rest area and keep going."

Kid and Jess scrambled back to the truck. The group sat in silence as the bus came ever closer. They all crouched low in their seats. Kid's heartbeat pulsed in his ears.

Without hesitation, the bus turned into the rest area.

As Kid reached for the keys in the ignition, Jess said, "New Jersey license plate?"

"We are being followed." Kid turned the key. He put the truck in gear and went to back up. The bus came right up behind them and stopped, pinning them in.

All the soldiers stood in a line with weapons drawn, ready to exit the bus and attack. They were stalled as the front door would not open. Elder-108 continued to hit the open button, but the electronically-activated door would not respond. He started pressing other buttons.

"The back door is open!" Elder-59 called out.

Elder-44 ran up the aisle and pushed past the line of members. "Follow me!"

Seeing that he could not reverse, Kid put the truck in drive and yelled, "Hold on!" The truck lurched forward and jostled them as they climbed the curb. Turning quick to avoid ramming into the rest area building, he drove on the sidewalk.

Jumping to the snowy ground out the rear door, Elder-44 put a hand up to stop the rest of the members from coming out, "Back! Now! They are on the move again." He climbed back in, ordered the members to sit, and ran to the front of the bus.

Kid drove off the curb and the truck bounced as he headed toward the exit. Cruising in the virgin layer of snow, Kid was having difficulty discerning whether he was driving on asphalt or grass. He then spotted a line of snow plow markers and followed them to keep on the pavement. Within moments, he had made it back onto the highway and was heading north on Route 87. "Did that bus look full?"

"I couldn't see much, but with the commotion inside the bus, it seemed like a pretty large group. At least 15 or 20 soldiers," Jess responded.

"Large enough they needed a bus to transport them all." Maria was unable to hide the panic in her voice.

Go Kid! Step on it! General Hyland urged.

Elder-44 ran to the front of the bus and yelled, "We're losing them!"

"Sir, we are out of fuel," Elder-108 advised.

"Pull up to those buses in the back! Quickly!" Elder-44 said as he went down one step toward the front door. Reaching down, he muttered something inaudible and stood with an umbrella in his hand. Turning around, he hit a button and the front door opened without hesitation. "Seems the tip of this was stuck in the swing arm for the door." He held up the umbrella and turned to the other elders, "Where did this come from?"

General Hyland spoke up, knowing Elder-44 was directing the question at him. "It was on the floor when we got on the bus. It must've slid forward," the general noted, trying to sound sour. In reality, the general had picked up the umbrella from next to the driver's seat when he first got on the bus. He had positioned it on the floor in front of him so that a simple push from his foot would wedge it between the control arm mechanism and the door.

"Given the odds, it seems most unfortunate." Elder-44 had a hint of disbelief in his voice as he threw the umbrella out the open door. "And it cost us a perfect opportunity to eradicate this group once and for all."

Parked behind the rest area, the elders found a plush, silver tour bus. It was full with fuel and devoid of passengers. The entire group switched vehicles in a swift and orderly manner, and within moments they were back on the road.

The general looked back at the group of 18 members. He nodded as he made eye contact with numbers 81 and 19, who were sitting in the same row.

As they pulled onto Route 87, the rear of the silver tour bus fishtailed. Looking down at the signal locator, Elder-44 scowled, "They are again five miles ahead. Increase our speed, now!"

CHAPTER 14

January 4, 2045
Wednesday, Dawn
Near Rutland, Vermont
Nine days after the event

As dawn was climbing the nearby Green Mountains, Chris guzzled a cup of coffee and stared out the kitchen window. Snow blanketed the rolling fields in his view and offered a peace and serenity his heart would not accept, not at the moment anyway. He was more than ready to embark on the mission to rescue Karen. He would wait two more minutes before waking James, Wendy, and Tim. They had all stayed at the Hyland house last night with the entire group sleeping in the living room like a hippie commune. While Chris, Tim, James, and Wendy were going after Karen, the Moore's were going to tend to Evelyn and facilitate the move to the Mahler farmhouse a half-mile away.

At that moment James, Wendy, and Tim walked into the kitchen, already awake and prepared to leave.

After saying a tearful goodbye to his wife, Chris and the group set off on snowmobiles for Killington.

January 4, 2045
Wednesday, Morning
New York State
Nine days after the event

After a few hours of driving on Route 87, it dawned on Kid they were leading the group chasing them right into the area of Vermont that was supposed to have survivors, including the Hylands. He checked his coat pocket and felt the hard outline of his 38-caliber pistol. "Jess, do you still have your gun?"

"Yeah, I still have a Glock and some extra ammunition. Why?"

Looking out the front windshield, Kid said, "If we split up, we'll better our chances, well, Grandma Hyland's chances. One of us needs to lead that bus back there away from Vermont while the other grabs a vehicle and makes a beeline for the Hyland house."

"Good idea. I have no problem being the decoy so you can get to Vermont," Jess offered.

"Alright. At the next overpass, me and Heidi will get out and find another vehicle."

After passing a sign for Saratoga Springs, Kid pulled over and stepped outside with Heidi. Jess moved to the driver's seat and Maria jumped into the passenger seat.

Kid emptied a tool bag he found behind the seat and filled it with 30 of the pill bottles. Walking to the driver side window, he handed the bag to Jess. "You keep half of the medication, and we'll take the other half. Don't lose this bag. It equals more than seven years of life."

While they stared at him, Kid continued, "Lead them well past Exit 20, which is the exit heading toward Rutland. Maybe head north and west, lose them, and then double-back and meet us at the Hylands. There's a road map in the glove box with the United States on one side and Canada on the other. It only has major roads, but it should help you find your way."

Jess nodded. "What if they see your footprints and get off at this exit to follow you?"

"Then we become the decoy and you guys head straight for the Hyland house. That's why you have half of the medication," Kid stated and then held up a finger. "Don't pull out yet. Let me see if there's anything in the back I can use to erase our tracks."

Kid handed the box with the other half of the medicine to Heidi. "Watch for headlights coming up the road." He ran to the bed of the truck and found a four-foot section of PVC pipe. All he needed was a piece of rope, or even string, so he opened the mounted toolbox. Rummaging around he said, "Come on now!" All he could find was an unopened spool of fishing line. "It'll have to do," he muttered as he used his teeth to remove the plastic wrapping and started unwinding the line. He ran up to Jess and asked, "Do you have a knife?"

"Yeah, remember I found that cool Swiss Army knife back at the marina?" Reaching into his pocket, Jess pulled it out and opened the blade. "It is super sharp."

Unwinding a length of fishing line, Kid said, "Cut it here."

Struggling, Jess looked like he was trying to sever steel.

"Sharp huh?" Kid quipped. "Anyone coming Heidi?"

"All clear."

"There is no way. This blade could split a hair..." Jess stopped and took the spool. Reading the label on top he said, "Shit, no wonder. This says it's the latest generation of Zylon line. It's 1/16th of an inch thick but, get this, it has a 5,000 pound breaking point! A knife isn't cutting through that unless I saw it for an hour."

"Talk about overkill. What were they fishing for out of Good Luck Point Marina? Great Whites?" Kid took the spool back and held it in his hand. "We will make it work. You can go."

Maria leaned over Jess and said, "You guys stay safe."

"You too."

"Let us get far enough ahead before you hit the road," Jess suggested. "You don't want them to see you behind them."

"True," Kid agreed. "After they pass here, assuming they do, I'll wait another 20 minutes. It may take me a while to find a vehicle anyway."

Jess waved his hand out the window as he started motoring up the road.

Kid fed the Zylon line through the section of pipe and pulled it out the other side. He laid the PVC on top of the snow and while holding an end of the line in one hand and the spool in the other, he dragged it as he walked backward. It functioned like a roller for smoothing the surface of the snow and erasing their footprints. "Head up the embankment and take big steps," Kid instructed.

Heidi obliged and while walking in front of him, she asked, "Do you really think they could spot footprints in the snow while driving by?"

"It's possible. Look around. Except for the tire tracks, the snow is perfectly smooth and undisturbed," Kid said as he rolled the snow behind them.

As soon as they reached Union Avenue, he dropped the PVC pipe. He almost let go of the line, but he was so impressed by its strength that he wound the Zylon back around the spool and stuck it into his coat pocket.

He took the box from Heidi and they walked across the overpass into Saratoga Springs. Halfway across the bridge Kid stopped and stared at Route 87 heading south. The bus was nowhere in sight. Turning around and scanning the same highway to the north, Jess's taillights seemed to be floating in a sea of white in the distance.

They continued across the overpass and headed toward the Saratoga Race Course. Kid turned and walked backward in the calf-high snow so he could keep an eye on Route 87. As they neared the horse racing track, Heidi spotted a couple of vans parked alongside one of track's maintenance buildings. They ran over to the building and Kid was able to shoulder the door open. "Damn, we forgot to grab a flashlight," he said. "Can you hold that door open so I can see?"

On a desk he found a pack of cigarettes with a blue, butane lighter resting on top. He took the lighter and ignited it so he could look around the darkened areas. He could not find any vehicle keys.

Stepping outside, he recognized the silhouette of the legendary grandstand. He realized that no more horse races would be run here. It was a sobering thought.

Turning around, he spotted some houses up the road. "I'll be right back. Just keep your eyes on route 87 in case they pass by or turn off the highway," Kid said. "If they come this way, hide."

Several minutes later, Kid pulled a pickup truck to a stop and Heidi opened the passenger door. "Sorry, it took a few minutes to find the keys," he said.

"I'm just glad you found something, and hopefully it has heat." She handed him the box with the medicine bottles.

"Check it out. We get two for the price of one." He tilted his head toward a black quad with large knobby tires sitting in the bed of the truck. "The key for the quad is right here, on the same key chain. Who knows, we may need it. This truck is a dinosaur, circa 2030, and it's only two-wheel drive."

They motored at a slow speed as they neared Route 87. Kid pulled to the side of the road and shut the truck down. He leaned back against the seat. "Now, we wait."

"You always seem so…calm, and ready to do whatever needs to be done next, no matter what the danger." Heidi almost sounded exasperated. "What if they get off the exit? It may be us they come after."

"I'm as scared as anyone else. It's not like I've ever been in this…" he hesitated, "…situation before."

The awkward break in his speech made Heidi look over. "What?" she asked.

He shifted in the seat and exhaled. "Nothing. It hit me that I actually have been hunted before, but it was years ago."

"What happened, if you don't mind me asking?"

"It's not something I like to talk about. I haven't told many people."

"Alright." She turned away. "I'm not pushing you."

A few seconds passed and he decided to open up to her.

Kid cleared his throat and started, "When I was 16, I went to summer camp for a week. I was the senior patrol leader of the Boy Scout troop. One night, we were attacked by two 19-year-old derelicts with hunting knives who had snuck up on us in the woods. They said they would give us a ten second head start before they started stabbing and we knew they were serious."

Heidi exhaled sharply. "Oh my God."

"I was scared out of my mind, so I took off and hid in a pitch black, disgusting smelling latrine. I dialed 911, but a few minutes later, I heard a 12-year-old kid named Brett scream. Actually, it was more like a screech. The sound still gives me the chills when I think about it."

"You must have been freaking out!" Heidi exclaimed.

"I sat there frozen in the latrine and didn't do anything, not a damn thing, until I heard the police sirens. Only then did I run out to check on Brett. He was still breathing, but heavy wet sounding breaths. I put pressure on Brett's stab wound until medical help arrived."

"I am so sorry. That is scary. Did the kid make it?"

"Brett? Yeah, he fortunately only had a punctured lung. One other kid wound up in the hospital with stab wounds as well, but nobody died. They hailed me as a hero for helping save Brett and keeping him from bleeding out, but I was the leader of the group, and should have taken on the derelicts. Because I didn't act, we nearly lost a 12-year-old kid. It haunted me for a long time, still does, but I swore I would never sit by idly ever again. I would never let fear keep me from acting and doing what needs to be done."

"Well, you've certainly been able to practice a lot recently." Heidi shook with a sudden chill. "Did we have to shut the truck off? We have no heat."

"Yes. We need to stay completely invisible for now, including the smoke from the exhaust." His eyes refocused on the highway in front of them.

"Without the heat in vehicles, we would be in big trouble," she noted. "They are like our little life pods." As they sat, Heidi moved closer to him. "I'm freezing."

He opened his coat so she could rest her head on his chest. She wrapped her arms around his waist and pulled in closer. With her head against his shirt, he lay his coat across her upper body and put his arm over her.

"Thank you, Kid," she said.

"You'll warm up."

"Not for that. I mean for that too, but thank you for sharing such a personal story with me."

Ten minutes later, Kid tensed and sat up straighter as he saw a silver tour bus in the distance. It cruised on Route 87 and was approaching the Union Avenue overpass.

"Down!" he whispered.

Heidi put her head on his lap while they ducked down. He grabbed the ignition key, ready to high-tail it if the bus made the turn into the jug handle. Time seemed to stand still as the sound of the bus faded in the distance. They sat motionless for two minutes.

"They kept going," Kid whispered. "Time?"

"10:15."

"Alright. We sit tight until around 10:35, and then we move. We have 20 minutes to kill," Kid noted.

"What can we do for 20 minutes?" Heidi exhaled. She again wrapped her arms around his waist and put her head on his chest.

Kid put his arm around her and watched the road for ten minutes. "I hope Jess sees them tailing and stays far enough ahead." He looked down at her. "Do you feel a little warmer?"

She nodded her head. "Much."

"Your cheeks are hot, I can feel them through my shirt," he concluded. With his hand, Kid felt his face. "Mine are like slabs of ice." After rubbing his cheek with his hand for a minute, he touched a palm to Heidi's face. She jumped.

"You weren't kidding!" she exclaimed as she sat up. Unzipping her coat, she put her hand behind Kid's neck and guided his head toward her. "Here. Quid pro quo. You can lie on my chest for a while and warm up."

Kid did not resist, and as he lay across her lap, his face was nestled between her warm breasts. He breathed deep and felt like he was floating for a moment. He smelled the remnants of body wash, coupled with the slightest hint of perspiration, but it was a nice smell. It exuded femininity, and it soothed and relaxed him.

As he lay against Heidi's chest, he looked up at her. She dropped her head and returned the gaze. With her arm cradling his head, their faces were just inches apart. Their eyes locked. Kid blinked, and in that second, their lips came together. Her lips offered a warmth, but it was more than that. It was like an emotional outpouring, all being funneled by her through a passionate and powerful kiss. They moved their heads in slow circles and warmth radiated throughout his body as the tip of her tongue met his. After a few long, slow kisses, they paused. Kid was lost in the moment as he stared into her alluring blue eyes.

"Oh no, it's already 10:50!" she said.

Kid sat up straight in his seat and ran his hands through his hair. He had to snap out of it. Turning the key, he felt a little dazed and disoriented, like he had just come out of a trance. He couldn't believe how much time had passed. "Time to go."

She kissed him again, but he pulled back after a second and said, "We have to stop. We were supposed to leave 15 minutes ago." In truth, he felt something else starting to swarm inside.

Guilt.

Heidi stared deep into his eyes, and her manner was playful, but the underlying promise sounded iron-clad. "You just wait until later."

CHAPTER 15

January 4, 2045
Wednesday, Morning
New York State
Nine days after the event

Jess cruised up a long, straight stretch of Route 87. "Are they gaining on us?"

Maria checked out the back window and said, "No, they haven't even hit the straightaway yet."

"We don't want to get too far ahead though, not until we get past Exit 20. I want us to stay in their sights, but from a long distance."

"How much fuel do we have?" Maria asked.

Jess looked at the fuel gauge. "A quarter of a tank, but we have two full 5-gallon cans in the back of the truck. Once we get past the exit, we'll hit it and get far enough ahead that we can pull over and gas up."

As soon as Jess came upon Exit 20, he slowed down. "There's the mark." After headlights appeared behind him and he knew he was spotted, he accelerated until they were again a few miles in front of their pursuers in the silver tour bus.

Kid and Heidi reached Exit 20 and slowed down. He spotted multiple sets of tire tracks continuing north on Route 87. Jess had continued on as planned with the bus still following, which was a relief.

Kid got off the exit and maintained a reasonable speed for quite some time, even while dodging several trucks and cars scattered along

Route 149 and then Route 4. After crossing from New York State into Vermont, they were coming around a sharp bend between Fair Haven and Castleton when Kid yelled, "Hold on!"

He was squeezing the steering wheel in a death grip and was tapping the brakes. At his rate of speed, Kid would not have had time to stop on dry asphalt, let alone the snowy mess they were traveling in. Right in front of him, the east-bound side of Route 4 was entirely blocked by a jack-knifed tractor-trailer at a point where the lanes were nearly infringed upon by rock formations on both sides. He turned the wheel and his truck slid up an incline and came to rest against a flat granite rock face.

"Just our luck. You alright?" Kid asked.

"I'm fine, but I think we're stuck," Heidi surmised.

Looking in the side mirror and shifting into reverse, Kid could see the back tires spinning freely. "We have rear wheel drive, but the back tires are in a gully. I knew not having four-wheel drive was going to come back and haunt us," he muttered as he let off the gas.

Stepping out of the truck, Kid surveyed the situation. "The median we need to cross is lined with guardrails and rock formations in front of us and behind us, as far as the eye can see."

Heidi's side of the truck had come to rest against the front cab of the tractor-trailer. She grabbed the box with the medication, slid across the seat and went to exit Kid's door. "It's a good thing we have that quad back there."

"You won't be saying that for long," he responded. "We still have a 15-mile ride in 30-degree temperatures."

"We'll just wrap our faces with scarves." She took his hand and stepped down to the ground.

"And we'll have to stop for fuel. At least once anyway," he noted.

Kid knew the truck was on an incline, but the second he touched the latch, the tailgate came crashing down. He climbed up, freed the tie-down straps securing the quad, and put the key in the ignition. He started the engine and revved it until he had a good feel for the throttle. Dropping into gear, he crouched and leaned back. He hoped the angle of the truck-bed would make for easy unloading. He gave it gas and released the clutch. The quad almost jerked out from underneath him, but he held on and launched off the tailgate. The front and back tires hit the ground at the same time, completing a perfect jump. He braked and came to a sliding halt. "Hey baby, need a ride?'

"Do I have a choice?" She stood with the box of medication in her hands, eyeing the quad. "How are we supposed to carry these pill bottles?"

Pulling a flap back and peeking inside the box, Kid said, "Hold on, wait here." He dismounted and walked toward the tractor-trailer, muttering, "This is going to be disgusting."

Climbing under the trailer to get to the other side and opening the passenger door of the cab, Kid breathed out his mouth. He eyed the front driver's seat, knowing what he was going to see. Without fixating on the disgusting mess in the front, he turned his sights to the back. In the dim light, he could see that two people had been in the sleeper cab when the destruction came. Two flesh-less skulls rested peacefully on pillows, as if asleep when the destruction came.

Getting back to his primary mission, Kid searched until he found a couple of small plastic supermarket bags. He took the bags and went to close the door. He stopped as a picture caught his eye. On the dashboard was a picture of a man, woman, and young child at an amusement park, and they all looked so happy. Kid felt saddened as he presumed the three mounds of flesh in the truck were the remnants of the smiling family in the picture. But as he went to step out, he second-guessed that assumption when he noticed a whip and couple of pairs of handcuffs on the floor.

As Kid tied the double-bagged pills to the handlebar, Heidi climbed up behind him. They both pulled down their winter hats and pulled up their scarves, covering as much of their faces as they could. She groaned as she tried to pull up close behind him on the small carry-rack behind the quad's seat. "This is obviously not made for two riders," she said through her scarf as she shifted her rear-end back and forth, trying to get comfortable. He inched forward and Heidi pressed into him and wrapped her arms around his waist.

Taking off, Kid headed back west until he found a gap between a section of guardrail and the edge of a rock formation. The quad barely fit through the opening. "Lean forward and hold on tight, and I mean, tight," he said and started up the rock formation.

"You are not…" Heidi buried her face in his back.

Fighting gravity, they drove up the bumpy and uneven side of the rock formation until they reached a fairly level plateau. Kid slowed down when they were right next to the jack-knifed tractor-trailer. He turned around to see Heidi staring down with wide eyes at the steep slope next to them.

He looked up the road and as far as he could see, the truck could not have crashed at a more narrow section of Route 4. Although he knew it wasn't a rational thought, Kid felt like it was an obstacle that was just too perfectly placed.

January 4, 2045
Wednesday, Morning
Killington, Vermont
Nine days after the event

Sid Sherman stirred and woke up. *Where am I?* he wondered. *Oh yeah, the restaurant at K-1.* He lay on the floor in front of the fireplace for another minute and then threw his blanket aside. Staring at his pants, he muttered, "Morning wood." As he stood, he reached his arms to the sky and yawned, and then tried to pat down his bushy mess of red hair. Shuffling his bare feet, he opened the side door and went to walk on the landing for the outside steps.

"Whoa!" His hands snagged the doorframe while his foot dangled in the air. He looked down at the large mat covering most of the top platform. He recalled that under it was a large square cut-out with a 12-foot drop to the sloping ground below. "Almost stepped into my own booby trap."

Tiptoeing with caution along the edge of the platform, he unzipped his pants and urinated off the side of the tall set of steps. While doing his business, he tried to focus his sleepy eyes on the slopes. The sun shining off the sea of white powder made him squint. After zipping his pants, he stepped around the mat and went back into the restaurant.

As Sid headed toward the fireplace, he stopped and gazed upon their captive, Karen Stone. Her hands were tied behind her back and around a pole. Her mouth and her ankles were duct-taped. The noose around her neck was affixed to the top of the pole in such a way that it would tighten and choke her if she struggled too much. Sid was proud of that design. His dark eyes met hers. Karen appeared to be wide awake.

Kneeling down, Sid glanced over at Scott. His brother was snug in his ribbed sleeping bag and looked like a caterpillar in a cocoon. After hearing a rhythmic snore coming from the bag, he glared down at Karen. Getting close to her face, he whispered, "He'll sleep all day if I don't wake him up, and we're not going to wake him up now are we?

He pulled out his hunting knife from a sheath on his belt and held it by its thick, camouflage-decorated handle. He admired the forged stainless steel blade as he twisted it around in his hand close to her face. "You make a sound and so help me, I'll kill you."

Her eyes shone fear and dread, which only aroused him more.

She started to struggle and tried in vain to free her hands. He wasted no time unzipping her coat. Her blouse was already bloodstained near the neckline. After backhanding her face at the Mahler farmhouse and giving her a bloody nose, he had lied to his brother and said she had fallen. At the sight of the dried blood on her outfit, he licked his lips and stared down at her. Using the blade of the knife he sheared off the buttons at the top of her blouse. He slipped his hand in, pulled down her bra and squeezed her breast, hard.

She shook her head and made a sharp noise through the duct tape covering her mouth.

Sid lifted the knife in the air, threatening to slice her throat as he mouthed, "Shh."

Karen remained silent. She blinked several times, and like a fast-moving slide show, the panic in her eyes seemed to grow with every new frame.

Glancing over his shoulder, his brother was still snoring. Turning back around, Sid moved quicker. To free both of his hands, he bit down on the hunting knife and held the flat of the blade between his teeth with the sharp edge facing out. His eyes warned Karen not to struggle as he unzipped his pants. He lowered his head until the blade was less than an inch from her face.

Her legs trembled as she pressed her knees together. *Fight all you want, bitch.*

As he roughly pulled her pants down to her ankles, she strained to free her hands from behind her back. Her efforts were futile. He forced her legs apart and fell in between to keep them spread. For several minutes she fought, but every time she moved, the noose around her neck pulled tighter, and she had no way of loosening it. With her mouth taped closed and the noose squeezing her neck, she exhaled in bursts through her nose as panic seemed to swarm over her. She let out a muffled cry as tears streamed down her cheeks.

Sid glared at her, full of lust and rage, and feeling high from the power he had over her. He nuzzled her breast with his cheek, and as he turned his head, the knife blade sliced the surface of her areola. As an even line of blood appeared on her tender skin, his arousal peaked. Karen let out a muted shriek. He tried to stifle the sound by covering her mouth, but it was too late.

He heard Scott yawn, and say, "Quiet."

Slipping his knife back in its sheath, Sid climbed off of her. He hurried to adjust himself and then Karen, starting with her pants.

As he pulled her bra back over her cut breast, another shriek escaped her lips.

Scott thrashed out of his bag and jumped to his feet. "Dude, get the hell away from her!"

"Shut your face, bro, before I kick it in."

"I said get the hell away from her. She's my girl," Scott stood rigid and his face was red.

"She's not yours anymore. She's our captive so she's *ours.*" He stood to face his younger brother.

Grabbing an iron poker from the fireplace and holding it like a baseball bat, Scott yelled, "Back off!"

With his face getting hot Sid pointed his finger. "Try it. I'll shove that poker straight up your ass. We better find me a hot chick pretty soon, like your little Karen here, or you'll have to get used to sharing, whether you want to or not." Turning away, he added, "I'd rather ski anyway, so we have to go down and get the gondola going. Now that you're up and off your lazy ass, go get some firewood."

Scott hesitated, but went outside.

Sid walked up to Karen, peeked over his shoulder, and then reared back and kicked her in the thigh. "I told you to shut up!"

A scream of pain vibrated the duct tape covering her mouth.

Grabbing and squeezing her cheeks between his thumb and pointer finger, he shook her head a couple of times. Every time he jerked her head, the noose pulled a little tighter. "I hate little skanks like you. Always treated me like I was invisible, or worse." With his face an inch from hers, he sneered, "Can you see me now?" He stood and turned as the door opened.

Scott walked in with a handful of logs, and dropped them in the round iron ring next to the fireplace. He dragged a chair over to Karen and helped her into the seat. After loosening the noose, which was very snug around her neck, he pulled the duct tape off of her mouth.

While panting and gulping for air, she yelled, "That stings!"

"Sorry honey. I didn't mean to hurt you. You know I love you.

And you told me once you loved me back, right?" he said in a soft voice as he took her hand.

Sid was sickened by his brother's coddling of the little bitch.

"Well, alright, you didn't say that exactly, but you did say you cared about me. It's kind of the same thing, isn't it?" Scott tried to kiss her cheek.

She pulled away and had a look of disgust on her face. "If you really cared about me, would you treat me this way, or let your brother treat me this way, and hold me against my will?

"Are you upset, honey?" he asked.

Karen sounded flabbergasted and her voice had a fierce edge. "Am I upset? I'm being held against my will. I'm in pain. I'm starving. I have to pee, I haven't showered in days, and I..." She looked up as Sid turned around while standing at the window.

He met her eyes and shook his head once, while wrapping his fingers around the handle of the knife on his belt.

"I feel...disgusting," she concluded, with a quiver in her voice as she looked away.

CHAPTER 16

January 4, 2045
Wednesday, Midday
Vermont
Nine days after the event

Driving through Castleton, Vermont, Kid and Heidi had to stop and refuel the quad. While Kid siphoned gas, Heidi grabbed some food and drinks from inside the gas station.

"How much further?" she asked as she handed him a powdered doughnut.

"Still ten miles or so, but we shouldn't need any more fuel stops."

"Good. I just hope that Jess is taking the bus far away from here," she commented.

Kid took a bite of his doughnut and started pacing.

"What's wrong? Are you worried about Jess?"

"No, I have complete faith in Jess. I was just thinking of having to tell Grandma and Grandpa Hyland about Sara. We're delivering life-saving meds with a gut-punch of bad news. It's going to be brutal. She was their only grandchild."

Heidi sighed. "Kid, I know it's a touchy subject with you, but please don't blame yourself when telling them about what happened."

"Don't worry," he said with his voice sullen. "I've accepted it's not 100 percent my fault. Let's get back on the road."

Thirty minutes later Kid drove the quad up the snow-packed road to the Hyland residence. As he pulled up, he saw a white pickup truck parked in front. It was loaded with food and supplies. At first he thought nothing of it, but then a possibility put him on high alert. *What if the Hyland house is being ransacked?*

Kid reached into his pocket and pulled out his 38-caliber pistol. He flipped the safety switch and motioned for Heidi to stay with the quad. With the pistol in his hand, he crouched down and walked toward the house. The front door was ajar. Peeking in the sliver of an opening, he could see the small foyer. Beyond that he saw the living room with an oddly placed bed.

"Hello?" he whispered. He could see a motionless form lying in the bed. His stomach turned sour at the thought it might be Evelyn Hyland, already deceased.

"Hello?" he called a little louder. No response, and the body in the bed did not stir. He pushed the door open and froze as a prolonged creak emanated from the hinges.

The door was yanked open by someone standing behind it.

Kid raised his weapon.

A heavy-set woman African-American lifted her hands high in the air and yelped before screaming, "Don't shoot!"

Vaguely recognizing the woman, Kid raised his hands and the weapon toward the ceiling. "Aren't you…"

At that exact moment, an African-American man jumped out from behind the section of wall separating the foyer from the living room and plowed into Kid's midsection.

Wrapping his arm under the attacker's armpit, Kid swiveled and flipped him onto the floor. The man was on his back and had a bandaged arm, but also looked familiar.

The woman shouted, "No!" She turned on Kid, her fists and jaw tightly clenched.

"Stop!" Evelyn yelled as she raised her hands and sat up in the bed. "He's not an enemy!" She swung her legs over the side and got to her feet. Shuffling across the floor, she put her arms around him. "It's Kid, Sara's boyfriend."

“You’re still…here!” Kid said with relief and hugged her. “And seem…fine.”

“That’s more than my poor Clarence can say,” the other woman muttered as she checked the bandage on the man’s arm.

Hearing the name jogged Kid’s memory. He knew it was one of the Hyland’s neighbors. Putting his gun inside his coat pocket, he ran over to Clarence’s supine form and knelt down. “Sorry. That was a reflex. Are you alright?”

“I think so. As a retired police officer, I will tell you that was a great defense on your part. But I am at a slight disadvantage.” Clarence nodded toward his bandaged arm.

After Kid helped him up, they shook hands. “You’re Kid? I’m Clarence Moore, and this is my wife Marissa.”

Marissa seemed to relax a notch and also shook Kid’s hand. “We’ve heard a lot about you.”

He hesitated. “Nice to meet you. And again, I apologize for my entry. I didn’t know if someone was ransacking the place.”

“No problem. And we apologize for the less-than-warm welcome,” Marissa responded.

At that moment, Heidi appeared at the door. Seeing her, Evelyn said, “Well hello. Please come in…” and then she snapped her fingers.

“Heidi.” She held out her hand.

“Heidi, right. I’m sorry.” She took Heidi’s hand in hers. “My memory just isn’t what it used to be, but I did recognize your face.”

“I was with the group that came with Kid to ski last month. You made us hot chocolate, which really hit the spot,” Heidi reminded.

“That’s right. It’s nice to see you again.” Evelyn turned back to Kid and gave him her warmest smile. “Anyway, I’m alright…for now. But after taking my last pill this morning, I’m now out of the medication I need to take every day. I’m afraid my time is up.”

“Or is it?” Taking the plastic bag that Heidi was holding, Kid gave it a shake. It sounded like they came bearing maracas. “Not if we can help it.”

“Is that…don’t even tell me!” Marissa darted over.

He untied the bag, pulled a small medicine bottle out and held it up. “Anyone in need of this?”

Evelyn peered at the label and placed her hand across her heart.

Taking the bottle from Kid’s hand, Marissa let out an excited yell and looked up. “This is a gift from the good Lord above.”

“What is it?” Clarence asked.

“Levonesex 212! The medication Evelyn needs to take every day that she just ran out of. And a huge supply of it!”

A smile came to his face. “This truly is a miracle.”

“And it is only half of what we found,” Kid added. “My friend Jess will be along at some point with the other half.”

Opening her arms, Evelyn embraced Kid. “I can’t believe this. I thought my time was up. Today was going to be my last day on this planet. I wasn’t really ready to go, but I had accepted my fate. Now that you’ve brought my medication, I have another chance at life. I can never thank you enough.”

“It wasn’t just me, a group of us made it happen,” he said and turned to Heidi.

“Well I thank you. I thank you all.”

Kid suddenly felt overwhelmed with emotion. He went to speak and found he was unable, so he put up a finger to ask for a moment and he walked away. He could not stop the tears from rolling down his cheek. He was unable to save Sara, but he had saved Evelyn Hyland, and just in time. He hoped the general would learn of this and at least give Kid some credit. It would never make up for what happened to his daughter, but absent Kid’s focus in getting the medication to Vermont, General Hyland would have also lost his mother. The extreme highs and lows were disorienting and Kid held onto the door jamb to keep steady. He wiped his face and steeled himself. He had to snap out of it as he had yet to tell Sara’s grandparents of her death. He summoned every ounce of resolve in his body and walked back to join the others.

The room fell silent. Swallowing hard, Kid's stomach felt sour and his heart started thumping in his chest. He knew what Evelyn's next question was going to be. There was no avoiding it. "Kid?" she started.

Sweat formed near Kid's temples and he exhaled. *Here it comes.*

"Where is my darling Sara?"

Kid had practiced in his mind 100 times, but he still felt unprepared. He was supposed to remain calm, factual, and steady in explaining what happened. And then, be an emotional support for the inevitable breakdown, like he had to do with his friends at the New Jersey beach house when he told them about their loved ones after the destruction. This time, he was struggling to maintain the integrity of his hard outer shell. It had serious cracks and was coming undone. Tears started rolling down his cheeks. He fought to keep it together, but as he looked into Evelyn's eyes, he saw the sudden realization come over her. He was telling her without saying a word. Her eyes flashed distress, panic, dread, and disbelief in quick succession. Her hands started to shake.

"Sara..." Kid squeaked out, "...didn't make it."

"What?" she whispered. "No. It can't be. I mean, you made it..."

"But Sara didn't. She survived the initial destruction, but the bastards behind all of this captured her. I tried to save her, but we didn't get away fast enough when we were escaping and they shot her."

"No..." she uttered in disbelief. "It just can't be."

There was nothing Kid could say that would have offered any consolation.

She burst into tears, "No, not Sara! Not our Sara!" she wailed. Kid hugged her tight, and together they cried for several minutes.

Evelyn said with a trembling voice, "I have to lay down." She began to walk toward her bed on the other side of the room and after two steps, she started to collapse.

Kid and Heidi rushed over, but Marissa pushed past them and said, "I've got her." As Kid opened his mouth to speak, she added, "I'm a nurse, just stand back." She single-handedly carried Evelyn to the bed. "Clarence, pour a cup of water, quick."

Marissa cut a Levonesex 212 pill in half with her teeth. She used the bottom of a solid table lamp to crush it to powder. As Clarence handed her the water, she brushed the powder into the cup, swished it around and put the cup to Evelyn's lips.

After a few minutes, Marissa whispered, "I think she's stabilized."

Kid breathed a sigh of relief.

"Lord knows with a cardiac trauma like that, she may have been a goner without the medication you just brought."

Clarence came over and put his arm around his wife, who dropped her nurse demeanor and started crying. She mumbled, "Oh Clarence, Sara didn't make it."

Alone in the kitchen of the Hyland's Vermont home, Heidi was hugging Kid. She whispered, "There was no way to soften the blow."

"I know," he said. "But did you see the look in Grandma's eyes when she realized? It was horrible."

Marissa came into the kitchen, so Kid and Heidi separated. Grabbing his hand, Marissa said, "I was sorry for Mrs. Hyland, but I should be sorry for you too, and I am. My most sincere condolences about your Sara." She gave him a firm but sincere hug.

Nodding his head, Kid whispered, "Thank you, Mrs. Moore."

"Please, call me Marissa. Sara's grandfather will be devastated when he finds out. And Chris Hyland is such a good man. As we speak, he's risking his own life trying to save Karen Stone."

Kid's eyes narrowed. "What do you mean *save* Karen Stone?"

"She was taken captive by the Sherman brothers, Sid and Scott."

"Those derelicts?" he responded with disgust.

"I guess you know them," Marissa quipped. "We believe they have her up at K-1 peak in Killington. I just pray she is still alive."

"You've got to be kidding me." Kid was shocked. "And Sara loved Karen. They were like sisters. I have to go over there and help," he said without hesitation.

"Be careful. The Sherman brothers are armed and they've killed already. They even shot my Clarence, which is why his arm is bandaged."

"Did Grandpa Hyland, Chris, go alone?"

"No, he had a few of our neighbors with him; James and Wendy Levy, and Tim Mahler, who was the Sherman brothers' foster parent."

Once outside, Kid climbed on the quad and turned to Heidi. "Are you sure you don't want to hang back? The situation sounds dangerous."

"Hang back and do what?" she asked. "There's only so much grief one can handle."

"Understood."

Heidi sat behind him and wrapped her arms around his waist. "Now we have to go save the…freaky girl."

"I wouldn't say 'freaky,' maybe a little eccentric."

"Eccentric? Her hair was purple, and she had her belly button pierced in two places. Remember, she said she wanted to load up on piercings, but because her mother would have a conniption, she had to get them in areas her mother couldn't see?" Heidi added.

"Well, she was a little rebellious, but she seemed like good hearted kid." Kid started the quad.

They motored through downtown Rutland where they would pick up Route 4 to Killington. As they turned a corner, Heidi yelled, "Stop!"

Braking hard, Kid brought the quad to a sliding halt. He stared in wonder at a herd of moose standing in the middle of the road. It was not the kind of place you would expect to see the largest of the deer family. The animals, who must have wandered out of the forests of the Green Mountains, all looked anxious.

"Look at that," Heidi said in awe. "Are they all females? I don't see any with antlers," she continued with her Brooklyn accent coming through.

"No, they could be males too. Every winter, the males shed their antlers and grow new ones in the spring. What's odd is they're in a herd. I count six of them, but from what I understand, they're usually pretty solitary creatures," Kid responded.

"Maybe they're spooked by whatever happened, so they're sticking together? And how does a guy from New Jersey know anything about moose?"

"Just from talking to Grandpa Hyland. It became a topic of conversation after one ran across the field behind their house," he answered.

"Can we go around them?"

Seeing a long stretch of sidewalk, Kid said, "We can try, but watch out. If they panic and start charging everywhere they're big enough to do some damage." At that, he throttled up lightly and got on the sidewalk. He was trying not to startle the creatures.

As he came alongside their position the animals all turned their heads and watched him with suspicion, but did not move. As Kid hit a gully, his steering was thrown a little to the right, and he bumped into a metal garbage can. All the moose crouched a bit, their tension growing. Then Kid did something he thought was innocuous. He put up his hand and said, "Sorry, mates."

That was all it took to start the stampede.

One moose let out a bellow and started to run and the entire herd scattered in every direction. One ran in between two buildings. One broke a storefront window and dove into a building. The others sprinted up the road.

"Hit it!" Heidi yelled as a large moose headed their way.

Kid throttled up and followed the sidewalk. As he hit a curb-cut for wheelchair access, the quad caught air. He struggled to maintain his path on the sidewalk. It felt like he was moving at blazing speed, but glancing to his left, the two moose running in the road were outpacing him. He throttled even more and sped side by side next to the large creatures. He felt an odd thrill. The moment was simultaneously frightening and exhilarating.

"Look out!" Heidi yelled and pointed to a pallet of bricks obstructing the sidewalk ahead.

He had no choice but to make the jump onto the main road. As he did, he landed right next to the largest one. The animal shook its head and sprinted ahead of him. Driving behind, Kid could not slow down because the other was charging at him from behind.

"Move, move!" Kid yelled and waved his hand at moose in front of him.

The creature slowed and turned aggressively toward them.

"Duck!" Kid yelled as the moose let out a bellow. They slipped underneath its large jaw and were slapped by its dewlap. The animal again gave chase.

Just as Kid thought they might outrun the moose, a sizeable dog bolted out from in between two buildings. *Not good,* Kid thought as he realized it was a Doberman Pinscher. With bared teeth, the canine joined the pursuit.

Heidi looked back and screamed.

"Pull out your gun!" Kid yelled. As he glanced back, the large moose came within a few feet of the quad before slowing down and turning off. Fortunately, the dog followed the other animal. With a vicious lunge, the canine tried to snap at the moose's hind leg, but a well-placed kick sent the dog flying. The canine rolled, yelped, and retreated into an alley between two buildings.

"Didn't expect that," Heidi yelled in his ear as they drove east on Route 4.

"We're lucky that moose are not distance runners, and they look like a better meal than we do." He shook his head. "This rescue has already been treacherous and we're not even at the starting gate yet."

CHAPTER 17

January 4, 2045
Wednesday, Early Afternoon
Killington, Vermont
Nine days after the event

Coming into the ski resort, Kid stopped at a point where they had a view of Killington Peak. He was in disbelief as he squinted and tried to focus.

"The gondola is working?" Heidi sounded as surprised as he felt.

Kid blinked. "I thought I was seeing things. It must be running by a backup engine. No other explanation. And is that smoke rising above the restaurant on top of the peak?"

"There's definitely smoke," she confirmed. "And where there's smoke…"

"The question is, where is Grandpa Hyland?" Kid glanced all around. The overcast skies were beginning to break up overhead.

"Marissa said K-1 peak," she responded. "Maybe he already has the situation under control up there."

Kid went to speak, but paused. "I don't know. Somehow when I look up at this picture-perfect scene, I feel like something's lurking." He felt a sudden sense of foreboding.

"Maybe you're just projecting, after all we've been through," she offered.

"Only one way to find out. Let's get over to the gondola base." Kid revved the engine and took off.

Knowing the layout of the Killington Ski Resort fairly well having been there multiple times, Kid knew the gondola departed from behind K-1 Lodge. He pulled up next to the building, shut down the quad and dismounted. He grabbed Heidi and ran toward the back. As they hid behind the corner of the lodge, he gazed at the adjacent gondola base building. "Let's see if someone is inside working the controls." He crouched down and took off in a sprint.

The door to the gondola's mechanical room was held open by a couple of cinder blocks, which allowed some light to creep inside. He pulled out his weapon and motioned for Heidi to stay behind him. He led with his pistol, but nobody was in the first room.

He approached a door labeled, 'Authorized Employees Only.' Putting his ear against it, he heard the loud engine. If someone was inside, they never would have heard the quad approaching. Having the element of surprise, Kid pushed open the door and jumped forward. "Hold it!" he shouted with his pistol aimed straight in front of him.

A man inside raised his hands, holding a walkie-talkie in one and a flashlight in the other.

With the faint stream of light coming in through the open door, Kid squinted his eyes. The man was about five-foot-ten and was slightly overweight. His head was bald except for the gray crown of hair running over both ears. "You're not one of the Sherman brothers."

"That is for certain," the man stated.

"Are you helping Chris Hyland try to rescue Karen Stone?"

"Yes, I am helping out on the ground."

"We're here to help too." Kid put his weapon inside his coat pocket and reached out his hand. "Kid Carlson. I was dating Chris Hyland's granddaughter, Sara. This is Heidi Leer," he said as she walked in the door.

"Tim Mahler," He shook both of their hands.

"Sorry about the gun," Kid added. "You can't be too careful."

"Don't worry. I understand. The Sherman brothers are on a rampage, so we need to be armed."

"What's the status here?" Kid asked.

"Chris and two of our younger neighbors, Wendy and James Levy, made one heck of a climb, but they are now ready to move in on the restaurant at the peak. We are pretty certain the Sherman's have Karen up there. I just hope it isn't too late."

"Why do you have a string tied to that walkie-talkie?" Kid asked.

"I didn't do that. The Shermans' did. Those boys were able to engage the backup diesel engine to get the gondola working, and then concocted a shut-down system with this," he said as he threw the walkie-talkie on a folding chair. He then shined a flashlight on the face of his watch. "Listen, one of the Sherman brothers, I think Sid, is riding up in a gondola car right now and I need to shut it down and trap him up there. He should be about halfway up by now."

Kid watched him turn the ignition key and shut the gondola engine down. After a mechanical thump, an eerie silence followed.

Tim, Kid and Heidi all ran outside to look. The gondola had stopped and the cars were gently swaying.

Holding another walkie-talkie, Tim depressed the call button. "Are you there?"

"Go ahead," Chris responded.

"Wait!" Kid snapped.

"What is it?" Tim whispered. "Chris's group is ready to storm the restaurant at the peak."

"If you mention me, tell him I came here alone to help with the rescue," Kid spouted. "Believe me, it's too much to explain right now." He didn't want Chris to ask about Sara.

Tim nodded and depressed the call button. Without pausing long enough for Chris to ask any questions, he told them to move in, and noted that Kid was now there to help with the rescue. Before Chris could respond, Tim said, "Signing off."

At that, Kid exhaled, but he knew the relief was only temporary.

Moments later, Tim's walkie-talkie came to life. "Come in!"

"Go ahead, Chris."

"We moved in, but they got behind us. They were hiding behind a woodpile and escaped. I guess Sid is the one trapped in the gondola car because Scott is heading down the mountain on a snowmobile right now, and he has Karen with him," Chris huffed. "James has a busted ankle from one of the booby traps up here. He fell through a hole at the top of the steps covered by a mat, but Wendy is putting on skis and going after them. If you can get a clear shot without Karen or Wendy being in harm's way, you have to take it."

"I will be ready," Tim radioed.

"And send the gondola up to get us. There is no other way for James to get down," Chris added.

"We will, but we have to make sure Sid remains stuck."

"If we get in a car and you turn the gondola on, even if Sid jumps out up top, he will be all alone," Chris noted. "First things first, let's save Karen. They are flying down the slope as we speak!"

Kid jumped on a snowmobile. "Heidi, wait here with Tim. I'm going to try and head them off." He throttled up and took off, casting snow in a powdery white arc.

January 4, 2045

Wednesday, Early Afternoon

Outside of Champlain, New York

Nine days after the event

Parked on Route 87 in New York State, Jess threw the now-empty gas cans in the bed of the truck. Turning the vehicle back on, the gas gauge needle had a quick burst and then stopped. "Only half a tank," he muttered.

He turned to Maria. "See anything?"

Watching the long straight-away behind them, she said, "Nope. How are we ever going to lose this bus?"

Jess shrugged. "We can probably outrun them and erase our

tracks. Now, if they are getting satellite feed, it doesn't matter what we do. They'll find us anyway, and Kid and Sara's grandparents too."

"Are you still with us, 801?" Maria asked as she turned.

"Yes," came from the back seat of the crew cab.

"Don't worry, we'll pick up your vocabulary lesson in a minute."

Checking his watch, Jess said, "We've driven for more than an hour and a half since we passed Exit 20 toward Rutland so we're going to hit the Canadian border pretty soon."

Maria turned to him. "We are definitely doing our job, leading them far away from Rutland."

"I know, but look at this map." Jess opened it on his lap. "If we don't turn off, we'll wind up right in the heart of Montreal. That is a big city, so I could see us getting bottled up. If we alter our route, we can cross the Saint Lawrence River at Cornwall, which I assume would not be so congested. We'll lose them in Canada and then double back," Jess concluded as he put the truck in drive and continued north on Route 87.

"So we are crossing the border?" Maria confirmed.

"Yes. At least now we don't have to worry about what we have to declare."

Having crossed into Canada after hours of pursuit, General Hyland knew he had to catch up with Kid and Jess and get back to Vermont. He hoped they had found the medication, but time was running out for his mother. He had been incorrect in assuming the chase would lead straight to Rutland. He had a plan to take out the other elders when they got there, but he had not contemplated the chase moving further and further away from Vermont. He had to do something, and fast.

"Distance?" the general asked, while they traveled west on Canada's Route 401.

Elder-44 looked at the handheld tracking device, which continued to read the chip in 801's scalp. "The distance has grown again, now to eight miles. They have stopped once, and we have not, and yet we still lose ground. This behemoth can't catch up to them."

"We're pushing it as much as we can without losing control," Elder-108 countered.

"It's not enough." Elder-44 snapped.

"At some point if we are unable to catch up to them, we may have to move on to our second mission and go inspect the Green Mountain area near Rutland, Vermont," Elder-108 concluded.

With a sour expression on his face, Elder-44 said, "That would require us giving up on our first mission and it being considered a failure."

As they approached an exit in Brockville, Ontario, the general stood and announced, "Elder-44 is right. Since we are just going to keep losing ground, get off at this exit. We need to find a smaller vehicle that can catch up to them, a map, and walkie-talkies to communicate and coordinate our attack."

Ransacking stores in a long strip mall, the elders picked up walkie-talkies, batteries, and several area maps. In the parking lot they secured an unoccupied brown four-wheel drive sport utility vehicle with a full tank of gas. While the items were being gathered, the members were given food and drinks from the large chest of rations they had brought with them on the mission.

The general handed the maps to Elder-44 and finally grabbed the tracking device. Peering at the four-inch by six-inch screen, a red dot marked 801's position within a 50-mile range. Without any current satellite feed, they had to use their fingertip to manually adjust the cached map and follow the tracking chip.

"We must move, quickly," Elder-44 said. "How much ground have they gained?"

Reading the screen, the general answered, "They are now thirteen miles ahead, still on Route 401." He raised his eyes from the device and assumed a more rigid stance. "Let's split up the group. Me and Elder-59 will drive the SUV and take…411, 705, and 19 with us. Elder-44 and Elder-108, you will follow behind in the bus and stay in constant communication via walkie-talkie."

Elder-44's face reddened. "Elder-41, we should be in the lead vehicle."

"No, it is more important you lead the larger assembled group on the bus."

"That would be foolish. The bus cannot keep up. We should be in the faster lead vehicle, where my training and experience would be the most beneficial, and maybe even necessary, in terms of eliminating our target when we catch up to them," Elder-44 continued to press.

"Do not underestimate me or Elder-59. Now, we are losing time. We will proceed as outlined, immediately!" the general said with authority.

"Yes, Sir," Elder-59 said and climbed into the SUV.

"Yes, Sir," Elder-108 echoed from inside the bus.

Elder-44 took a step toward him. "Again, we must disagree with the course of action you are dictating."

The general knew this moment was coming and had known it from the very second Elder-44 was assigned to the mission. His eyes and resolve were steadfast while saying, "So noted, but as the ranking elder here, my orders will be followed."

Taking a step back, Elder-44's teeth were grinding as he forced out, "Yes, Sir."

After motoring in the brown SUV for an hour, the general was gaining ground. He knew he was driving at dangerous speeds given the snowy road conditions, but he felt like too much sand had accumulated on the bottom of the hourglass. On Route 401 heading to Kingston, he encountered the northeast edge of Lake Ontario as he followed Kid and Jess's tire tracks.

The walkie-talkie on the seat came to life. Elder-44's angry voice burst through. "Elder-41, what is your current speed?"

The general grabbed the walkie-talkie and responded, "Approximately 45 miles per hour, where possible. We are gaining ground."

"With the road conditions, we are barely maintaining 35 miles per hour." Elder-44 sounded disgusted.

"Carry on and push it harder if you can," the general advised and tossed to device back onto the seat.

A few moments later, Elder-59 glanced at the tracking device. "One mile and closing!"

January 4, 2045
Wednesday, Afternoon
Killington, Vermont
Nine days after the event

The snowmobile ride up the slope was frustratingly slow for Kid. He was more than halfway up Cascade Trail, but he already had to travel in a zigzag pattern to make any progress since the hill was so steep. Glancing up, he stopped when he spotted a snowmobile with two riders speeding toward him. As it came closer, he could see Karen sitting in the front with her arms behind her back. The younger Sherman brother was pressed up against her as he held the handlebars. He slowed and stuck his hand in his coat pocket.

Suddenly, a gunshot rang out in Kid's direction. Ducking down, he pulled out his own weapon, but it was no use. Scott had a human shield in Karen. Still, Kid fired a shot above them to give the impression that he was not shying away from a firefight.

Scott stopped his snowmobile in the middle of Cascade Trail and again raised his weapon. He seemed to be having difficulty getting his hands in a natural shooting position with Karen's body pressed against him. Kid noticed that gray duct tape was wrapped around both of their waists, which he assumed the Sherman brother did to keep Karen from jumping off.

As Scott tried to aim, Karen threw her head back and slammed into his chin. He reached for his face and his expression turned from agony to anger. Scott slapped her with the palm of his hand. She screamed and buried her face into her shoulder. He raised the weapon again, aimed, and pulled the trigger.

Kid hit the gas and turned into the woods. He leaned back and throttled up as the snowmobile jumped over a fallen tree and flew through the air. When it came down, he rode on one ski for a few seconds. A gunshot pinged off a nearby tree at head level, so Kid crouched down and both skis settled onto the ground. The low brush was trampled or pushed aside as he carved a path through the woods toward Downdraft Trail, which ran parallel to Cascade Trail. He stopped and peered out from behind the cover of a thick tree.

Karen was clearly trying to disrupt Scott's aim every time he tried to fire his gun. With her hands behind her back, she must have grabbed at his crotch because he tried to jump back. Scott reared back to smack her again, but stopped mid-swing as something caught his eye.

Wendy was racing down the double-diamond trail toward him. She swayed her hips gently from side to side, kicking up puffs of powder, but barely breaking speed.

Looking around, Scott seemed unsure of what to do. He yelled, "Sid? Where the hell are you?" Gunning the snowmobile, he continued down the slope.

Watching through the trees, Kid descended Downdraft Trail parallel to Scott. He would soon run out of tree cover as the trails merged in a large clearing and became a straightaway down to the K-1 Lodge.

Kid saw Wendy was now right behind Scott and Karen. Her ski pole dangled from her wrist as she reached inside her coat pocket and drew her weapon. She was flying down very much under control even without using her poles. Her strawberry blond hair flapped behind her as she swayed from side to side. At that moment, Kid agreed with James's assessment that Wendy could be an Olympic skier.

Glancing over his shoulder, Scott pulled his weapon and fired behind him. Karen again bucked her head and hit him square on the bridge of his nose. With the gun still in his hand, he pulled his arm back and covered his face, yelling something inaudible.

Slowing down, Kid could see Karen bouncing up and down on the seat. He then noticed that she was tearing at the duct tape around her waist. *Clever*, Kid thought. Finally, she fully ripped the tape and freed herself. Scott threw his arm over her shoulder and across her chest to hold her in place.

"Stop!" Wendy yelled from right behind him.

Scott looked back but did not slow down. Kid could see blood running from the Sherman brother's nostrils.

"Now!" she snapped.

As Scott turned and faced forward, he looked distraught and defeated. He tugged the handle of the snowmobile to the right and pushed Karen off the left side, dropping her in the snow in front of Wendy.

CHAPTER 18

January 4, 2045
Wednesday, Afternoon
Killington, Vermont
Nine days after the event

After climbing out of the stranded gondola car, Sid had narrowly escaped severe injury or death after leaping to grab the branches of a White Pine. He missed the limb he was reaching for, but a cluster of thick lower branches slowed his descent to the ground below. He landed on his back, and although the wind had been knocked out of him, he was still alive and nothing was broken. After catching his breath, he made for the lodge below. Whoever shut down the gondola and trapped him was going to pay. They were dead meat.

Working his way through a patch of woods, Sid turned down Flume Trail. This allowed him to approach the K-1 Lodge from the side. He then snuck in the door of the gondola control building. Tim was showing some hot chick the shut-down system Sid had made for the gondola, explaining how a walkie-talkie was placed strategically on a half-closed folding chair. When called, the device would vibrate and slide off the seat, pulling a string that was attached to the emergency shutoff switch. The old scumbag wasn't as stupid as he looked, but class was over. Sid stepped into the room and leveled his pistol at them. "Ingenious, isn't it?"

Tim and Heidi turned and both froze.

"Sid?" Tim started and went to take a step forward.

"Don't move! Hand me any weapons you both have on you."

They complied and as Sid pocketed their guns, Tim again tried to speak.

"Don't do this Sid. We should be…"

"Shut up old man. Don't give me any more of your bullshit lectures. I was sick of hearing them. Sounded just like all the other foster parents we had before you. Not to mention, I hated working on that so-called farm of yours. Did you see what happened to your favorite cow, Nutmeg? Did you notice she was missing something, like her head?" Sid laughed.

Tim's face turned bright red. Despite being a cow, Sid knew that Nutmeg was more of a family pet than livestock. The old man loved that stupid animal.

"But don't worry, her head isn't really lost. It's tied to the front of our snowmobile. She was our favorite too, and what better way to keep her memory alive?" He laughed again.

The chick grimaced. "That's sick."

Sid felt a flash of rage and grabbed her by the hair. With his face an inch from hers, she shrank back as he said, "What the hell do you know?" He looked her up and down, and his grip on her hair loosened. He had seen her before, and recognized her from somewhere.

Turning to Tim, he grabbed him by the flap of his jacket and pushed him hard toward the door. "Let's go next door and wait for my bro to get down the hill." He led them into the K-1 Lodge and had them sit on the floor with their backs against the front counter. Sid took a seat on the counter top, keeping a weapon aimed from a safe distance. He could see them on the floor below him, but he could also see the lower portion of Cascade Trail out the door. "Come on, bro, let's move it," he muttered while he waited, swinging his feet.

Without even a split second to react, Wendy plowed into Karen at full speed. With her hands still tied behind her back, Karen was rammed in the stomach with a ski. The impact knocked her further and faster down the hill.

Kid watched in dismay as Wendy launched high into the air when both skis disengaged from their bindings. Her hand still clutched her gun as she soared for several seconds and then crashed head first into the snow. The hand holding the gun rolled over and bent awkwardly. Her body slid for several feet before coming to a stop.

After witnessing the girls' violent collision, Kid navigated through the strip of forest between the two slopes. Once he reached Cascade Trail, he sped over to check on Karen. She had stopped rolling and was curled into a ball with her hands taped behind her back. She was gasping, like a fish out of water fighting for its last breath. Her face was contorted and showed her pain. "I'm alright...go check on Wendy," she croaked.

Kid drove further down the hill and pulled up to a sprawled out form. Wendy sat up and raised her hands to indicate that she was fine. She grabbed her wrist and let out a sharp, involuntary yelp. She was not fine.

Turning his head, Kid saw that Scott was speeding down the slope toward the K-1 Lodge. Heidi and Tim were down there and would now be in great danger. Bending down, Kid grabbed Wendy's ski pole from the snow. He planned to use it as a lance to knock Scott off his snowmobile. He slid the pole's wrist strap over his hand and throttled up.

Scott slowed down for a moment. He seemed to be searching for someone, but as soon as he saw Kid behind him, he crouched and accelerated.

Soon Kid was traveling at a dangerous speed but was gaining ground. Both snowmobiles were traveling nearly 50 miles per hour. Kid wanted to reach for his pistol, but he was moving so fast and was being jostled and thrown about so much that he couldn't let go of the handlebars for a second.

Scott tapped the brake, which made Kid swerve and almost lose control. Speeding downhill side by side, they glared at each other. The

Sherman brother looked savage as he gritted his teeth, which were stained red from the blood running out of his nose. Scott turned the handlebars and tried to ram Kid.

Kid turned away. As he did, the ski pole strapped to his wrist bounced around erratically and whipped him across the cheek. He instinctively grabbed the pole, but for a second was driving with just one hand. Right then, Scott rammed into him. Kid's snowmobile turned hard to the left before he could regain his grip, and he flew off as it began a barrel roll down the slope.

In mid-air with the ski pole in his hand, Kid had no time to think, but he reacted in an instant. Unable to raise the pole enough to knock Scott off his snowmobile, he thrust it into the track assembly. He tried to pull his hand free before it was dragged under the Kevlar tread, but the strap was still around his wrist. Just in time, the aluminum pole broke at the hilt and Kid rolled away.

The tread locked as the lance became wedged and the snowmobile stopped short. Scott was holding on, but his forward momentum threw him over the handlebars. The now unmanned snowmobile turned sharply and also started rolling down the hill. After the first dramatic mid-air spin, it came down hard and the front right ski snapped off.

Scott landed and rolled a few times. When he stopped he pulled out his gun, but it was too late.

"Don't move!" Kid yelled as he lay in the snow, propped up on his elbows with his pistol perfectly aimed. "Put the gun down!" He did not want to kill the younger Sherman brother.

Appearing distraught, Scott tried to swing his weapon around and fire. As soon as he moved, Kid fired off two shots and hit him right in the chest. Scott fell back into the powdery snow, dead.

"No!!" A blood-curdling scream from the bottom of the hill was followed by gunshots. Sid was standing in the doorway of the lodge, firing wildly. Kid was in the middle of the slope, completely exposed. *I am a sitting duck!* Fueled by desperation, he took a few steps and went airborne, trying to find cover behind a fallen snowmobile.

"You fucking son of a bitch!" Sid screeched.

"How did he get out of the gondola car?" Kid uttered in shock. As he went to peek around the front of Scott's damaged snowmobile, he grimaced. From the crash, a severed cow head tied to the front stared straight ahead with dead eyes. A rope was pulled tightly between the animal's teeth, like a bit for a horse, and the front of the snowmobile was stained red. Sid fired a couple shots in Kid's direction. The first bullet pinged off of the snowmobile, but the second lodged into the cow's head through its eye with a quick, sucking sound, like someone jamming a spoon into a container of cottage cheese.

Sid stormed inside the lodge.

Turning his head, Kid yelled up the hill to Karen and Wendy, "Take cover! Get to the trees!"

Karen was already doing just that, but Wendy just stared at him for a moment, dazed. Then she started patting the snow around her.

Kid's eyes turned to the K-1 Lodge at the bottom of the hill as Sid brought Tim outside. He threw him on the ground while waving a gun around. Tim tried to stand up and screamed in agony as Sid shot one of his knee caps.

After staring in shock and horror for a second, Kid's eyes turned toward the slope rising behind him. After securing the gun she had dropped in the snow, Wendy was crouched and limping to the tree line. "Hurry, Wendy!" he urged, willing her to move faster.

Kid turned back around to take aim with his pistol, but Sid was not there. Seizing the opportunity, he sprinted out from behind the snowmobile and made for the tree line. Without any shots being fired, he made it over to Wendy's position.

A few seconds later, Sid shoved Heidi and she stumbled out of K-1 Lodge. Kid's heart jumped and he pulled back his weapon and pointed it toward the sky.

"Hey! Down here!" Sid yelled. He stood over Tim and yelled up at the slope, "You like shooting people, do you? Watch this, you scumbag!" Without hesitation, he stuck the pistol against the back of Tim's skull and pulled the trigger.

Heidi screamed.

The bullet and some brain matter exited out the front of Tim's forehead and his limp body fell forward into the snow.

"An eye for an eye!" Sid yelled.

For a second Kid was shocked and sickened, until his anger swelled. "Bastard!" he snapped and raised his weapon.

Sid pulled Heidi in front of him. With a gun against her temple, he forced her to walk up the slope toward Scott's fallen body. It was a slow and strenuous uphill march, but he kept her pressed against him the whole time. Getting closer to his brother, Sid looked at the tree line and called out, "Don't even think about it. I'll shoot the bitch!"

Kid had no clear shot, not with Heidi being used as a shield.

After confirming his brother was dead, Sid's face was as red as his hair. "Don't worry, bro. They are going to pay!" He backed down the hill still holding a gun at Heidi's temple. She looked scared as she backpedaled in step with him.

They reached the bottom of the slope and he grabbed her hair harshly. Glaring at the mountain he screamed, "Listen to me, and listen good, you fucking scumbag. You are going to pay!"

Twisting Heidi's head and getting in her face, he bellowed, "You are all going to pay!" With a thrust of his arm he threw her inside the lodge and slammed the door closed.

CHAPTER 19

January 4, 2045
Wednesday, Late Afternoon
Outside of Belleville, Ontario, Canada
Nine days after the event

While driving on Route 401 West in Ontario, General Hyland suddenly snapped with just the right pitch and tone, "*Ion*!"

The members in the back seat of the SUV went limp as if they were fainting. For a change, he found it a good thing that all Utopia Project members had been conditioned to fall into a deep meditative, trance-like state upon this one-word command.

Still holding the tracking device, Elder-59 appeared surprised. "What…" He stopped speaking when he saw the barrel of the general's weapon aimed his way.

Without hesitation, the general said, "Sorry," and pulled the trigger. The bolt from his weapon hit Elder-59 in the chest and he ripped the tracking device from his comrade's frozen fingers. With great difficulty he swiveled Elder-59's neck so his head was facing forward and looking down. After pulling the eyelids mostly closed, he was satisfied that Elder-59 appeared to just be sleeping.

He proceeded to yell the conditioned word that broke the trance, "*Fleson*." He turned to see two of the three occupants behind him struggling to climb back into their seats after having slipped to the floor.

19 had remained in her seat, but was sluggish. She pointed at Elder-59. "What happened to him?"

"He seems to have fallen into a deep sleep. Members, listen up. Here are your new orders…" The new orders included ceasing all hostility toward the group in front of them. As the general spoke, he leaned closer to the windshield. The vehicle ahead was now in sight, pulled over at a gas station.

Maria was in the bathroom when Jess yelled, "Come on! We have to go! There's a vehicle coming!"

She hurried out and jumped in the truck. As Jess gunned the engine and started driving up the road, she peered back. "It's not the bus."

"I know, but who is it?" he asked.

"If it's them, they now have a smaller vehicle."

"And a faster one. That could be a problem." Jess looked in the rearview mirror. "Why are they flashing their lights behind us?"

Maria turned around and saw a person leaning out the driver's side window. "Whoever it is wants us to pull over and they're waving something!"

"What? Here, take the wheel," Jess said. While Maria held a steady course, he leaned his head out the window and squinted his eyes.

"Jess, you're slowing down!" Maria yelled.

"That looks like Mr. Hyland!"

"They're catching up!"

"I think it is him."

"Here, take the wheel back!" Maria yelled and turned around. She stared for a few seconds. "I'll be damned, you're right. It is him."

Jess stopped right in the middle of the road as the brown SUV pulled up behind them and General Hyland stepped out. Opening their doors, Jess and Maria ran out to meet him.

Thank God! General Hyland was beyond relieved at the sight of Jess and Maria. "Where is Kid?" he asked. Upon learning that Kid should already be in Rutland with his mother's medication, the general exhaled as he doubled over and muttered, "Thank you. Thank you." He waved the members, 19, 411 and 705 out of his vehicle.

Jess and Maria greeted the members and the interaction was nothing short of bizarre.

The general stated, "We'll catch up on everything once we're out of harm's way, but a bus full of our members is still behind us. We only have a few minutes to hide before it gets here. That is what we have to focus on, and now." Looking around, he noted, "There aren't many places to hide around here."

"What about behind that gas station back there?" Jess suggested.

'We don't have much choice." The general thought for a second, and then an idea hit him. "We can hide my vehicle there, but Jess, we need your vehicle as a decoy."

"What do you mean?"

"We need them to keep chasing your red truck, so they keep moving further away."

"So I have to keep driving?" Jess asked.

"No, I'm going to have 411 drive it."

"Wait," Maria said and ran back to their truck. She came back with a tool bag that sounded like it was filled with rattlesnakes. "The other half of your mother's medication."

411, who seemed to have fully recovered from his response to the word *Ion*, was ordered to get in the driver's seat of the red marina truck. Elder-59's corpse was carried over and belted into the passenger seat.

The general stuck his head in the driver window. The vehicle still had more than a quarter tank of gas. He turned on the ignition and the headlights. "Take the steering wheel," he said to 411. "You will drive this vehicle, and stay on this main road. Do not make any turns."

"Sir, we have never driven before."

The general gave a quick tutorial on how to drive. He then pointed at the speedometer. "With your foot on the gas pedal, maintain a speed of 30 miles per hour. You will not stop for any reason. Do you understand your orders?

"Yes, Sir," 411 said. Reaching for the transmission shifter, he glanced at the corpse belted into the passenger seat.

"And do not wake Elder-59, whatever you do." The general said as he stepped back from the vehicle. "Go!"

411 shifted into drive and hit the gas. After peeling out and then sliding when he hit the brake, he again started traveling down the road.

"Lord help him," the general muttered.

Jess backed the general's brown SUV behind the gas station, shut it off and jumped out. "801, throw snow all over the truck."

"Where are you going, Jess?" the general asked.

"To get a broom from inside so we can try to erase our tracks."

For the next few minutes, Jess used a broom to smooth out as many tire tracks and footprints as he could. Meanwhile, the general and 801 covered the roof and hood of the truck with snow. Although it was hidden behind the building, the general was confident that even if someone spotted the truck, it appeared as if had been there for a long time.

The general took one last look up the highway. 411 was already out of sight. Turning and staring at the road behind them, he could swear he saw blips of light, like headlights, shining in the distance. He walked around the building to the SUV. Jess followed him and used the broom to smooth over their footsteps.

Now inside the vehicle, the general said, "Everyone, sit tight. They will be by any minute."

Just a few minutes later the bus came bounding up the road, but it seemed to slow as it passed the gas station.

"Nobody breathe."

January 4, 2045
Wednesday, Late Afternoon
Killington, Vermont
Nine days after the event

With Sid and Heidi inside the lodge, Kid tried to keep his fear at bay while he gathered his thoughts. Seeing Tim so brutally executed had him shaken up. His thoughts turned to Heidi, and he felt a sense of dread with her being held hostage, especially given Sid's state of mind after the death of Scott. Kid did not want to fire on the younger Sherman brother. He was hoping Scott would drop the weapon and surrender. It did not work out that way. He would have to deal with that, and himself, at some point, but for now Kid had to figure out a way to save Heidi.

First, they had to get down to the lodge without being seen. They could take cover behind the tree line that continued down the slope for a few hundred feet, but the tree line ended at a wide expanse leading down to the lodge. With so much open space, a frontal charge would be disastrous. Kid needed to figure out another way. And the only people available to help at that moment were the two battered girls. *Where is Grandpa Hyland?* he wondered.

"You must be the infamous Kid," a voice said from behind. "I heard over the radio you were here. I'm Wendy Levy. I would shake your hand, but I hurt my wrist when I fell."

"Hey, nice to meet you Wendy. Obviously I wish it was under better circumstances. Do you know where Mr. Hyland is?" he asked.

"Last I knew he was at the restaurant at the peak, taking care of my husband James who broke his ankle..."

"Wendy!" Karen called out as she made her way down along the edge of the woods. Her hands were still tied behind her back with duct tape.

"Are you alright? I couldn't avoid hitting you. He threw you right in front of me."

"It's alright. What's a few more knocks? I'm beat to crap already." Karen turned to Kid, and despite her condition and the circumstances, she seemed pleased that he was there. "Hey stranger. Long-time no see."

"Hey Karen. It wasn't that long ago. Come here and turn around."

While Kid unbound her hands, she said, "That's right. The night I broke up with Scott." Rubbing her chafed wrists, Karen said, "I guess you guys found the letters I wrote on the back of Mr. Mahler's barn door?"

"We did," Wendy answered. "Very ingenious. It made finding you easy. Now rescuing you, that's another story."

"Thank you for saving me. I thought I was doomed to a lifetime of being the Shermans' pet if they didn't kill me too. I can't believe what Sid did down there to Mr. Mahler. It makes me sick."

"Me too," Wendy agreed. "How could he do something like that?"

"Do you realize your one eye is swollen and your cheek is cut?" Wendy asked as she lowered her wrist and cradled it.

"I know, and it hurts like hell. But it looks like I'm not the only one beat up." Karen pointed at Wendy's hand.

"I'll be alright. I just wish this was all over and we could go home."

"I'm finally free, but now Sid is holding that friend of Sara's hostage," Karen started.

"Heidi," Kid clarified.

"Heidi's probably not too happy about that exchange, since I could tell when you guys were up in December that she really didn't care for me at all," Karen noted. "I'm not sure why. Actually, she didn't seem to like you much either, Kid. All you did was argue with her if I remember right."

"Back then, yes, that was the way of things," he acknowledged as he examined their surroundings, searching for a way to get to the lodge without being spotted. Then defending Heidi, he added, "I don't think she disliked you. It just takes a while for her to warm up to people."

"That's what Sara said too. Speaking of, where is…"

Tired of running this emotional gauntlet, Kid just plopped down in the snow. Another person who was going to be heartbroken.

"…Sara?" Karen finished. "What's wrong?"

"She didn't make it." Kid's voice was somber. "She passed away in New Jersey."

Karen was motionless for a minute. "Son of a bitch." She also dropped her rear end into the snow. "First my mother, and now Sara," she mumbled. After a minute, she jumped to her feet. "What do we do now? I have to do something, or I'm going to just come apart here. I can't think about it."

Knowing he had to do something and fast, Kid tried to speak but the words got caught in his throat. His one second delay proved to be too long.

Karen sputtered and brought her hands to her face to try and stop the flood, like someone grabbing their nose to keep from sneezing. But, it was too late. She plopped back down in the snow and through her sobs she repeated the same words, "First my mother…and now my big sister."

With his hand on Karen's shoulder, Kid felt numb. He groaned as he stood. "We need to save Heidi and then get Grandpa Hyland and Wendy's husband down from the peak."

"I'm ready," Karen muttered.

Looking down at her, Kid could see her pretty, young face was battered. She had dried blood under her nose, and her one eye was swollen and raw. Although her eyes were red, she met his gaze with a resolve. He sensed it would be an affront to question her readiness, so he moved to the primary dilemma. "How are we going to take out Sid Sherman?"

"I wish he was the one you already took out. The wrong Sherman died back there."

"So you did care for Scott?" Kid asked.

"I wouldn't go that far. But, his heart wasn't as black as his brother's. Sid was the real mastermind and was definitely the more destructive of the two."

"What will Sid do now? Run, or stay and fight?" Kid wondered aloud.

Karen shrugged her shoulders. "Not sure. He's crazy, but not dumb. He knows he has to sleep at some point and we have enough people on our side to wait him out. He may be ready to fight, but he will not wait forever. He may just kill Heidi and run."

Kid stared at the K-1 Lodge below and felt a familiar sinking feeling. "It's a tough call. Moving in may also prompt him to kill her, and possibly us." He had to act, and act now, despite his fear. "But it is a chance we have to take. I am going in."

It was then that he gazed at the late afternoon sky and saw that dusk was muscling its way in. He noticed there were half a dozen Turkey Vultures very much alive and circling above their heads. They must have been living within the boundaries of the 'Green Mountain wildlife tract' that Maria had mentioned at the beach shack in New Jersey. He was surprised the creatures were present so far north in the month of January. But he also knew these large birds had the unique ability to sense a dead carcass from several miles away; an ability that baffled even scientists. Kid realized that with the bodies of Scott Sherman and Tim Mahler still lying in the snow, the vultures' senses were in fact dead on.

CHAPTER 20

January 4, 2045
Wednesday, Late Afternoon
Outside of Belleville, Ontario, Canada
Nine days after the event

On Route 401 in Ontario, General Hyland continued to hold his breath for several agonizing seconds. The silver bus with Elder-44 and the members seemed to be idling right in front of the gas station. After an uncomfortably long pause, a loud mechanical clunk sounded, followed by the whine of an engine. The bus was accelerating and pulling away.

The general allowed himself to breathe. A few minutes later he got out of the vehicle. Running to the front of the gas station, he noted the silver bus was up the road and already out of sight.

"Jess, can you drive? I have to do some surgery," the general asked when he came back.

"Sure. Where are we heading?" Jess was already in the driver's seat, so he turned on the vehicle and put it in gear.

"East. We're back-tracking and heading for my parent's house in Vermont."

Pulling out a knife, the general waved his hand. "801, come here and look down."

Jess's eyes opened wide. "What kind of surgery are you talking about?"

The knife was used to carefully cut 801's scalp. Holding up the blood-laced locator chip, the general said, "To remove this."

"What is that?" Maria asked.

"A locator chip. Whether you realize it or not, with 801 in your custody we've been able to track your every move. But that will no longer be an issue." He opened the passenger window and threw the tiny, blood-laced chip outside.

"We never had a clue," Jess muttered.

"Lucky these are older, simpler trackers that need to be manually monitored. We had more modern devices that would have been tracked via the satellite system if it was still operable." Rubbing the back of his neck, the general was relieved the rice-sized tracker and tiny bomb had been removed a few days prior.

Grabbing the hand-held tracking device from his coat pocket, he also tossed it out the window. "Fortunately, back in New Jersey, before we could send out an attack team, your group and 801 were already on the move. Otherwise, you were sitting ducks at the marina you were holed up in."

"You knew we were hiding out at Good Luck Point Marina?" Jess sounded surprised.

"Yes. You got out just in time. The next morning, you would have been ambushed."

Jess and Maria turned to each other and both said at the same time, "Drex!"

The general gave them a questioning look.

"We didn't *all* leave. We left one person there," Jess clarified.

The general remained silent and chose not to speculate as to the fate of the person they left behind. Still holding the knife he waved his hand. "705, come here. You're next."

He cut a locator chip from the scalp of 705 first, and then 19. Rolling down the window, he tossed away the bloody trackers.

"Disgusting." Maria turned and rested her head against the window, staring outside. "Here comes the dark again, and we barely got any sleep last night."

"We can sleep in shifts on the way. But first," the general raised his hand in the air, "I need silence. I am going to check in one last time." Putting the walkie-talkie to his lips he snapped, "Elder-44!"

"Yes, Elder-41," came an impatient voice.

"The target is on the move again and is continuing west on Route 401. They are still a couple of miles ahead of us," the general lied.

"We thought you were gaining on them, yet you were unable to catch them?"

"Affirmative. They have increased their speed."

"Maybe we should have given more consideration to who was driving in the lead vehicle," Elder-44 radioed back, his voice thick with sarcasm and arrogance.

Rolling his eyes, the general said, "Just follow your orders and continue your pursuit." He then heaved the walkie-talkie out the window and stated, "To the contrary, Elder-44. Much consideration was given."

"He is going to be surprised when he finds out who he is actually chasing," Jess noted.

"Let's hope he doesn't catch 411 until they are both far up the road. What I would give to see the look on Elder-44's face." The general sat against the seat back and turned to Jess and Maria. "Well, I guess I have some serious explaining to do."

With shock still lingering about their faces as they cruised along Route 401 East, Jess and Maria both nodded their heads assuredly.

Outside of Kitchener, Ontario, Elder-44 threw his walkie-talkie on the bus seat as his frustration continued to grow. "Why is Elder-41 not responding?" He stood and squinted his eyes. "Stop!"

Elder-108 hit the brakes and the bus began to fishtail in the snow. As the bus came to a halt, Elder-44 yelled, "Weapons ready! Now! Open the door and follow me."

Off the road and stopped against a large tree was a red truck with its taillights still on.

With his weapon in front of him, Elder-44 crouched as he approached the vehicle. He pulled open the driver side door and saw member 411 at the wheel. Looking past him to the passenger seat, he asked, "What happened to Elder-59?"

"He is sleeping," 411 answered definitively.

Walking around to the passenger door, Elder-44 opened it and stared closely at Elder-59.

"Who said he was sleeping?"

"Elder-41."

Grabbing Elder-59's coat and pulling him out of the truck, Elder-44 tossed the rigid corpse onto the ground. "Damn Elder-41!"

That night, with darkness settling in, Elder-44 decided that his group would stay parked on Route 401 outside of Kitchener. His plan was to pick up the enemy's trail at dawn. They used the bus as a shelter and turned on the heat every half hour to combat the plummeting temperature. In battling the elements, which they were not used to doing, he noticed that none of the members seemed concerned with games or sexual activity periods.

As Elder-44 paced up and down the aisle of the bus, he stopped and glanced around. "Where is 19?"

"She is in the other vehicle with Elder-41," Elder-108 said.

Elder-44 grunted as another spike of anger ran through him. "Figures. We wanted 19." He pointed to an 18-year-old female member with dirty blonde hair. "81, come with me to the back of the bus, now."

While walking up the aisle, Elder-44 took off his belt and unbuttoned his pants. "Well Elder-41, we don't know what kind of game you are playing, but we can now appreciate your idea about bringing female members."

When he was done, Elder-44 got to his feet and put his belt back on. Satisfied that he had fucked up 81 while fucking her, he fought to suppress a smile as he glared down at her now swollen face.

January 4, 2045
Wednesday, Early Evening
Killington, Vermont
Nine days after the event

Kid waited for sky to darken. He zipped his coat all the way up and hugged himself, trying to stave off the chill.

"What is the plan?" Wendy asked. "I don't know about you, but I can't stay outside much longer. I'm freezing and it is only going to get worse."

"I'm ready to go in," Kid said and squinted as he looked down the slope. With nighttime falling and no lights anywhere, the lodge and the gondola control building were now faint outlines. "I just needed it dark enough to sneak up to the lodge without being seen."

"Why don't I come with you, Kid?" Karen offered. She turned to Wendy. "Will you be alright by yourself?"

"I guess. I still have a gun," she said. "How are you guys going to get down there without them seeing you coming?"

"I was thinking we go down the next trail over…"

"Flume Trail," Wendy clarified.

"Yes, and approach the lodge from the side," Kid finished.

"Makes sense," Wendy observed. "Good luck and I hope you end this quickly so I can get down from here."

Without hesitation, Kid and Karen took off through the trees and ran down Flume Trail. At times Kid's downhill momentum was so great that he had to fight to slow himself before tumbling to the bottom. They came up behind the gondola's control building and stopped to catch their breath.

"He's probably inside waiting for us to attack," Kid huffed. "So rather than going in, we need to draw him out."

"How?"

"If I go inside this building and turn the gondola on, I assume he will come over to check it out."

"You know how to turn it on?" Karen asked.

"I watched Tim operate it when I first arrived. It seemed pretty simple. I just wish we had a flashlight." He patted his pant pocket and felt the bulge of the butane lighter he had secured in Saratoga. "But listen, as soon as Sid sees the gondola moving, I assume he will come running over here to the control building to see what gives. I may be trapped inside, so you need to wait behind the corner of the building and take him out when he comes. Even if he has Heidi with him, you'll be close enough to get a clear shot. Here," he said as he pulled a 38-caliber pistol from his coat pocket.

"Kid, I hate to bring this up now, but I've never fired a weapon before."

"Aim and shoot, like a camera. The safety is off and the gun is loaded, so be careful. Just hold it tight with both hands, aim, and fire while exhaling. Don't hesitate and don't close your eyes."

She took the gun and aimed at a tree nearby, "Eyes open. Exhale. Got it."

"Let's do this. Every minute Heidi is with Sid, the worse the odds become, and we already had to wait for it to get dark enough. Take your position." After ensuring Karen was hidden and set, Kid entered the gondola control building.

Pulling out the butane lighter, Kid could not ignite it with a gloved hand, so he put his glove in his pocket. Navigating in the pitch-black engine room, he had to extinguish the flame before the lighter became too hot to hold.

In complete darkness, Kid's hearing seemed more acute. For a second he thought he heard breathing, but listening closer, he heard only silence. After reigniting the lighter, he headed toward the diesel engine. As he approached the control panel, he stopped short. The key had been removed, but by who, and when?

Right then, without any particular visual or auditory trigger, he sensed something.

He extinguished the flame, dropped flat on his stomach, and

crawled a few feet away from where he had been standing with the lighter. He heard a muffled yelp. He could not tell which direction the sound came from. A second later, he heard another quick shriek and then silence. The next sound made him freeze. It was the click of a pistol trigger being cocked.

Kid then jumped as a piece of metal bounced across the floor.

CHAPTER 21

January 4, 2045
Wednesday, Early Evening
Killington, Vermont
Nine days after the event

Kid was chilled further as a voice emanated from the darkness. "Missing something? Like maybe…the key?"

It was Sid. Kid turned his head in every direction, not having any clue where the voice in the room was coming from.

"Don't even think about making a move. I have a gun to the… girl's head." Sid snickered, and then lowered his voice. "They actually came in here. I am glad you mentioned they would need the gondola to get some of their injured from the peak. Our booby traps up there worked like a freaking charm."

That isn't why we came in here, at least not now, Kid thought. But he quickly realized it did not matter. They were in here all the same.

Another muffled yell cut through the darkness.

"Let her go, Sid, and drop the gun. You'll never make it out of this building alive. I have several backups armed and waiting outside," Kid bluffed.

"Do I care? What's the worst that happens, I die? Big friggin deal."

A stifled volley of, "Mmm," came from Heidi in varying pitches, as if she was trying to speak through something covering her mouth. Kid heard her shuffling around.

"What are you saying?" Sid whispered.

"Mmm!"

"Hold on. He knows we're here now anyway." Kid heard a *zip*.

"Ow! I can't believe you taped my mouth!"

"Hey, I'm in danger and I'm not going to have some little bitch…" Sid paused, and then continued, "I'm not going to have some *girl* blow it and get me killed."

As Kid tried to reposition himself, his walkie-talkie tapped against the floor and produced an audible click.

Hearing the noise, Sid yelled, "Don't move! I still have this gun cocked and stuck against her friggin temple!"

"It's cool, I was adjusting myself. I'm not making any moves."

"Don't do any more adjusting, or move a single muscle, or I'm pulling the trigger on her, and then you, and by the way…" Sid paused, and his next words chilled Kid to the bone. "…I can see where you are."

Now he's bluffing. Sid can't see me, Kid thought. Bringing his eyes down and looking at himself, he noticed the walkie-talkie clipped to his belt. Since he was lying down, the unit was resting against the floor but the power button was illuminated like a red beacon. Sid did know where he was.

"So what do you want, Sid?" As he spoke, he quietly pinched the belt clip without covering the illuminated power button. "What is your end game?" he asked while pushing his body backward on the floor.

"Something a putz like you could only dream of. Me and Scott were going to find the biggest castle in the world and take it over like rulers and keep women chained up in the basement, when they weren't serving us."

While Sid talked, Kid continued to move backward. The walkie-talkie was free, but he was holding it in place with his hand. He opened his fingers, hoping he would not jostle the unit. To his relief, the walkie-talkie stayed in place.

Sid's voice lowered and became throaty. "But now Scott is dead."

Kid started crawling away from the walkie-talkie, now trying to follow the sound of his adversary's voice.

The Sherman brother roared and his words echoed in the darkness, "You are the scumbag who shot my brother, aren't you?"

"Sid! Haven't we been over that?" Heidi sounded more compassionate than reproachful.

"Shut up!"

For a moment, Sid was silent. Then he said in a quiet voice, "You would be raging too."

Kid was not going to answer the question, fearing it would trigger an explosive rage. He steered the dialogue in a different direction. "What is your plan now?"

He continued crawling toward the sound of the voices. At least, he hoped he was heading that way. The darkness was disorienting and voices seemed to come from all angles. He could tell his eyes were as adjusted as they were going to be. The black had taken on a softer shade, but was still black.

"I don't need no castle now, that was more Scott's idea, but I do like the part with the women, especially the chaining them up part. I'll tell you what. My first slave can be this…girl right here."

"Real nice," Heidi muttered.

"Sorry. Just speaking my mind. Hey, you told me to before."

He's sorry? Why would he say that? What the heck happened with Sid and Heidi over the past couple of hours?

"And I'll take that bitch, Karen, too. I'll screw her on behalf of my brother and then beat the shit out of her on behalf of myself," he said and snickered.

Suddenly, the door swung open and Karen screamed, "Like hell you will!"

Not now! Kid jumped flat on his stomach and snapped, "Get out of here, Karen!" He searched in vain for movement in the darkness.

As Heidi yelled, "Wait…" Sid fired a shot and it pinged off the door. His second bullet hit the walkie-talkie on the ground. Luckily,

Kid was well out of harm's way.

"Kid? Are you alright?" Heidi yelled.

Having seen the flash from the gun's barrel, Kid honed in on the location. Sid and Heidi were holed up in a corner of the room to his right. He would not answer and give his position away.

"Are you alright?" she repeated.

Kid crawled as fast as he could toward the flash, fearing that Heidi was now in grave danger. He could hear her struggling, but he couldn't come in firing, not in the dark. He also hoped Karen had jumped back through the door and out of harm's way.

"Put the gun down, Sid!" Heidi's voice was strained.

"Let go of my arm!" he snapped.

Closing in, drawn to Heidi's voice, Kid had a split second to decide whether to stop or to act. The odds of finding any reasonable ground with a bitter and angry Sid made the decision easy. He rose to a crouch.

"Stop! Put it away," she repeated.

Kid was closing in and lurching. The sound of the gun barrel clicking against the wall allowed his senses to further refine the trajectory of his lunge. He hoped he was on target, or he would be ramming full bore into a solid wall. As he pounced on Sid's chest, Kid threw an elbow head-high and connected. He then wrapped both of his hands around Sid's arm, which was the side where he had heard the pistol tap the wall. His hands squeezed and slid down his combatants arm and he got a firm hold on the pistol. "Get out of the room Heidi! Go!"

Sid punched him in the back of the head with his free hand. Had it not been pitch black, Kid was sure he would have been seeing black. With his limited sensory perception, he relied on his sense of touch and would not let go of the weapon. Sid pulled the trigger and a bullet fired across the room, ricocheting off the engine housing.

Grabbing Kid by the hair with his left hand, Sid started yanking hard. Kid yelled in pain but kept his grip on his adversary's wrists. As his hair started ripping from his scalp, he released one of his hands and threw another elbow, catching Sid across the face. He quickly reestablished his grip on the pistol with his second hand. For a split second, Sid lost his strength, as if he temporarily blacked out. But he would not let go of the weapon.

Heidi then piled onto Sid's right arm and screamed, "Let it go!"

Instead, he continued to struggle and then tried to push his body away from the wall. Kid dug his toes into the ground and pushed back, using his weight and leverage to keep him pinned.

"I don't want you to die in here, Sid!" Heidi yelled. "I don't want you to die like your brother. Remember us talking about that?"

Sid's ferocity seemed to come down a notch.

"Come on! Let go of the gun and let's get out of here. Tomorrow we'll have a proper funeral for Scott like I promised we would," she added.

Softening ever more, Sid would still not entirely give up.

Heidi was holding on tightly so Kid took one hand and reached into his pocket. He ignited his lighter and moved it toward Sid's hand. In the dim light their combatant appeared conflicted, with his eyes toggling between grief and fury. Blood gushed from his bottom lip.

As fury again took hold, Sid threw another punch and caught Kid's temple. The world started spotting with even darker shades of black. Kid needed to defend himself before his own light was out, so he gave the lighter to Heidi. With his hand now free he threw a jab underneath his body and found an unsuspecting solar plexus. His strike was just in time as it weakened the punch that landed against his head.

Heidi ignited the butane lighter and put the flame right to Sid's hand. The struggle continued as Sid jerked his arm and wrist, but the flame was now also licking at Kid's hand. Finally, Sid yelled in pain and let go of the gun. The smell of his burning flesh wafted in the air.

Heidi jumped back and held the pistol with one hand, while holding the lighter in the other.

With the illumination, Sid snarled, "You *are* the scumbag who shot my brother!" He lashed out and his knuckles caught Kid on the cheek.

"Stop! Now!" Heidi yelled. "Kid, come over here."

While Kid rose, his adversary stood and reached for him.

Heidi aimed the weapon and shouted, "Sid, I said stop! That meant both of you. Don't make me shoot."

Taking a step forward and challenging her, Sid looked stunned as Heidi fired a shot off the tip of his shoe.

"I told you, I don't want you to die in here," she repeated. "Now put your hands in the air."

Staring at Heidi, Sid raised his arms and surrendered.

"Kid, take the flashlight and the other guns from his coat pockets. Hurry, this lighter is hot."

After grabbing everything, Kid clicked on the flashlight and yelled, "Karen?"

"I'm here," she called from outside.

"Walk slowly to the door, Sid," Heidi said.

As they left and made their way across the snowy ground to the lodge. Kid's voice echoed in the night as he yelled up the slope, telling Wendy to come down.

Inside the lodge, Sid was tied up while Heidi kept a gun on him at all times.

Kid put batteries in an electric lantern and put it on the counter. Next he needed to try and contact Chris, so he turned on the flashlight and stepped outside. Trying to keep his eyes averted from the bloody carnage sprayed across the snow, he removed the walkie-talkie from Tim's belt and pressed the call button.

A beep sounded and Chris came across, "Tim! What's the status? What the hell is going on down there?"

"Hi, Grandpa Hyland. Kid here. We have Karen with us. We captured Sid and are holding him inside the K-1 Lodge. Scott Sherman is dead, and unfortunately, so is Tim Mahler."

"Oh no, not Tim!"

"Yes, I'm sorry." Kid responded. He had to avoid mentioning Sara. He didn't want to break that news over a walkie-talkie. But he did want to share the good news. "Listen, we stopped at the Merck plant on the way up here and grabbed more of Grandma's special medication, that Levonesex, several years' worth. Your son told us to get it and bring it up here. We dropped it off to her today."

"Oh my God. Thank you, Kid! I am so relieved to hear that. You don't even know."

Kid knew Chris would feel quite the opposite when he heard the other news. It was such an extreme of highs and lows. Before he could be overrun by emotion, Kid tried to focus on the problem at hand. "We are going to get you down in the gondola. Wendy said James's ankle is pretty busted up?"

"It is. Whatever we're doing, we better hurry. The temperature keeps dropping," Chris noted.

"Can you get James into a gondola car?"

"One way or another, I will."

"Alright. Then radio down when you are in and we'll turn on the lift and get you down."

Kid walked back in the lodge to tell them he was heading over to the gondola control building, and he noticed that Sid's chin was resting on his chest. "What happened to him?"

Heidi seemed annoyed as she pointed her finger.

"I pistol-whipped the son of a bitch," Karen said without any hint of regret.

Kid gave her a disapproving look. It made him feel like their side was stooping to the level of their enemies. It also seemed out of character for Karen.

"Sorry, but you don't know what he put me through up there." She was on the verge of tears as she looked away.

Must've been pretty bad. He decided to let it go. "I'll be right back. I have to go to the gondola building and find the key."

Kid found the engine key on the floor of the control room. A moment later Chris called to say they were ready to roll. Kid activated the gondola and ten minutes later the enclosed car arrived at the bottom of the hill.

As Kid helped them out of the car, Chris said, "I have to commend you. Despite what you were up against down here, you were still able to save Karen. Time for us all to get back to a warm house with food." Chris hesitated. "Well, not all of us. Sid can have a house all to himself."

Chris drove the quad to a nearby parking lot, secured an extended-cab pickup truck and came back for the rest of the group. Before heading to the Mahler farmhouse where the others had moved that day, they took Sid to the jail downtown. When Chris and Kid entered the station carrying the Sherman brother, they both gasped upon seeing, and smelling, the remains of the clerk serving as the receptionist or dispatcher. The only thing clear in the gory mess covering the chair behind the window was the dark-brown Rutland Police uniform. Fortunately, the jail cells were in a separate room with a door that could be closed. Sid was locked in a cell for the night, but was given a sleeping bag and some food and water.

It was not until Chris arrived at the Mahler farmhouse and went to greet his granddaughter that he learned of Sara's fate.

He too crumbled.

III:
CONCATENATION

CHAPTER 22

January 4, 2045
Wednesday, Evening
Near Rutland, Vermont
Nine days after the event

At the Mahler farmhouse, with Heidi and Karen now safe, Kid's focus turned to Jess and Maria. He anxiously awaited their return, assuming their pursuers were not close behind.

After eating steak and potatoes for dinner, Kid could not wait to take a bath. He desperately needed one. Unlike the beer basin at Ironside cabin in New Jersey, they were utilizing a full-size tub, which seemed like a luxury, comparatively. He had worked on the assembly line bringing in bucket after bucket of water from the well outside. The cold liquid was then tempered by pots of water heated in the fireplace.

Kid plopped down on a couch next to Karen, and both waited for their turns to bathe. Evelyn approached and handed him a small duffle bag. "Toiletries, including a new toothbrush, and some clean clothes. We are lucky you are roughly Tim's height and weight."

"Thanks, Grandma. You are a life-saver."

"Oh, it's nothing." She patted his cheek and said, "No, a life-saver is someone who brings a poor old lady the medicine she needs every day to live."

Heidi exited the bathroom, so Kid offered the next turn to Karen, but she insisted that she bathe last. Karen said she felt 'really unclean' and would assume the chore of thoroughly cleaning the tub when she was done. He found the strength of her insistence odd but was not about to question her in front of anyone else.

After a refreshing and necessary bath, Kid was exhausted and ready for some sleep. He inquired about the sleeping arrangements. The living room downstairs was being shared by the Hyland's and the Moore's so that Nurse Marissa could keep an eye on Evelyn. They slept with their beds close to an open-hearth fireplace that was so large that Kid could have stood inside the opening. Wendy Levy and her husband were offered the other bedroom downstairs since James had a broken ankle. Kid was then advised by Evelyn that he had his own bedroom upstairs, so he headed up without delay.

Two of the four bedrooms upstairs had fireplaces; one was for Heidi and Karen and the other for Kid alone. The two other bedrooms up there had previously been occupied by Sid and Scott. Karen had mentioned that Mr. Mahler put them in rooms without fireplaces because they both had arsonist tendencies.

After giving Heidi a hug and saying good night, Kid grabbed a brass candle holder from a small table. He opened his door and ran his hands through his long, brown hair to feather it back. He froze as his heavy wood door creaked. With his hair still wet from his bath, he shivered. "Feels like the windows are wide open," he muttered. Scanning the room through the dim light offered by his candle, he could see the windows were all closed.

Heading straight for the fireplace, he was relieved to see it was ready to be lit. He put down his small duffle bag, hung his coat on one of the oak bedposts and pulled the butane lighter from his pocket. He put flame to the wads of newspaper stuffed underneath the stacked logs and waited for the wood to start burning. Sitting in front of the hearth, he stared at the lighter in his hand. Today, the small, blue butane flame-maker had served a greater purpose, and had been the weapon that made Sid drop his gun. As he relaxed and warmed up, the fatigue that was lying in wait began to course through his bones.

He closed his eyes and started humming his own song. *Angels Never Cry…unless they're falling down to earth…*

He turned and glanced around his room, which was now more visible in the firelight. Despite a double-bed being placed in the middle of the floor, he noticed the space was fairly ornate for a small upstairs bedroom. The dark crown molding circling the top of the walls matched the two prominent, and fully stuffed, cherry bookcases. It appeared the room was once a small library or reading room. For a moment Kid felt like he was in a different era, just like he always did in Ironside cabin in New Jersey. The room had a charm to it, as if it retained the ambiance of a simpler time. The heavy natural wood had a certain look, smell, and feel. It was comfortable and welcoming. The Mahler house reminded Kid of an upscale version of Ironside. No wonder he felt so at home.

Groaning while standing up, he walked over and dragged the heavy wood framed bed closer to the fireplace. He lifted the brass candlestick holder and also moved the small end table. Sitting on the edge of the bed, he took off his shoes and socks and slid them under the heavy frame. Stripping off his shirt and pants, he hung them over the thick oak bedpost. He pulled back the colorful flower-patterned quilt and lay on the soft mattress. Relief washed over him and he felt his body relax. As the soft flame of the candle swayed, he felt himself being hypnotized. He was barely able to blow out the flame before plummeting into a deep sleep.

A creak sounded and Kid's eyes popped open. It took a second to remember where he was as he lay motionless in bed. The fire had burned down to embers and the room was dark. Then it registered that a strange creak had woken him up. Alarmed as he came to his senses he remembered that his gun was in the pocket of his coat, which was hanging from a bedpost near his feet. His bedroom door shut and a click sounded. *They're locking the door.* As his eyes adjusted to the darkness he spotted the fireplace poker close by. That would be his play.

Then the intruder spoke. "Kid?"

Sitting up straight, he could make out a silhouette by the door. "Heidi?"

She tiptoed across the room. "Who else would it be?" she mused.

Kid relaxed and rested on his elbow. "You mean, you're not Lucy Lips from the escort service?"

"Ha…ha…ha. Wow, it's colder in here than in my room." Despite wearing a winter coat, she crossed her arms and hugged herself. She grabbed a couple of logs from a metal ring. Dropping them into the smoldering fire, she used the poker to stoke the bed of hot coals. As she jabbed, she blew at the embers, making them glow.

"What time is it?" Kid asked.

"About 3:00 a.m.," she answered.

Grabbing a tissue from a box on his end table, Kid balled it up and took aim. Firing the small wad against some glowing embers in the fireplace, it started to shrink and then caught. With a quick poof, flame arose from the entire bed of embers.

"Nice trick," Heidi mumbled as she put the poker down. She again sat on the edge of the bed and crossed her arms.

Kid lifted the edge of the heavy quilt. "Do you need to warm up?" He was thinking of the warmth they shared under the blanket at Ironside cabin. Heidi slipped off her coat and threw it over the bedpost. With her standing in only a bra and panties, he realized that she had a perfect hourglass figure. What struck him was that he noticed, so he reacted by closing his eyes. Maybe his adrenaline was still pumping from the day's events.

She crawled under the blanket. They faced each other, both in partial fetal positions and not touching.

"You must be sore as hell after today," she noted.

"I am, but I know I'll feel worse in a couple of days. Takes a while to catch up sometimes. How about you? How do you feel?" He was trying to further the conversation and get past the visual of Heidi's scantily clad body.

"Drained, mostly from being scared. After Sid killed Tim, I was sure I was next."

Although she was almost nonchalant about it, he was stung by the reminder of how close she was to losing her life today. "Given his mental state, we were all afraid." After a pause, he noted, "It's strange, when we were battling with him, he seemed to respond to you. When you talked to him, he seemed to listen, at least a little, and it took some of the fight out of him. What the heck happened in the couple of hours you were his captive?"

She shrugged. "We just talked. He opened up to me about his pain with his brother dying. Scott was probably the only person in the world Sid genuinely cared about. It was interesting how at first, he kept calling me 'bitch,' and then in time, he would catch himself and try not to refer to me that way. I didn't tell him to stop. I wasn't in any position to tell him to do anything, but I think he actually developed a conscience about it."

"And just because you gave him the time of day and talked to him?"

"I mostly just listened, but I guess he felt like nobody ever really listened to him before. He told me that he and his brother felt abandoned by society, and by the system." She paused. "I actually started to feel a little bad for him."

"You felt bad? Almost like a form of Stockholm Syndrome?"

"I said 'a little.' Believe me, I know the guy brought all of his pain on himself."

After a few moments of silence, Heidi eased out of her fetal position and straightened her body under the covers. "I'm finally warming up." She pulled the covers tighter under her chin. "It feels good under here."

"Under he-ah?" he joked nervously as he felt the heat of her body.

"Are you mocking my Brooklyn accent? You got something against New Yorkers?"

"No, us homegrowns down the New Jersey *shaw*, we…"

"Shaw?" she asked.

"Shore. I was speaking your language. We loved it when the

bennies came to pollute and desecrate our beaches every summer. We welcomed the tourists with open arms."

"You know, in the old days I would have not found you a bit funny." She chuckled and pinched his thigh. He jumped as she said, "You locals down the *shaw* had no problem welcoming our cash every summer."

"Couldn't you just wire us the money and stay up in New York? I'm just kidding anyway. Some of the tourists had as much respect for the beaches as the locals. It all depended on the individual. I met a lot of great people from New York."

"Like…me?"

"I also met a lot of people who were quite…interesting."

She pinched him again.

"Yes, like you," he conceded and laughed.

"You know what hurt me the most today?" She had turned suddenly serious.

"What's that?"

"Not so much the physical strain, but I think some emotional nerves were hit when I was Sid's captive. He got me talking about my own life, and we actually did find some common ground when it came to feeling abandoned."

He almost asked her to clarify, but at 3:00 a.m., his brain was not ready for such a heavy discussion.

She reached out and took his hand. "But it made me realize how much I need you, Kid. That's why I had to come in here tonight."

Through the hazy firelight, her blue eyes emerged, and he got lost in them.

Putting her hand on the small of Kid's back, she pressed until his body was also straightened. "Relax," she whispered.

She stated the obvious as she rubbed her leg against his, "You're not wearing pants." She ran her fingers up his thigh and started to ask, "Are you…" and then her voice turned seductive, "…wearing anything at all?"

Her question was answered as she encountered the edge of his boxers.

"Barely," he muttered as he laid his arm over the curve of her waist.

She propped herself up on one elbow and hovered right over Kid's face. "Remember when we were in the truck today in Saratoga?"

"Yes," he whispered. He remembered all too well, but Saratoga seemed like a lifetime ago.

Brushing her swaying blond hair off of her face and pinning it behind her ear, her next question sent a mild electric current through every nerve in his body.

"And I said, 'you just wait until later'?" Face to face, her eyes glinted even in the dim light.

There was no need for Kid to answer. The conversation was over as she lowered her soft lips to his and began a slow kiss that felt like it lasted for hours, just like in the truck in Saratoga. After some gentle petting, Heidi squirmed and then pulled her hand out from under the covers. She held her hand high until Kid could see what she was holding.

What the... In the soft glow of the firelight he saw white lace and a deep blue, silky fabric. He caught a faint but intoxicating scent and felt flush. A realization came over him and he turned to her. She tossed her panties to the floor. As if not believing what he just saw, his hand dropped and found that her backside was bare. A surge of blood rushed to his already tingling genital area. She whispered with a desperate lust and something deeper, "I'm yours. Completely...yours."

A part of Kid fought against giving in. His conscience was throwing him a line and giving him a choice. Her hand brushed against his skin and he let out a deep exhale. At that critical juncture, he did not grab onto that line and within a second it was too late. He had to let go. He pulled off his underwear and before he could hold them up, Heidi took them from his hand and heaved them across the room.

She then climbed on top of him and lowered her hips. As they shared another kiss their movements were slow and firm, but in perfect rhythm. Tears ran down her cheeks and seemed to convey something much deeper than just a physical connection. The heat and intensity swelled, and appeared to be overwhelming her as they reached a crescendo. She trembled for several seconds, as if she had released every ounce of her being and let all of herself go.

Kid had willingly received her outpouring and even reciprocated. Too late, a small part of him wondered if he should have held something back.

CHAPTER 23

January 5, 2045
Thursday, Morning
Near Rutland, Vermont
Ten days after the event

Kid opened his eyes and squinted against the sunlight penetrating the drawn curtains in his room. Before even comprehending where he was, he was overcome by feelings of guilt and regret. He reached out to find that he was alone in his bed, which was a relief. Having Heidi in his bed would not have been right with the Hyland grandparents just downstairs.

His thoughts turned to Sara and he did not need a mirror to see that his cheeks were red. He felt ashamed and raised his hands to cover his face. He knew, without question, that in those wee hours of the morning he should have taken the line and stopped it before it went that far. It was too much, too soon. How could he know that so definitively now, but not in the wee hours? How is it that Heidi was such a temptation that his judgment was disabled? And what about contraception? *Don't blame her*. He had the ability to stop himself and didn't. What now? He did not want to run away, but he had to take a few steps back without making her feel rejected or abandoned. That would not be easy to do…

A knock at the door made him jump. He sat up and after ensuring he was covered by a blanket, he rubbed his face and yelled, "Come in."

Heidi walked in, already washed up and fully dressed. She seemed to have a glow about her. She closed the door behind her and walked over to the bed. She sat on the edge, leaned over, and kissed him. "You look a little worn out."

"Well, I had an action-packed dream. It was exhausting," he said.

"A dream huh? I only want to hear about it if it was a hot dream. Full of passion and the most powerful love." She stroked the hair on his head.

"Oh," he stated and turned his eyes down. "Sorry. In this dream I hit the home run that won the World Series."

She gave his hair a little tug. Putting her forehead against his, she said, "That must've been *after* the other dream you had, the one with the powerful love? You know, the one where you dreamt you lost your underwear?"

Reaching under the blankets, he stated, "As a matter of fact, I did lose my underwear!"

"Well, in the dream the beautiful, sexy girl you were with most likely grabbed them out of your hand and tossed them…" she stood and walked behind the headboard of the bed, "…somewhere over here." Walking back, she handed him his boxers. "Time to get dressed. Clarence is making breakfast."

"Heidi, let's talk for a second." He patted the bed.

As soon as she sat, he took her hand. "Listen, for a while when we're in front of the Hylands, I think it best we not act like we're more than friends. They did just find out about…you know."

Heidi nodded and seemed to understand. "I get it. It will be hard to keep my eyes and hands off you though," she admitted as she caressed his face and planted kisses on his cheeks and forehead. She gazed for a long second into his eyes. "Kid…" she started and became ultra-serious. "Thank you."

"For?"

"Last night. And I don't just mean some sexual release. Last night, for the first time in many…" she emphasized the word, "…*many* years, I no longer felt abandoned by this world."

The conversation was interrupted by a sudden knock. She took her hands away from Kid's face.

Karen opened the door. "Hey, Kid, time for break…" she stopped as she saw Heidi sitting on the edge of the bed. Heidi had separated, but was caught off guard and it showed.

"Oh, sorry. I should have waited for you to answer my knock. Anyway, breakfast is ready downstairs," Karen finished. As she turned to step out the door, she looked back at them, her eyes questioning the circumstances.

"Thanks, Karen," Kid yelled out as she closed the door.

"Yeah, you could've waited for an answer," Heidi whispered with contempt in her voice. She took his face in her hands, kissed him gently and then jumped off the bed. "So what is the plan for this morning?"

"After breakfast, I guess our mission is to retrieve Tim's body and have a proper funeral?" he said as he dressed.

"Yes, as well as Scott Sherman. I promised Sid we would do that." Glancing back at the closed door, Heidi quickly kissed him again. "Wow. I think I've fallen in love with you, Kid. No need to respond. I'm just saying…" She opened the door and walked out.

In an instant his feelings of guilt and regret were back in full force. Kid was glad she did not turn around, lest she see how red his face must have been.

A short time later, Kid was sitting at the cherry wood dining room table eating scrambled eggs.

As Karen was rehashing her K-1 hostage ordeal, she stopped eating and put her fork down. "Sorry, I'm not feeling too good. I need some air." She got up from the table and walked out the back door.

Putting down his silverware, Kid got up. "I'll be right back." Heidi stopped chewing and peered at him questioningly. He pointed in the direction that Karen had gone. "Something is really wrong with her."

"How do you know? Maybe she just needs some time alone." She seemed uncomfortable that Kid felt the need to check on Karen.

"If I get that sense, I'll leave her alone. But right now, my sense is that she needs help." Before Heidi could counter, he added, "I'll be back."

Kid opened the back door quietly. Karen was sitting on a wood porch swing that overlooked an expansive yard with scenic rolling hills beyond. She used her toes to push off and started a gentle sway. As he pulled the door closed behind him, she turned in surprise. He could tell she had been lost in her own world. "Mind if I sit?" he asked.

"Not at all," she said with her slightly raspy voice and moved over on the seat. She turned away, but not before Kid saw the tears running down her cheeks.

Sitting down, Kid put his hands in his coat pocket. Feeling a lump, he pulled out the spool of Zylon line he had been carrying since stopping with Jess on the highway in Saratoga. Slipping it back into his pocket, he asked, "Something bothering you?" He did know if she wanted to talk, but everybody always told Kid he was a good listener.

"Is it that obvious?"

"It's obvious you're upset. Listen, I'm truly sorry about your mother."

"Thanks. I'm still trying to cope with losing her. The last thing I needed to deal with was the hell the Sherman's put me through. And then to lose Sara?"

"I know you went through a lot up at K-1, but I get this feeling there's more to the story." He knew there had to be. She had been unable to hide it when recounting her ordeal as a captive.

"I'm just trying to process it all." She was being elusive. "It was brutal. Not the kind of situation you want to rehash."

He felt like she was starting to retreat, and at that point, she would have shut right down if he pried. He was about to leave her so she could be alone.

"This is when I would usually have a heart to heart with Sara, to help me process it all and make sense of things," she started, sounding despondent. "I think the girl may have saved my life when she helped me see the light with the Sherman brothers, especially now that I've seen what they are really capable of. Heck, then you saved my life over at Killington. I really owe the both of you, big time."

Kid stood. "You don't owe me anything. Just know that if you need to talk to someone, I'm here for you."

"Thanks..." She then seemed uneasy that he was leaving. Grabbing his arm, she said, "Oh, I'm sorry Kid. I shouldn't have mentioned Sara. That was totally insensitive. You've had your own hell to deal with."

"Don't be sorry."

"It puts my abuse at K-1 into a different perspective," she continued.

"Abuse?"

She froze and covered her mouth. The words had slipped out, but he knew she couldn't turn back now.

"You don't mean sexually?" he pressed.

Her eyes and body language answered before she did. She crossed her legs. "Well, some, but compared to..."

"Wait, don't belittle something as serious as that." He sat back down next to her. "To the...extreme?" he said. He was not sure how to question the degree of abuse without being blunt about it.

She squirmed and moved her rear end to the edge of the seat and anchored her feet on the porch. The swing came to a halt. She seemed to be fighting herself, choosing between letting go and shelling back up. In a moment of decision, she turned to him. Tears ran in torrents from her eyes and her lips were quivering.

Kid felt a wave of dread, knowing what she was going to say before the words even left her mouth.

"While tied up, I was raped." Her voice was raw with pain. "By Sid." For a second, she sat up straight and acted as if she might sustain the allusion that she had it under control, but she broke down and started sobbing. "I can still see, and feel, the knife he threatened me with."

He reached out and held her tight. He wanted to say something to soothe her, but was surprised that even he couldn't find the words. He did not know if there were any words to be said. Just when he thought she had encountered the most serious degree of abuse possible, she pushed the bar a little further when through her sobs, she added, "And I had been saving myself."

He knew what she meant and it broke his heart. The girl's virginity had been stolen from her and nothing could bring that back. There is only one first time. Even with the world in shambles, he worried about the impact that may have on her for the rest of her life. *That sick, heartless bastard.* He was disgusted. If Sid was in front of him at that moment, he would have punched him in the groin so hard that he would have been forever a soprano, if he could still speak at all.

"I know it's hard to believe right now, but in time, you will come to terms with this," he said.

"I hope so." She sighed. "Because right now I'm having a pretty damn hard time with it."

After sitting in silence for a few minutes, Kid asked, "Are you alright?"

"No, but I do feel better now that I was able to confide in someone about it. I'm sorry, Kid. You're the last person who needs this."

"Like I said, I'm here for you."

"Listen, please keep this between us. I'm just not ready to talk about it with anyone else. I'm not ready for all the sympathy and pity."

"Not a word. When you're ready to talk about it, you can. Come on. Our food is probably cold." He led her back into the house.

As he reached for the doorknob of the front door, she grabbed his hand. "Kid, thank you."

He gave her a quick hug and messed her hair. Brushing off a few strands that came loose and were stuck to his hand, he said, "You're welcome. Hang in there."

"Wait!" She used her sleeve to wipe the wetness from her face. "Do I look alright? Can you tell I've been crying?"

"No, you look fine," he fibbed.

CHAPTER 24

January 5, 2045
Thursday, Morning
Near Rutland, Vermont
Ten days after the event

Kid returned to the table and took his seat, while Karen did the same. Raising his eyes, he saw Heidi peering at him. "Is everything alright?" she asked.

"Yes," they both said at the same time.

As they all conversed at the table, it was Chris who posed the necessary question. "So, where do we go from here? What do we do?"

All eyes turned to Kid, who asked, "Who is still up here, besides everyone staying here in this house?"

"Just the three other families. The McDermott, Spatz and Ryan families."

Marissa added, "We need to stay close to the McDermotts. Doctor Craig McDermott is a cardiologist at Rutland Regional Medical Center. He's the only survivor I know who is a doctor, and a pretty young one at that. Maybe in his mid-forties?"

"He's a young man with quite the Irish accent. He only came to this country when he was going to medical school," Evelyn noted.

"Dr. McDermott and his wife, Pamela, have a 17-year-old boy and 13-year-old girl," Chris continued.

"17 years old?" Kid repeated and cast an inquisitive glance at Karen.

She raised her eyebrows. "The son, Dylan, was a grade behind me in high school. He's a nice guy, but kind of a hermit. Although he would probably say the same about me."

Chris continued, "Then there is the Spatz family. Melanie Spatz is a single mom with two young girls. Katy is six years old, and Karly is five. Never married, and her boyfriend, the father of her children, took off when she was pregnant with Karly. She never saw him again."

"At her core she is a good-hearted woman," Evelyn said. "But she never lost the bitterness about her boyfriend leaving her and the kids. It kept her on edge, so that she hardly ever laughed and always sounded angry."

"But to Melanie's credit, she wasn't the type to wallow in self-pity," Chris said. "She was an incredibly hard working woman. During the day she had an office job. By night she had a second part-time job and in her 'free' time learned how to fly. She got her pilot's license this past summer."

Chris continued, "Then finally, there is Rick and Katherine Ryan and their 11-year-old son, Robert. The family had another son but lost him to Leukemia."

Evelyn exhaled. "That was so sad. The worst funeral I've ever attended."

"Rick Ryan is a certified electrician," Clarence said as he stuck a forkful of eggs into his mouth.

"Without operational power plants, there's probably not much use for those skills," Marissa quipped.

"I wouldn't say that," Kid responded. He proceeded to tell them about the electric hot water heater and shower back at Good Luck Point Marina. "A skilled electrician comes in handy when you need to connect a generator to an electrical panel."

"Why did you settle at a marina?" Karen asked.

"Now, that is a long story."

"I better make us more coffee." Evelyn went to stand up and Marissa grabbed her arm to help her. "I got it Marissa, but thank you."

Over the next half hour Kid told the group the entire story from the night of the destruction up until the present moment. The group was staring at him, mesmerized.

"Man, that is quite a sequence of events," Clarence said.

"So my son is with the Utopia Project Group, and they will be setting up a base camp on Long Beach Island?" Chris clarified.

"I am so relieved he is alive, but I am still shocked, and…disappointed," Evelyn muttered, with pain evident in her eyes.

"Well, let's hear him out before making any judgments. If we know our son, he would never willingly participate in something this destructive. There must be more to the story."

"But he's there, and from what Kid said, the group Eric is with is responsible for the death of our granddaughter," Evelyn pursed her lips and fought back tears. Chris went to respond, but stopped and remained silent.

Kid changed the subject. "There's more." He proceeded to tell them about Jess, Maria, and 801 being chased by a bus load of Utopia Project soldiers.

"So these Utopia Project soldiers are up our way now? We need to be on the lookout." Chris got up from the table. "I know you said Jess was supposed to lose them, but what if they follow him here?"

Kid nodded. "You're right. We should definitely have a lookout posted. Not only in case they follow Jess, but I suspect they will come and search this 'Green Mountain' area anyway, to make sure there are no survivors." The group around the table looked at him expectantly, so he added, "They know the location of the areas missed by the neutron beams."

"So one way or another, they will come here. It is just a matter of when," Chris noted. "What are you guys going to do when Jess gets here?"

"Since we got Grandma Hyland's medication to her, we'll head back south to New Jersey," Kid explained. "We left a friend named Drex down there to keep an eye on the progress of the Utopia Project base they are going to be setting up."

"Why would you want to be so close to them?" Clarence looked surprised.

"We are working on a plan," Kid said.

Heidi shared her story about being a captive on the ships, and then Kid laid out the concept they had discussed at Ironside cabin about reigniting the humanity in the members of the Utopia Project.

Marissa's eyes were wide. "Sounds dangerous. Do you really think you can succeed?"

"I don't know our odds, but when we thought about our future, I guess we wondered what else there was to live for. To sit around and watch humanity become extinct and do nothing about it?" Kid asked. "If we could free the 20,000 members of their society, then we've changed the future and given humanity a chance. We could definitely use the help and expertise of the survivors up here if you're willing. We would have a much better chance if we banded together."

"We would be the underdog. Rebels with a cause," Karen said as she wrapped her arm around Kid's.

Heidi squirmed a little as she looked across the table. "You've seen too many movies."

Evelyn put her coffee cup down and grabbed Chris's hand, "I would go to New Jersey because I want to see our son. I want him to explain what happened. Plus, with what happened to Sara, he must be devastated."

Chris nodded. "We will have to think it through and discuss it as a group, and get some of the other neighbors in on the discussion. Especially if we're sitting ducks up here, we should strongly consider banding together and going south to New Jersey," he said as he stood.

"And we are using firewood all day and night at this point, so we will run out of it long before we lose the cold up here," Clarence added. "Although New Jersey isn't exactly the equator, I would imagine the winters aren't quite as harsh there, or as long."

Karen pulled close to Kid. He glimpsed a streak of purple in her dark brown hair as she leaned over to him. "One way or another, you can count me in."

"We have a little time to decide," Chris concluded. "At least until Jess shows up anyway."

After breakfast, Chris stepped outside and gave a walkie-talkie to Kid. "You and Heidi just relax and recover for a day. Besides saving my wife with her medication, you've been through hell."

"I can help with any work that needs to be done here. What about digging graves for Mr. Mahler and Scott Sherman?" Kid asked.

"We've got it covered. No manual digging. We still have the backhoe out in the barn since me and Tim used it to dig a grave for Alice..." he cut off his sentence as Karen walked over. Clearing his throat, Chris continued, "Don't worry, Clarence and I will handle it. Just take a break. Let it catch up to you, and then gather your strength, especially with the big plans you have for when you get back to Jersey. Give Heidi the grand tour of Rutland or something. If we need you, or if Jess shows up, we'll reach out to you on the walkie-talkie."

"Do you want me to give you a tour?" Karen offered.

Kid hesitated for a second. Heidi did not and said, "Thanks anyway, but we'll be fine. We won't be going far."

Karen looked disappointed but waved as she turned and walked away.

Mounting a two-person snowmobile and taking off, Kid decided he would take Heidi for a short tour based on his limited knowledge of the area. "Check this out," he said as he pulled to the side of Kendall Hill Road. A 139-foot bridge crossed Otter Creek and led to nowhere, with the road on the other side having been closed many years ago.

Heidi approached the tourist placard. "What's the story with the...Hammond Covered Bridge from 1842?"

Walking into the covered structure, Kid glanced around as he waited for her to read the placard. He examined the diagonal wooden support planks of the town lattice truss bridge, all the while watching where he stepped since the floor was rotting away. He noticed there were deeply carved initials on the crossbeams dating back to the 1800's.

"Holy cow!" Heidi exclaimed. "In 1927 this bridge was actually carried away in a terrible flood and wound up a mile downstream," she said as she walked in and looked around.

"Yep. The bridge floated away. It actually stayed intact and they towed it back on a barge of empty barrels. They used it until the 1990's when they paved a road right around it and built a modern overpass." Kid added and put up his hand. "Hold up. Watch your step."

She stopped and peered down at the creek flowing under the bridge. "I'm surprised they even allow people in here with all these gaping holes in the floor."

"I know. Some of them are big enough to fall through."

Kid made sure his walkie-talkie was still on his hip. "I wish Jess and Maria would get here. I'm worried about them. I hope they've been able to stay a step ahead. And I hope they see the walkie-talkie taped to the Hyland's door when they get there. Otherwise, they won't know where to find us."

It had been Kid's idea to tape a walkie-talkie to the door of the Hyland house so Jess could call and get directions to the Mahler farmhouse. He did not think it was wise to post directions on the door in case the enemy got there first.

"Don't worry. Jess will get here soon." Heidi sounded optimistic.

They mounted the snowmobile and went up the road to the New England Maple Museum. Kid had been there a couple of times before and figured it would have been closed and empty when the destruction came. Prying open the back door and finding some candles, Kid gave Heidi a tour of the inside. He showed her all the sugaring artifacts and explained how they turned the sap of maple trees into syrup. "Believe me, we can learn from the past. Looking at the simple way they did things may come in handy for us now."

"You don't suppose they would miss them if we borrowed their..."

she pointed to a couple of labeled artifacts, "…sap buckets and taps do you?"

As they walked around inside the museum, Kid purposely kept the candle light away from a large diorama in the middle of the room. "Just walk that way." He pointed. "But walk slowly."

Heidi shuffled in the darkness toward the middle of the room. She had her hand in front of her and stopped when she encountered something in her path.

Kid stepped up and shined a flashlight on a sign. "It says, 'Do Not Touch.'"

She retracted her hand and as she turned around, she found herself face to face with a stuffed bobcat. Its teeth were bared and one of its paws was extended.

"Shit!" she yelled and jumped back, slapping at Kid, who was already laughing.

Glancing over her shoulder at the bobcat, Heidi's smile disappeared and she shuddered. "Christ."

"Are you alright? I was just messing with you," Kid said, unsure of why she seemed so bothered.

"Get that thing out of here! Throw it outside!"

"What, this?" Kid pointed at the lunging animal.

"Yes. I'm serious. Get it out of here." Her distress seemed to be growing.

"Alright, but…"

"Now, please."

Complying, Kid took the stuffed life-size bobcat off the diorama and tossed it out the back door. When he came back in, Heidi was still tense, but she explained, "The mascot at my first high school was a bobcat that looked just like that one. Let's just say I have some bad memories and leave it at that."

He did leave it at that, but it would be a half hour before Heidi could relax enough to even sit down.

Kid got the wood burning stove inside the museum going until it was warm enough to take off their coats. He then cooked pancakes on a cast iron griddle. While eating, they grabbed a sample pack of the different maple syrups.

"Remember, we told Drex we would bring him back some genuine maple syrup," Kid said.

Heidi was the first to cast a vote on the sample pack varieties. "Definitely the Grade A Dark Amber. We need to take a stash of it when we leave."

"I hope you have a lot of cash? Real maple syrup isn't cheap," he quipped.

"Don't worry. I'll haggle with the cashier."

"Do you have anything to barter with?" he asked as he put his plate on the hearth.

While grabbing the front of his shirt, Heidi said, "Oh, you just wait." She leaned in and put her lips to his.

The kiss had a maple sweetness to it and he didn't know if it was from his lips or hers. While engaging in a rapid fire series of kisses, Kid uttered, "Seems…I've heard that…threat…before." Separating himself and stepping away before the sexual tension could continue to build, he capped and organized the maple syrup sample bottles.

With the warmth of the fire and the scent of maple syrup, they laid together on a thick area rug. She took his hand and whispered, "Kid, you do realize how much I care for you already? It almost scares me."

"I don't know why," he mused and she smacked his cheek.

After talking for more than an hour, they noticed a chill had taken over as the fire in the wood stove had burned down to embers. Kid untangled himself from their embrace and got up.

"It's freezing!" she voiced and hugged herself.

Kid grabbed her coat and laid it across her shoulders. "I'll go grab some more wood from outside."

I have goosebumps! Heidi thought. Hearing Kid's footsteps as he walked toward the back door, she adjusted the coat over her shoulders.

As she moved it, a lump slid out of the pocket and fell to the floor. Propping up on her elbow, she picked up General Hyland's diary.

"Why do I still have this?" she groaned as she flipped through it. Something registered, and she stopped fanning the pages.

Sitting bolt upright, she repeated, "Oh my God, oh my God..."

CHAPTER 25

December 29, 2044
Thursday, Before Dawn
New Jersey coast, Utopia Project Ship Number One
Three days after the event

Before dawn on the third morning after the event, General Hyland sat at his desk on Utopia Project Ship Number One. He could not fall back to sleep, not after seeing Kid on Sara's hall. And certainly not after Kid revealed that he was going to attempt a rescue the next night. The general had his own plan to get Sara off the ship before her conditioning went too far, but that was days, if not weeks, away. Now he had to throw his plan out the window and come up with a new one, and fast. He had little time.

He still could not fathom how Kid had been able to get aboard the ship and find the girls, but he had to give him credit for whatever stealth maneuvers he had employed to get so far, so fast. He was good, but good enough to pull off a rescue without them getting caught or killed? After all, Kid did not seem to realize that his every move was being captured by video cameras. The general took control of the camera at the end of Sara's hall and using the tilt and zoom feature, he spotted Kid and Jess. They were crouching under a video camera, pointing up to it. *Attaboy. Took you a while to catch on, but you got it. But what would've happened if I was not the first one to see this video?* Although the cameras were not actively monitored after 9:00 p.m., the video of any activity on the ship through the night was reviewed the next day as a matter of protocol. Were they to see Kid and Jess, a full ship lockdown and search would commence and the stowaways would be found and killed.

As he watched video from a camera in the circular staircase, he could see Kid enter a supply closest on the 29th level. A couple of barely audible thumps could be heard on the audio feed as the sound reverberated up the stairwell. *What is he doing in there?* The general watched as Kid stepped out with keys hanging from his pointer finger. *And how is that going to help with a rescue? What are you up to Kid?*

He followed their footsteps as Kid and Jess went back up the stairs to the engineer's room next to the bridge and approached a hatch on the floor. They opened it and descended what the general knew was the emergency ladder that led down to the engine room in the bottom of the ship. *So that's where you're hiding.* They had avoided detection because only member rooms and common areas were covered by video cameras, which did not include the bottom level of the ships.

The general worked to erase all footage of Kid and Jess. Using the video camera program, he was able to trace their footsteps around the ship. After removing all the incriminating video and ensuring the guys were done snooping around for the night, the general again set the camera system to alert him if anyone approached Sara's door.

As he lay down in bed, he thought of his wife, Amanda, and the familiar wave of guilt passed through him. He would forever feel responsible for her death. He was the one who insisted they participate in the Child Conditioning Program, or CCP when his wife was pregnant with Sara.

Back in December of 2024 in Georgia, one month before Amanda's due date, then 30-year-old Major Eric Hyland had said to his wife, "About my appeal to General Barnes..."

Amanda had looked at him for a second and then appeared to be hit by a sudden realization. "Don't even tell me..." she started to say. He could see the fire growing in her eyes.

"You know with the CCP, the baby will only be gone for a few months," he reminded.

"Months?" she exploded. "Months, conditioned like one of Pavlov's dogs?" Amanda sounded disgusted.

To Major Hyland, it didn't seem so traumatic that parents would have to give up their baby for an initial three-month social conditioning period. Everything about the regimen seemed so logical and rational.

"That's not entirely fair or accurate," he responded, but with her being eight months pregnant, he did not want the discussion to evolve into a full-on argument.

"Come on Eric, we watched the informational video together. You know how I feel about it."

He had incorrectly assumed that his wife would find some level of comfort and reassurance after watching the informational video. The segment described the harmless conditioning techniques to be used. Social conformity and respect for authority would be seemingly innate qualities in the conditioned children. Any rebellion would cause intense anxiety, thus forcing conformity and obedience. The video went on to say that with the conditioning techniques, children would benefit for the rest of their lives, as would the whole of society.

"The video showed all the safety measures they have in place," he countered.

"Why would our baby need conditioning anyway? What happened to parenting?" she asked.

"Look at this world Amanda. The parents need help."

"We wouldn't."

"I know we wouldn't. General Barnes knows it too, but he was insistent."

"What does Barnes know about parenting, or family? He has never been married, has no kids, and has excommunicated his family. Come on Eric, they said this was voluntary!"

"Yeah, but for a major, it really isn't. I need to be a good example for others." Initially he had summoned resolve by reminding himself that as a member of the armed forces, like his father before him, it was his duty to support the military's initiatives, even CCP.

"Knowing Barnes, he was probably worried about how it would reflect upon him," she countered.

"No doubt about it," he said. She knew General Barnes all too well. "He admitted that, but it's a valid concern and I have to respect that. If I don't participate, it reflects poorly on him too."

"Eric, we can't let them take our baby." Amanda started to cry. She reached her hand out to him, as if begging for help.

He realized that no informational video or any other medium could fully prepare the parents for the emotional aspect and what the mother and father would feel. For his wife, those feelings had been instantaneous and strong from moment one. For him, with his baby due in a month, his feelings were growing exponentially. He now realized, and felt, that he wasn't just giving up a baby for a time, he was giving up *his* baby.

He held her hand and looked into her tormented eyes. "I do understand. Please, Amanda, try to calm down. You and the baby do not need the stress." He worried about the harm it could do to the baby, or his wife, especially since she was in the third trimester.

A little more than a month later, his wife was past her due date and he was becoming increasingly anxious. She had been in the hospital for a few days now and there was no indication the baby was ready to enter the world. He went to the military base at Fort Gordon, Georgia, to take care of some important work while he impatiently waited. For the entire morning, he buried himself in printouts for the weapons program to ensure the recent software updates were installed correctly. Despite his rank of major, he was always hands-on, and even more so when he needed to keep himself distracted.

The blare of a ringtone from his hip stopped him in his tracks. After taking the call he dropped everything and scrambled to get to the Eisenhower Army Medical Center.

"You're going to have to give a good push," the doctor was coaching as the major entered the delivery room.

He ran to his Amanda's side and grabbed her hand.

She squeezed his fingers tightly, "Eric! You made it," she gasped, in obvious unbearable pain.

"Just in time, but I'm here," he said as they both took a deep breath. His wife yelled out, clenched her teeth, and pushed with all her might.

"Almost there, one more good one!" the doctor directed.

She pushed hard, squeezed the major's hand until his fingers lost all sensation, and then she screamed.

The doctor held the baby up in his hands. "You have a…" he started, as if feeding on Amanda and Eric's excitement. He then cleared his throat and said in an even, monotone voice, "We have a healthy baby girl."

Amanda's mouth was open and her eyes were fixated. She put her hand over her mouth and cried, "Look at our baby, baby…Sara."

They had decided they would not know the gender in advance. If it was a girl, her name was to be Sara, named after Major Hyland's deceased little sister.

Amanda cried uncontrollably and seemed utterly exhausted. He and his wife just hugged and stared at the baby they had brought into the world. The major was choked up. In front of his eyes a living being had taken her first breaths of life; a being made from him. His blood. His genes. His own…little girl.

After a few moments, the doctor told Amanda to rest as he walked out with the newborn. Eric was waved out into the hall by the attending nurse.

"Is my wife alright?" he asked before the door even closed.

"Yes, exhausted, but she is fine," the nurse responded.

"And the baby?"

"Fine as well. They will do the usual tests, but she seems completely healthy."

"What a relief," Eric said as he hunched over. *No damage from the stress of their heated CCP discussions.* He was too relieved to even speak. As he went to push the door back open, the nurse stopped him.

"When your wife wakes she must meet with the psychologist, who should be here any minute. That is mandatory and you cannot be present."

"Can I at least go in and kiss her goodbye?" He tried not to sound like he was pleading.

The nurse looked up the hall. "If you hurry."

Eric ran in and kissed his wife on the forehead. She stirred and struggled to raise her eyelids. Amanda looked exhausted.

It was mere seconds later when the door to her room opened. "Sir, Dr. Carmelo, the psychologist, is here." The way the nurse held the door open, it was more than just an invitation for him to leave.

In almost slow motion, Amanda took his hand. Her other hand moved to the cross hanging around her neck. She whispered to him, "We need to watch over our baby, and keep her away from the Devil's hands." A tear ran from the corner of her eye.

He did not know what to say and found himself relieved the psychologist was there. He kissed her forehead again and whispered, "Rest hon. I love you."

The door was closed firmly behind him when he stepped out. He turned to see a woman with a crisp white overcoat walking up the hall and coming his way. As she neared, she raised her head and made eye contact. Dr. Carmelo had the most stunningly green eyes he had ever seen, and he found himself unable to look away. After introductions were made, Eric spoke to the green-eyed woman for a few moments until the nurse interrupted their conversation. "Major, it is probably best you go home and get some rest yourself."

Peeking in through the small window in the middle of the door, Major Eric Hyland blew a kiss to his groggy wife. He said good bye to the green-eyed psychologist and went home.

At 6:10 p.m., the ringing of the phone startled the major from a moment of deep thought. After answering and hearing the news, he just dropped the phone and held his face in his hands in utter shock. He paced around the house until midnight. Finally, his shaky legs collapsed and he fell to his knees, unable to outrun reality any longer. Tears poured out of his eyes. His heart and soul were crushed by despair and bottomless agony.

Amanda Hyland, his beloved wife, and mother of baby Sara, was dead.

Days later, the now mother-less Sara came home from the hospital. Amanda's belongings came home too, including the cross she wore every day. Eric Hyland immediately put the cross around his own neck and kissed it. While taking baby Sara in his arms, he had looked to the sky and made a pact that he would never break. The words emanated from somewhere deep in his soul. "Amanda, I swear, I won't fail you again."

Those words he had always taken to heart. Always.

As he lay in his bed on the ship, the general again questioned his own participation in the Utopia Project from nearly its inception, especially since Amanda was so much against the CCP and government conditioning. It was his duty and where he was assigned, but he realized that he had always been able to differentiate the Utopia Project from the CCP in one critical aspect. With the Utopia Project, women were not raising their own children, so there were no mothers who were distraught and heartbroken at the prospect of their baby being taken.

General Hyland tormented all day at the thought of Kid's rescue attempt planned for that very night. It was as if he already knew the final answer but had to run the mental gauntlet anyway. Conflict and guilt gnawed at his insides and he felt damned no matter what course of action he chose. His promise to his deceased wife right after Sara was born kept replaying in his mind, *Amanda, I swear, I won't fail you again*. In the end, he made a gut-wrenching call. Despite the implications and risks of such a decision, he had to protect his little girl.

After dinner, he walked over the unsteady rope bridge to ship number three. As he returned to ship number one, five female members walked with him. Having adjusted the member rotation schedule for the five girls, he directed four of them to report to their assigned rooms on the tenth hall. He instructed 19 to follow him.

Once back in his own room, he had 19 sit in a chair while he pulled out his thermographic scanner. He scanned her face and kept her thermographic signature on the screen as he clipped the device back on his belt.

"Please take that over to the door and wait," he instructed. She got behind the handle of a mobile cart and pushed it to the door.

The general pulled up the video camera program. In room 2912, Sara was laying on her bed with her hands resting on her stomach. The general froze the camera image in the system, cutting off the live video feed. After waiting for her hall to be empty, he also stopped the live video feed for the cameras at each end and froze the image of an empty corridor. Anyone looking at the video feed would see still-frames of Sara lying in bed and an empty hallway.

He checked his watch and gave 19 a pill to swallow. The neurological drug would quickly work into her system, so the clock was now ticking. "Let's go. Push the cart and follow me. Keep your head down," he instructed. She did so without question.

As they exited and went up the hall they passed a couple of preoccupied elders without arousing any suspicion. They had to walk closer to the wall as a large group of members filed past but none of them glanced their way.

Entering a service elevator, the general hit the button for the 29th floor. As they came to a stop and stepped into the hallway, an elder walked toward them with strands of wire and pliers in his hand. The general took quick, purposeful steps, not wanting to engage.

Glancing back, the general watched as 19 pushed the cart, which held a coffee pot and a single cup. Her steps seemed labored as the drug had started to take effect. She stared down at the pot as she had been instructed to do. *Keep your head down, but move quicker.*

"Elder-110," the general acknowledged as he passed.

"Sir." Elder-110 nodded his head. Looking down at the cart, he inhaled a deep breath, "We are not used to smelling the aroma of coffee at night."

The general realized he should have brought some other beverage down, but it was too late. He did not break stride but changed the subject as he called over his shoulder, "Why all of the wires Elder-110?"

"Power and generator trouble-shooting. We needed to access the electric distribution panel on this floor," Elder-110 shouted back as the general continued walking.

"Understood. Carry on."

"Yes, Sir."

Approaching room number 2912, the general slowed and glanced back. Elder-110 was at the end of the hall opening the exit door but had paused and turned around. The general could tell the elder found the late coffee delivery unusual and that a curiosity had been aroused. What the general did not want was for that curiosity to grow into a suspicion. Once the hallway door closed and Elder-110 was gone, the general stopped and turned around. Backtracking up the hall, he returned to room 2912. He had to hurry.

Waving his hand across a scanner, the door slid open. The general turned around and backed in so Sara would not recognize him. He waved for 19 to also back into the room. With her head lolling, 19 dragged the mobile cart over the door's threshold.

The general reached his hand over to the scanner inside the entrance and the door closed. Turning slowly, he put his finger to his lips. "Shh."

Sara jumped off her bed and covered her mouth. "Dad? Dad!" she uttered and ran over to him.

He was thankful that he had paused her two-way monitor, effectively shutting it down.

She wrapped her arms around him and they embraced. Sara was crying and he realized he was too. "I thought you didn't make it!" she said through her tears.

"I know, hon." He wanted to keep holding her but he had to stay on task or their tearful reunion would be for nothing. He grabbed her shoulders.

"How did you get here?" She looked at his outfit. "And where did you get the…Elder-41 uniform?"

"It is mine. I have been working in this project since shortly after its inception."

"And you never told me? I thought you were going to work at the base every day!"

He took her face in his hands. "I am sorry and will explain it all, but we don't have time right now."

"And who is…" she went to look behind her father.

"Hold on." He held her face tighter in his hands. "Sara, listen to me. We only have a minute. For you to survive, you need to do exactly what I say. No matter how difficult it is, you have to."

"I will, Dad, but you're scaring me."

"I'm sorry, but you have to trust me. First of all, sit. There's something you need to know now." As he sat her down, he was careful to keep himself between Sara and 19. "When you were born…"

As the words left his mouth, a bang made the general and Sara reflexively look over. The cup from the cart was bouncing on the floor. 19 dropped to a knee and before the general could react, she lifted her head and peered directly at Sara.

Sara's eyes flew open wide and a gasp escaped her throat. Her eyes rolled back and she crumbled forward into her father's arms. As he caught his fainting daughter, 19 simultaneously collapsed to the floor, having been knocked out by the neurological drug.

CHAPTER 26

January 5, 2045
Thursday, Morning
Near Rutland, Vermont
Ten days after the event

Inside the New England Maple Museum, Heidi held General Hyland's diary and continued to utter, "Oh my God…" She closed her eyes and heard wind whistling through the trees of the forest. She knew the wind was approaching and getting closer and she shivered. She had encountered the same sense of foreboding before. That was at the cabin in the woods in New Jersey, but this time it was stronger. The howl of the wind drew closer and closer and she put her hand to her chest, as if her heart might explode.

She gasped as the back door slammed shut and Kid entered the rear of the building. Before finishing the entry, Heidi tore out the diary page and crumpled it in her closed fist.

She held the book in her other hand as he came into the room. "Here, this fell out of my coat pocket." Her voice had a tremor.

He stopped short. "You have that? I thought we left it back in the widow's walk at the marina?"

"Remember you gave it to me? I forgot I put it in my coat pocket until just now."

Kid seemed reluctant to take it.

"You're acting like it's cursed," she chided.

He grinned and tried, unsuccessfully, to laugh it off as he

reached out and grabbed it.

She discreetly stuffed the balled-up diary page into her coat pocket.

After slipping the book into his own coat pocket, Kid opened the front of the wood stove. "We'll warm up for a bit, and then we should get back to the farmhouse."

Heidi nodded in agreement.

Although she tried to maintain casual conversation, she could not shake the disturbance she was feeling. She avoided making eye contact with Kid and a couple of times he asked if something was bothering her. He even pointedly asked if it was because she saw General Hyland's diary again. The last time they had it out was during a very emotional interaction. She would not admit it, but he was right about it being the diary. Not due to any prior associations but because of the words that she had just read, words that chilled her to her core as she squeezed the crumpled diary page inside her coat pocket.

That afternoon, Kid sat on a sill inside a cold, empty church, where he could watch the second funeral from a distance. He made the first one for Tim Mahler, but choose not to be at the funeral for Scott Sherman. Sid would have been enraged if the man who shot his brother was in attendance. Chris and Clarence had picked up Sid from the jail and while under constant guard, they allowed him to bath and change into fresh clothes for his brother's funeral. Kid noticed that Sid, whose wrists and ankles were tied, was sitting next to Heidi and talking to her. In front of them was a freshly planted granite tombstone with the chiseled initials, 'S.S.'

While Kid watched the proceedings, his mind drifted like the snow that was swirling around the cemetery. His confrontation with Scott was a close call. The Sherman brother was raising his pistol when Kid shot him. Even after, Kid had another close call with Sid in the darkness of the gondola engine room. Before that was the battle atop the fire tower in the New Jersey Pine Barrens. *I never had to worry about life or death confrontations before. And now they are happening regularly.*

In his half dream-state his thoughts turned to Sara, as they always did when he took pause. For a prolonged period of time he was alone in the silent church and was a captive audience for his own grief. Suddenly, a bell rang overhead and Kid almost fell off the window ledge. He had forgotten they would ring the church bell at the conclusion of the funeral services. Clarence must have come in the back door and gone up to the bell tower. Kid made sure his coat was zipped up all the way as he watched the group disperse from the fresh graves. Chris had his pistol drawn and was escorting the grieving Sid Sherman back to the jail. A chill passed through Kid. He wiped his cold cheeks and was surprised to find them wet. Walking through the nave of the church, he absently whispered, "Sara, Sara…"

For the second night in a row at the Mahler farmhouse, Kid heard his door open.

In the waning firelight he watched as Heidi slipped off her coat and hastily tossed it over the tall bedpost. "It's cold!" she whispered as she crossed her arms.

Kid hesitated, but then lifted the blanket to let her in again.

She slid under the covers. With her back to him, she squirmed until she was rubbing against his body. A few minutes later, her hands started to wander. She reached back and caressed his hip and then took her finger and hooked it under the waistband of his underwear.

He put his hand over hers. "Hold on. For tonight, let's just lay together, alright?"

"Are you alright?" She sounded a little taken aback as she tensed up.

"Yes, and don't think it's you. It's just that things are moving so fast."

She was silent and he could tell that her mind was processing and contemplating. He sensed that she wanted to go full-speed ahead and he hoped that she understood his need for a pause.

He felt her relax and nestle against him. She pulled his arm across her chest and hugged it. "It's alright. But Kid, promise me last night wasn't just a moment of weakness."

His stomach hollowed because he could not answer that question, not honestly. Instead, he said something that made him cringe the second the words escaped his lips. "If it was, why would I tempt myself again by letting you into my bed?"

"Especially when I'm all yours and want to be taken," she whispered. She kissed his arm, and he felt the tip of her tongue on his skin. He felt a stirring in his genital area. He fought it, but being pressed up against her, she had to feel it too. She turned to face him and had an expression of desperate and insatiable desire.

He fought his own urges and was nearly in a panic as he moved his hips back and sat up. "We have all the time in the world. Let's pace ourselves."

"If you feel a need to fight it..." she huffed and he felt her legs move, like she was ready to kick out of the blankets and leave.

Kid took her face in his hands and stopped her. He had a split second to make sure she did not feel completely rejected, so he gave her a kiss that was warm but not deep. Her eyes still longed for the deep passion and love they had shared the previous night. He laid his head on the soft pillow and put his arm around her. To his relief, she eased up and put her head down next to his.

Sometime before dawn, Heidi awoke with a start. Her mind was racing. Kid was sound asleep, so she carefully slipped out of the bed. Putting a few logs in the fire, she waited until the logs caught and provided some light. Tiptoeing to her coat on the bedpost, she gently reached into the pocket and pulled out the crumpled page from General Hyland's diary. Sitting in front of the fire, her heart rate continued to increase as she quietly smoothed out the creases in the paper. She exhaled and willed herself to look down and read the words again. Her hand clenched and she leaned forward to toss the wad in the fire.

She stopped herself and put her fist to her mouth. The same wind that taunted her at the cabin had come again and it would not be held back or turned away. Racing through the trees in the forest it was now upon her and she could not escape.

She turned and made sure Kid was still out cold. Unfolding the paper, a sick feeling coursed through her but she forced herself to read the words one more time. Tears started streaming down her face as she reached the final words of the entry.

'…I guess by now it should not be a shock, but it is—every time.'

Heidi's hand drooped to her lap and she sobbed in silence. Pulling her hands away from her face, she braced as if the wind was literally whipping her, casting words and revelations into her ears and brain. She whispered, "No. Please, no…"

Kid stirred and sat up. "Are you alright?" he mumbled.

She froze. Moving in slow motion, she squeezed the diary page into a tight ball and flipped it into the fire. It bounced off a burning log and settled in the corner of the fireplace.

"What was that?" he asked.

"Just some garbage." She did not move and continued to stare at the ball of paper. The wad was in reach of a flaming log and finally ignited. Relieved, Heidi slipped back into bed.

Moments later, she said, "Kid?"

"Yes?" he moaned.

"I need to talk to you. Something is on my mind and it's keeping me awake."

"So now it's going to keep us both awake?"

"Yes."

Kid rubbed his eyes. "What's bothering you?"

"Well, I've been thinking. Remember our idea about taking on this new society? I'm just starting to wonder if I felt that way because I had nothing left to lose. But now, I have something to lose…you and us. All of a sudden I'm wondering if it is worth the risk. Let's face it, the odds are really against us."

"I'm surprised you would feel this way now. It's like a complete 180-degree turn from just a few days ago at the cabin."

"I know, but I've been thinking a lot about it and I guess I'm conflicted now. Why do you think I can't sleep? Maybe we should consider just getting as far away from that Utopia Project society as we can. Go across the country, go to another country, and get out of harm's way." Pulling close to him, she said, "Think about it. We could live our life together in peace wherever we want."

He wiped his eyes and sat up, leaning on an elbow. "Heidi, it wasn't just about having nothing left to lose. It was about having nothing left, period. Nothing left of humanity."

"Why take that risk now?" she asked.

"If not now, when? The longer they get entrenched, the stronger they will be. Listen, we've had to deal with some serious traumas here recently, so it's understandable we might be a little gun-shy. But let's sleep on it."

I am getting nowhere, she thought. Heidi paused and exhaled heavily through her nose. "Alright, as long as we can talk about it in the morning."

"We have time. Jess isn't even back yet." His head dropped on the pillow.

"But I don't want to wait. I want to chart our own course. I can envision us spending every day together. My heart and soul would be in perfect peace and harmony."

"I hear you, Heidi. I do, but let's get some sleep," he whispered as he pulled her against his body. "That'll be our more immediate peace and harmony."

She nestled against him, her back arched in unison with his. His arm was wrapped around her waist. She laid her arm over his and held on, afraid to let go.

Just after dawn, Karen was lost in thought while helping prepare breakfast.

Evelyn said, "Well, it's almost ready. Let's get some people fed, starting with the folks upstairs. Why don't you get Kid, and…umm…"

"Heidi," Karen answered.

"Heidi! Sorry, that's right. I keep forgetting her name. Sara's friend."

"Yeah, by association."

Eying Karen, Evelyn wiped her hands on a dishtowel.

Feeling the gaze upon her, Karen knew her face was a little flush as she tried to clarify, "I mean, she was part of their friend group, but she's not at all the kind of person I could have ever seen Sara being close to."

"I don't know. My granddaughter was the kind of girl who could find the good in anyone."

"*Anyone* is right," Karen spouted and then bit her lip.

After a minute of silence, Evelyn offered a pained smile. Her face seemed to indicate that she had all the answers to life's questions.

Karen said, "I'll be cordial to Heidi, but to be honest, between you and me…" and then she lowered her voice to a whisper, "…something about that girl really bothers me. I don't know why, but I get a bad vibe."

The smile on Evelyn's face disappeared, leaving her with an expression that was just pained.

CHAPTER 27

January 6, 2045
Friday, Early Morning
Near Rutland, Vermont
Eleven days after the event

Knock, knock, knock!

With the room bathed in the morning sunlight, Kid inhaled as he sat up straight. He shook Heidi and whispered, "Wake up! We fell asleep and you never made it back to your room!"

"Oh no! I'm sorry," Heidi said as she swung her legs over the side of the bed.

Knock! Knock!

"Yeah," Kid yelled. "I know, breakfast is ready."

Marissa called back, "No, Jess is here!"

"What?"

"I said Jess is here! Come on."

"Be right there!" Kid jumped out of bed and started dressing.

"Have you seen Heidi?" Marissa yelled.

With his eyes open wide, Kid watched as Heidi got out of bed wearing just a bra and panties. "Yes!" he blurted out, louder than he meant to. "She's in here with me. We were talking for a few minutes. We'll be right down."

They both dressed and shared a quick kiss.

Heidi pursed her lips. "I know we're both relieved Jess's back, but after we catch up with him, can we talk like we said we would?

About our plans for the future?"

"Sure," he forced out. He was hoping that particular conversation had just been a bad dream.

Leaning into him, she gave him a deeper kiss and whispered, "Back to being just friends, but I love you."

"You too, friend," he whispered back, trying to hold back the wave of guilt and regret, wishing that for the time being they could really just be friends.

When Kid saw Jess, he felt an incredible wave of relief. He shook his hand and gave him a firm man-hug. "Did you bring the other half of Grandma's medication?"

Jess smiled. "Already gave it to her."

Kid then shook 801's hand and said, "Good to see you."

801 gave him a brisk man-hug, mimicking the interaction with Jess. "We are glad to be here. We are hoping there is food to eat."

"Don't worry. Grandma Hyland and Karen will take care of that."

When Kid embraced Maria, she said, "You will *never* guess who came back with us."

"You don't look worried so I assume it is not a bus full soldiers."

"Nope. Well, there is a soldier, but he was with none other than... Mr. Hyland."

"What?" Heidi blurted out as she snapped her head toward Maria.

"Mr. Hyland? Are you serious?" Kid was stunned.

"Even I wouldn't joke about something like that," Maria responded and patted his shoulder.

"Is he outside? Where is he?"

Jess answered, "He wants us to meet him at 9:00 a.m. He's out gathering some things."

"Why didn't he just come here?" Heidi sounded suspicious.

Good question. Kid turned and peered at Jess.

"I don't know." Jess shrugged. "He told us he had a few items to pick up first and that he may need our help to bring everything back to the house. He dropped us off and kept going. He also said to tell everyone to pack up because we're moving out and heading south."

"How did Mr. Hyland get up here?" Kid asked.

"He was in that bus full of soldiers that was chasing us. He splintered off, grabbed a smaller truck, and caught up. He had 705 with him." Jess pointed to the soldier. "We actually rolled into town last night, but we didn't get here until the middle of night so we just stayed at Mr. Hyland's parent's house."

Over the next half hour, there was a palpable excitement as Kid and the others ate and washed up.

Jess seemed restless and unable to sit still. "Kid, it's 8:30. Ready to move out?"

"I'm ready. I think." Kid breathed in and then slowly exhaled, trying to keep himself calm. Although the general knew about Sara's fate, it would be the first time he was facing him.

Pointing at 801 and 705, Marissa asked Jess, "Can these two be trusted? They scare me. They don't act…normal."

Jess chuckled. "They are fine, harmless, believe me. Unless an elder from the Utopia Project gives them specific orders, they will not be hostile in any way. Maybe give them something to do? They are pretty easily amused."

Clarence chimed in and said, "They can help us pack to head south. Come on guys." He left with 801 and 705.

"Maria, are you coming with me?" Jess called out.

"You bet. Wouldn't miss it!" She threw her coat on and casually touched Heidi's arm as she passed by.

Kid saw Heidi flinch.

"Whoa, easy there, Mrs. Jumpy," Maria said as she put her hands in the air. "Are you alright?"

"Yeah. I'm just a little tense these days," Heidi uttered as she looked away.

For a split second Maria's face showed pity and even sympathy. She offered a half-smile and said, "I hear you. Hang in there."

"You coming, Heidi?" Jess asked. Maria shot him a glance,

which Kid found odd.

"Assuming Kid doesn't mind," Heidi answered timidly.

"Why would I mind? Come on." Kid turned to Jess. "So where are we supposed to meet him?"

"Somewhere on Killington Road. We'd better go because Grandma and Grandpa Hyland want us to hurry back so they can see their son."

Freezing for a second, Kid felt the blood drain from his face. *Killington Road? Couldn't Mr. Hyland pick somewhere else to meet?*

His reaction went unnoticed by everyone, except Heidi. She pulled Kid to the side. "What's wrong?"

"Nothing, I guess it's just hitting me that I am going to finally be facing Mr. Hyland." He did not want to share the real reason.

"I know you're dreading it, but you don't have to do this. Remember what we talked about last night? We could leave right now." She took his hand and held it tight.

He was in fact dreading that he would have to face the general, but he had to.

"Can't we just go, and chart our own course?" she pleaded.

Kid turned away and said in a solemn voice, "Heidi, I'm not ready to make that choice. Especially not now. Come on, Mr. Hyland is waiting."

Passing the living room, he saw Chris hugging his wife. They separated and Evelyn met Kid's eyes for a second. She smiled at him but then brought her hand up to wipe the tears running down her cheek. Chris spun around and his eyes opened wide. "Oh Kid, didn't see you there. Listen, we'll see you when you get back."

"Alright. See you soon." He shrugged his shoulders and resumed walking. *What was that all about? Why is everyone acting funny?*

While driving over in Tim's pickup truck, Jess radioed the general, who instructed him where to go.

Upon hearing the general's voice, Kid broke into a sweat. They pulled up in front of a tourist gift shop and he felt even more uneasy as he stared out the window. Kid did not budge, and neither did Heidi next to him.

General Hyland walked outside from a small store, so Jess jumped out to greet him.

"There's Mr. Hyland, come on." Maria said and got out.

While Kid reached for the door handle, he turned to see Heidi sitting with her arms wrapped across her chest, hugging herself. "Coming?"

"I'll wait here. I'm not feeling well."

Taking her face in his hands, he tried to meet her eyes.

She looked the other way and gently took his hands from her cheeks. "They're waiting for you," she whispered.

"Alright, but we'll talk when I get back."

"I'm sure we will."

Kid opened the door and jumped out. The wind rustled his hair as he squinted against the early morning sun. Mr. Hyland was walking straight toward him. Kid swallowed hard and closed the vehicle door. Without hesitation, the general embraced him. Unable to suppress the tears in his eyes, Kid tried to speak, but no words would come out.

With his arm around Kid's shoulder, the general said, "Let's talk. Jess and Maria explained everything that happened with your rescue and escape and with your time at the cabin. In the end I was quite stunned about the sequence of events. Let's sit for a moment." He motioned to a bench with a view of the Green Mountains.

Kid froze. "Mr. Hyland, you do realize that this is the bench where Sara and I first met?" He was sure the general knew that.

"Yes, Kid. I do."

Is this the general's way of hurting me for what happened to Sara? Kid felt confused and uncomfortable.

"Please, sit," the general continued.

"It is incredibly strange to be right here." Kid bent over and brushed snow off of the all-too-familiar bench. He ran his fingers on the wood slats comprising the seat back, and he could swear he felt a stickiness, as if a piece of tape had just been removed.

Kid exhaled a shaky breath as he sat. In front of him, the snow-covered Green Mountains loomed and just as he remembered, they were far enough away to offer an incredible panoramic view but were close enough to make him feel like he was sitting in their shadow. The first time he sat on this bench, he felt magic. This time, he felt nausea.

"On the ship, after the girls were captured, I was faced with an impossible choice," the general started and paused.

"What choice are you referring to?"

"Whether I should try and intervene and save my daughter."

"You were going to intervene?" Kid asked in surprise. He hung his head. "I wish we knew that before we went ahead with the rescue attempt. But at the time we didn't even know you were alive, let alone on the Utopia Project ships. All I can say is…I'm sorry."

The general paused for a long second. "Not only was I on the ships, but with our video camera coverage, I was able to follow what you and Jess were doing. I'm still amazed at how quickly you were able to locate the girls. I saw the whole thing unfold, but never in my wildest dreams could I have ever foreseen the final outcome, or the pure happenstance that would come into play, sometimes before my very eyes."

"Kid, close your eyes," the general directed as he touched Kid's arm. "Imagine what I am about to describe. Seriously, close your eyes, tightly."

He complied.

"The morning of your well-planned and executed rescue, there is absolute chaos everywhere as you grab the girls and get into an escape boat. You immediately take off. I watched you leave from the deck of the ship. In the mayhem, Sara is shot by one of our weapons. You witnessed that, didn't you?"

"I did. The shot grazed her shoulder," Kid said. He could still see Sara's face as he tried to pull her to the bottom of the boat, but he took a second too long. And if only he had reached out and caught the bolt before it hit her…

"From talking with Jess and Maria, it seems that after Sara was shot, she was never the same and never recovered. At the cabin, her physical and mental health rapidly declined. Do you remember Sara in her last days and hours? Can you see her?"

"It hurts like hell, but I can see her all too clearly." Kid's heart was pumping like a locomotive speeding uphill. He could see his helpless girlfriend lying in bed at the cabin, her cute upturned nose and her alluring hazel eyes. He recalled how her lips had involuntary pursed, as they always did, when she got upset. He could see her smiling through her pain. His nostrils flared for a second as he absorbed the olfactory recollection from when he had bent down to kiss her after she had had a bath at the cabin.

"How different things would've been…" the general said, "…if my intervention was not too late." He exhaled and paused. "I have to stand up, but keep your eyes closed and sit tight."

Feeling the bench seat ripple, Kid folded his arms and fought the painful churning in his stomach. This discussion was not what he had expected at all. He was stunned and could not grasp that the general knew Sara was on the ships and he was ready to intervene. As bad as it was that she passed away, it was even worse knowing the general was ready to save her. "I'm sorry that our rescue attempt wrecked your plans to save her. If I had only known." Kid shifted his rear end on the bench.

"When was the last time you saw Sara's face?"

Kid clenched his teeth. "When…" His voice was quiet and strained as he continued, "…we buried her. I can take you to her grave when we're back in New Jersey."

"Alright, Kid, but please, describe her face the last time you saw it."

"She looked very much at peace."

The general said, "Close your eyes tighter, gaze deeper into your memory."

Silence followed, and despite the temperature outside, Kid's face was hot as confusion reigned.

He felt the bench seat bow slightly as the general sat back down.

"I can't close my eyes any tighter! I promise you, I can see her clear as day!" Kid was frustrated and dropped his open palm to his thigh. So this was how the general was going to make him pay for not taking care of his little girl. He began to understand. "Mr. Hyland, with all due respect, why are you doing this to me?" As much as he tried, he could not hide the pain and emotion as his voice trembled.

A few seconds passed and no response was given.

"Why?" Kid repeated. His breaths shortened and his heart was in his throat.

Oddly, the general's next words came from right behind him, not next to him. "What if in fact, my intervention was *not* too late?"

'Not too late?' But he was too late. Kid's heart was pounding to the point of being painful. *In the end, his intervention was too damned late and he failed! So why does he keep bringing it up? If he didn't fail, then…* With his eyelids twitching, a tingle started in his spine and spread throughout his entire body.

"Open your eyes, Kid."

Kid turned and opened his eyes.

His breath and his heart both stopped.

CHAPTER 28

December 29, 2044
Thursday, Evening
New Jersey coast, Utopia Project Ship Number One
Three days after the event

Sara fainting in her room on the ship was not part of the general's plan. She was not supposed to see 19 until after he had given her a short, yet necessary, speech. He had to ensure she was prepared for the inevitable and unavoidable shock.

He needed her to know that clones were grown from the cells of a group of children who were born around the time of the Child Conditioning Program, or CCP, in January 2025, and Sara was one of those children. Her replicated fetus developed as Utopia Project member number 19.

The general had checked the member rotation schedule two days ago to ensure 19 was not on ship number one. He knew that Sara crossing paths with her mirror image would be disastrous. He had succeeded in keeping 19 away from the ship until bringing her over tonight as part of his new plan.

Carefully laying Sara on the ground, he pulled out his thermographic scanner. He did a profile edit as he waved the device over Sara's face, capturing her facial heat point data. He then did the same for 19. Clipping the scanner to his belt, he had succeeded in switching the thermographic signatures for Sara and member number 19 in the computer system. This swap was essential. The members were always identified by thermographic scans, not by visual recognition or even uniform numbers.

He needed 19 to be in bed as Sara would have been. By morning, with the drug dose he had given her, she should be dead. In the unlikely event she survived, 19 would at best be in a vegetative state and would be terminated anyway. The general felt a pang of sadness about sacrificing 19 and found it hard to look at her without feeling guilt and pity. Since she was a clone of Sara, it was like watching his own daughter wither and perish.

He moved 19 away from the cart and laid her out on the floor next to Sara. Despite the pressure and intensity of his mission, seeing the two bodies side by side momentarily stunned him. With the exception of a few tiny blemishes on Sara's face, the two girls were identical twins. They had the same face, the same build, the same shape, the same bone structure, and even the same fair skin color.

He took off 19's uniform and picked her up. After he laid her in bed, he pulled the blanket up and rested her hands across her stomach. From being her father and as confirmed by the video feed, he knew this was how Sara slept. He was surprised as 19 moaned and turned her head. It made him question if he used a large enough dose of the neurological drug. His intent had been to give her a dose large enough to kill her, but small enough to avoid detection during a routine physical examination of the dead body.

He ran to the sink in the back of the room. Filling a small paper cup with water, he ran over to Sara lying on the floor. He hated to do it, but he had to wake her, so he splashed her face. She jerked up and inhaled deeply. Her hands reached for her father. He held her and said, "Stay calm. I know it's a shock."

"Dad, she's…me."

"She's a clone of you, yes, made from your cells. An exact replica. It stunned me every time I saw her."

Getting to her knees, Sara gazed at the bed. She seemed more curious than shocked. "Talk about freaky. It was like I was looking into a mirror, seeing my own face and eyes, but the reflection was acting independently. Wait, a clone? She is one of the original 23 members of the society, developed in test tubes?"

"How would you know about that?"

"My first night on the ship, Elder-1 and Elder-76 said the cells for the first 23 members in the project came from kids who were in what I knew was the Child Conditioning Program. How could I, or my cells, be part of the original 23? I was born *after* the CCP ended," she asked.

"They were still able to harvest some your cells, but don't worry about that now. We have to go. You are switching places with her. I'll explain more when I can, but from here on out, until we can escape and get to the mainland, you have to *be* number 19. You have to act like one of them. Do what they do. Act like they do. You have to be detached emotionally."

"I have to be her, 19? How can I pull that off?"

"Hey, you were in school to be an actress. You'll have to put on one hell of a performance. Just follow what everyone else does. Physically, you are a carbon copy of 19, so as long as you can act like them, you'll blend in. And make sure you avoid eye contact with all elders."

Sara jumped to her feet. "Oh no. Wait Dad, Kid is going to try and rescue me tonight!"

"I know. I'm going to do everything I can to help him escape."

"But he's going to come for me and I won't be here."

"We will catch up with them on shore as soon as we can," The general looked around the room as he spoke, avoiding eye contact. He did not want to give any indication of how he really felt about Kid's odds. He had to be reassuring. Sara's life depended on it. Her being distraught about Kid and the others would impair her ability to blend in with the members of the Utopia Project society. "We're getting ready to set up our base on the mainland. As soon as we're over there, you and I can safely escape ourselves and we will find them."

"But he may not leave this ship without me."

"He will," the general stated. "Once he sets the rescue plan in motion, he will not be able to stop or turn back."

"What if it goes awry and he gets killed trying to find me! Let me stay here and take my chances. If you're helping the rescue anyway, we could…"

The general snapped his head up. "Sara, no more. I'm not taking that chance. Not with your life. I swore I would never fail your mother again, and I don't plan to."

"What?" A torrent of emotions seemed to flood over Sara and left her speechless. Her eyes were absent and her mouth was open.

"I told you, I will help their rescue," he added, trying to provide more reassurance. He did plan to help, including causing a delay with the primary alarms on the girls' hall that night. He could buy them a 59-second head start.

As the general stood and faced the door, he said, "Before sending you to your room on the seventh floor, we should go back to my room. I'll give you more instructions as to what you need to do to blend in with them. I'll also explain your schedule of activities…" and then he fell silent as a shadow passed the door and slowed down. They had already taken too long and he was anxious to leave. A second shadow passed by and also slowed.

The general tensed. They had to get out of there right away.

Sara went to speak and the general swung around with his finger to his lips. "We have to go. Change into her uniform, quickly," he whispered as he picked it up from the floor.

She disrobed, took the uniform number 19 from him, and put it on.

He hung her uniform number 19794 on the wall hook. "Just look down and bend over while pushing the cart. Don't make eye contact with anyone."

He hugged and kissed Sara affectionately. "Act mechanical, emotionless, and whatever you do, don't say any word that starts with the letter I. Talk monotone and lose that southern accent of yours. This is the biggest acting gig of your life, but you can do it. I know you can.

Push the cart over here and face the hallway."

Sara picked the fallen cup off the ground, placed it on top of the cart and moved to the doorway as he waved his hand over the scanner. Stepping out, the general saw the backs of the two elders who had walked past. Elder-110 had returned to the hall and was accompanied by another elder. He was relieved that Elder-110 still had tools in his hand, indicating a purpose other than just following up on a suspicion. He waved his daughter out with the cart.

The general glanced back in the room as the real 19 exhaled and rolled over on her side. Although drugged, she did not seem as debilitated as he expected her to be by that point. She should have been knocked out cold, but she would be soon enough. Once she went into a deep sleep, she would never wake up. With the drug dose he gave her, by morning she should be dead and the elders would conclude the new captive, number 19794, had expired.

Only then did it hit him. He hoped that Sara's DNA did not have a strand containing the strength and resiliency she had demonstrated throughout her life, because he did not factor that into his drug dose calculation for her clone, 19.

January 6, 2045

Friday, Early Morning

Outside of Rutland, Vermont

Eleven days after the event

Still sitting inside the truck, Heidi rocked back and forth as tears continued to run down her face. She refused to even glance outside and stared down at her hands. She was coddling the gold arrowhead locket with Kid's picture inside that she had taken from Sara's dresser.

Although the air in the vehicle was still and tomblike, the same whistling wind engulfed her. Heidi could not fight it anymore, especially after reading the page she had torn out of the general's diary.

Finally, it was time for her to face the wind that had taken to taunting her.

Closing her eyes, but with the sights of her memory open wide, she allowed herself to see a moment that she previously could not, and would not, look at again. Her mind threatened to freeze as it had done time and again, as if reality would bend under the collision, but this time she would not stop. Her mind forced aside the heavy curtains and held them back so she could see the memory that lay beyond.

It was less than a week ago. She saw herself inside Ironside cabin, helping Sara take a bath in the metal tub. The curtains in her mind became heavier and tried to force themselves closed. Heidi shivered as the memory came into focus. Maria had said, "Go ahead and say it Sara, 'Leave me alone. I feel like hell.'" Sara reacted by shaking her head once, then she mechanically raised her hand and pointed at the corner of her eye with her finger. Maria was behind her and thought Sara was mocking the Utopia Project members. But Heidi was face to face with Sara and something had registered right then.

Sincerity.

She couldn't shake the recurring vision of Sara's expression and no matter how many times she saw it, she could not find even a hint of mockery in it. The girl's response was 100% sincere, as would be the response of any fully conditioned Utopia Project member; just like 609 when they were able to converse with her while eating lunch. Then suddenly the wind was coming through the trees toward the cabin, carrying the implications of such a realization. She could not face it. It was too much, as if asking her to consider the possibility of some alternate reality. Like trying to accept the earth is actually flat, or the moon is not real and is just a trick of light. A wisp of that wind had reached her before she could turn and run, but she had refused to acknowledge it.

But now, as the scene unfolded, she realized that no amount of denial could alter the stunning reality.

The girl who died at the cabin was not who they thought she was.

On the bench, Kid opened his eyes to see the number 19 embroidered on a Utopia Project uniform and then his eyes turned up. An apparition so beautiful and so real had to be a cruel and torturous penance. The vision leaned toward him with tears running down her face and grabbed his hand. Desperate hope and disbelief mixed in every cell in his body, like mixing bleach and rubbing alcohol. As they combined, black curtains came down over his eyes and he felt like he was falling. He had never fainted before and it was a strange and helpless feeling. But even as he fell, he could see his Sara sitting next to him on the same bench where they had met. She looked so real and sounded so real, but what stuck with him was the touch of her hand as he blacked out. It was an emotion and sensory overload and a shock that made his body shut down lest he might spontaneously combust.

A vision of Sara emerged through the haze, standing behind the frosted glass window of her room on the ship. He was then reliving a dream he had had where Sara's outline in the opaque glass was filled in by a hideous creature. A feeling of panic choked him, but then the scene switched and he saw her lying in bed at the cabin. Panic was washed away by sadness and helplessness. Then a sickening feeling rushed through him again as he felt in vain for her pulse. After putting her in the grave, he pulled the blanket back far enough to take one last gut-wrenching look at her face before burying her. He was unable to say good-bye. He could not even finish the inscription on her grave marker.

He floated in a sea of darkness, but it seemed a distant part of him was conscious of what was happening. Sara simply could not be alive. It was beyond the realm of comprehension. Accepting such a change in reality came with the risk of irreparable harm. He would never survive another trip through the same vicious emotional gauntlet if she was in fact an apparition. It was not a simple leap of faith.

"Kid?" A sweet and familiar voice cascaded through his soul and sounded so real. *Kid, Kid, Kid...*

As he came to, he went to sit bolt upright and was restrained by a pair of arms. He stiffened, afraid to glance behind him.

"Shh, it's alright, Kid. Relax," Sara whispered. His upper body and head were in her lap, and she was holding him tight. "It's really me."

He willed himself to turn and look at her face. Tears were running down her cheeks. He touched them and stared at the drops of salty water on his fingertips. He touched his fingertips to his own cheek. The spot turned cold in an instant from the chilly breeze. He closed his eyes for a second and absorbed the feeling.

Sitting up, Kid turned and whispered, "Oh my God. It really is you." As the shock subsided, waves of relief, love and pain coursed through his body in powerful bursts. "Sara?"

"Kid…" She choked up and started bawling.

He was unable to stem the emotional tide and also erupted into tears. His knees slid to the ground and he pulled Sara with him. He held her tightly and they both fell sideways into the snow.

For several minutes they cried and clung to each other. As he held her head in his hands, he kissed every inch of her face and rested his forehead against hers.

The general sat on the bench with tears in his eyes and a smile on his face.

Reality and reason started coming back to Kid in small waves. He turned to her and asked, "How is this possible? I," he swallowed, "buried you."

The general cut in, "You buried someone, but it wasn't who you thought it was."

Shaking his head with confusion, Kid tried to form his next question but was stumbling. "But, how…"

"Almost 20 years ago, right after Sara was born, her DNA was taken and used to develop another living being in a test tube. That living being grew up as number 19 in the Utopia Project. She was one of the original 23 members."

Sara interjected while staring at her father, "Despite the fact that my DNA never should have been taken, since the Child Conditioning

Program ended before I was even born."

He ignored her questioning gaze and continued, "Anyway, it was number 19 you buried. She was an exact replica of Sara, especially when their hair was cut the same way, except for two tiny, tiny details."

Kid peered at Sara and then turned to the general.

"Sara's clone, number 19, did not have the two tiny freckles Sara has near the bridge of her nose. And neither did Sara until she spent too much time in the sun."

"That's right!" Kid knew the two freckles he was talking about. "You pointed those out last summer when we were both giving her a hard time about laying out in the sun."

With Kid and her father turning to her, Sara put her hand in front of her face. "Can y'all stop staring at me?"

Hearing the familiar southern accent coming through, Kid smiled. He turned and asked, "So that's why you wanted me to gaze more closely at her face in my memory?"

The general had a knowing look.

"I would've never noticed that when we were at the cabin unless I was specifically looking for it, but why would I?" Kid asked.

"It is truly amazing you didn't know the girl you rescued wasn't Sara, but after talking to Jess and Maria, I understand. The sequence of events unfolded in a way that could not have been scripted with more precision."

In his defense Kid said, "She, number 19, was only with us a few minutes before she was shot when we scrambled off the ship. Why would number 19, a Utopia Project member, even come with us when we escaped?"

"She was heavily medicated and likely not of sound mind. With the drugs I gave her, I expected her to die in her bed. I still cannot believe she was able to function at all. Once out of bed, if she was disoriented, I could see her clinging to a group since the members are not used to being alone."

Shrugging his shoulders, Kid continued. "After she was grazed by a shot when we were trying to escape, we knew she wasn't right, but we figured it was because of whatever ammo was in those crazy weapons your people use. We knew they didn't fire bullets. Had I thought to ask her, 'Are you really Sara,' I guess I would have known." As he reflected for a moment, he added, "But what's strange is that number 19 made a lot of the same facial expressions as Sara and had some of the same mannerisms."

"I know. I noticed the same thing when I saw 19 on the ships. But given that she has the same DNA as Sara, I guess it shouldn't be a complete surprise. They both had a lot of my wife, Amanda, in them."

As Kid recalled 19's face, her voice and her body, a chill ran through him. She was truly a replica. In retrospect, if he had doubted she was the real Sara, even for a second, any number of simple tests would have revealed the truth. A random inconsistency from the cabin crossed his mind. "You hate weak coffee!"

Sara had a perplexed look. "You know I do. Where did that come from?"

General Hyland got up from the bench. "Why don't we give you a few minutes alone to catch up and then we'll head back." He and the others made their way back to the gift shop.

Speaking through pursed lips, Sara said, "I can't believe how that all went down. My greatest fear was you would attempt another rescue when you realized it wasn't me you were saving. They would have been ready for you the next time. I'm so sorry you had to go through that, Kid. I swear, I will make up for it every minute of the rest of my life. I have been so, so worried sick about you."

Kid gazed into her beautiful hazel eyes and ran his fingers through her dark, soft hair. He kissed her lips, which were red and succulent despite the cold. It was a feel and taste he had thought he would never experience again. He could not stop kissing her and touching her as if she was a ghost that might suddenly disappear.

"And the worst part," Sara started as she ran her fingers through her hair and pulled the strands from her face. "My dad didn't realize we would be flash blinded by the neutron beams the night it all went down, and I wouldn't be able to read the note he left. Even still, with the alarm he put in it, I should have opened the gift box as soon as my vision returned. We would have known we needed to hide and I never would have been captured. I also would have realized that my Dad was still alive." Staring down, she muttered, "And that he was part of that Utopia Project."

"You never knew he was?" Given how tight she was with her father, he did not think there were any secrets.

Sara looked embarrassed. "I'm surprised I didn't, but no. I had no idea. I thought he went to the base to work every day." She took his hand as she continued, "But I'm sorry Kid. If I had only followed my father's instructions, this crazy sequence of events after the destruction never would have happened."

"Don't be sorry. How could you have known what was going happen, or how it was going to unfold?" he asked. "What matters is you are here now. And so am I, although I'm still in a state of shock."

Their emotional reunion lasted for several minutes more until the general came over and said, "Come on. Sara, your grandparents can't wait to see you."

CHAPTER 29

January 6, 2045
Friday, Morning
Outside of Rutland, Vermont
Eleven days after the event

Kid took Sara's hand and they walked side by side. Since they were both not wearing gloves, he was able to absorb the warmth of her touch.

Heidi had left the confinement of the truck and was walking toward them. Sara opened her arms and wrapped her in a warm embrace.

Kid met Heidi's eyes as she was hugging Sara. Although he was still stunned and could not acknowledge it at the moment, he knew the implications of Sara's impossible survival. Despite feeling instantly complete again after reconnecting with his soulmate and regardless of the unbelievable fortune fate had provided him, he knew deep inside he would have to confront an unavoidable reality. His time with Heidi was over, and even through his shock he felt a dull ache. But at that moment, the hurt and sorrow he glimpsed in her eyes was downright brutal, if not ominous. He felt a wave of frustration. *How could there be any negative implications to this most incredible turn of events?*

Heidi was sobbing as she kissed Sara's cheek and whispered, "This is truly a miracle."

As they walked to the general's brown SUV, Kid tried to tamp down his raw emotions and get his bearings. He turned to Jess, "So this morning, you already knew Mr. Hyland's plan for today?"

"Not about the bench, but we knew Sara was with him and you were in for a surprise. Kind of like we were when Mr. Hyland caught up to us in Canada. Maria and I both screamed so loud when we saw Sara that 801 covered his ears and ducked," Jess said as he adjusted a brown leather aviator cap on his head, making sure his ears were snug inside the fur lining.

"And listen to this one," Maria started, "Heidi, remember when we reached Mr. Hyland on the walkie-talkie that night in the widow's walk at the marina? He thought we were asking about Sara to find out why she wasn't in her room on the ship when the guys came to rescue us. He was actually apologizing to *us*, for moving her out of her room and switching her with someone else. He had no idea that when we rescued 19, and after, we all fully believed she was Sara."

Shaking her head, Heidi could only say, "What are the odds."

The general clarified, "I didn't know you thought Sara was dead until I met up with Jess and Maria. That's what gave me the idea about Sara reuniting with Kid at the bench where they met."

While grabbing Kid's hand, Sara noted, "When I found out from Jess you thought it was me who died after your rescue, my heart fell through my stomach. I just broke down. I felt so terrible about it."

Another implication hit Kid and he felt a spike of anger. He stopped and turned toward the general. "Wait. If you switched Sara with 19, weren't you kind of putting me and the others in danger? If I realized it wasn't Sara, I would have probably started searching for her and got myself killed in the meantime."

"I'm sorry, Kid, for putting you at risk. That was an unfortunate implication of the impossible choice I had to make. I do not want to get into it right now, but I swore I would never fail Sara's mother again and I just couldn't take the chance." The general's tone was firm, but apologetic.

With the unusual emotion in the general's voice, Kid said nothing more and merely nodded his head.

The general continued. "It is no consolation, but I have to say, your rescue was methodical and well-planned. I am still not sure how you pulled it off, but it was impressive. If history repeated itself, which it better not, I would not hesitate to leave my daughter's fate in your hands."

At that, Kid's anger started to taper off. He did not have the emotional energy to carry it anyway. He was still in shock and drained. "Ah…her double didn't fare very well," Kid reminded.

"No, but the real Sara would have immediately taken cover in the boat when you were escaping. Right?" He turned to his daughter.

"Right, Dad. The clone's problem was that she had good sea legs. Forget taking cover. I would have fallen over."

"So, how long were you on the ships before coming up here?" Kid asked.

"Five…long…days!" Sara huffed.

"Were you hidden away?"

"No, that's the worst part. After the switch with my clone, I had to take her place and act as if I was number 19. I actually lived as a member of their society."

"So you had a true firsthand look," Kid noted.

"Yes, but I am glad we left when we did. I don't know how much longer I could have pulled it off."

"You'll have to fill in the details of what it was like to…" Kid was cut off by a sudden beep from his walkie-talkie. Before he could even pull it from his belt, Clarence spouted frantically, "Come in! Emergency, do you read me?"

Kid stopped in his tracks and lifted his walkie-talkie. He tried to shake himself out of his present state of shock from Sara's incredible survival. "What's wrong, Clarence?"

"They're here! Karen went downtown to look for stronger antibiotics and spotted a bus full of those soldiers you told us about. They parked the bus and secured a bunch of snowmobiles. They are on the hunt in downtown Rutland and are supposedly following every quad and snowmobile track they come across. It's just a matter of time before the tracks lead them to us!"

"Get rid of anything that would give away you're in the farmhouse. Put out the fires, arm yourselves, and stay inside," Kid said. "We're on our way."

"Got it. Avoid downtown when coming back!" Clarence warned.

"We will. Over and out."

General Hyland said to the group. "I know some back roads, so everyone get into my vehicle. We can all fit."

"What do we know about this group on the bus? How many are there?" Kid asked as he hopped in the front seat and Sara sat on his lap. Jess, Maria, and Heidi piled in the back.

"Around 17 or so, but one of them is Elder-44, a cold hearted and well-trained bastard. He is formidable," the general noted as he sped away.

Heading back toward the Mahler farmhouse, the general was driving down a steep snow-covered hill when he saw a log had fallen across the road ahead. He hit the brakes, which were doing nothing to slow him down. He tapped the brake pedal while turning the wheel and was just able to get around the log as the ground leveled off.

"Now that we're north of Route 4, we're in the official borders of the Green Mountains, which means this was an infrared scanning zone. Wait until we turn the corner up ahead," the general added. "They had their own tent city out this way, which was inhabited by more than forty homeless people."

"I always wondered why homeless people wouldn't migrate south to where it was warm. If I had to live outside, that's what I'd do," Jess commented.

They turned the corner and saw nearly twenty tents arranged in a circle. One brown and green camouflage tent had blown away and was caught in a tree, flapping in the breeze. While driving past, the general pointed to the central fire pit. "If we cleared the snow around the fire, we would find the remains of one body after another, probably all melted together. They used to huddle around the fire, shoulder to shoulder, trying to stay warm enough to survive."

The walkie-talkie attached to Kid's belt chirped to life. He grabbed it and brought it to his lips. "Go ahead."

"Listen up. Here's the status report," Clarence started. "Karen went out to track their movement. From what she could see, the enemy group is searching every building in downtown Rutland."

"Got it. We are avoiding downtown and should be there in just a few minutes. Hold tight, and tell Karen to keep her distance," Kid said.

Upon reaching the farmhouse, Kid was touched as he watched the hurried, but emotional, reunion of the general and Sara with Chris and Evelyn. While Evelyn held Sara tightly and rocked ever so gently, Chris hugged his son quickly and got right back to business, "We need to grab every weapon we have."

After securing several handguns and one pump action shotgun, the group met in the foyer by the front door. The general stated, "I don't want to go to war with them, at least not here and now. They have too much of an upper hand in terms of weaponry and the physical condition of their forces. If we could get around them, we could head back down south to New Jersey and regroup."

"We can do that if we take the right route," Chris said. "But with the enemy crawling around up here, we need everyone to get out of the area, and now. I have to go warn the neighbors."

"Wait, what about Sid?" Heidi blurted out. The room went silent. "We can't just leave him."

"The jail is downtown," James noted. "Karen said the place is crawling with soldiers. It's bad enough she is down there."

Chris exhaled. "It would be a risk. Can the guy be saved, or will we just move him to another jail for the rest of his life?"

"I can tell you how Tim Mahler and Karen would answer that," Kid said bitterly. *And if they only knew what Sid did to Karen…*

Heidi countered, "It's possible he can be saved. I spent enough time with him when I was a captive to know that. He has some real problems and insecurities, but most of them are traumas from how he grew up. And even Kid noticed, for whatever reason, he responded to me."

"So you think his soul can be saved?" Chris asked.

"Right now I'm not the right person to make judgments about anyone's soul, but I know he has one, and there are not many left on this planet," she answered.

Chris sighed. "I'll go get him."

"Dad, why don't I go?" the general offered.

"Son, I know my way around here better than anyone, except maybe Wendy. Besides, I need to round up Dr. McDermott, Melanie Spatz, and Rick Ryan, and I know where they live."

"I'll go with him," Kid offered.

This seemed to provide some reassurance to the general, who stopped pressing and said, "I hope your neighbors are ready to leave on a moment's notice. Do they even have suitable vehicles?"

"Dr. McDermott has a large Cadillac SUV with four-wheel drive. It'll be tight if all the families cram in, but a few are small kids, so he should be able to fit everyone. Let me radio Karen and make sure the area around the jail is clear."

"We need Karen to get back here too," Kid noted.

Chris nodded. "Yes. She's downtown close to the jail. We'll have her meet us there and we can come back together."

Walking up the hall, the general yelled, "Let's get to the van! Everyone, grab a change of clothes, blankets, food and drinks, and only the bare necessities! And Mom…"

"I know, bring my medication." Evelyn called out. "I will bring all of it."

Running upstairs to his room, Kid kneeled down and hastily stuffed his clothes into a small duffle bag. Starting to cough, he buried his mouth and nose in the crook of his arm. He realized that he had drafted smoke out of the fireplace while whipping his garments around, but all fires were supposed to be extinguished. In front of him, the fire still smoldered, so he grabbed a half-full cup of water from the end table. The liquid sizzled as he poured, but he stopped as something behind the logs caught his eye.

Reaching the back corner of the fireplace with the tip of the poker, he dragged out a crumbled piece of paper which was browned on the outside but not burned through. The thick paper looked familiar. Unfolding the page, he stiffened as he realized it was from the general's diary. He read the creased paper with his mouth agape. His eyes flicked left to right, over and over, as he read the words.

In the entry the general is describing Sara's clone on the ships, number 19. The entry ended with the general running into 19 on the ship that day and noting, '…I guess by now it should not be a shock, but it is—every time.' Bringing his eyes back to the top of the page, Kid read the words again. He did not have time to ponder the implications, but had he read all of the general's diary, he would have been aware that Sara had a clone on the ships. *If I had only known.*

"But how did a diary page wind up in the fireplace?" he asked aloud as he stared at the smoldering ashes. He then remembered the crumpled ball being tossed in there in the middle of the night. *Just some garbage.* His eyes opened wide with the realization and he whispered, "Heidi."

Dropping his hand to his lap and letting the diary page fall onto the small hearth, he gazed straight ahead, shocked and dismayed. His lips tried to form words but only twitched, as if he was chewing a piece of gum. It took a full minute to get the words out.

"She knew."

CHAPTER 30

January 6, 2045
Friday, Morning
Outside of Rutland, Vermont
Eleven days after the event

Kid ran down the stairs and met Sara by the door. She was now wearing a sweater and blue jeans. "Where did you get the clothes?" he asked.

"I grabbed them last night when we stayed at my grandparent's house. I have my own designated closet there," she answered as they stepped outside.

Heading around to the open back door of the van, Kid saw Heidi, James, 801, 705, Clarence and Marissa, ready and waiting. They were sitting amongst cases of water and boxes filled with food. Wendy was also there, but was handing a blanket to Evelyn in the passenger's seat.

From the driver's seat, the general called out, "Let's move. Time to go."

Kissing Sara's cheek and handing her his small duffle bag, Kid whispered, "Now that I have you back, please be careful."

"Have me back? I think it's the other way around. You too," she said as she climbed in the back of the van.

"Come on Kid," Chris called while starting up his snowmobile.

Kid jumped on the back and Chris throttled up. Arriving at the McDermott's, Chris gave them directions for a route to the west and advised them to leave immediately and pick up the Spatz's and the

Ryan's. Before Chris and Kid were even halfway up the road, Dr. McDermott already had his family in the vehicle and was pulling out.

Chris and Kid headed toward the Rutland County Jail in downtown Rutland to get Sid. As they were heading along Kendall Hill Road, Chris made a sudden turn and pulled into the historic Hammond Covered Bridge. The snowmobile ground to a halt on the wooden boards. Before Kid could ask, Chris jumped off and said, "Trouble is coming our way. Two snowmobiles. I don't think they saw us." He hid behind a beam just inside the structure and pulled out his pistol. Kid lined up next to him and followed suit.

"We have the element of surprise, and with the weapons I understand they have, we'll need it," Chris said. "As soon as they pass the bridge, I'll aim for the first one, and you aim for the second one. Got it?"

"Got it."

He glanced at the 38-caliber in Kid's hand. "Are you fully loaded?"

Kid double-checked his weapon and nodded.

"Make at least one of them count."

The whir of the approaching snowmobiles was getting louder and louder. "Get ready," Chris whispered. A second later he said, "Now," and jumped out with his pistol aimed forward. Kid leapt out next to him.

Shots rang out in rapid succession from both guns. The first soldier took a bullet in the chest from Chris. While slumping over the steering arm of his speeding snowmobile, the soldier careened into the woods and smashed into a tree.

The second soldier was hit in the leg by one of Kid's bullets and fell off of his snowmobile. While on the ground, the soldier pulled out his weapon and took aim.

Without hesitation, Chris swung his arm and slammed Kid across the chest, knocking him through the opening of the covered bridge and out of the line of fire. Kid felt like he had been hit with a baseball bat. Chris ducked and stepped inside the bridge as a bolt flew past him.

Crouching and leaning his head out, Chris immediately jerked back as a bolt soared inches from his face and hit a diagonal cross brace inside the structure. "Jesus. He's a sharpshooter," he noted with alarm.

Holding his gun out, Chris said, "I only have time to step and shoot in one quick motion." As he led with his gun and stepped out, a bolt struck the barrel. He reacted by shaking his hand, but in doing so he whipped the pistol in the snow outside.

"Not again!" Kid muttered. "Can you move your fingers?"

Chris clenched and unclenched his fist. "Yeah, I can. But I lost my weapon."

"I'm going to the other side of the bridge to try and get a few shots at him before he spots me," Kid whispered.

"Remember, you only have a few shots left!"

Tiptoeing to the other side of the bridge, Kid encountered a large hole in the floor. He could see the steadily flowing creek below as he stepped wide of the rotted section and sprinted the rest of the way. On the other side of Otter Creek, Kid tried to get around the corner of the structure so he could see the soldier, but he had to wade through bushes and small trees. As he separated two small shrubs, he gasped. The soldier was limping to the opening of the covered bridge. Chris and the soldier could not see each other, but were now just a few feet apart.

Kid urgently waved him over and Chris started running across the bridge. A realization hit Kid and he uttered, "Watch your step!" He started frantically waving and pointing, but he was too late.

The floor disappeared under Chris's feet right as the soldier stepped onto the bridge and fired, barely missing his target. Kid stepped back around the corner and through the tree branches, he saw a body plunge into the creek with a heavy splash. Chris surfaced and began to swim toward shore.

It was now just Kid and the solider, and the uneven pounding of feet indicated the enemy, despite the bullet in his leg, was running across the bridge. Kid knew he would never win a firefight so he slid down the steep embankment toward the creek. As soon as he had a clear view of the rotting underside of the structure, including the large hole in the floor that Chris had just fallen through, he dug in his heels to stop his slide. Pulling out his gun, he held it with both hands. "Steady," he coached himself. "One chance," he whispered as he extended his arms a little farther.

The footsteps on the bridge stopped and the soldier simply followed Chris by jumping feet-first through the hole in the floor. Given Kid's experience with these soldiers, he was expecting this and he timed his shot perfectly. After taking a bullet to the chest, the soldier splashed into the creek below.

Kid kept his weapon trained on the surface of the water, but the soldier was floating face down in the stream.

"Kid!" Chris yelled from the bank.

Running back carefully across the rotting planks, Kid came out the other side of Hammond Covered Bridge. He first waved to Chris and then ran over to ensure the other soldier was dead. Rolling over the body lying next to the battered snowmobile at the edge of the woods, he saw a large blood stain covering the entire chest area of the uniform. Despite the discoloration, he could make out an embroidered 'Elder-108.' The elder was clearly dead, so Kid ran across the road.

As Kid slid down the embankment toward the creek, he yelled, "Grandpa Hyland! Are you alright?"

Chris sat up and said with his teeth chattering, "Yes, nothing broken. I had no idea the bridge floor had deteriorated that much."

Kid stared at the blood running from a gash on Chris's face.

"But when I fell through the floor, one of the planks caught my cheek. Help me back up the embankment. Johnny Ritter's house is just up the road. I can stop there and grab some dry clothes."

After Chris quickly changed his clothes and dressed the wound on his cheek at his friend Johnny's house, they set out again. Chris suggested going wide and he took the snowmobile on a path through backroads, fields, and forests to avoid the main roads as much as possible. This time, they did not encounter any more enemies and they made it unabated to the jail in downtown Rutland.

Running inside the building and heading to the cells, they both stopped in their tracks.

January 6, 2045
Friday, Morning
New Jersey coast, Utopia Project Ship Number One
Eleven days after the event

Aboard Utopia Project Ship Number One, Elder-2 was confounded. She was meeting with a group of elders, including the one in charge of the video and surveillance system on the ships, and she wanted answers. "How is it possible that a rescue was carried out by a couple of stowaways on the ship, yet we have no video of it anywhere? You have had a week to get to the bottom of this."

"We believe we have. It appears the video system was tampered with."

"Who had access and could do this?"

"The changes were made under a Test User ID that has existed in the system for years that any elder with access could modify. And with us taking captives, someone reviewing a data log would not have seen a change in the video system settings as unusual."

"How was the system tampered with? What was done to it?" Elder-2 demanded, her frustration growing.

"When we checked the video to see how one of the new female captives, 19794, escaped, we could not find footage of any such activity. We knew that just could not be. So when we focused on times and places where we knew there had to be activity, including her room and her hallway, it was then we discovered live footage for several cameras had been replaced by still-frames." Elder-133 stopped and peered up, "Sir..."

Elder-3 picked it up from there and said, "But when we looked at the history of member 19794 in our database, it jumped out at us there was a change in her thermographic signature just before she escaped. It seems her signature was switched with that of our own number 19, but interestingly, the signatures of 19794 and 19 were nearly identical. Impossibly close. So, we researched the history of our 19 and found some…enlightening information. As we know, 19 was one of the original 23 offspring who were developed in test tubes. The captive, 19794, was in fact the host whose stem cells were used to create our number 19."

Elder-2 looked perplexed. "The female we captured on the beach, 19794, just so happened to be one of the original 23 offspring whose cells we used?"

"Yes, but not by coincidence or happenstance. The elder who fathered her, is one of us. In knowing that, it became obvious that he was responsible for tampering with the video and aiding the stowaways in their escape."

Elder-2 turned and snapped, "Who is this traitor in our midst?"

Elder-3 paused for a second. "We know him well, and even sent him ashore to…eliminate…the survivors."

"He seemed unusually uptight, so we would guess…Elder-41?"

"Yes, Elder-41. United States Army General Eric Hyland," Elder-3 confirmed, his voice sounding bitter. "Unfortunately, we are unable to even reach Elder-44 and warn him. And if that is not bad enough, remember we allowed Elder-41 to take three females with him on the mission?" He turned and faced Elder-2. "One of them was 19."

"It cannot be so."

"It is. And since we now know the thermographic signatures were switched, and the captive *became* 19, it appears he really took…"

"His own daughter," Elder-2 snarled, seething with anger.

January 6, 2045
Friday, Late Morning
Rutland, Vermont
Eleven days after the event

In downtown Rutland, Kid was perplexed as stared at an open cell door in the jail block. Sid was gone. He shook his head. "There is no way he could have reached the spare keys."

"Then how did he get out?" Chris asked. Almost on cue, his walkie-talkie beeped and came to life. "Karen here! Come in!"

"Go ahead, Karen. Where are you?" he radioed back.

"On the third floor of an office building on Route Seven. I just saw a large group making their way north in the direction of Mr. Mahler's farm and you'll never guess who was with them? "

Staring at the empty jail cell, Chris said, "Sid Sherman?"

"Yes! He was on a snowmobile leading them."

"They must have just found him here and let him out," Kid concluded.

"Yeah, in return for him leading them to us. And to think we're here risking our asses to save him." Chris pressed the call button. "Come down to the jail, Karen, and we'll get out of town and meet up with everyone."

"Lucky you took the back way coming here," Kid noted. "You were right about going wide. If we had taken Route Seven, we would've run right into them."

Driving snowmobiles west on Route Four and away from Rutland, Chris, Kid, and Karen came upon the van and the large SUV waiting along the side of the road. The general and Jess had their weapons out and were hiding behind the front of the vehicle. Chris waved as he approached.

"Clear!" the general called out.

The back door of the van opened and Heidi asked, "Where is Sid?"

"Seems he's decided to join forces with the enemy," Kid said as he climbed in. "I guess they found him in the jail and freed him and he was leading them to the farmhouse. Lucky we left when we did."

"Yeah, so much for saving that soul," Chris added as he also climbed into the vehicle.

"I can't believe it." Heidi appeared deflated.

"I watched him leading the whole group, heading north up Route Seven toward the farmhouse," Karen said as she stood at the van's back door.

"But you didn't see him actually go to the farmhouse? Maybe he wasn't taking them there. You're assuming," Heidi countered.

Silence followed and as Karen went to respond, she stopped and just sighed. Kid glanced around the back of the van and saw the expressions on everyone's face. Except for 801 and 705, who were expressionless, it was clear that nobody believed that for a second.

Breaking the uncomfortable silence, a smile came to Karen's face as her eyes settled on one person. "Sara!" she called out. Kid realized that Karen had heard that Sara was still alive, but had not seen her yet.

Sara jumped out the back of the van and hugged her tightly.

Karen said excitedly, "I cannot believe you actually survived."

"I heard you had a pretty harrowing experience yourself."

"I did. But let me tell you, you are a sight for sore eyes."

After a solid embrace, Sara leaned back. She had her back to Kid, but he heard her say, "Wow. Speaking of sore eyes, what happened to you?"

"Oh that," Karen said as she touched her bruised eye. "It's a long story, but I took a heck of a beating the last few days."

"That's putting it mildly. That's quite a shiner," Sara replied.

"I can sum it up in two words and I don't think you'll be real surprised."

"What two words?"

"Sherman brothers."

Sara cocked her head. "Not surprised, at all."

Kid heard Karen sniffling and it sounded like she was crying.

"What is it?" Sara asked with concern as her friend turned away. "What did they do to you?"

Inside the back of the van, Kid heard Heidi exhale and mutter something. "Are you alright?" he whispered and touched her arm.

Heidi flinched and then tried to recover by forcing a smile. She said in a quiet, sullen tone, "Should I be, Kid?"

He did not know how to respond.

She exhaled and while turning away she mumbled, "No need to answer."

"Everyone get inside please," the general called out. "Both vehicles have full tanks of gas, and we're ready to roll."

"We'll talk later," Karen said to Sara as they got into the back of the van.

After everyone was in and the back door was closed, the general waved his arm out the window and began driving up the road. The SUV, with the McDermott, Spatz and Ryan families followed and the convoy started the trek south to New Jersey.

Almost an hour later, and now well clear of the Rutland area, Kid noticed that everyone's anxiety had come down a notch, including his own.

From the front seat, General Hyland spoke. "I have to say, the behavior of those Sherman brothers was symbolic of much of what was wrong with society. Such destructive behavior patterns would have been headed-off and prevented by some level of social conditioning. It's why I believed in it, to some degree, in the first place."

"Maybe they would not have been so destructive if the system, and society, hadn't let them down," Heidi responded, sounding bitter.

"Well, there are many people in the world who face incredible challenges and instability," the general noted. "That is why it is critical that everyone has some stabilizing force in their life. When people feel completely...abandoned, they are much more prone to fall into a dark place."

Kid turned and looked at Heidi.

She went to respond, but her face turned red and she bit her lip.

CHAPTER 31

January 6, 2045
Friday, Afternoon
From Vermont to the New Jersey coast
Eleven days after the event

The drive down south to New Jersey was slow but uneventful, save for the occasional hydroplane on the slippery roadway and the few vehicle pileups they had to navigate around. They kept a close eye on the road behind them, never seeing any vehicles trailing.

Kid met Sara's eyes and they stared at each other for several minutes. He squeezed her hand tighter. *I cannot believe she is alive.* He smiled and kissed her cheek. Still holding her hand, he said, "Tell us about that society you had to live in."

Shrugging her shoulders, Sara said, "As far as a typical day, I followed a schedule, which they posted on the screen in the room for all 10 of us every morning. Six days a week, every day but Sunday, the work schedule was the same, but the activities changed."

"I remember counting 10 beds in the rooms when I was on the ship," Kid noted. "Bunkbeds, right?"

"Yes. And although they didn't get used often, each room had a toilet and a sink. If someone had to go to the bathroom, they went in front of everyone. I only saw it happen a few times, but nobody there batted an eye."

"Did you ever use the toilet in the room?" Kid asked.

"I should have, but no, I held it in until the next morning when I could use the gang bathroom in the Hygiene Station. It was bearable because we woke up early. Each morning you wake up at 6:00 a.m., put on your uniform and go straight there. Besides using the bathroom, we had to take a shower and get a clean uniform. They were fanatics about hygiene. But you went to the bathroom and showered in the open and always in sight of somebody, so I had to lose my humility and quick."

"Sounds…uncomfortable," Karen noted.

"And get this, they have no mirrors anywhere. Imagine trying to comb your hair or check your face. I had to be conscious not to look for one out of habit. Heidi, do you remember your comment when Elder-1 told us there were no mirrors?"

Heidi was sitting across from her and it seemed to take a second for the question to register. "I remember," she responded.

With no more elaboration forthcoming, Sara filled in the blank. "After Elder-1 tells us there are no mirrors, Heidi says, totally deadpan, 'And he calls this Utopia?'"

This generated laughter in the back of the van. Maria said, "I remember that! I'm surprised there was no backlash for that comment."

Forcing an awkward smirk, Heidi replied, "Me too, but in retrospect I understand why they don't have mirrors. You never know what you're going to see in the reflection."

For a moment, Kid stared at the floor. Breaking the uncomfortable silence, he turned to Sara and asked, "So…after the wake-up shower, what did you do next?"

"Then we went to a breakfast buffet at 7:00 a.m."

"Does anyone speak to each other during meals?"

"Sure. It was no different than any other group of people. Mostly people talked about their work, activities, what they were eating, how good it was after they finished, etcetera. It was constant small talk, and people seemed perfectly content to do just that. Then my work shift was from 8:00 until 1:00 p.m., and 1:30 was lunch time."

"What was your job? I remember we saw some work stations

when we were walking around the ship," Maria asked as she repositioned her rear end on the van floor.

"I was part of the 'Offspring Conditioning Team.' Fortunately, my dad prepped me for the work I would have to do, especially mentally. I had to help tend to the babies, or 'offspring' as they referred to them. I had to watch them, feed them, take care of toileting, keep them harnessed during trainings, the whole nine yards. But the workers weren't exactly warm and fuzzy in handling the kids there."

"With how caring and compassionate you are, I don't know how you dealt with that," Kid noted.

"It was only for five hours a day, but even that took an Academy Award winning performance. My heart was broken 10 times a day for those poor kids and I couldn't show it."

"Wait, what worker Type were you, Sara? I remember that speech from Elder-1," Maria said.

"I was categorized as a Type B worker."

"I'm surprised," Maria said. "How could your clone not be a Type…C? Weren't they the smart ones?" Nudging Heidi, she added, "I'll bet you guys are surprised I remembered that."

It seemed to take all of her effort, but Heidi flashed a smile. It evaporated instantly.

From the driver's seat General Hyland said, "She is a bright girl Maria and so was her clone, but all of the original 23 clones were categorized as Type B because the fetus testing was not perfected yet. Actually, from what I observed, at least five of the original 23 would have been Type C."

"So what did you do after lunch?" Karen asked as she turned to Sara.

"The afternoon included a mandatory period of physical fitness in the gym. With how hard they pushed you, I would've been ready for a triathlon in no time. And then after that you might have massage therapy, or a conditioning session if it was your turn in the rotation. Fortunately, it was not number 19's turn for conditioning, although that time was coming up if we didn't get off the ships. They also assigned everyone tasks in the afternoon, cleaning, organizing, or some other menial job. Then 6:00 p.m. was dinnertime. After dinner, they showed a one-hour video every day."

"Movie-time?" Karen asked. "See anything good?"

"They weren't entertainment films, more like training videos, or even just more brainwashing. Most were of the mainland, but the videos were strange. They had edited out all the people, but showed different places throughout the world. They also showed different utility systems, water treatment facilities, power plants, and even solar arrays. They seemed to be prepping the group for inhabiting the mainland to help get them familiar with their future environment off the ships. Then everyone had either assigned activities or games and then went to bed."

"You said the schedule wasn't the same on Sunday, and you were there for a Sunday, so what did you do that day?" Karen asked. "Was it a day of rest?"

"Not really, no. You still woke up at 6:00 a.m., showered and ate, and then you were required to participate in activities. But you could choose your own since that was their 'free' day. You wouldn't believe how exciting it was for them to choose their own activities. They loved it."

Kid heard Jess whisper, "For your activity, did you choose one of those orgies?"

Maria heard him too and smacked his arm. "Jess! It's pretty bad when even I think that was in bad taste." Turning to Sara, she whispered, "You didn't, did you?"

"No! I chose the hang gliding simulation and a dice game that resembled Yahtzee, but they called it Sixes. The activities were actually a lot of fun and there were a lot of choices."

"I know you are a good actress, but how were you able to pull off being one of them for five days?" Kid asked.

"I have no idea. A couple of times I was sure I blew it."

"How so?"

"Besides my southern accent flaring up a couple of times, I slipped during lunch one day and started a sentence with, I. They all stared at me and were freaked out. Then another time, at dinner, all I did was make a harmless comment, or so I thought, about how an elder's hair was sticking straight up. They all went silent. It was a show stopper. Fortunately, I recognized right away that I had crossed some foul line in their world and I immediately got them chatting again when I commented on the pasta I was eating."

Kid shook his head. "I don't know how you were able to do it. I would have been a nervous wreck."

"Trust me, I was. I don't know how much longer I could have played the part. It was like performing in a never-ending live show with no breaks. They only way I got through it was by constantly reminding myself what my high school drama teacher used to say, 'You will never fall out of character if you are the character. Don't play the role, be the role.'"

Sara's mind drifted back to her first play after transferring to a high school in New Jersey for her junior year of high school. Her performance as the lead was compromised by a puddle of oil on the stage, intentionally placed by Tanya White, a physically imposing girl who Sara displaced in the class rankings when she transferred in. Sara slipped on the oil and fell out of character for just a moment. After the performance, her drama teacher drilled into her head, 'You will never fall out of character if you are the character. Don't play the role, be the role.' Sara had confronted the much-larger Tanya and nearly got into a fist-fight. With the courage of her convictions, Sara stood her ground. It helped that her father had mandated from an early age that she be regularly trained in self-defense. Tanya finally broke down, admitted to her horrible actions, and went straight to the school counselor. During senior year, they actually became friends, even studying together, which helped Tanya finish as the second-ranked student in the 2042-43 graduating class. Sara never begrudged finishing one place behind in third. Tanya had worked hard and deserved it and Sara felt better knowing the girl had learned about subjects not measured by class rank. Of course now, Tanya was just another one of the billions of puddles of flesh and bone.

General Hyland called out, "New Jersey state line. And we need gas."

Thank God, Kid thought. *I need to stretch my legs.*

When they stopped to fuel their vehicles. Kid conversed with the occupants of the Cadillac SUV. They all appeared haggard and tired, taxed by hard winter days without the creature comforts to which they were accustomed. Dr. McDermott, with his Irish accent, swore they would never again take such comforts for granted.

Before getting back into the vehicles, Kid turned to the general, "What can we do to throw them off our track since you know they'll eventually come back down this way?"

"Let's just worry about getting to the Jersey Shore and setting up somewhere first. It will be dark by the time we get there. We should be fine for a while." The general jumped back in the driver's seat. "But, I am not saying we can let our guard down. We still need to be vigilant, especially with Elder-44 leading their group."

It was already dark when the two vehicles pulled into Ocean County, New Jersey. The sky was overcast and the temperature gauge in the vehicle now read '30 degrees' after falling three degrees in the last half hour. The vehicle headlights cut through the ominous black of night.

"Should we just go straight to Water Street?" Jess asked.

The general seemed inquisitive as he looked over.

Kid clarified, "The Water Street Grill restaurant was the rendezvous point with that guy Drex we left behind, if he had to abandon the marina. You mentioned that with the tracking chip in 801's scalp, you knew we were holed up there. Would they still search the marina if the tracking chip had moved away when we left for Vermont?" Kid asked.

The general turned to him. “They would have sent a force, even a reduced one, to ensure that no survivors were left behind.”

“Then, with any luck, Drex left there and made for the rendezvous point, so let’s head to Water Street.”

“I just hope that poor Drex is alright,” Maria muttered.

“He seemed like a wily old bird. I’m sure he found a way to survive,” Kid tried to reassure her.

CHAPTER 32

January 6, 2045
Friday, Early Evening
Toms River, New Jersey
Eleven days after the event

Pulling into the parking lot of the Water Street Grill, Kid jumped out of the back of the van. As soon as he took a breath, he knew Drex was there. Or at least, he hoped it was him. There was a faint smell of something burning, although no plumes of smoke were visible. The odor registered as burning charcoal, rather than wood. He walked up to the front door of the restaurant and knocked. "Drex!"

The front door of the restaurant swung open and Drex stood with a pair of grill tongs in his hand. Somehow the old guy appeared even more unkempt than Kid remembered him. "That's how you were going to defend yourself?" He pointed at the grill utensil. "Maybe you should upgrade to a mightier weapon, like a basting brush."

"Kid! So glad you are back!" he yelled as they shook hands. "I knew it had to be one of you. The enemy wouldn't bother knocking." Leaning closer, Drex's voice became a whisper. "Did you make it in time?"

After a second, Kid responded, "To save Grandma Hyland! Yes. We made it. In fact she's outside with the others."

"What did you think I was referring to? That was the whole reason you went up there."

"It took me a minute. That mission was accomplished, but a lot, and I mean a lot, happened after that. What about you? How long have you been here?"

"I came here the day after you left. Lucky for me I am an early riser, or I would not have spotted the group of soldiers coming across the water and heading straight for the marina. They had a problem getting through the ice near the docks, which gave me time to get away unseen. I don't know how they knew I was there. I never went outside where I could be spotted."

"Actually, they had already targeted the marina because of a locator chip in 801's scalp, which has since been removed. Thanks to that chip, they chased us the whole way up to Vermont. I'll fill you in, but let's get everyone inside first." Kid waved over at the van and the SUV in the parking lot.

Kid walked into the lobby of the restaurant, which Drex seemed to be using as his camp. A couple of large blue tarps had been affixed to the ceiling and hung to the floor, enclosing the space, and separating it from the main dining area. Kid noticed the significant increase in temperature. He did not know if it was actually warmer, or if it was just the absence of the frigid winter breeze. He then spotted two propane heaters. "This is a pretty large space," Kid noted. "It might be a little cramped, but if we move the tarps back some and move out some of the lobby chairs, we'll all fit."

"What? How many people did you bring back with you?" Drex peeked outside the front door. He watched as people poured out of the van and the SUV. "Holy mackerel! I guess a lot did happen up there. Who are all of these people?"

"Other survivors, from the part of Vermont that wasn't hit."

"Speaking of, did we lose any of our group up there, you know like M..." Drex hesitated.

Kid could hear the concern in Drex's voice and knew who he was worried about. The question was answered a second later.

"Drex!" Maria said as she came in the door and hugged him.

"I was just going to ask about you," he said as he embraced her.

His eyes opened wide as he looked over her shoulder and saw the others parading in through the front door.

Maria moved the tarp aside and cased out the restaurant. "Nice digs, and we have a bar in here to boot!"

"Anyway, Drex, we all survived, including Jess, Heidi, and 801," Kid said.

"Barely, in some cases," Maria uttered and turned back around. "We were worried about you though, Drex, especially after we found out they had us pegged at the marina. You're alright?"

"I'm fine. As a matter of fact, I've eaten better in the last few days than I ever did in my life. This restaurant is top notch. Come back to the kitchen and I'll show you the food stock."

"Listen, Mr. Maitre D', skip the tour and just feed me. I'm starving," Maria said.

Drex patted her cheek. "That's one of the first things I noticed about you. I love the fact you're not afraid to say what's on your mind."

"Ever the diplomat, our Maria." Kid rolled his eyes, but smiled. "Drex, I'll come with you and check out this food stock."

"Don't take all day. I'm feeling a bit shaky. I think my diabetes is kicking up," Maria called after them.

"Diabetes?" Drex stopped and looked concerned. "Type 1?"

"No, Type 2. I take pills, but I'm trying to conserve them and control my blood sugar by watching my diet."

Drex looked relieved. "That is fortunate. If you're insulin dependent, within the next six months your greatest survival challenge will probably be finding insulin and keeping it at the right temperature."

After a pause, Kid tapped Drex's arm. "Come on, before she gets cranky."

In the back of the kitchen Drex had a small kettle grill with smoldering charcoal briquettes. A window sash was raised so the smoke from the grill could seep out. As Kid stoked the briquettes, Drex put a pot of water and a couple of cans of imported soup on the cooking grate.

"Let's put a few more cans on there." Kid pointed back over his shoulder. "We have a lot of people to cook for, and they're half-starved."

"So much for my food stash," Drex lamented.

During dinner, Kid looked over and watched as Jess played with his chunky chicken soup. "Are we sure the neutron beams didn't affect the meat in these soups?" his friend asked.

Kid was wondering the same thing.

"I asked my Dad the same question," Sara answered. "The amount of neutrons emitted from the beams only affected living tissue, so soups should be fine."

Jess shrugged his shoulders and kept eating. "Good enough for me."

General Hyland added, "Not only that, but the neutron beams swept so fast there was minimal offing of radiation. Only trace amounts were left behind, unless someone was standing right next to a beam. Otherwise, we all would be in trouble."

As if struck by a realization, the general sat up and turned to Kid. "Where did you guys put my laptop computer?"

"It was at the marina." Kid turned to Drex. "Did you bring Mr. Hyland's laptop when you came here?"

Shaking his head and pursing his lips, Drex said, "No, I didn't have time to grab it."

"Not good," the general muttered as he put his face in his hands.

"But it is safe," Drex added quickly. "Kid, you told me to protect it, so I put the computer bag in the oven. I don't think anyone would ever think to look in there."

This seemed to provide some comfort to the general, who noted, "Good. I need to sleep, but I have to get it tomorrow morning."

Drex gave a quick snap of his fingers and leaned forward to get up. "Speaking of sleeping, Kid, we have to go to the County jail up the street and secure a bunch of pillows and blankets for everyone. We just need to avoid the cell block, which is a disgusting mess."

“Can we wait a little while? I want to relax for a few minutes.” Kid did not want to move.

Sitting back, Drex pulled his blanket over his lap. “Alright. We can do that.”

“Good. I’m fed and warm. Let me savor this peaceful moment.” Kid wrapped his arms further around Sara’s waist as they sat in one of the plush lobby chairs.

Kid’s body and mind begged for a pause. He had been through an emotional storm and needed to get his bearings. As he gazed absently, the moment suddenly reminded him of a car ride he had taken in the fall, a ride that started out as anything but peaceful. The night was dark and suffocating as he motored through a heavy thunderstorm. His knuckles were white and aching as he gripped the steering wheel. He had never been so tense driving, but with the windshield wipers at full speed, he still could not see a thing. In the blink of an eye, the storm just stopped. The loud pounding of the rain torrents on his car ceased and he could see clearly out his windshield. His grip on the steering wheel loosened and he flexed his fingers. A feeling of calm and peace swept over him, just like he felt now sitting in the lobby of the restaurant. He wanted to stop the memory right there and hold onto that feeling, but he knew what happened next. As soon as he came out from under the other side of the overpass, the storm picked up right where it left off and he had resumed his chokehold on the steering wheel.

As Kid’s recollection ended, he realized he wasn’t staring absently at all. His eyes were on Heidi as she sat against the wall in the candlelit room. Her arms were wrapped around her shoulders, as if she had crawled into herself. Maria sat next to her, trying to make conversation. Since Sara’s resurrection, it seemed that Maria was sticking close to Heidi, trying to be a friend and support for her. For a second Heidi glanced up and met Kid’s eyes. Just like when his car had come out the other side of the overpass, his moment of peace was over in a flash and he was back in the throes of a raging tempest.

He couldn't sit still a second longer, so he tapped Sara's leg and she got off his lap. He stood and said, "Drex, come on. Let's go get those blankets and pillows."

"What happened to relaxing for a few minutes?" he asked as Kid walked to the door.

With Kid stepping out, Sara sat alone in the chair. Everyone else was preoccupied, which gave her a rare but welcomed moment to herself. She exhaled and peered around the waiting area of the restaurant. Clarence was trying to explain a card game to 801 and 705. The soldiers seemed content and engaged.

Her eyes then fixated on a picture on the wall. It depicted an 18th century sloop riding heavy ocean swells in a storm. The top portions of the sails were illuminated by a flash of lightning in the sky. For a second she could feel the ship captain's anxiety. There was no telling whether the sloop would make it through the storm or not. Sara figured such an assessment was dictated by the mood of the person looking at the picture. Someone feeling hopeless would see the ship as doomed. But at that moment she saw the sloop pulling through the storm and coming out the other side, battered, but still intact. It was that kind of optimism and hope that got her through her days on the Utopia Project ships.

When her father had briefed her the night she switched places with 19, he had given her quick training for 19's position on the 'Offspring Conditioning Team.' He didn't cover every detail, but the job was manageable because there was a team leader of the highest intelligence category, Type C, who would provide directions and specific assignments. And Sara, or rather 19, functioned on a team of ten members so it was easier to blend in.

After covering all facets of life on the ships, he gave her a 10-day birth control pill. She had hesitated, but he insisted that she needed to take it 'just in case.' Her father had told her the rules and morals of the old world did not apply and that she needed to go with it, no matter what. The vagueness of this warning was disconcerting to her. Was she going to be abused by the elders? Was she going to be forced into having sex to further the 'offspring' production? Her father tried to ease her mind by saying the hardest part would be getting used to the peace and serenity of the daily life of the members.

She soon realized that her father was right. 19's life was not complicated and it did not take long to settle into a simple routine. Life was regimented, but the food was good, the people were pleasant, and she was always clean and rested. The usual life tasks were simple, although some were handled in a way that would have been downright unbearable to most people who grew up in the old world. She could never get used to showering or going to the bathroom in a stall with no door, where other members routinely walked by and could see everything. Urination and defecation were normal bodily functions and were nothing to be ashamed of. She struggled to follow suit and even when it wasn't her sitting on the toilet, she forced herself to not look away modestly when passing others doing their business. At one point she smiled as she realized her bathroom conditions sounded much like Kid's college dormitory. She felt for him if that is what he had to deal with every day.

On Sunday night, January 1, 2045, Sara was moved to a different room on Utopia Project Ship Number Three. All nine of her new roommates appeared to be within a few years of her age. She found it odd, but her father said that every week they shuffled member groupings to avoid attachments between any two members. Sara was just getting used to the current group and she found the familiarity comforting. She had regular conversations with one female member in particular, number 332. Although their conversations were superficial, she was actually beginning to like the girl. She knew 332 always brightened up a bit more when she saw Sara, but the girl was used to the shuffle routine and probably formed a temporary bond with someone else every week. Sara recalled that when Elder-1 had initially briefed her after she was captured, he mentioned the member's needs were met by the system, not other individual members. She knew that if 332 formed too much of a bond with any individual, she would be sent for further conditioning to cure her of her affliction. While sitting in the chair in the restaurant, Sara chuckled aloud. "Her…*affliction*."

For the first few days as 19, Sara fought to not slip and show the worry she had for Kid, Jess, Maria and Heidi, but it was not easy. Until Monday afternoon, January 2, 2045 when her father again met with her alone in his room, Sara did not even know Elder-1 and a large group had gone ashore in pursuit of Kid and the others when they escaped. But her father told her that Elder-1 had not reported in and was presumed dead. This gave Sara a much-needed glimmer of hope.

That same night, her last one on the ships, she had endured a grueling and traumatic activity period. After, she had been unable to sleep and was still wide-eyed long after the 9:00 p.m. sleep tone. For several hours that evening, despite all rational defenses, she battled feelings of guilt and shame. Even now, those feelings had not left her and she realized they wouldn't.

Her moment of reflection was broken as the door of the restaurant opened, and Kid and Drex walked in. Sara turned around as she stood. Catching the portrait of the sloop, she let out a tired exhale, feeling a little less sure the struggling ship would pull through.

After distributing the blankets and pillows, Kid still felt restless. He needed a few moments to gather his thoughts so he could confront himself and then Heidi. He pushed aside the blue tarp and walked through the empty dining room. He passed the dark mahogany bar and headed to the back corner of the restaurant. At first he saw only darkness out the windows overlooking the river until he peered down. The white snow on the deck seemed to be glowing. With his eyes adjusting, he could now make out the docks and pilings. He wished his thoughts would come into similar focus.

He could not deny that he and Heidi had embarked on a relationship. They jumped in too quickly, but that was irrelevant now. The tugging at his heart reminded him that he had developed some feelings for her and it was creating an emotional maelstrom within him. Life was easier to navigate when people, situations, and even choices could be evaluated and easily categorized as black or white, good or bad, right or wrong. This situation did not qualify. He could not act like nothing had ever happened and simply abandon Heidi. Not when real emotions were involved. She seemed to have fallen for him completely and had established in her mind they would be inseparable for the rest of their days on this planet. He had let himself go for a moment, but had backpedaled and retreated almost immediately and was in a different place.

"Hi, friend," Heidi said as she walked up next to him.

He never heard her approach, but somehow knew she would follow him back there. Unable to meet her eyes, Kid continued to stare out the window. "Hello, Heidi. Did you eat?"

"I tried to, but I'm having a tough time keeping anything down these days."

"Well maybe…" he started.

"Maybe, we could skip the small talk," she cut in, her words biting.

Turning to her, he could not fight the wave of emotion and remorse that was passing through him. "I don't know what to say, Heidi. Who could've ever predicted it would work out this way?"

As soon as his eyes met hers, Heidi's harsh edge evaporated and her voice sounded somber. "Kid, I know fate played the biggest part here, but I'm convinced I was destined to live an empty, bitter, and lonely life."

"That's not true," he whispered.

"Don't tell me it's not true!" she snapped, struggling to maintain whisper volume.

He said nothing. This was a war he could not win.

"Are you going to tell her?"

"Yes," Kid responded without hesitation, knowing she was referring to Sara. "I have to."

"Of course you do because it would be the *right* thing, wouldn't it?" she jabbed. "Don't worry about me, I might as well lose a friend too!" She threw up her hands and seemed exasperated. "Now I'm going to feel funny around her."

"You're already acting funny around her."

"What do you expect? Every time I see her it's like I'm seeing a ghost!"

"I don't think you'll lose any friend," he concluded.

"Oh no? Let me guess, she'll understand? You don't know much about women do you?" she derided.

Softening, she put her hand on his forearm and whispered, "Kid, now that Sara is back, your feelings for me are gone, just like that?"

"Of course not and it hurts. It does. But you know what Sara means to me and the special place she held in my heart before you and I got closer."

"There is no special place for me?"

"I can't go there now. I'm sorry, but the largest part of my heart had already been spoken for back when."

Heidi hung her head. "I knew you were going to say that. I loved you, Kid. I gave myself to you and in such a short time. I held nothing back and now I'm empty, lonely, and dammit I'm bitter."

The pain, resignation, and solemn surrender in her eyes were upsetting, even chilling, to Kid. "In time you'll…" he started.

"Don't…patronize me!" she said while raising a hand, as if she could block the sound waves traveling through the air. "And don't tell me it will be alright in time. It won't. The part of me I gave you, which was basically *all* of me, means nothing to you now. It's dead to you, so it's fucking dead to me too!" Angry tears ran down her face and she started to walk away. "There's not enough room for the both of us so I guess I'll have to go…" she froze in place and whispered with a heavy shivering breath in an eerie timbre, "now."

IV:
LIBERATION

CHAPTER 33

January 6, 2045
Friday, Evening
Toms River, New Jersey
Eleven days after the event

"I guess I'll have to go now…" As the words rang hauntingly in Heidi's ears, she could not fight the surging recollection. The memory was like a vial of poison she had buried deep inside her and kept protected, until now. She felt the thin glass crack and dark matter quickly coursed through her soul. Her mind and body not only replayed, but relived the events of her darkest day. The day of the…accident, when she was 15 years old.

For her early life, Heidi had been close with her father, Richard Leer, and she loved him more than anyone in the world. She had grown up in Brooklyn, New York as an only child and she was undeniably a daddy's girl. Her father made her feel like she was the center of the universe and he doted on her, giving her everything she wanted and more. He was always there for her and never let her down. And then, out of nowhere, he filed for divorce. Not only did he break their stable family, her father had fallen in love with a woman who also had a 15-year-old girl. New step-sister Lisa, much like Heidi, had grown up as an only child and was also used to being the center of attention.

With the trauma of the divorce and without any love or support from her mother, Heidi needed her father more than ever, but she felt like he had left the planet. She remembered feeling abandoned night after night, even when she was busy with friends and activities. She had loved her dad more than anything, but she felt anger and resentment growing with the realization that he had left his old life behind, including her.

She saw her step-sister Lisa at school every day and at cheerleading practice. While Heidi's insides churned and ached, her step-sister seemed so damned happy and content, probably because Richard Leer's attention was now fully focused on her. While Heidi's face was contorted from the strain of trying not to vomit from the stress of it all, her step-sister would fuss about a small pimple intruding on her perfect complexion. She could see the whiny bitch pouting with her pom-poms on her hips, wearing a uniform with a lunging bobcat in the center, just like the one in the diorama in Vermont. It's not that Lisa was mean to her. It was quite the opposite, but her step-sister wasn't the one who was being tossed to the curb. Lisa being nice only infuriated Heidi more. She wanted to hate the bitch.

After staying overnight at her Dad's a few times and having to sleep on the lumpy, smelly fold-out couch while Lisa had a large bedroom with beautiful heavy wood furniture, Heidi had resolved to stay away from that house. Her dad did not seem to have the time of day for her now anyway. Once in a while he would focus his attention on her, but his pathetic efforts seemed empty and patronizing. Heidi felt like an outsider and even worse, she felt like she was being pushed out of her father's world; a world that used to exist for her and her alone.

Then came the darkest day.

Richard Leer was going on vacation with his new wife and Lisa. Her father had insisted that Heidi to come visit and stay the night before they left, but he had not even offered to take her with them to Mexico. Begrudgingly, she spent the night at her father's house, sleeping on the hideous fold-out couch.

That night, Heidi had the most beautiful and peaceful dream. In it, her father's divorce was just a nightmare and her world was still perfect. She cried tears of joy in her sleep and felt at peace. She awoke to see her Jezebel step-mother glaring at her. Her dream came crashing down in an instant and she threw up all over herself. Her step-mother had a look of disgust on her face while throwing Heidi out the front door and telling her to go to her father.

Richard was changing the tire on the car when she stumbled over. He threw the lug wrench into the open garage and said, "That better hold, at least until we get to Newark Airport."

As he ushered her inside to get her a new shirt, she was welcomed by Lisa's perfect smile. The only shirt Lisa or her mother were willing to give her was a rag they used to wipe down their shoes. Heidi was despondent as she watched them finish packing for their trip. They were singing James Taylor's old song, 'Mexico' while dancing around the house. Her father did not even consider how hurtful it all was to her, and didn't even notice that she had left the house. For a half hour she sat on the front steps and cried until her sadness was replaced with rage and worse. She could not take it anymore.

She recalled walking like a zombie over to the car after grabbing the lug wrench. Fueled by fury, she started removing the lug nuts on the tire that her father had just tightened. She had thought somebody would come out and would realize that she was falling off the edge. In step with the loud creaks made by the protesting lug nuts, she was screaming for help. Like someone having a stroke in their soul, she knew that if she was not saved quickly, the damage would be permanent and irreversible. Her dad never came out and never saved her.

She finished unscrewing the last lug nut and was about to throw it into the bushes with the rest, but she stopped. With the lug nut in her trembling hand, she waited and through heavy tears, whispered, "Help."

Nobody came.

Hearing her father and Lisa singing James Taylor in harmony, "I guess I'll have to go now…" she knew she had been replaced and was no longer part of her father's world. He had abandoned her and the damage was irreversible.

She screwed the lone lug nut one complete turn, and left.

The police report noted that while driving on the New Jersey Turnpike heading for Newark Airport, Mr. Leer's car hit a patch of bumpy road and a front tire flew off. As the axle on the front passenger side skidded along the pavement, the car cascaded in front of a speeding eighteen-wheel truck. The report noted the car was crushed, winding up under the jack-knifed tractor-trailer. Her father and his wife had massive injuries, including multiple fractures and internal bleeding. Both were in intensive care for a week.

Her father survived, but his new wife did not. Heidi's step-sister, Lisa, had two broken arms, and her entire head was bludgeoned. She underwent ten plastic surgeries to reassemble her face, and her one eye socket. In the end the surgeons had performed miracles, but Lisa was left with damaged facial tissue, which left the skin of her right cheek appearing cratered and uneven. Her lips were reasonably aligned, but they appeared stretched and did not match up perfectly like they used to. When she smiled, the scar tissue around her one eye and cheek prevented one corner of her mouth from turning up. Even on her best days, Lisa still looked damaged and deformed.

After initially being ruled an accident, the police investigators soon discovered the car had been sabotaged. When the investigators questioned Heidi, the last person to see the car in one piece, she broke down and confessed. She started her confession by citing the James Taylor lyrics that finally broke her and became the final nail in the coffin. "I guess I'll have to go now." At first, what confounded the lead investigator was the question of why she had left one loosely fastened lug nut on the vehicle. "If you had removed all of the lug nuts, the tire would've probably fallen off before they even got out of the driveway and nobody would have been harmed. Didn't you realize how much more imminently dangerous it was to leave on just one?"

Her fate would be sealed with her soft spoken but incriminating one-word response. "Yes."

At the time she could not deny that she wanted the tire to fall off at a high speed, the higher the better. She knew this would likely bring harm to them. She admitted to hoping that her father and step-mother would be maimed, and that her step-sister, Lisa, would die a horrible death. That way, her father and step-mother would forever feel Heidi's pain from being utterly abandoned. They would have to live with that agony for the rest of their lives. But it had not worked out that way. Lisa was maimed and it was the step-mother who died the horrible death. Under questioning Heidi was unable to express any remorse at all the death of her step-mother. This was the Jezebel who had stolen her father and horded all of his love and affection for herself and her needy daughter.

Lisa wanted Heidi tried as an adult and charged with the murder of her mother and the attempted murder of her and Richard Leer. Heidi was able to avoid being tried as an adult, but she was still found guilty of voluntary manslaughter and was sent to a juvenile detention and rehabilitation center in Florida for a year.

When Heidi came back to New York, her mother had moved out to Long Island with her new boyfriend and was already pregnant. Heidi found some level of hope and maybe even a chance at redemption, in that she would have a sibling to care for and love, but her mother would give birth to a stillborn. Heidi believed her deeds had brought a curse and killed the child, and that God was making her pay. For that, she hated God, to the bottom of her tormented soul.

She quietly finished high school in a Long Island district where she felt like a new student even during graduation ceremonies. Her father was conspicuously absent from the ceremony, which was no surprise since he hadn't communicated with her since the crash.

Heidi never spoke of the 'accident' to anyone, and since she was a juvenile when it happened, her identity and records were well protected. She had not allowed herself to relive those dark days, until now. Even when she had gone to her former high school's website looking for contact information to get transcripts and had seen her step-sister in a picture on the home page, she had been able to shut the memory out. Lisa was still an honorary captain of the cheerleading squad and stood in the center of the photograph with the prominent bobcat mascot leaping off of her uniform. She shuddered as she recalled Lisa's disfigured face in the picture.

All of a sudden, Heidi could no longer suppress the memories. She not only found herself reliving the horrific incident, but dwelling on it.

Standing frozen in the restaurant, Kid uttered, "Heidi…" He was stunned by her level of hurt, which was evolving into uncontrollable rage before his very eyes. As she walked away, she stopped and raised both hands.

"Don't!" she snapped as she turned around and took a step toward him.

He braced for a physical assault.

"Don't!" She covered her face with her trembling hands and stormed away, walking into the kitchen.

Standing with his head hanging down, Kid wiped his eyes. This was a gauntlet he knew he had to run and no amount of preparation could have readied him. He had tried to steel himself for this moment, but the pain was excruciating. He could do nothing to sooth it. He wished he could hold Heidi and tell her it would be alright, but showing her any love or affection would only gouge the wounds and inflame them, even within himself. He remembered how Heidi had tried to get him to, in essence, elope and run away somewhere. He then recalled the crumbled diary page he had found in the fireplace at the Mahler farmhouse. These recollections should have provoked anger in him, but instead he felt pity.

"Kid?" the general called while holding back the edge of the blue tarp on the other side of the room.

Spinning around, he answered loudly, "Yes?"

Walking over and glancing at the kitchen door, the general whispered, "I heard a loud voice. Were you and Heidi…fighting?"

“Well, we were having a conversation about an emotional topic.”

“It is not my business, but I will just say this. Please be careful about…upsetting her too much.”

Kid was about to question what he meant by that, but was cut off.

“Don’t ask. Just trust me.”

Not wanting to push it, Kid relaxed his shoulders and nodded. “Alright.”

“Come on.” The general started to walk back toward the blue tarp. “We need to talk as a group and we need your input.”

CHAPTER 34

January 6, 2045
Friday, Evening
Toms River, New Jersey
Eleven days after the event

Upon returning to the living area, Kid realized why the general had wanted him there for the discussion. The topic centered on the future direction of the group of survivors. As Kid looked around the room, he did a head count. Their group was small, 26 people in all. They had seven New Jersey and New York survivors: himself, Sara, General Hyland, Jess, Maria, Heidi and Drex. They had 17 Vermont survivors, Chris and Evelyn Hyland, Karen Stone, Wendy and James Levy, Clarence and Marissa Moore, Doctor and Pamela McDermott and their son and daughter, the Ryan's and their son, and Melanie Spatz and her two young daughters. They also had Utopia Project soldiers 801 and 705.

That night they started working on their road map for a new society. The general fully supported the plan to free and awaken the humanity in the Utopia Project society members, and had presented some of his own ideas along those lines. He also agreed the Utopia Project's 20,000 members might be the only chance for the survival of humanity. A group of 26 people of varying ages might not be enough to propagate and survive. With such a small group, there was no margin for error and any number of calamities, diseases or tragedies could befall them. The general had voiced what Kid also felt in his gut—

and disable any aircrafts and take any weapons that could be used against us, then what do our odds look like?"

"Much better. At least for the time being. If they can't find what they need at the Joint Base, the closest base with military aircraft such as an M3 is several hours from here. We would at least buy ourselves time to develop and enact a game plan."

Kid nodded his head, encouraged.

"But..." the general started.

There is always a 'but.'

"...even if we engaged in guerilla warfare, let's not underestimate the difficulty in eliminating elders and machine-like members, especially since they have the advantage in terms of numbers and weaponry. Our only advantage would come from having a better tactical game plan."

"I don't suppose that group would just get discouraged and leave us to live in peace?" Maria asked.

"No," the general stated flatly. "The Board of Elders was adamant about wiping the slate 100 percent clean and wanted zero risk of any influence from the old world. They will not stop."

"Who is the Board of Elders? A governing body of some type?" Karen inquired.

"Exactly. It was originally a 9-member governing board, but a few years ago we added two more members when two countries refused to join unless they had a place on the board."

Jess shook his head. "Politics. It never ends."

"No, it doesn't. But this 11-member board, comprised of six males and five females, made all decisions relative to the project, and as we found out in the end, they are merciless, cold, and black-hearted."

"I'd say so. But to be involved with a project like that I guess you would have to be," Karen noted.

Looking down at the floor, the general exhaled.

"I'm sorry, Sir. Skip that."

Evelyn took Karen's hand and seemed to be assuring her that her comment was not out of line. In fact she was peering at her son awaiting a response.

"No, Karen, it is a reasonable perspective, and is something I need to explain." He peered around the dimly lit room, which had soft light emanating from candles in two brass wall sconces and three tabletop candleholders.

"First and foremost, I had no idea the lead elders were so sick and evil. The bottom line is that from the start I was involved in the project not only because it was my military duty, but because I believed in the concept of using *some* social conditioning to help manage the world and society."

Rick Ryan exhaled loudly in obvious disgust.

"The official mission of the Utopia Project had always been to perfect our social conditioning techniques and peacefully infuse them into society at large in several countries. I repeat, peacefully. I had believed this would be successful. If infused into society at large, people still would have been free to be individuals and make individual choices, but conformance with laws and rules would have been innate qualities in everyone. Where social conditioning was implemented, crime and murder would have been virtually eliminated."

Karen asked, "You mean, like a police state?"

"No, the opposite. People would've lived in peace and harmony in an orderly and conforming society, without needing to be policed."

"Sounds like an internal policing," Kid noted.

"I genuinely believed that was still the legitimate plan of the Board of Elders until a highly confidential memo about the project fell into the hands of the press a week before the destruction and public outcry erupted in several countries. In response, the newly elected American president and his team vowed to shut the Utopia Project down as soon as he was sworn in."

"Not soon enough, obviously," Rick muttered, angrily. His patience seemed to be at a breaking point.

"Anyway, after the uproar started, diplomatic efforts with the new president and his advisors broke down right away, and at that point we all knew the project was over, done. I was also stunned and devastated, but I hoped the core of the project could be assumed and carried on within another existing project, or that it would continue but with a lesser scope," the general said and then paused.

"But the Board of Elders obviously did not share such hope about the survival of the core of the project. Several of them were going to be removed from their powerful government posts and possibly be prosecuted," he continued. "I never could have imagined the collective leadership would go to such extremes as to destroy the world, even if the Utopia Project was being shut down. There had to be some evil seeds in that group and if the Board of Elders had some surreptitious, destructive plan behind the scenes all along, I never had an inkling of it."

"When did you find out, or realize?" Evelyn asked.

"The board presented their devastating plan to the other elders after the leak of the confidential memo about the project and after diplomatic efforts failed. All of that was less than a week before the December 26 event. Many of the other elders had unknowingly given them the capability and tools to carry out such a level of destruction, including me. But before revealing their plans, the Board of Elders inserted trackers, which were also tiny bombs, in the necks of every elder to ensure nobody would out them, or try to escape the project. Several elders who took off were killed right away."

Evelyn looked horrified. "What kind of people would do something like that?"

"Spawns of Satan," Rick snapped. "That's who."

The general continued, "After the plans were revealed to us, they used the trackers to follow us very closely for that final week, monitoring our every step, every word and even every sight. At that point they had already linked up to the U.S. neutron beam satellite system and had the power to initiate the destruction in a matter of minutes if they had to. The only chance we had to stop it was if more than one of the top four elders could be simultaneously taken out at the moment of the commencement of the attack. I devised a plan with the only other elder I could explicitly trust. With a communication code that only he and I shared, I proposed we shoot two of the four highest ranking elders at just the right moment. We would be killed in the process, but the plan would have worked. In no time, the United States would've regained control or shut down the satellite system and the world would have been saved."

Sara brought her hand up to her mouth.

"Then the other elder who was in on it with me, General Van Pelt, went home to Texas, killed his entire family and committed suicide. That left me to fight the battle myself. I was powerless since the technological systems and protocols in the project were structured and layered in a way so that no one person could stop the destruction alone. If I could have stopped it, or even part of it, I would have. I was fully prepared to give my life, but acting alone, it would have been in vain. The world still would have then been 100 percent wiped out but none of us would be sitting here right now."

"The *entire* old world would have died that night," Kid concluded.

"Yes, it would have. I was fortunate just to be able to save the three small areas I did." The general held up a finger. "We'll pick it up in a minute, but I need to grab a water from the kitchen. I'm talking myself dry."

No one said a word as they waited expectantly. As Kid looked around, he felt like he was in a box full of jurors during a recess at a trial.

CHAPTER 35

January 6, 2045
Friday, Evening
Toms River, New Jersey
Eleven days after the event

As Sara lay against Kid, he heard her sniffle. He knew it must be painful for her to watch her father defend himself and try to justify his actions, given his participation in the Utopia Project.

The general walked back in and looked at Karen. "I crucify myself every day for the choices I've made in life, but did I at least address the question as to why I was involved in the project, and why I couldn't get out or stop it?"

"Yes, you did. I just can't believe how quickly it escalated," she said with a somber voice.

He glanced around at everybody, as if seeking the feedback of the entire room.

"I have a question," Kid chimed in. "Why did you only save three areas?"

"The system controls would only allow me to make three adjustments, and small ones at that. And since I only had margins to work with, the three areas had be at the edges of large bodies of water or protected wildlife tracts. That is why I needed my daughter to be at beach that last night."

He seemed to be anticipating the next question and continued as he stepped forward, "With only three adjustments, my choices were impossible. I wanted to save as much of the old world as I could and I know it was selfish, but the areas I chose spared the people I was closest to. The real goal though, was to save a piece of humanity."

At that moment, Kid thought of his own loved ones and felt a spike of anger at the general's selfishness.

"What about the people we were closest to?" Heidi sounded disgusted.

Kid turned to her and she would not even look his way. She still seemed to be fuming after their recent conversation.

Suddenly, Heidi erupted and yelled, "What about my mother? Or all of our mothers? They're all dead. Seriously, who are you to determine who should live and who should die?"

Evelyn opened her mouth, prepared to take up for her son, but the general held out his hand and stopped her. His tone was even as he responded, "I could only save a handful of people."

Rick Ryan jumped to his feet, no longer able to contain himself. "Today is my father's 65th birthday and we were supposed to go bowling. But he's gone thanks to this bullshit project you were involved with. He beat cancer twice just to go out like that? Tell me you didn't know they were planning something that destructive!"

"I did not know."

"Bullshit! I don't buy it. And then you handpick three small areas to survive? It's just by dumb luck that my family is still alive and only because we live up the street from your parents. I wish I had been slaughtered with the rest of the world. Then I wouldn't have to feel so God awful about all my relatives being dead."

"What would you have done in my place?" the general asked. "What three areas would you have spared?"

Rick had nothing to say for a moment. He waved his hand dismissively. "I would've tried to stop the whole thing."

"Like I said before, I couldn't stop it by myself. I would have given my life in a second, taken a bullet to the head, if I could have stopped it."

"Well, if you felt the way I do now, you would have welcomed a bullet to the head." At that, Rick stormed outside, and his wife and son followed him.

Kid's anger was more controlled, but he really could empathize with Rick and shared his frustration. Having also lost many loved ones, Kid felt sick to his stomach every time he thought of them all; his parents, his brothers, his other family and friends. There were so many that he had to engage in a form of collective grieving because it would be too much to grieve for them all individually. He wondered if he was still in a state of shock and would suddenly collapse from the grief. The thought of his family triggered a seemingly random memory. After his high school graduation, his mother had tears in her eyes as she whispered, "Billy…" since she refused to call him Kid, "…you are a good man." She had never referred to him as a man before, and it choked him up at the time. But it was his mother's next words that would always stick with him. "One day you'll understand what it took to get you there."

Sara touched Kid's arm and he flinched. He turned to see her eyes welled up. She was clearly having a tough time watching people lash out at her father. As he blinked, Kid found that his eyes were watery too after the recollection of his mother. Trying to compose himself, he wiped the tears, and the memory of his mother, away.

"My father is not a monster," she squeaked out.

"I know he's not," Kid said, trying to be supportive. Unfortunately, her father associated with monsters, but he would keep that comment to himself.

For the next several minutes the group sat in silence. Kid could feel the torrents of sadness and anger flying about the room like restless ghosts.

Looking around, 801 did not understand the behavior of this group. Some people had screamed at each other with tones that bothered his ears. Someone had said that people were 'angry.' It was explained to him that when people were not happy or did not like something that happened, they sometimes became angry. That is why they yelled in loud tones and their faces sometimes turned red. He had never felt that way. Sometimes he did not like it when his food was too cold or when the shower water was not the right temperature, but he never became, 'angry.' When something happened that someone did not like, they fixed it or went away from it. Angry as a response did not seem to help anything. He did not see the benefit of angry.

He also did not know what could cause someone to have water coming from their pupils while having facial expressions he had never seen before. He stared at Heidi, who had water running down her face. These responses from the group on the mainland were hard to interpret and understand. Water did come from his pupil one time when he had squeezed a piece of lemon for his chicken dish. It hit his pupil and as he rubbed it, it began to water. He searched for a lemon, or something that may have splashed Heidi in the face.

"What are you looking for?" she asked.

"A lemon," he responded.

"Why?"

"Something has made your pupils' water."

"Seriously? I'm crying because I'm upset and angry so can you please stop staring at me?"

"Yes." He turned his eyes away, still perplexed. Angry and upset caused water to flow from the pupils and caused people to speak loudly with strange facial expressions. He did not understand these responses.

Seeing Sara with water coming from her pupils, 801 again looked around for a lemon.

Everyone remained quiet and still.

Kid glanced around the room. Drex was sitting next to him doing the same thing. When their eyes met, Kid raised his eyebrows. He slid over a bit and whispered to the former attorney, "What is your read on the jury?"

Drex scratched his beard and after making sure nobody was in earshot, he said, "I was just trying to read that myself. For Mr. Hyland's participation in the Utopia Project, guilty. That was more of a plea because he fully admitted it and even defended his participation, but that was based on the original intent of the project. I think the vast majority of the jury believes the project was inhumane and cruel, but not enough to hang him for it."

"That's my read as well," Kid answered.

"Next charge, for the general being selfish when making his three small adjustments, guilty, but everyone would have done the same thing in his shoes. They would have a hard time hanging him for that one either."

"Agreed."

"For the most severe charge, the general *knowingly and willingly* taking part in the world's destruction…" Drex paused, "…not guilty."

"Ditto. Due to coercion, right?"

"Very good. Are you sure you weren't heading to law school?"

Kid shrugged. "My final read is that more than anything, the group condemns the leaders of the project, the 11-member Board of Elders who unleashed the destruction."

This time it was Drex who said, "Agreed. Court adjourned, although not necessarily case closed."

The general wiped his brow. "Let's take a break for a few minutes and if we're up to it, we can talk about what to do going forward."

As the group dispersed, Evelyn got to her feet. Kid watched as she walked over and embraced her son. Displaying all of a mother's love and pain, she held him tightly. As she let him go, she put her hand on his cheek. "In my heart, I know you would have sacrificed everything, including yourself, to stop it, hon."

A half an hour later the group was reassembled. Kid noticed that after getting some fresh air and having tea, coffee, and cookies, the group seemed a bit more settled. The only ones who were not were Rick and Katherine Ryan. They refused to join any further discussions.

"Where did the 20,000 people in the project come from?" Dr. McDermott asked as he lifted his thick, black winter hat and ran his hands through his thinning brown mane. His hair was disheveled, although the perfect side-parting had somehow been maintained.

"The first group of members developed in test tubes..." the general said and looked at Sara, "...but that was a small group. Our members then came from adoptions of kids that would have been aborted or even abandoned. On the ships they at least were cared for, and were well fed and secure."

The doctor looked curious. "I thought there was an incredible demand for adoptions in the world?" Kid thought the same.

"I think that was a generalization. There was a great demand to adopt children of certain ages, and from select backgrounds and ethnicities. Why do you think so many shelters and child care centers were bursting at the seams with unwanted children?"

"Point taken," Dr. McDermott acknowledged with his thick Irish accent.

The general continued, "Then finally, the female members in the project were getting old enough to have their own offspring..."

"Children!" Sara corrected him.

"Children," he finished.

A few seconds passed and Jess muttered, "20,000 humans and not one soul." He put his hand on 801's shoulder. "No offense intended."

Grabbing Jess's shoulder back, 801 said in his monotone voice, "Right on, jackass."

Everyone burst out laughing and seemed to welcome the break in the recent tensions.

The laughter was contagious and even 801 smiled, which prompted Clarence to say, "That's a first."

It seemed that every time the mood lightened, even for a second, Kid felt like they were letting their guard down. He immediately tensed up and felt a wave of nervous fear. Although he hated feeling that way, in a sense, it was necessary. Becoming lackadaisical, even for a moment, could cost them their lives. Rick Ryan, his wife, and son were in the widow's walk keeping watch and refusing to participate in the discussions. Kid had little confidence in Rick at the moment, but he felt better knowing their 11-year-old son, Robert, was with them. Without understanding all of what was going on, Robert had yelled while running up the stairs, "I'll be the lookout!" Kid could tell the boy thought it was a cool and important job, so he was probably more focused than his parents.

Drex turned to the general, "Are you sure they're still going to set up camp at Long Beach Island? They seem pretty well settled at Seaside Heights."

"They will eventually move down there, yes. The Seaside peninsula was not even an option as far as a base camp. They only anchored there to inspect the area. Right now they are not moving because they are replenishing their fleet of tenders since Kid and Jess cut all of theirs free."

"We need to keep our eyes open for them coming this way," Kid reminded.

"I am just as worried about Elder-44. His group will find their way down here from Vermont eventually. I don't see that happening tonight, but we need to be vigilant. Between me, my father…Kid and Jess, we should take turns standing post throughout the night."

"Just tell us what we can do to help," Dr. McDermott offered.

"It sounds like it has been a long day, and week, for you all. Thanks for asking, but for tonight, please, just try and get some rest. We'll handle it." The general clapped the doctor on the shoulder.

The third shift would be Kid's, so he had time for some sleep. He laid out a blanket on the floor, almost against the hanging blue tarp.

As Sara lay down, she chuckled. "Could you set us up any further away from the heaters?"

"I figured we would have to hold each other tighter to stay warm," he whispered as he lay next to her and pulled two blankets over the top of them. He was being mindful that Heidi was in the room, although she was right next to the heater.

Sara flinched as the blanket was dragged over her head. "That spot is still a little sore."

He realized she was referring to where her father had removed the tracking chip from her scalp with a knife. "Sorry," he said as he carefully lifted the blanket over her head.

"Doctor Hyland was not very gentle with that procedure," she added.

After a few moments, Kid whispered, "I'm afraid to fall asleep."

"Why? You must be exhausted and you have to be up in a few hours."

"I guess I'm afraid I'll wake up and find out your survival was just a dream."

Cradling his head and pulling it to her chest, she whispered, "Sleep. I'll hold you so you know I'm here. When you get up for your shift, wake me. I'll sit with you."

Kid felt slumber coming upon him. It was that sudden need to sleep when no matter how hard he tried, he could not keep his eyes open. He welcomed the feeling and begged for it to take hold, hoping it would clear a subconscious that was still disturbed by his earlier conversation with Heidi and the depth of the hurt he had glimpsed in her eyes.

CHAPTER 36

January 7, 2045
Saturday, Morning
Toms River, New Jersey
Twelve days after the event

After a two-hour lookout shift in the middle of the night, Kid and Sara went back to bed. At dawn, Kid woke up again, shivering. Sara was wrapped so tightly that he did not want to wrestle any blanket from her so he pulled her closer and tried to glean as much warmth as he could. Unable to fend off the chill in the air, he decided to get up and start his day. First and foremost he would find more heaters.

He whispered to Sara and then to the general that he was heading to the store, the police station, and the county jail. He walked up to Jess who was on watch, staring at the white world outside the front door's glass panes.

While Jess and Kid talked, the general approached and said, "I'll keep watch, Jess. You can go back to bed if you want."

"As much as I would love to, I'm up now. I'll go with Kid," Jess responded as he got out of his chair.

"Don't forget to grab more walkie-talkies," the general reminded as he sat. "And after Clarence wakes up, remember, he and I are heading to the marina so we might not be here when you get back. I need to secure my laptop and get to work." He absently patted his hip to ensure he had his weapon.

Kid pointed. "Do you really think that is better than a standard gun that fires bullets?"

"This?" the general asked as he put his hand on his holster. He pulled out the coal-black weapon and pointed to it. "This magazine contains hundreds of doses of the neurological agent that it fires." He looked at a readout on the handle and tapped a tiny screen. "I still have nearly 400 shots left."

"So it hardly ever requires reloading," Kid concluded.

"No. And the neurological agent freezes every muscle in the body, which is why the weapon was named, Medusa. The agent will get through even the thickest layers of clothes and garments, and you don't even have to hit a vital organ with this to take out your enemy. A shot that hits a finger is every bit as lethal as a shot that hits a chest. The enemy is frozen either way."

"That much I already know, all too well," Kid said, having seen the effect first hand with Sara's Utopia Project twin. "And no matter what we tried, we couldn't stop its effects."

"The only way to stop it is with the antidote."

"We heard there was an antidote, but it could only be found on the ships." Kid recalled his conversation with Heidi on the roof of Ironside cabin.

"Not any more. The medical group on the ships quickly made a compact distribution system for the antidote which could be used like an epi-pen. Each elder who embarked on a mission off of the ships was given three vials." He lifted his shirt and tapped the vials, which were affixed to his belt. "But it has to be administered quickly once someone is shot. After two minutes, the odds of survival drop precipitously with every passing second."

"Why would you even want to have an antidote handy?" Jess chimed in.

The general pondered for a second. "For a couple of reasons. First to save our own from friendly fire, which happened during Medusa firearm training. It took too long to retrieve the antidote and a member died. Second, so the enemy could be revived if we needed to gather information. Using Elder-1 as an example, had he been able to revive your friend Brian on the beach, he could have retrieved information about the existence and location of other survivors."

"Meaning us," Kid clarified.

"Yes, so from that angle, it is fortunate that elders did not yet have antidote vials."

"But if they did, Brian might still be alive," Jess noted bitterly.

Driving to the police station, Kid and Jess grabbed 38-caliber handguns, 12-gauge Remington semi-automatic shotguns and all the ammunition they could find. Heading to the county jail, they found even more weapons and ammunition. With a substantial arsenal aboard, Kid drove away, turned a corner and came around the block.

"Why are were driving in circles?" Jess asked.

"We are leaving tracks in the snow all over town, in case anyone tries to follow us."

They made their way across town to a sporting goods store and secured several walkie-talkies and a supply of spare batteries. They also snatched a dozen small propane camping heaters, three propane camping stoves and forty spare propane canisters. On their return, they again drove in a zigzag pattern to lay tracks in every direction. When they arrived at the restaurant, Kid was comforted by seeing someone posted as a lookout.

Melanie Spatz held the door open so the guys could bring in the supplies. Although wearing a full-length coat with furry edges and thick winter gloves on her hands, her head was uncovered, and her brown hair flowed over her shoulders. Having slept in relative warmth, she appeared stronger, younger, and less aggravated than when Kid had met her the night before. She looked her 33 years of age this morning. As she greeted them, Kid noticed that her smile, regardless of how slight, made her entire face pretty. Her smile disappeared when she saw the shotguns he was carrying under his arm. "More weaponry," she muttered.

He pointed. "Don't worry, weapons will go behind the bar. We just need to keep the kids out of there."

"Yes. Guns and booze are usually a bad combination," she noted.

"Mr. Saturday Night Special," Jess quipped as he walked by.

While passing Heidi inside the restaurant, Kid said, "Good morning."

She turned but would not meet his eyes. "Morning," she mumbled and walked right into Sara.

"Oh, hello, Heidi."

"Hey."

"Did you already eat?" Sara asked.

"I have no appetite," she said and walked away.

Sara made eye contact with Kid and pinched her brow. She shrugged her shoulders and kept walking. "So Kid," she started, "I got a firsthand account from Karen of your heroics up in Vermont."

"I don't know if I would call them heroics." When he met Sara's eyes, he knew without asking that Karen had told her everything, including the part about her being raped.

Sara answered, "Maybe not in your version of what happened, but in her version they sure were."

Kid's eyes turned down. He never was comfortable receiving accolades. "She's lucky to still be alive with me as her rescuer. Did your dad and Clarence go to the marina?" He was quick to change the subject.

"Yes, and they will be there a while. After Dad found out the widow's walk had a perfect view of the Route 37 bridge, he figured that while he worked on the laptop, Clarence could keep watch for both Elder-44 and anyone coming from the ships."

That morning tasks were given to some of the adults, while the rest took turns sitting at the door and serving as the lookout. Jess and Maria had left right away after being given the task of securing more food, beverages, toiletry items, and supplies.

Kid, Dr. McDermott, and Chris were responsible for identifying the best location for a new home base. Water Street Grill was a good place to regroup, but they needed a home base where they could have a shower and separate bedrooms. They plotted for a few hours with a map of Ocean County opened on a rectangle table in the dining room. In trying to determine a suitable location, Kid remained guided, as he had previously, by the principle they needed to be far enough from the Utopia Project base camp to be out of harm's way but close enough to keep an eye on them.

Sara was sitting with Melanie, keeping her company while on lookout duty. Sara smiled as she watched the kids running around. It warmed her heart to see them having fun.

Drex was busy entertaining the young children. After a while, he needed a break, but the kids would not hear of it.

"You've made yourself some new friends," Melanie said while sitting in a chair at the front door.

"Children are a lot easier to relate to than adults," Drex mused as he cuddled the children's stuffed animal, a blue-eyed Husky puppy. He then ran around the lobby with it.

The two Spatz children stayed at his heels, laughing with every step. "Come back Santa Slim!" they called out.

"Santa Slim?" Sara asked.

"A little while ago, young Katy here touched my whiskers and told me I had a Santa beard. Well, they had to know the truth. So I told the girls the tale of how I actually used to be Santa Clause. But, a bratty little boy put a thumb tack on my sleigh seat and when I sat, I popped. So now the kids all call me Santa Slim."

Drex flopped into a chair, leaned a little to the side and broke wind. "See, I'm still deflating."

Shrieks of little-girl laughter followed while Katy and her younger sister, Karly, waved their hands in front of their noses and ran away.

"Now, Drex! Behave." Melanie appeared serious, but the corners of her mouth turned up.

Sara laughed outright. She turned as Chris and Dr. McDermott came out of the dining room and sat in two of the plush lobby chairs.

"At least we made a final decision," the doctor muttered.

"What about?" she asked.

"The location of our new base camp."

Kid peeked in and waved Sara over.

"If y'all can excuse me for a few, I'd love to hear about it when I come back," she said.

They nodded, so she ran over and took Kid's hand. He grabbed a portable camping heater and they walked to the riverboat next to the restaurant. On the top deck of the River Lady, a replica of a 19th century Mississippi River paddle-wheel steamer, Kid sat in a lounge chair. He pushed himself to one side so Sara could slip in next to him. Huddled together, they looked out over the Toms River, watching the current flow in the center of the river between sheets of ice. Kid put his arm around her shoulders as she rested her head on his chest. The only thing obscuring their otherwise perfect view was the slight haze that had settled on the upper deck's clear vinyl window enclosure.

After a few moments of silence, Kid said, "Sara, there's something I need to talk you about."

"I know," was her simple, yet assured, response.

CHAPTER 37

January 7, 2045
Saturday, Midday
Toms River, New Jersey
Twelve days after the event

Does she already know? Kid wondered.

With her head on Kid's chest, Sara said, "You told me most of what happened to y'all while I was on the ships, but what happened with you and Heidi?"

Kid stiffened a little. She seemed to sense it as she moved her head back and stared him in the eye.

"That's what I need to talk to you about, but how did you know?"

"It's not too hard to sense these things. There's an obvious tension between you and her, but not like the old days when you couldn't stand each other."

"It's hard to explain," he muttered.

She continued to look at him expectantly.

"After I thought you died, me and Heidi kind of latched onto each other, almost out of necessity since there weren't any other people to hold onto."

"Latched on…to what extent?"

He felt a wave of discomfort. "A *fairly* serious extent. It happened so fast, it was kind of a blur."

"Serious as in, you had become a…couple?" She seemed incredulous.

Kid hesitated, but that was crux of it. "Sort of, but of course that's over." No choice of words could minimize the substance of his answer.

"Heidi, the same girl you couldn't stand to be around?"

"I know."

"And so quickly?" she asked, with mock amazement. She propped herself on her elbow and fixed her eyes on him. "When did you bury the woman you thought was me?"

Feeling a generalized ache in his stomach, Kid tried to think. "I don't know. I actually couldn't remember the date when I tried to make an inscription on your grave marker."

With the silence that followed, Sara made it clear that he was not going to get away without answering the question.

"Maybe a week ago or so?" He cringed. When said aloud, it did sound absurd.

"So, all within a week you conquered the grieving process and developed a relationship with Heidi of all people?" she summarized. Her tone was sharp and her eyes were piercing. In that moment he noticed a resemblance between Sara and her father. They both had gazes that first froze you and then saw right through you. He wanted to crawl into a corner, but with how they were laying, he was pinned in.

He tried to reposition his body.

Sara noticed. "You should squirm."

"I wasn't even close to conquering the grieving process. It was killing me. Those were raw and desperate moments. We initially were clinging to each other for comfort and support..."

"Comfort? That's your idea, both of your ideas for that matter, of comforting someone? I must have been raised wrong," she said in jest but did not smile.

"I'm sorry, Sara."

He looked at her and saw the same emotional shell forming that he had seen one time before early in their relationship, after he had called her bitchy and hung up the phone on her. It had taken much effort to chip through that hardened exterior and if he thought that was tough, he could not imagine the thickness and density of the shell forming now. He tried to grab her hand. He was surprised that she did not pull away, but the hand he held was unresponsive and cold.

She got up from the lounge chair and stood at the deck rail, staring at the docks behind the restaurant next door.

"I guess I was using my interactions with Heidi to distract me from the pain of the grieving process. It was too much." His anger at the whole happenstance came to the surface. "How was I supposed to know you weren't actually dead? If I thought there was even the slightest possibility you were still alive, it never would have happened. Never. I knew at the time it was moving too fast, but I didn't stop it. I was trying to move on and with how I felt, it couldn't happen quickly enough. In my heart I really believed that's what you would've wanted!"

"Of course I would've wanted you to move on, if I was actually dead, and…"

"How was I supposed to know you weren't?"

She turned toward him and raised her voice. "…*and* after the body in the ground, the one you thought was mine, was at least cold!"

An uncomfortable silence followed. Kid was not used to Sara lashing out and it stunned him. What scared him was that she had no tears in her eyes. She appeared emotionless and distant.

"Alright. My final words will be this," he started. "I love you, Sara, more than anyone could love another human being, and I would never betray the love and trust we share. I thought you were gone forever, and with Heidi I gave much more than I needed in return because at the time, I felt like it was necessary."

"I need time to process all of this," she said in a quiet tone and to his dismay, she left.

For a half an hour, Kid did not move. He had hoped Sara would understand what happened, but Heidi was right, he obviously did not know much about women. Did he make an unforgivable blunder, given the circumstances? Sara meant more to him than anything in the world. He felt horrible about how the circumstances played out, but he would never knowingly betray her, and he didn't. This he knew deep inside. The question was, did Sara know? That was a question that words and even actions could not answer. If she did not come back, it meant that she had already made up her mind and accepted an answer, even if it was the wrong one. And she may never open her heart and soul to him again to revisit the question. So for the next several minutes, he begged for her to come back.

Kid's eyes wandered and stopped as he spotted a gazebo on the other side of the river. It was inside that very gazebo, so long ago, that he and Sara spent time the first night after they had reconnected, subsequent to meeting at the Lakehurst Diner. A wave of sadness coursed through him and he closed his eyes.

His eyes shot open upon hearing a sound. *Sara?* No luck. It was just the wind slapping at the clear vinyl window enclosure, as if taunting him.

On the verge of giving up all hope, he started to sit upright and froze as Sara came around the corner. Maybe all hope was not lost.

She did not even look at him as she walked past and again stood at the deck rail, staring at the river. Then again, maybe all hope was lost.

They both remained motionless and silent for several minutes. Finally, she asked, "What did you mean when you said you gave much more than you needed in return because at the time, you felt like it was necessary?"

His voice was sullen. "I was destroyed when I thought you died. I was coming to pieces and I really needed someone for comfort and support, and who was there for me? Her, as crazy as that sounds. But in making those ties with her, I found that she needed a *much* deeper connection. That was the price I wound up paying for what I needed."

"Please don't tell me you were just using her."

"I think we were kind of using each other, at least at first, since we both had lost our partners and were alone."

"In some strange way, I'd feel better knowing you actually cared about her." Sara seemed to be softening. "Did you develop feelings for her?"

He needed to be 100 percent honest. "I was starting to. But for me it had not gone too far or too deep. Nothing could touch the depths of my feelings for you. All the while, she knew the biggest part of my heart would always be yours, regardless."

"Oh no. The girl probably developed strong feelings for you and thought y'all would spend the future together, and then suddenly I reappear." Despite the circumstance, Sara seemed to feel bad for Heidi. "No wonder she's acting funny toward me."

"She was afraid that would happen," Kid stated.

"You already talked to her?"

"Yes, last night after dinner for a few minutes. I needed to make sure she understood it was over. I was hoping to smooth things over enough so we could all function together, but I have to say, it was pretty ugly."

"I'm not surprised. You have to realize how quickly and deeply some people invest themselves in a person or relationship. You two have probably lived many lifetimes together in her mind. But like you said, you thought I was dead. She thought I was dead too, so why wouldn't she grab onto you?"

"Well, I am a keeper." Kid smiled.

Sara said flatly, "You're not out of the woods yet."

"Sorry."

"I'm struggling to make sense of it all, but at least I understand how it happened."

"I told her you would understand," he noted.

Exhaling, she sat on the lounge chair and grabbed Kid's hand. To his relief, her fingers and palm were warm again.

"Just because I understand doesn't mean I'm alright with it, or that it doesn't hurt. Listen, Kid, I love you with all my heart and I always will. I can't imagine life without you. But I also can't imagine sharing you either. I need to know your love is for me and for me only. I need to know I'm your only soulmate."

In that moment, with truth and unspoken words conveyed through his eyes, Kid did not even have to answer the question.

They shared a loving but firm embrace. While holding her, his voice was raw with emotion. "You're truly my one and only soulmate."

Pulling back, Kid rested his finger under her chin and kissed her cheek. Looking at her face, his eyes were drawn to the clear vinyl window behind her. It sucked in and bowed out as the wind whirled around the riverboat.

While he put his head down and nestled against her neck, Sara stroked the back of his hair and said, "I know you didn't betray me, or us, and you never would."

Lifting his head and meeting her eyes, he said, "I have to know you truly believe that."

"I don't have to believe. In my heart I know." After a pause, Sara added, "I'm sorry, Kid."

"Why are you sorry? It's me who should be sorry."

"I don't know. I guess because I can't stand it when you're hurting or in pain…among other things." She looked away.

"Even when it's you who's dishing it?" he asked.

She smacked the back of his head.

"This is going to hurt me a lot more than it's going to hurt you, said the man with the whip?" he mused.

After holding each other for a few more minutes, his eyebrows pinched and he turned to her. "What are the 'among other things,' you are sorry for?"

This time it was Sara's body that stiffened.

CHAPTER 38

January 7, 2045
Saturday, Midday
Toms River, New Jersey
Twelve days after the event

D*oes he already know?* Sara wondered.

Feeling uneasy, she said, "There is something I need to tell you too."

Leaning back, Kid stared her in the eye. "I don't like the sound of this."

"It's hard for me to talk about, and something I wish never happened. For five days on the ship, I had to pretend I was member number 19. I had to follow her schedule exactly and had to live her strange, regimented life. Including, well, going to one of those sexual activity periods."

"You got to sit in on one of those?" He seemed curious.

"I had to do more than just sit in."

"Are you serious?" Kid looked shocked.

"Unfortunately yes."

Continuing to stare at her, he repeated, "Are you serious?"

"I just said I was!" She sighed. "It's not that I wanted to. I had no choice. I had to be number 19 and act like one of them or risk being discovered."

"What was it like?" he asked in a serious tone.

"Scary. It was unnatural, although I guess to them, it's completely natural. To me it seemed almost ritualistic. Those people, the males and the females, are unadulterated and shameless. They are 100 percent comfortable walking around naked and touching whomever they want however they want. When I came to the door, I saw a girl hang her uniform on one of the hooks, and just stroll over to the first male she saw and start fondling him."

"So what did you do?"

"I tried to hide my shock, but I stood there gawking for a second. Do we have to get into the gory details?"

"You did what you had to do, but I still have a morbid curiosity about it," Kid said.

"I'll just say you know it's going to be a bizarre gathering when they're handing out drugs at the door."

"What kind?"

"A sensitivity enhancer called Viameen," she answered.

"You took one?"

"I took five actually, but only ingested one. My hands were trembling when I walked in and reached for the tray of pills, so I wound up grabbing a handful by accident. I stuck the extras in my uniform pocket, but I'm glad I did swallow one. I was so nervous that I was sure my cover was going to be blown right there. When I took a pill I started to relax almost instantly. Maybe it was because it was the first time I had ever taken a drug like that, but it hit me quick. From that point I just chilled out, and the next thing you know, it was time to shower and go to bed."

"Did you on some level, find yourself, you know, aroused?"

"What kind of question is that?" she huffed and felt insulted, although she had yet to fully confront that question even within herself.

Kid waited without saying a word.

She shifted her position as she sat next to him.

"You should squirm," he said. *Touché.*

"Smart-ass," she muttered as she again smacked his head.

She really didn't want to delve any further into the details of that strange evening. When briefing her on the ship, Sara's father had not warned her enough regarding this activity. She assumed that was on purpose because it would have freaked her out. All he said was that if there were any 'sensual activities,' he wouldn't even use the word 'sexual,' that she should immediately take a Viameen pill to chill her out. He told her the old-world rules do not apply, and that she needed to just go with it no matter what. He had omitted some pertinent details, like the protocol that every female in the room was required to accept a full ejaculation to further the impregnation initiatives. That explained her father giving her the 10-day birth control pill on the Thursday night when she had switched places with 19. He knew her daily schedule, and knowing she was in for a sexual activity period the following Monday, he had the forethought to prevent her from getting pregnant.

She was lucky she followed his advice and took the Viameen. She would not say it, but after she took the drug, she had felt the full aura of sexuality from the activity. Everyone else was absorbed in it and she had no choice if she was going to blend in. She felt like she was in a dream state, thrown back into a Greek-era orgy. The members were shameless, fearless, and utterly comfortable in their own skin and sexuality. It didn't hurt that they were in great physical shape, but she suspected it would not have bothered them if they were not. Members were engaged in slow intercourse, in varying positions, although there were not many one-on-one entanglements. Most members were in groups. She saw three females caressing the same male all over his body. As soon as the male was ready to climax, the closest female lay on her back and let him enter. Sara wanted to turn away in embarrassment, but she forced herself to smile as if she was delighted.

Having no idea what she was supposed to be doing, Sara caressed her body to appear like she was into it. Watching the members interact while she walked slowly, she noted not all activities were overtly sexual. Some were just body massages. The members were still nude, but she thought she could better handle that. As she was approaching a group engaged in massages, she came to a sudden stop as she made eye contact with a younger male. He looked her up and down and despite the urge to cover herself and turn away, she stood frozen.

During her pause, another nude male came up behind her and wrapped his arm around her bare midsection. She was falling into a state of relaxation from the pill taking effect, but still let out a weak gasp in surprise. She played it off by chuckling playfully. Unabashed, the male started fondling her. She quickly sat on the couch and the pursuer sat next to her and continued his approach. From her other side, multiple hands began to caress her bare skin. She turned to see a male with a female in his lap, both reaching for her.

Although the Viameen was increasingly chilling her out and enhancing her sensitivity, it was not altering her state of mind and she was fighting back pure panic. She could not stiffen, tense, and go cold. Half of her wanted to scream and run, while the other half wanted to let go. The sensitivity was becoming too acute and she could not take it anymore. If she did not release herself, she would be revealed. She closed her eyes and willed herself to let go. In retrospect, she had to admit the activity period was erotic, but it was also…wrong. Unlike the other participants, she left that room burdened with guilt and shame.

Sara broke her reflection and said to Kid, "I had to act like one of them and appear like I was enjoying myself. I tried to fight it but became kind of clumsy and nervous. The easiest way was to just play the role. At that point, I treated it like an out-of-body experience, like it was a fantasy. I had to completely detach myself, like it wasn't me in there. I don't think I could have done it without that little pill to chill me out."

"So you're blaming the drugs?"

"I'm not. They just helped me endure." She patted her pocket. "Actually, I still have the other four Viameen pills. I'm going to slip you one and then take advantage of you," she tried to joke.

He did not smile.

Kid's reaction was unsettling to Sara. His eyes were dark and distant, so she continued to hold them until he came back. He softened as he stated, "Why would I need a pill anyway."

Her body relaxed and she rested her forehead against his. He was receptive. She ran her fingers through her hair and answered, "You wouldn't."

She gently brushed his face with her fingertips and then stopped. She nibbled her lip and lowered her eyes.

"What's wrong?" he asked.

"Well, to come full circle with the role reversal here, I now find myself in the hot seat. I also need to know that, in your heart, you honestly believe I didn't betray you either."

"I don't know…" He let the seconds linger.

"Kid, don't do this to me!" She put her palm against his chest.

"You went ahead and did that knowing *I* was still alive." He looked serious.

"Yes, but with my life depending on it, I had no choice. Now *you* had a choice," she responded.

"Yeah, but that choice was based on a false reality. I thought you were dead."

"You're much closer to death right now than I ever was," she said, wide-eyed.

A moment passed, but she could tell he was holding back a smile.

Finally, he chuckled and grabbed her hand. "Well, as a beautiful girl once said not so long ago, I don't have to believe. In my heart, I know."

"As well you should." Before he could respond, she gave him a warm, gentle kiss.

Standing in the empty dining room of the restaurant, Heidi gazed out a window through a thin gap between the blinds and the glass. From where she had positioned herself and after shifting the blinds, she had a perfect angle to view Kid and Sara on the top deck of the riverboat docked next to the restaurant. She rested her head against the frame of the window and sobbed, no longer caring if someone came in and saw her. She slammed her fist against the window frame and the wood and glass vibrated. She swatted the blinds, turned, and stormed toward the kitchen.

On the way, she barreled through a few chairs, knocking them over. As she walked past a table, the Ocean County map got hung up on her leg. Without slowing, she swung her hand and grabbed it in a death grip, crinkling the paper tighter and tighter. As she approached the kitchen, she passed an opening and whipped the crumpled map behind the dark mahogany bar. Heidi used her palm to ram the kitchen door, drilling it into the corner of a stainless-steel table. A few cans of vegetables tipped over and rolled onto the floor.

Crouched over the grill, Karen turned her head. She stood and asked, "Are you alright?"

Not breaking stride, Heidi plowed straight ahead. "Move it, you freaky bitch," she hissed and slammed into Karen's shoulder.

Karen stumbled back and tripped on the grill. While falling, she knocked over a steaming pot of water and it poured over her lower leg. She yelped as she reached down.

Got what you deserved!

Heidi shoved open the door behind the kitchen, angrily muttering all the while.

What the hell was that? Having heard a loud bang, Kid looked up. Through the clear vinyl he could see the windows of the restaurant. The blinds appeared to be swaying. He stared for a minute, fully alert.

Upon hearing an engine start and over-rev, he jumped to his feet. His defenses kicked in as he reached for his pistol. He ran to the deck rail and peered over. From there Kid spotted an SUV roaring out of the parking lot and driving up the road, power sliding and kicking up snow all the while. "Who is that?" He watched as the vehicle slid around the corner and headed south on Main Street. Running along the deck rail to get a clearer view, he squinted against the glare of the sun off the snow on the ground. Trying to shield his eyes with his hand, he still could not make out the driver. "Come on, Sara, quick."

Running down to the restaurant, a group stood in the kitchen around Karen. Dr. McDermott was examining her bright red leg through his gold-rimmed octagonal glasses. "It is already blistering up. I'm not a dermatologist, but I don't think there'll be any permanent damage."

"Karen, what happened?" Sara asked.

"And who tore out of here like that?" Kid hoped his gut was wrong.

"The girl's lost it, completely! She flew out of here in a rage!" Karen uttered. "She was mumbling about how she is not wanted here."

"Who?" Sara asked.

As the first sound left Karen's mouth, "Hei…" Kid ran for the door with Sara close behind. He stopped and turned. "Was she armed?"

"I think all of us are."

"Why would you ask that?" Maria inquired.

Kid was trying to be nonchalant. "Just wondering, that's all."

Seeing the expression on his face, she said, "I'm coming with you."

Jumping into Drex's red marina truck, Kid, Sara, and Maria took off.

Driving south on Main Street and following Route 9, Kid noted, "I don't know where she's going, but she's following the existing tire tracks."

"And driving fast. Look at the fresh tracks. She's fish-tailing all over the road." Sara pointed.

Following Heidi's erratic path, Kid had a lump in his throat. *She flew out of here in a rage?* He did not know what was going on inside her head, but she seemed to be losing it. Was it about the ending of their relationship? *She is not wanted here?* Where would she go? As he fought the sickness blossoming inside his stomach, he depressed the gas pedal further. He had to get to Heidi before she did something she would regret.

CHAPTER 39

January 7, 2045
Saturday, Early Afternoon
Ocean County, New Jersey
Twelve days after the event

Turning onto Ocean Gate Drive, Kid was confounded. "Heidi's heading for the marina."

"Maybe she just needed to get away from everyone for a while," Maria suggested.

Wishing that were so, he sounded dispassionate. "Yeah."

"I'm trying to be optimistic, Kid."

Had Maria seen the same anger in Heidi's eyes that he did, she would not be overly optimistic either.

Pulling up to the marina, they spotted the SUV. It was parked with its front end nudging a shrink wrapped boat, lifting it and the trailer on which it rested. The SUV's driver door was left wide open as if the person had bailed out in a hurry. Exiting the marina truck, the disorder of the Heidi's vehicle stoked Kid's sense of dread. Sara and Maria seemed to now be feeling it too.

The general and Clarence ran outside. "What's going on?" the general asked.

"I was hoping y'all could tell us," Sara said as she hurried over. "What happened when Heidi showed up?"

"We saw a vehicle flying up the road. We were armed and ready, but when Heidi stepped out, we stood down and relaxed. She looked up and saw me in the widow's walk, and she waved. Then she pointed to the workshop and lifted her finger in the air, as if saying she'd be back in a minute. I didn't think anything of it. But then we saw you coming up the road too. What is going on?"

"It's a long story, but Heidi seems to be losing it. We're afraid she's going AWOL."

"AWOL?" Clarence seemed perplexed. "Where would she go? We're the only people left."

"Are we?" Sara asked as a high-pitched whine cut through the air.

Knowing where the sound emanated from, Kid yelled, "Oh no!" as he broke into a sprint. He ran full speed on the dock but when he tried to stop, his feet slid out from under him. If the wood surface wasn't so encrusted with layers of snow and ice he would have had splinters galore, but instead he glided. His feet found purchase just before he launched off the end of the dock. "Heidi!" he yelled.

She was in the 28-foot center console boat that Jess had spotted when they first arrived at the marina. Kid recalled that his friend had taken the time to ready it for a quick departure, if that became necessary. This was not the departure it had been prepped for. Heidi had the boat at full throttle, but the craft was encased in ice and locked in place. From the whine of the engine, she was clearly trying to bull her way out. With a sudden crack, the ice in front of the bow gave, and the boat lurched toward the flowing water of the bay. The Boston Whaler bounced up and down as she made some headway, but was soon blocked by another sheet of ice.

"Heidi! Come back!" Maria yelled.

Heidi glanced over her shoulder.

Maria dropped to her knees on the bulkhead. "Come back!"

Tears ran from Heidi's contorted face. She yelled, "No!" at the top of her lungs and started thrusting her body into the steering wheel as if she could push the boat through the ice herself. The next sheet cracked and gave way, allowing the boat to make forward progress.

Kid cased out the splotchy frozen surface that extended out from the dock toward the middle of the bay. He hoped it would hold him as he jumped down on the ice and started running. As the surface began to crack and give way, he jumped to the side and continued on another intact section. Looking ahead, the surface was broken into large floating chunks. If he could zigzag across a couple of them, he might be able to reach her boat. He had to move fast. Heidi was stuck again, but it was the last obstruction before she would reach the free-flowing channel.

He jumped to the next ice sheet and it began to pitch and roll. Falling face down, he extended his arms and legs and waited for the slab to stabilize. As the sides of the floating block dipped into the bay, water breached the edges and drenched his pants and shirt. Almost instantly, his clothes began to freeze to the surface.

Getting on his knees, he yelled, "Heidi, please. Wait!"

Turning his way she let out a blood curdling yell. "No!"

Maria and Sara were both calling Heidi's name from the dock.

Leaning over the bow, Heidi hammered the frozen surface with the hard-plastic head of an oar. A couple of swings later, Kid heard a crack, and it wasn't the ice. Turning toward him, Heidi yelled, "Get away!" and whipped the now headless handle, just missing him.

He had to make his move. Now fewer than 15 feet away, if he could get to his feet and reach the next ice slab, he could make a running jump into the craft.

She reversed the boat several feet and put the throttle in neutral. She seemed to be preparing to get a running start at the last frozen barrier keeping her pinned. Her hand gripped the throttle tightly, but his movement made her turn her head.

Kid was finally able to get to his feet and stabilize himself by holding out his arms.

She pulled out her pistol. "Don't even think about it!"

"Heidi! Put that down!" He was fighting to maintain his balance. "Let's talk about this. Let me just get on the next chunk of ice and I'll stop right there."

"No! Stay away or I swear to Christ I will blow you to pieces," she said with her back to the bulkhead.

"Where are you going, Heidi?" Kid was pleading. He could see, and feel, the conflict in her tormented eyes.

"What do you care? No longer your problem or concern. Now for the last time," and her voice lowered, still seething with rage, "I said, back...off!"

"Heidi, if you turn back..."

"There is no turning back for me now," she responded, sounding regretful, but definitive.

Sara's voice came from the bulkhead, pleading, "Heidi! Please. It will be alright."

Kid's eyes opened wide. *Damn! Wrong thing to say.*

"No it won't!" Heidi yelled, her voice hoarse. With her rage peaking, her eyes turned black and cold as she turned to the bulkhead. "For you maybe," she screamed as she lifted the pistol.

"Down!" Kid snapped loudly. "Everyone!"

Sara dropped to her stomach behind the lip of the bulkhead. Clarence followed suit.

Maria didn't react right away. She stood on the dock, seemingly stunned at what was transpiring until Sara grabbed her arm firmly and pulled her down.

Heidi's eyes locked onto General Hyland. "And who do you think you are, playing with people's lives? You God damned manipulator," she spewed and swung the pistol toward the general just as he dropped on his stomach behind the bulkhead. "It will all come full circle one day," she added, her tone bitter and caustic.

Kid had to act right now.

He crouched and was about to leap onto the next ice sheet. Heidi turned and aimed her pistol. The gun trembled in her hand as she pointed at his head. She then dropped the barrel toward his feet, and fired. A couple of shots in a row slammed into the ice between Kid's shoes, cracking the frozen surface under him. As he tried to stand and thrust forward, the ice sheet cracked in two, leaving him with one foot on each of the separated chunks. He pushed off with his left foot and dove for the larger piece. He held on as the ice sheet canted like a raft in a wave pool.

"Hey!" Sara screamed.

Kid turned to see her leaning on the bulkhead and taking aim with a pistol. She had a clear shot at Heidi.

"Sara! Don't shoot!" Kid yelled.

Hearing his words, Heidi ducked. She dropped her gun and pushed the throttle all the way forward. The boat roared ahead and burst though the last ice sheet blocking her from getting into the channel. She kept her head low as she drove across the bay.

Kid turned to see Sara running out on the dock. "Are you alright, Kid?"

"Yeah." He was on his stomach hugging the chunk of ice.

"Don't shoot? If she's firing at you, I'm shooting," Sara stated firmly.

"She wasn't firing *at* me. She could've but didn't," he responded.

"Crawl over to the next ice sheet. You should be able to drag yourself to the dock," the general said.

"I will. Just give me a minute to catch my breath." Physically he was tired, but mentally, he was downright whipped. *What the hell just happened?* He was upset beyond measure and did not want them all to see it. He rested his head on the ice, breathing heavily. The ache in his stomach felt as if a cannon ball had been fired right through him at point-blank range, leaving a gaping hole. *What have I done?*

Pulling himself across the ice and getting back to the dock, he turned and looked out at Barnegat Bay. In the distance Heidi was speeding north, toward the inlet.

"Certainly didn't expect that," the general said. "Let's get inside and get you out of those wet clothes."

As soon as Kid had his clothes off and a blanket around him, he ran up to the widow's walk. He watched as Heidi's boat turned into the inlet. "Damn," he whispered. "That's what I was afraid of."

"What?" Sara asked.

"She is going through the inlet and I'll bet she is heading to the ships."

"Why would she ever do that? Doesn't she realize the danger?"

"She doesn't seem to care right now," he noted.

"Maybe she'll come to her senses before she gets there and turn back."

Exhaling, Kid could not muster enough conviction to even utter a hopeful grunt. "Seems too much to hope for. You saw her. She's lost it completely."

"It's all so irrational," Sara stated as she pulled the blanket tighter around his body. "Maybe she had some mental problems we never knew about."

"I don't know. I just know I'm responsible for triggering her breakdown."

"It wasn't you so much as the circumstances. I know she was upset, but she is responsible for her own actions."

Kid shook his head. "Now we have to get everyone away from the restaurant."

"Why?"

"Because Heidi knows we're hiding there, and who's to say she won't give that away." He started down the stairs. "Accidentally or otherwise."

"I would hope..." Sara froze with her mouth open.

"What's wrong?" Kid stopped.

Snapping out of it, she said with a sense of urgency, "Kid, come back up here, quick."

They both gazed out the window at the Route 37 bridge. A bus was traveling east over the span, heading toward Seaside Beach.

"It must be Elder-44!" Kid grabbed his walkie-talkie. "Jess, do you read me?"

A second later, "Go ahead, Kid."

"Did a bus come by there?"

"Not that we've seen, and someone has been on lookout at all times."

"The same tour bus that chased us to Vermont just crossed the bridge on Route 37 east. I assume they're heading back to the ships. Listen, I'll explain when we get back, but get everyone ready to leave. We have to move out and quick."

"Why do we need to leave so fast?" Jess asked. "You said they are heading back to the ships."

"It's not them I'm worried about at the moment. It's Heidi."

"Heidi? Why?"

"She took the boat from the marina. I think she is heading out to the ships."

"Are you serious? Why would she do that?" Jess sounded flustered. "What is she thinking?"

"She's not at this point. I'll explain that too as best I can, but we can't stay at Water Street another night, not when she knows we're there. Be ready to move out. We'll be back soon. Out."

At the restaurant, the survivors were scrambling to load their belongings and supplies into the vehicles when Kid and the others returned.

"Where are we going?" Jess asked as he peered at Kid. "And why are you wrapped in a blanket?"

"Long story. I'll explain that later too. We are going to Mallard Island in Stafford Township," he answered as he ran to grab some clothes to change into.

Although Kid, Dr. McDermott, and Chris had not communicated their final decision after reviewing the map earlier in the day, they had made a choice. Kid and Chris thought the proximity and view from Mallard Island would serve them well. From the tiny Island they could see Long Beach Island, where the Utopia Project base camp was supposed to be established. They could also see the Route 72 bridge, which was the lone span serving the island. If the soldiers came after them or made for the Joint Base, Kid and the group would spot them well in advance. Dr. McDermott went along with the choice, but voiced his concern about setting up so close to the enemy encampment.

Kid jumped into the driver's seat of the van and waved to Dr. McDermott at the wheel of the other vehicle. "Stay with me!" he said and headed south on Route 9.

Following a plan of diversion devised with Jess and Kid, Drex took the marina truck and turned west. His mission was to lay tracks in different directions to confuse anybody trying to follow them. After, he would double back and head down to Mallard Island.

As Kid drove, he took as many back roads as he could. Dr. McDermott and the group from Vermont followed close behind in the SUV.

"I can't believe Heidi tore off like that," Jess muttered. "And headed out to the ships?"

"I know. I'm still in shock," Maria stated.

"She turned on us."

Kid stared out the window and said nothing.

"Are you alright," Sara whispered as she leaned over from the passenger's seat and touched his arm.

"Yeah, I'm fine. Just trying to contemplate their next move and ours," Kid answered.

He wasn't fine. But he wasn't going to talk about how distraught he was over Heidi's leaving and how she left. Despite all of his rationalizing, a part of him still felt responsible, and he wanted her back with the group.

CHAPTER 40

January 7, 2045
Saturday, Afternoon
Mallard Island, New Jersey
Twelve days after the event

Cruising on East Bay Avenue, Kid approached Mallard Island. The small piece of land, well under a mile square, was nestled in an alcove and was surrounded by creeks and waterways on all sides. Kid thought the island was like a small-scale Pangaea, with the land mass just beginning its drift away from the main continent. From a distance, all he could see were clusters of houses rising out of what appeared to be a large field of marsh grass. He could not fathom how any structure weighing more than 10 pounds could remain standing in such wet, swampy ground.

"Are we there?" Jess inquired as he crawled up between the front seats and crouched between Kid and Sara.

"Almost," Kid said as he spotted a bait and tackle store down the road. A box truck was parked out front with huge letters on the side indicating, 'Fresh Catch,' prompting him to think of clams. "It looks like there might be some serious steamers just waiting to be taken over there."

"Yeah, I know I've taken some serious steamers in those," Jess responded.

"What?" Sara asked.

Jess pointed to a blue stand-alone structure within a construction site at the end of the road. "The outhouse over there."

Kid shook his head.

Sara had a smirk on her face as she smacked Jess's arm. "When Kid said steamers, he meant clams. See the truck in front of the bait and tackle store up the road?"

Turning onto Heron Street, Kid stopped on the arch of the Mallard Island Bridge as an expansive view opened up before them. Sara leaned forward in her seat. "This is perfect."

Kid nodded. He was glad he had taken the time to study the map. He was correct in his presumption that from Mallard Island they would be able to clearly see Long Beach Island—the landmass across the bay where the Utopia Project base camp was to be established. They would also have a view of the long Route 72 Manahawkin Bay Bridge, which was the only road to and from Long Beach Island.

Still stopped on the arch of the small Mallard Island Bridge, Kid looked left and right. Under the span, Manahawkin Creek looked to be 40 to 50 feet wide in both directions. The water along the banks of the creek was frozen over, but a wide swath of current still flowed in the center of the channel. He took note the section of unfrozen water was too wide to jump or easily get across. That would help keep them protected and would serve as a barrier to accessing the island.

Continuing on, the vehicle approached an open grass field. Sara pointed to an oval welcome sign with a brightly colored duck. "Here we are, Mallard Island."

Heading deeper into the island, Kid slowed as he followed a bend in the road. He stopped upon seeing a pair of neighboring homes that appeared suitable.

Sara stared at the first house. "I'd be surprised to find any bodies in that...bungalow. It doesn't appear winter ready."

The general leaned forward between the front seats. "It doesn't look ready for any season."

Kid's first thought was he wouldn't want to ride out a hurricane in such a...bungalow, but it was low to the ground and out of sight, which made it desirable for their purposes. Although it appeared to be a small shack from the outside, upon shutting down the vehicle and busting inside, he was surprised by the generous sizes of the three bedrooms.

The house next door was more modern and had two stories but required Kid and the general to dispose of two melted corpses they found in the master bedroom upstairs. What struck Kid was the two corpses were melded together as if one person was on top of the other when the destruction came. Perched on the nightstand were two Happy 25th Anniversary cards and two quarter-full cups of champagne. They wrapped the pallid mounds of flesh in the soiled bedsheet and moved the bodies to a garage up the road. Next they threw out the mattress and remaining bedding, closed the door to the master bedroom and opened the windows to blow out the smell of death.

Meeting up with the group at the house they now referred to as the bungalow, Kid announced, "We can live in these two houses since they are side by side and can't be seen from Long Beach Island." He thought the location was ideal. If they could not see Long Beach Island, then presumably, those on the island couldn't see them either.

The group agreed, and Jess said, "One good thing is that between the houses across the street we can see a few small sections of Route 72, which is the only road on and off the island. If we are watching, we will know if they try to come or go."

"Perfect." Kid nodded his head. "Now all we need is a tall lookout house with a view that is not obstructed so we can keep an eye on the base camp they're setting up."

He stepped outside and glanced around. The last house on the block on the other side of the street caught his attention because it had three-stories. The siding appeared new and was brown, which was unusual compared to the lighter colors of the other homes on the island. The balconies also appeared to be recently renovated and were bright white, which made them stand out when offset against the brown siding. As Kid strolled up the road, he noted the structure was surrounded by head-high marsh grass in the back and along one side. He stopped and turned his eyes up. From the third level they should have a clear view of Long Beach Island across the bay.

Sara and her father walked up beside him. "Will it suffice?" the general asked.

"I think so. We need to get up to the balcony on the third story to be sure," Kid stated.

"That's pretty elaborate." Sara pointed to the mailbox in front of the house, which was held in the open hands of a decorative, life-size mermaid. "Maybe even a little creepy."

They turned as Chris walked up the road with a long box under his arm. Meeting him in the middle of the street, he showed them the package. It was a beginner's telescope, and appeared to be unopened.

"Hey, Gramps, you plan on doing some stargazing?" Sara asked.

"Enemy-gazing. This will help us keep an eye on Long Beach Island." He turned to Kid. "Which house did you think would give us the best view?"

He pointed over his shoulder. "That...mermaid house over here."

The general said, "This is all good, but rule number one is never hole up in a place with only one exit. The center of the waterways surrounding the island are still flowing and are too wide to jump across. We really need a secondary way off this island in case we need to escape."

"We thought of that. For now, our secondary exit is a footbridge," Kid said.

The general stared at him expectantly.

"There's a footbridge from this island over to the mainland at Bridge Street."

"Show me," the general said firmly. As they left he added, "It could make a life or death difference."

Kid hesitated, then resumed walking. He did not know why, but the general's words sent a chill down his spine.

On the top floor of the mermaid house, Kid waited for his turn as Chris peered through the telescope while wearing UV-rated sunglasses. The blinds were drawn and the sliding door to the balcony was cracked open just far enough so they could extend out the thin tube and point it at Long Beach Island.

Kid took the telescope and put on the sunglasses, but dusk was already falling. He peered through the eyepiece at Surf City where the base camp was being established. There was no activity at the moment. When he was done, he turned the telescope so it pointed at the ground. "We need to keep this facing down, and can't use it, until after midday tomorrow."

"Why is that?"

"Because the sun rises in the east. Until it is behind us the light will reflect off of the mirror inside the telescope. From the ships or even the base camp they could spot the pinpoint of light."

"Very astute," Chris complimented. "I'm glad you considered that."

As the sun dipped below the horizon to the west, Kid and Chris left the mermaid house and stepped outside. Chris stopped in his tracks. "Who is that?"

A vehicle with its headlights off crept toward them in the fading light. Seeing a beard that seemed to glow in the dark, Kid said, "There's only one person we know with chops that scraggly."

"With how long he was gone, he must have laid tire tracks across the entire county," Chris commented.

Meeting up with Drex, they all stepped into the bungalow. The living room was crammed full of people.

General Hyland walked into the room carrying his laptop computer and announced, "I am relieved to say the program works, and I'm ready to launch what I hope will be a final command. All I have to do is link up, hit a button, and once and for all we should be rid of the satellites."

Excited murmurs filled to room.

"How will that get rid of them?" Kid asked.

"The satellites will fire upon each other in sequence, like a chain reaction, until only one is left. And for the 48th and final satellite, it will continue to fire into space until it overheats, which will ruin the laser core and destroy the neutron beam system."

"Are we sure we want to destroy all of the satellites? Can't we use them later on?" Clarence asked.

The general's gaze was hard. "Haven't they done enough damage already?"

Nods and murmurs filled the room.

"Not to mention, if any of the satellites are left intact, there is always a chance the elders could recreate the codes to access them. So, come outside and watch the light show," he said as he walked to the back door.

Bundled against the cold and the wind, the group watched in silent anticipation as the general set his laptop down on top of a wood picnic table. In the middle of the small back yard he placed a solid square block on the ground and then fully-extended a telescoping antenna.

"What is that?" Kid asked.

"It is a special military grade antenna. So long as there is a satellite in orbit between both horizons, it will link up to it."

The general turned to the entire group. "Although the beams from the satellites aren't coming toward earth, just keep glancing and looking away. Don't stare at them. The beams should start there," he pointed to the sky. "We will lose sight of them as the satellites are activated in sequence and circle the globe, but it should end right about there." He again pointed to the sky.

"Ready?"

More nods and murmurs.

The general hit a button on the laptop.

Nothing could be seen in the sky at first. After a minute, Kid was getting worried the exercise was a failure. Then, a red line appeared on the horizon and stopped at a point, creating a line segment that seemed to hover in the sky. Suddenly there was a small, but bright explosion at the far tip of the line segment. Kid shuddered. The beams were a stinging reminder of the night of the destruction. Then another line appeared, aimed at the point of origin of the previous line segment, and a small explosion followed. In a clockwise sequence, bright line segments would appear in the sky until the tip erupted in an exploding circle. For the next few minutes, they watched in wonder as the red segments stepped across the sky over their heads.

On Utopia Project Ship Number One, Elder-2's monitor came to life. "Ma'am, Elder-51 here. There is something going on in the sky!"

"Clarify!" Elder-2 barked.

"From the deck-cam we spotted something unusual, so we adjusted the camera view. Red lines and small explosions are crossing the sky."

"The satellites," she uttered. "On my way. Don't move!" she snapped and ran for the high-security hall on the second level above the deck.

Inside, Elder-51 was at his workstation.

"Do we have access to the satellites yet?" Elder-2 asked as she approached him. "We need to access them right now!"

"No, Ma'am." Elder-51 turned. "We are still trying to recreate the codes."

"We have no time. The satellites are being destroyed! We need to stop it!"

"We can't, not without being able to communicate with them."

"Obviously someone is communicating with them!" Her frustration was growing.

Off the cuff, Elder-51 said, "Where is Elder-41 when you need him? If anyone could recreate the codes, it would be him."

"Son of a bitch!" Elder-2 stormed out the door and went down the circular stairs. The other elder followed behind. She opened the door to the ship's deck and stood at the railing. The cold wind blew against her face but she felt nothing but the growing heat of her anger. "Elder-41. General Hyland. Again," she growled as she spit over the rail.

"What about him?"

Grabbing the front of Elder-51's uniform and balling it into her fist, she pointed to the red lines tracing across the sky and snapped, "Who do you think is behind this!"

CHAPTER 41

January 7, 2045
Saturday, Evening
Mallard Island, New Jersey
Twelve days after the event

Has the circle been broken? Kid wondered as he watched the sky.

After waiting several minutes, General Hyland shouted, "There!" The satellite destruction sequence had circled the globe and was coming back over the opposite horizon from where it began. The group watched as the process continued.

Kid gazed in wonder, nearly spellbound.

"Last one," the general stated. A final red line segment burned bright for more than 15 minutes, aimed into space. The light started pulsating, blinking, and then died.

"It appears to have worked." The general did not sound victorious, just relieved. He closed his laptop and whispered, "Thank God."

The group stood for several minutes in silence until Dr. McDermott's 17-year-old son Dylan's teeth started chattering. His mother, Pamela, hugged him, but his body was shaking as if in the throes of a mini-convulsion. The temperature had plummeted and was less than 30 degrees. Kid realized Dylan may be used to the cold in Vermont, but he was not used to the relentless wind near the water. It was clear the chill had gotten into Dylan's bones. Kid could relate. He and the others fought the same struggle, day and night, and he knew it was taxing on the body. Everyone at some point had engaged in a bout with uncontrollable shivers. Helping Mrs. McDermott bring Dylan back inside, Kid made a beeline for the propane heater. Dylan sat on the floor, just inches from the heater's protective screen until his shaking subsided.

The rest of the group followed them and assembled inside the bungalow. General Hyland opened a coat closet and placed his laptop computer bag inside. While everyone sat in the living room, Karen and Evelyn used a camping stove to make instant coffee and tea. Given the destruction of the satellites, and the implications thereof, everyone seemed to be in a reflective mood.

Kid sat on a couch next to the general and said, "That takes care of that. For the first time in a long time, we are free from any eyes in the sky."

"Yes, free," the general repeated. He shook his head and also seemed wistful. "For centuries people and cultures have thrown that word around. Have you ever wondered what it really means?"

"What does free really mean?" Kid repeated.

"Yes, what does it mean?" the general asked, but not argumentatively, as he glanced around the quiet room. Some pondered. Some just shrugged their shoulders. Katy and Karly Spatz made faces at each other behind their mother's back, prompting Melanie to put them to bed.

"Let me ask it this way. Looking to the future, how should freedom be established with a new society?" the general prompted.

"All I can say is the society I envision would be free," Kid stated.

"Would the freedom be absolute?"

This made Kid think.

Before Kid could answer, the general added, "Do you think you had absolute freedom in America?"

"We were a free country," Maria chimed in.

"But was the freedom *absolute*?" the general repeated. He offered an example. "Kid, remember you told me the story about you playing your electric guitar late at night and the neighbors came over to protest so you turned it off?"

"Yes," Kid answered.

"Well, did you want to keep playing?"

"Sure, I could have played all night."

"Didn't they infringe upon your freedom to play?" the general asked and then answered his own question. "Yes, and how could that happen? Because your neighbor has freedoms as well, and they conflicted with yours. They are free to have peace and quiet after a certain hour. If you had absolute freedom, you could have kept right on playing, right?"

"I guess so." Kid paused and concluded, "But we were still free, relatively. I was free to play as much as I wanted and whatever I wanted until I hit the town's curfew."

The general moved to the edge of his seat on the couch. "Whether you know it or not, you nailed the crux of the concept of freedom in one word. You already said it."

Having to think for a second and retrace his words, Kid guessed, "Relatively?"

"Exactly!" the general responded. "How can one neighbor be free to make as much noise as they want while the neighbor next door is free to enjoy peace and quiet? Throughout the life of the project, these concepts were explored extensively and the conclusion was that freedom is always relative to something, whether it is established norms, environments or sets of rules. We used this to establish our own benchmarks for relativity."

"If you are talking about your people on the ships, what freedoms did they really have? They were so regimented every day. I know, I lived among them," Sara said.

"All of that regimenting seems horrible to you because of the environment in which you were raised. The people on the ships were raised differently and do not perceive regimens as constricting."

"But Dad, the people couldn't choose their work tasks, or even choose with whom they wanted to have relationships," Sara countered.

"And they didn't yearn for anything else because they have never known anything else. As for work tasks, in any society, necessary, and I emphasize necessary, vocations need to be covered to allow society to function. The better the allocation of duties, based on individual strengths and capabilities, the more efficiently a society operates. On the ships, did people seem discontent in their work? Even those doing tasks like cleaning bathrooms or removing garbage?"

"No," Sara admitted. "Even they seemed content and at peace."

"That's the point. With no financial reward and no negative social stigmas, people can be content just doing their part to help society. Every one of them felt like they had important and necessary jobs, and they did."

"Alright. I can at least *understand* the argument about the tasks necessary for society to carry on, but what about relationships? Why couldn't people choose their partners?"

"I did not agree with the extreme way relationships were addressed in the project," the general conceded. "But that was not my area of authority. I do believe that individuals should be able to choose each other, but I also believe they should not be tied together in any formal way, such as being bound by marriage. They stay together as long as they both want to stay together."

"Dad, why would you be so cynical about marriage?" Sara asked.

"I'm not cynical about marriage, but in raising you, I learned firsthand how much a good village can assist in raising children, and in taking the pressure off individual family units. When the village raises the child, that is the structure that needs to stay intact, and it generally will regardless of the status of any individual relationships or family structures within," the general responded. "Only couples who genuinely want to be together and are a great match should stay together. In that way, souls that are joined should not need to be formally bound by marriage."

"I would be worried about the stability of the family structure," Sara said.

"For many years, more children were born out of wedlock than through married couples anyway," Dr. McDermott chimed in. "So the traditional family structure was no longer the norm, or the standard."

"That only reinforces what I said about the importance of the village raising the children," the general responded.

Sara stood and walked behind the couch where her father was sitting. She wrapped her arms around his neck. "I am not 100 percent on board with your relationship and family perspective. A village is important and supplements, supports, and protects, but a family raises a child. And I would love nothing more than to be taken as the wife of the guy next to you, and raise our children together in a great family structure."

Maria turned to Kid. "Did she just propose to you?"

His eyes widened. "Oh…I do!"

Sara laughed, then bent over and kissed Kid's cheek.

The general patted Sara's arm. "Your perspective is duly noted. It's getting late, so we'll have to pick up the discussion at another time, but think about your own life, honey. Being raised by a single, widowed father wasn't necessarily a great family structure, but we did have a good village."

Kid and General Hyland divided the survivors into two groups. Since Melanie's young daughters were already asleep in one of the bungalow bedrooms, Kid figured most of the group from Vermont should stay there for the night. The group from New Jersey, plus Chris and Evelyn, Karen, and soldiers 801 and 705, walked to the newer house next door.

After the general established the lookout shifts, it was a relief to Kid that for a change, he was given the night off.

A large bucket of water was placed in the tub in the newer house so people could wash themselves before bed. Chris and Evelyn went first and then turned in for the night in a small bedroom up the hall. While the general was taking his turn in the bathroom, Kid and Sara sat on the couch in the living room and waited. They were facing each other having their own quiet conversation.

Jess and Maria were arm in arm sitting in the corner of the room and from what Kid could tell, they had shared more kisses in the last 15 minutes than he had seen in the past year. Although trying to be discreet as they sat in a corner, with their playful flirtation and subtle petting, Jess and Maria were surrounded by an unmistakable sexual aura. 801 noticed this, or sensed it, and crawled over without hesitation. Kid and Sara stopped talking and turned their attention to his movement.

"Are we being too mushy over here?" Maria asked.

Without answering, 801 lifted his hand and grabbed her breast.

CHAPTER 42

January 7, 2045
Saturday, Evening
Mallard Island, New Jersey
Twelve days after the event

When 801 touched Maria's breast, she smacked his hand.

Jess lurched forward, pushed 801's arm away, and stood. "What the hell are you doing?"

Kid and Sara were over in a second.

"Wait." Sara patted Jess's shoulder. "801 doesn't know any better."

"He doesn't know you can't just reach out and fondle people?" Jess huffed.

"In his society they actually promote it. That's just how he grew up," she countered.

"Well, he needs a crash course in the rules of our world."

The reaction of Jess and Maria seemed to confuse and bother 801. "We do not understand this reaction. We were hoping it was time for a sexual activity period," he said, but without guilt or apology.

"Listen…Romeo, this is a party of two." Jess sat back down. "We'll find you a piece of wood with a hole in it or something."

801 looked at him with curiosity. He was perplexed by Jess's reaction to his touching Maria. Touching was beautiful and natural. Jess seemed unhappy about it and 801 did not understand why. He had never encountered such a reaction before.

"We'll find a game for you to play, 801," Maria offered as she walked over to a built-in bookcase. She grabbed a cup and a pair of dice from the shelf.

Kid noticed that 801 appeared to brighten up when he heard the dice rattling.

She handed him the cup. "Here, I understand you like dice games. I figure you could amuse yourself with this."

801 took it and continued to stare at her.

"What?" She then appeared to have a realization. "That's right. You don't do anything alone." She sat across from him.

"I'm going to sleep," Jess grumbled as he lay on the floor and covered himself with a blanket.

While sitting across from Maria, 801 asked, "Why did he call me Romeo?"

Covering his mouth, Kid tried not to laugh aloud.

Contemplating, Maria responded, "Well, let's just say the real Romeo also touched women. Many women." She pointed at the cup with the dice. "So, what do you want to play?"

The general came out of the bathroom. "Is everything alright? I heard some commotion."

"Yes," Sara answered. "801 was just getting a little...restless."

Kid and Sara were next to use the bathroom, so they started walking up the hall. "801 is quite an effective...blocker," Kid commented.

The general stopped. "A what?"

Walking to the bathroom, Sara laughed. "Dad, don't ask."

Kid took one of the propane heaters and set it up in the second of the three bedrooms, which was a little further up the hall. Earlier, Jess had whispered to Kid, "We'll take the living room. If anyone could use a night alone together, it's you guys." He was sure Jess was regretting that offer about now.

As Kid stepped into the hall, he peered at the closed door at the end. Nobody wanted to occupy the master bedroom until it was aired out a few more days and was thoroughly cleaned again. Sara came out of the bathroom and kissed Kid firmly as she walked past him and into their bedroom. He changed places with her and stepped into the bathroom to wash down and brush his teeth.

When he came out, Kid checked on the group in the living room. Maria had finished her dice game with 801 and the group was preparing to get some sleep. They were setting up sleeping bags on the living room floor around the propane heater. The group was situated like a United States Army Marksman's Badge from World War II, with the heater in the center and the four protrusions being Jess and Maria together, General Hyland, Karen, and finally 801 and 705 side-by-side.

Sara was already lying in bed under the covers when Kid walked in and locked the door behind him. The heater next to the bed was cranking and the 12-foot by 12-foot square room was already warming. On the nightstand the flame of a burning candle was motionless, like an electric candle in a window during the holiday season. Sara's head rested on her interlocked fingers as she lay in bed facing Kid. She smiled and seemed to be watching his every move.

At that moment, it dawned on him. *Finally, we're alone.*

"Do you want to come over here?" she whispered. Her voice was seductive.

"For the second time tonight, I'll say...I do."

Sara smiled as she kept her eyes fixed on his.

Approaching the bed, he felt awash with sexual anticipation. The familiar tingle ran through his body. He realized how much he needed her, and how much he longed for that full and complete connection. Her alluring eyes said the same as the pace of her breathing started to increase.

Once Kid was close enough to the bed, she reached out and grabbed the waistband of his blue jeans above the zipper. While pulling him closer, the tips of her fingers slid below the band of his underwear. He felt like he was going to melt on the floor. He could not take it anymore and reached to unbutton his pants.

She snagged his hand and stopped him. Throwing off the blanket and standing up, she pulled his hand around her waist and rested it on the small of her back. Leaning forward, she kissed him gently but deeply.

Their kisses were like magic and weakened him in every way. He could feel time slowing down, and every touch and sensation seemed amplified and electrically charged. He felt he had walked into a massive spider web with threads carrying a mild current. He responded with a slow, passionate kiss of his own.

Her throat emitted an involuntary moan. She unbuttoned his pants and slid them down to his ankles. As she lay back down on the bed, she breathed deeply.

Kid sat on the edge of the mattress next to her. He blew out the candle, kicked off his pants and pulled his shirt over his head.

Sara took her top off. The heat from the propane unit offered a dim red glow, and as Kid's eyes adjusted to the faint light, he saw bare skin. A wave of heat and desire flushed through him. She arched her back and grabbed the waistband of her own jeans and started to slide them down. This time, he grabbed her hands and stopped her. She gave him a knowing smile.

He gave her a few playful kisses, but zeroing in on her most sensitive areas, he slipped his head under her chin and put his lips to her neck. She exhaled and another small moan escaped her throat. She raised her hand to cover her mouth.

Putting his forehead against hers, he whispered, "Shh."

She nodded with a playful, mock-serious look in her eyes, and then grabbed his hair and guided his lips back to her neck.

Kid pulled her pants off one leg at a time. As she lifted her leg she tugged his hair, the desire and need seemingly uncontrollable. Pulling off her second pant leg, he ran his fingertips gently under and inside her thigh. She clenched her hand and nearly ripped his hair from his scalp.

Leaning forward, she took his head in her hands, and he heard the desperation in her voice. "I need you, *now*."

He crawled up between her legs and lowered his lips and pelvis in unison. She rolled her hips to meet him. They both let out a hot breath as they became one. Kid felt their love and chemistry taking them to a dimension where time seemed to stand still. He was floating in a warm, womb-like capsule in an endless universe. Kid could feel a tingle in every nerve is his body as he reached the point of no return. He met Sara's penetrating hazel eyes, which became windows to the bottom of her heart and soul as the pulsations began. He knew his eyes revealed the same. Their gaze remained fixed during wave after wave until a tear ran down the corner of her eye. His own breath quivered with emotion from the power of their connection, and he knew they both felt complete in a way they could only feel with each other.

Waking a little before dawn, Kid did not want to stir. He knew the chill outside the blanket was just waiting to infiltrate his cozy and warm cocoon. His arm was over Sara's waist and he held her naked body against his. He nuzzled his face against her hair and absorbed her essence. He was still basking in the sweet aura of their intimate and powerful encounter from the night before. Without warning, a large wave of emotion crested and washed over him. Not that he consciously fought against such emotions coming to the surface, but it caught him off guard.

At that moment, he understood that he had shut down emotionally to avoid having to face the full depths of his grief when he thought he had lost Sara. He had grieved, but only to a point. He still had had a long way to go, much further than he realized. So much anguish had filled his heart and soul, and like a pressure release valve, with her alive he felt it releasing. But its path out rubbed the same nerve endings and triggered the same emotions as if he was grieving, which explained his tears.

She interlocked her fingers with his and whispered, "Kid?"

"Yes." Despite his efforts, his response came out choked.

She turned her head. "Are you alright?"

He paused for a second. "I'm better than alright now that we're back together. I'm never letting you out of my sight or my hands…" he gently squeezed her fingers, "…again."

"Nope. Never." She lifted his hand and kissed it. "I love you Kid," she said as she pulled his arm across her torso, just under her breasts.

"I love you too, Sara." He then drifted into the most peaceful period of slumber he had ever experienced.

Kid awoke upon hearing the faint sound of lowered voices coming from the living room. He squeezed his eyes shut, but could not fall back to sleep. Looking at his watch, he had only slept for 40 minutes. He leaned over and kissed Sara on the head, and got out of bed.

As he got dressed, his thoughts turned to Heidi. Even in his morning fog, it was somehow clear that her decision to leave and her state of mind were going to have a profound influence on the series of events that would unfold. Every scenario he could imagine made him sick from fear or deep regret. He walked out to the living room and with dawn making its entrance, the space was cast in a shadowy dark gray. He squinted his eyes and was able to discern it was Maria and Karen who were chatting as they sat close to the heater.

"Hey Kid. We were just talking," Maria whispered. "With Heidi going out to the ships, we are worried that she will talk and tell them where we are."

Karen said, "We were trying to figure out if she heard us mention Mallard Island yesterday before she took off."

Kid spoke quietly as he sat. "Before me, Chris and Doc went into the dining room to discuss where to go, the talk at that time was about heading west, not south down here."

They all turned as Jess breathed roughly through his nose and began to snore. Maria reached over and pinched his nostrils until he took a sudden deep breath through his mouth and swatted her hand away.

"That's good. Then she never heard you mention coming here?" Maria clarified.

"No," Kid said assuredly. "It wasn't until just before midday that we finally decided where we should go. We circled Mallard Island on the map, but had not told anybody yet," he clarified. He felt there was more to analyze, but his brain was still too foggy.

General Hyland was lying down, but was obviously not asleep since he asked, "Speaking of, where is the map?"

Silence followed. "Nobody grabbed it from the table at the restaurant when we cleared out of there?" Kid stood and started to pace. The morning fog was beginning to dissipate.

More silence, until Karen added, "I remember taking one last look around before we left, and I didn't see any map in the dining room."

The general sat up. "If we left the map at the restaurant that could be huge a problem. With Heidi heading out to the ships, the first thing they will do is interrogate her. After finding out we were hiding out at Water Street, she will most certainly take them there. And if they find the map, it directs them right here."

Kid jumped to his feet. "I'm going over to the bungalow to see if Dr. McDermott or anyone over there picked it up."

The general also got up. "I'll go ask my father since he was looking at it with you."

A few minutes later, Kid walked back into the house. "Nothing," he stated.

"Same here," the general responded.

"We must have dropped it, or left it," Kid concluded. "I have to get to the restaurant before they show up there. That map can't fall into their hands."

The general turned to him. "You can't go alone." His tone conveyed he was ready to come along.

"I won't go alone." Kid used his foot to nudge a form sleeping under a blanket.

"What now?" Jess groaned, sounding grumpy.

"I'll bring Jess." He nudged him again.

"Ahh, come on, Kid. Why are you up so early anyway?" He rolled out from under his covers.

Having come out of the bedroom, Sara stood with a blanket wrapped around her. Kid took her face in his hands and kissed the side of her head. He tried to be nonchalant. "We'll be back. We forgot the map at the restaurant. Come on Jess."

"Alright, but I'm not sure I should leave Maria alone with... Romeo over there," he quipped as he pointed to 801. The serious expression on the soldier's face garnered a tired laugh from Jess. "I'm kidding, 801. Lighten up."

CHAPTER 43

January 8, 2045
Sunday, Morning
Toms River, New Jersey
Thirteen days after the event

While making their trek north toward the Water Street Grill, Kid noticed that dawn seemed to be holding on just a little longer than usual, but it offered enough light to reveal the sky was gray and overcast. "As my father always said, another gray day in Jersey," he muttered as he drove along the snowy roadway.

Being cautious, Kid parked the red marina truck up the road from the restaurant. He and Jess crept up on foot, crossed the walking bridge at Huddy Park and peered in a window.

"Looks just as we left it," Jess concluded.

"For now. It won't be long before they come here." Kid went around to the front door of the restaurant. Pulling out a flashlight, he ran inside and back to the dining room. Scanning around the table on which they had spread the map, he crouched down and checked underneath. "Where the hell did it go?"

"I'm not seeing it," Jess said as he checked under the tables nearby.

After searching the dining room, the lobby and the kitchen, Kid concluded it was not there. He figured someone must have picked up the map and just didn't remember doing it. In the end all he knew was just like Heidi, it was gone.

Since her departure, Kid had been contemplating how he could get her to come back. There was no telling what happened to her after she left, but if she was still alive he had to try and seek her out. In the best scenario, she would come to her senses and return to the group of her own volition, if she was even able to. If she had really joined the other side, he was hoping for an opportunity to reach her before she was too far gone. The window of time might be very narrow. *If I could just speak to her for one minute…*

Kid stepped back into the kitchen. Flooded by many conflicting thoughts, he crouched down on one knee. For some unknown reason, he suspected she would come back today to the restaurant. He hung his head as a torrent of raw emotions flowed through him. Heidi had, in some ways, saved him at the cabin. He was dying from a broken heart after losing Sara, and she, of all people, was the one who helped him come back from the edge. He knew he could never repay her, but he also felt like he owed her something.

Standing up, looked around for a piece of paper and a pen. Opening an interior door in the back of the kitchen, he found a small room with a water heater, furnace and just inside the entrance, a cluttered desk. He grabbed a pen and paper and headed out to the dining room. Jess was still searching, so Kid sat at a table and began writing. 'Heidi, please hear me out…' He was going to craft a note in case she showed up and he could not talk to her. Maybe he could at least slip her the note. It would ask her to leave the Utopia Project and hide in the Riverboat next to the restaurant if she could escape now, and take refuge in Drex's beach shack if she had to escape later. He promised to check each of those locations every few days to see if she was there. As he put this all to paper, he couldn't help but plead with her, 'We miss you and desperately want you back with us where you truly belong.'

"Nothing. I even checked the restrooms," Jess said as he stepped over.

"I'll look once more for the map, but listen, why don't you take the truck and pick up some supplies and then come back for me," Kid started. "Keep your eyes open and radio first in case the soldiers come here. Stay away from Route 37. If they come, that's the road they'll take. If I need you, I'll call you."

Staring, Jess asked, "You want to stay here? You said yourself, there's a good chance of them coming here."

Turning away for a minute, Kid exhaled while folding up the note he had written. "Jess, it's hard to explain, but I hope they do."

"What?"

"And I hope Heidi is with them, and I can talk her into coming back."

"That's crazy!" he blurted out. "How would you even be able to talk to her if she is with them? You'll probably be killed, if not by them, by her!"

Kid waved his hand, dismissing the risk. "If I can hide, and get her alone for a minute, she'll at least hear me out. And if I can't talk to her, I wrote this note. I just need slip it to her somehow."

"I can't believe you would take that chance. The Heidi you knew might hear you out, but this isn't the same girl!"

"It's not too late, Jess."

"Now I know why you wanted to bring me. Mr. Hyland wouldn't listen to a word of this."

"He doesn't know the situation with Heidi. He wouldn't understand," Kid stated.

"I don't understand."

"Listen, I need to try. It's my fault she left."

"It's not your fault. It's hers. Don't feel bad for her. She choose to leave us and join up with the group that is trying to kill us. The girl is screwed up in the head!" Jess said.

"Leave it alone, Jess," Kid snapped, unable to contain his frustration. Although his friend was only trying to be rational, he was actually bothered by how Jess was speaking of Heidi.

Jess seemed downright flustered so he walked away and stood at the back window. He snapped his head around. "Kid! Kill the flashlight!"

Kid turned off the flashlight and then he saw it. For a second, a glare shone off a slushy snow bank outside, but then a second light appeared. He knew the answer before he asked the question. "What was that?" *Vehicle headlights, and more than one…*

Jess ran over and before he could say a word, they both fell flat and grabbed their guns as the front door swung open. They could not see who was in the lobby behind the blue tarp, but whoever was entering was not concerned about stealth.

"Search the premises," an authoritative voice barked. "And capture, but do not fire unless ordered to do so."

"Underneath, quick!" Kid whispered to Jess as they crowded together under a rectangle dining table.

"Where are they?" came an angry voice from the other side of the tarp. The timbre of the voice made Kid freeze. He had heard it before.

Sid Sherman.

"We better find the asshole who killed my brother!"

And with a vengeance.

Hearing the tarp being pushed aside, someone called out, "It appears they are a step ahead."

Kid could hear many footsteps as a large group searched the premises. "Elder-44! Nobody is here. Where did they go?" Sid yelled as his shiny new boots stomped past the table Kid and Jess were hiding under.

Kid's heart raced as he heard the voice responding.

"They might be holed up in the jail down the street. We had been going there too," answered Heidi Leer.

The soldiers hustled out of the room, and Kid assumed they were heading to the jail.

Heidi called out, "We'll catch up with you. Give us a few minutes in here. We may find a clue as to where they went."

Kid crawled out and risked a peek over the top of the table. He saw her back as she stood at the window. She was wearing a uniform and holding the blinds aside as she stared out. With his eyes and ears fully open, he realized she was alone, at least for the moment. He could not believe his good fortune, and was not going to let a golden opportunity pass by. Forget handing her a note, he could talk to her one on one. "Here's my chance," he whispered.

Jess held his friend's jacket. "No! Don't!"

Grabbing Jess's hand and removing it from his coat, he whispered, "I have to. It may be my *only* chance."

"Wait!" Jess hissed, but Kid left and stepped silently across the floor.

Heidi seemed to sense his presence right before Kid lunged. She had just started to turn when he threw his arms around her and pinned her against the window. She grabbed his wrists and turned her head enough to see his face. Appearing surprised and conflicted, she snapped, "What are you doing?"

"Shh," he uttered as he felt both of her hips for a weapon.

"Let go!" She struggled to twist her body out of his grip.

"Kid!" Jess snapped.

Finding a weapon on her hip, Kid pulled it from its holster. Without even looking back, he tossed it over his shoulder and reestablished his hold on Heidi. He glanced back to see Jess catch the weapon in midair and put it in his jacket pocket.

"Shh," he repeated and whispered, "Please, Heidi. Talk to me."

"There's nothing to talk about, now get off me before we scream and they come in and blast your ass. Now!" She struggled to free herself.

"No." He pinned her tighter against the window frame.

"Now!"

"No. Not until we talk for a minute."

The silent standoff continued for a minute, and then Heidi's intensity eased a notch. She let her head droop down, and Kid rested his cheek against the back of her neck. She no longer resisted and seemed to be relenting. It struck Kid that just a few days ago they would have found comfort and warmth in their bodies being pressed together.

"Hey!" Jess whispered.

Kid turned to see his friend shifting his weight back and forth from one foot to the other.

"Heidi, if I let you go, will you just talk to me for a minute?" Kid asked. "I just want to talk."

Her tone was sullen. "Yes."

"Promise?"

"Don't talk to me about promises, Kid," she said bitterly. She exhaled a deep breath. "You can let go. We'll hear you out."

We'll? Like the members of that society she was no longer using the long vowel, I? He loosened his grasp and she turned to face him. When she met his eyes, her lips pursed and he could see the conflict. She looked away, smoothed out her uniform and walked past him.

"I see they gave you one of their high-tech weapons and a new outfit," he said, having noted the embroidered 'Jr-Elder 2' on her uniform.

"When we went back, they made us junior elders."

"Us?" he asked.

"Me and Sid Sherman."

Bad news. "So you are elders?"

"Not full ones, and we are in training, but at least we don't have to deal with being fully conditioned like the members. Didn't want to go through that part again." She turned to him. "Just you and Jess are here?"

"Yes. Just us." He was focusing on his words, being careful not to give away any pertinent information. He was struggling with the thought of not being able to fully trust Heidi. Just a few days ago, he would have trusted her without reservation.

"Well, go ahead and talk, Kid. Why are you even here? We can't imagine you came back just to talk to me?"

"It wasn't the only reason, but deep inside, that's what I was really hoping for. I suspected you would come back here."

"Gee, should we be flattered?" Her sarcasm was thick, and angry. As she dawdled she glanced back over her shoulder. "So why else are you here? Did you forget something?" Heidi hesitated, and then strolled toward the kitchen door.

Kid felt a growing discomfort. Something seemed to click inside her and he caught the passing smirk that had come to her face. He followed behind her and said, "We wanted to grab more of the food and supplies we left here. Listen, I know you're angry and hurt, but don't do this. Come back with us, Heidi."

"Back where?" she asked. "Back to what?"

"To the group, you know, normal people. We're not too, too far from here," he said, making sure he was vague. "You know that group on the ships is trouble."

She peered at him and then turned away. "My life is all about trouble these days."

"Heidi, don't you remember our talk at the cabin? You said yourself their world is scary and people aren't meant to live that way."

"Maybe now we can see the benefits of their world, a world where they don't allow individual attachments. And it's the only other world out there. We sure as hell weren't staying where we were. Quick drink?" She pointed at the bar. "With all this chaos, we need one."

"No time, please, Heidi," Kid pleaded. "Come back to the world where you belong. We have to go, now."

"Belong?" Heidi scoffed, making Kid take a step back. She stepped behind the bar and grabbed a bottle of spiced rum. She crouched and muttered, "If we could only find a glass..."

"Come on. We can talk more when we're out of here." He approached the counter, as if he was a customer.

"Hold on, still looking," she said, still bent down behind the bar.

Glancing over his shoulder, Kid saw Jess on the other side of the room standing watch at the window. After waiting for another few seconds, which felt like an hour, Kid knew they had to go. "Stop worrying about drinks. Let's leave. When we get back, you can have all of the drinks you want..." and then he heard a strange crinkling sound.

He leaned over the bar as Heidi stood with two glasses and put them on the bar.

"What was that sound?"

"What sound?" She poured rum into the glasses. Lifting one, she held it out as if to toast him, and swallowed it in one gulp.

"It sounded like…paper being crumbled," he noted.

Reaching down she grabbed an inventory sheet from the floor. "Must be this. It was getting trampled under my feet." She started balling it up.

The sound was similar, but didn't quite match what he had heard seconds ago. He was about to inquire further when she said, "We don't feel like you are being completely forthright Kid, about why you're really here. And yet you want me to go with you, and trust you?"

Before he could respond, Jess walked over. "We should leave now."

"Yes, let's get out of here." Kid tried to usher her out with them. She didn't move.

"We're not going with you. We can't. We just can't."

"Heidi, please…"

All three snapped their heads as they heard voices outside the front door.

"We need to hide!" Kid whispered. He and Jess scampered behind the bar and crouched, but were now trapped.

Heidi did not move.

"Please, Heidi. Don't tell them we're here," he pleaded.

Jess frantically looked around. "Now how are we going to escape?"

"Heidi?" Kid repeated.

"Do you have weapons and walkie-talkies?" she asked.

"Yes."

"Give them to me."

"Wh…"

"Give them to me if you want to survive!" she snapped at whisper volume. "Fair is fair. We won't tell them you're here, but at the same time, we're not going to let you charge, or call in the cavalry either."

He so much wanted to trust her that he un-holstered his walkie-talkie and weapon, and handed them over. He turned to Jess and said, "Give her yours, hurry."

Jess stared at him in disbelief, "Are you kidding? You believe her?"

Without time for debate, Kid reached and grabbed the walkie-talkie from Jess's hand. He stuck it in Heidi's waiting palm. "Give her your gun."

Turned forward, Jess paused and then to Kid's surprise, complied without hesitation.

She dropped them into her coat pocket. "My gun! We'll have to account for that. Hand it back, quickly!" she whispered.

As Jess pulled her advanced weapon out of his pocket, Kid snagged it and paused. He realized she would have a weapon, and they were unarmed. It was a huge leap of faith. Despite the risk, he choose to hand it over. "Deal?"

She nodded as she holstered her weapon. Her fingers rested for an uncomfortably long second on the grip before letting go. Her eyes moved between Kid and Jess. Then she swiveled and hurried toward the blue hanging tarp.

Kid and Jess ducked further as the voices outside the door drew closer.

CHAPTER 44

January 8, 2045
Sunday, Morning
Mallard Island, New Jersey
Thirteen days after the event

In the kitchen of the bungalow on Mallard Island, Sara smiled as she washed the morning dishes. She mocked herself for being sappy. Kid had just left to get the map and she already missed him. Thinking of the love they made last night, she realized she needed to feel that closeness with him. She knew, and felt, how much he loved her. They were truly soulmates, and last night was a powerful reinforcement of that for the both of them.

It hurt to think he shared any of that love with Heidi, even if only briefly. And it pained her to see Kid crucifying himself for doing it. He would not say it, but she could read it in his eyes. He blamed himself for Heidi's breakdown and it weighed on his conscience. In time, Kid would understand it was unavoidable and the girl was seriously disturbed. Sara needed to help him get untangled from his self-spun web of guilt. She wished he was there with her at that moment so she could hug him and reiterate that Heidi's dark evolution was not his fault.

As she cleaned the plates and silverware, she handed them to 801, whose job was to dry them and put them in a cabinet. He seemed content in his role. In fact, he seemed content whenever he had any role and was helping out. Never once did he complain or roll his eyes. "So, 801, did you ever do the hang gliding simulation on the ships?"

“Yes. We love that one,” he said as he stacked heavy white plates in the cabinet.

“What do you think of the mainland?”

“It is fascinating and wonderful. We only wish we had a daily schedule. Our stomach hurts sometimes, and when we have no assigned tasks we do not know what to do. We have no schedule to follow.”

“Well, in those moments maybe you can think of something to do,” she suggested.

801 had a blank expression.

“For instance, the next time you have nothing to do maybe you could check the food supply and see if we need to go find more? Or, you could begin preparing the next meal, which would help your stomach too. You don’t have to wait to be assigned a task. Take the initiative to do something yourself. Try to think of things to do. Alright?” Sara patted his arm.

“Yes. We will try to think.”

Sara chuckled. “I know this world must be foreign to you, but I’m here to help. Just ask. Thanks for drying the dishes, 801. I got it from here. Jess had asked if you could help him when you were done. He’s setting up an outhouse in the shed.”

As Sara dried the final dishes, she watched out the back window. 801 passed her father and Drex, who were talking as they watched Jess. Sara’s hands stopped moving when she caught her father exhaling a cloud of cigarette smoke. For a second, she was 16 years old again.

It was a balmy evening during the summer of 2041, their last summer in Augusta, Georgia. Her father had been unusually quiet and mentally preoccupied while eating dinner. Afterward, he had stepped out back to have a smoke as he always did. She went to the sink and through the kitchen window, she saw him exhaling a cloud of cigarette smoke. She finished the dishes, but did not feel motivated to complete the rest of her chore list. She was drained from being hormonal and emotional all day. But she was also thankful because she had been able to confide in her friend's mother and get some good advice, which helped her cope.

Now standing at the sink in the bungalow, Sara realized that was the village her father was referring to in terms of helping raise her. Maybe there was some merit to his point, although growing up with a single, widowed father was not the great family structure she envisioned. She never would have said that aloud and made him feel bad. Given the circumstances, he had done his best and she loved him for it. The truth was, he needed the help of a village, especially in raising a daughter, and specifically, her.

Continuing her reflection on that one summer evening in Georgia, she had walked around the corner as her father came in the back door and they almost bumped into each other. When he looked up at her face, he actually gasped and jumped back. She was also taken aback, not from running into him, but by his reaction. The moment had always stuck with her, likely because nothing ever seemed to startle him, and he rarely went out of character in being a military officer or stern father.

"Sorry, Sara. Wait..." He took her face in his hands and seemed to be inspecting it.

"Dad, what are you doing? Am I breaking out or something?"

"You have two freckles," he said, almost absently.

"I've had them since I was 14, after I got that really bad sunburn, remember?"

Seeming to snap out of it, the general kissed her forehead. "Sorry, sweetheart. You're right, but I had never really looked that close." With his stern father voice he added, "You need to stay out of the sun."

She always recalled his behavior being strange that day. Now that she knew he was commuting all the way to the Utopia Project ships and there was a clone of her, something clicked. It took her breath away that a memory could be recast so long after the fact. It was not revisionist history, as it did not change what happened, but finding some missing piece can cast a memory in a different light. She tried to think of an analogy. It would be like discovering the Japanese did not really send Kamikaze's to crash into the ships at Pearl Harbor, but rather the plane engines stalled because of a pulse wave sent by the Americans as the enemy aircraft were approaching.

Sara now realized on that balmy evening in 2041, her father had noticed a mark on her face, two marks actually, that distinguished her from number 19 on the ships. With two Sara's in two different worlds and realities, maybe he needed such a distinction.

January 8, 2045
Sunday, Morning
Toms River, New Jersey
Thirteen days after the event

Facing the tarp, Heidi exhaled and lowered her head. She had to fully compose herself and fast. Her hand came to her heart, which was aching, and she felt like she might burst into tears. It was Kid. Seeing him again, and feeling him again, had triggered a surge of raw emotions, emotions she thought she would have to forever bury. She realized she had never fully let him go as she touched her chest. Underneath her uniform hung the arrowhead locket with Kid's picture, jewelry she was not supposed to be wearing as a member of the Utopia Project. But Kid actually came to the restaurant to seek *her* out, so he obviously still had feelings for her; strong feelings. Strong enough to risk his life. Her hand dropped protectively over her stomach. After her intimate one-night connection with Kid, she still had not had her period. There was still a chance…and then it hit her. He still had all of her, and she wanted it back. She wanted him back. But only him. Sara and her manipulative father needed to die, and the rest of the group could go to Hell with them. Heidi put her hand in her deep front pocket. She was prepared to make that happen, thanks to her slick maneuver.

Hearing her group outside the door approaching, Heidi raised her hand and grabbed the edge of the tarp. She stopped as her mind presented her with a rapid-fire series of options. She weighed them quickly and thought of the implications and required actions for each. *It might work. It just might fucking work!* She turned and looked at the bar. It would be so much easier if Jess was out of the picture and the look of disdain was wiped off of his damn face, but Kid would never forgive her if he thought she had anything to do with it.

The voices spiked in volume and clarity as the front door opened. She steeled herself, wiped her face and stood straight.

She knew what she had to do.

"Right here, Sir!" Heidi yelled out as she pushed aside the blue tarp and walked into the lobby area.

Outside the restaurant, after Heidi conferred with the elders, they were ready to leave right away. Elder-44, with Heidi's urging, ordered four members be left behind at the restaurant in case any survivors wound up coming there. At first, Elder-44 assigned the other junior elder, Sid Sherman, to stay behind. Heidi jumped in immediately and convinced the ranking elder that Sid needed to stay with the larger group. She had whispered, "He is too unstable to be left with such a small group." Fortunately, Elder-44 saw her point and acquiesced. In truth, she was concerned Sid would take vengeance for his brother's death and kill Kid on sight. Elder-44 then assigned Elder-101 to stay behind with three other regular members.

Turning to Elder-101 and three members who were to watch the restaurant, Elder-44's orders were clear. He wanted one person on each side of the building, hidden from sight. If survivors approached, they were to be captured and detained. If there was great resistance, then the elder and members were authorized to fire their weapons. Given that Elder-101 had three vials of antidote, some survivors were to be revived and bound so they could be interrogated.

Heidi was pleased. Since she took Kid and Jess's weapons, they would be captured, and not killed. That was essential to her plan. As she walked up to Elder-101 and the three members, she said, "If for some reason survivors are shot, and one is a younger man around 21 years old with long brown hair, make sure he is revived. He is one of their leaders and will have much information, which would be most useful."

"Yes, Junior Elder-2," Elder-101 responded.

"And some of them are sneaky bastards so keep your eyes on every direction, left, right, up, down, *front, behind…*"

"We know how to handle a stakeout," the elder said tersely.

Elder-44 called out, "Get in the vehicles. Let's move!"

Heidi said, "We will be right back. We left something in the restaurant."

"Hurry!" he ordered.

"Listen, Kid," Jess snap whispered while they were hiding behind the bar, "I know you feel bad about it, but she's lost it! You couldn't feel her anger?"

"Quiet. We won't have to worry about her betraying us with how loud you are!"

"At least we will be armed again."

"What do you mean?" Kid asked.

Jess pointed to a shelf under the bar. "Why do you think I gave up my weapon so easily?" Resting conspicuously on the top shelf were three handguns. "Remember we brought all those weapons from the police station and the jail and stuck them back here? We had more weapons than people, so there are still a few left. With how long Heidi was behind the bar, how did she miss these?" Jess asked as he pulled out a 38-caliber handgun, made sure it was loaded and handed it over.

Good question, Kid thought as he put the gun in his pocket.

After checking the second pistol, Jess said, "Also fully loaded." He flipped open the cylinder of the third revolver and dumped the five bullets into his palm. He pocketed two of them, and handed the other three to Kid. "For when you need to reload."

They both froze as the front door of the restaurant opened. "Kid!" Heidi whispered.

Kid and Jess stuffed the extra bullets in their coat pockets and scooted back.

Heidi leaned over the bar and whispered, "Stay here and don't move. We're inspecting the area between here and Good Luck Point Marina, but for only two hours at the most. We have to get back to the ships because they're starting to move them south down the coast today. So stay put until we leave the area."

"Stay put, meaning right here? Behind the bar?" Kid asked.

"Yes. You need to stay out of sight and stay quiet. They don't know you are in here, but four of our members are being left outside in case your group were to come back to the restaurant. We will pick our members up in a couple of hours and then you can go back to wherever you and the group are holed up. You got it?"

"Yes, we'll stay here," he responded. "I'm trusting you, alright?"

She looked at him with conflicting emotions running across her face. He saw sympathy and maybe even love, but he hoped he did not see an apology. "Would *I* betray *you*?" She was unable to disguise the pain in her voice. Her nostrils flared and she appeared to be fighting some turmoil inside as she turned and headed out the door. He also noticed she had slipped and used the long vowel, 'I.'

"We can't trust her!" Jess whispered. "We need to get the hell out of here!"

"She's upset, but she won't betray us," Kid answered as they heard vehicles pulling away.

While they waited behind the bar inside the restaurant, time seemed to drag. For every minute that passed, Jess seemed exponentially more restless. Kid checked his watch, "An hour has already passed. And don't worry, with how much area they have to search, and if they are following all the tire tracks Drex and I laid around town, they won't even get near the part of the county where the group is."

Jess did not seem to find any comfort in his words. "I'll be right back."

"Hey, where are you going?" Kid called after him.

"To look out the window back in the kitchen. Don't worry. I'll stay low."

Sitting against the cabinet behind the bar, Kid was tapping his fingers on his knees. With hazy daylight coming in through a side window, he noticed portions of the area behind the bar were now illuminated. At that moment Kid spotted many glasses under the bar. They were lined up, row after row in their stacked plastic dishwashing bins. As he leaned back and took in a wider view, it seemed there were glasses everywhere. *Heidi didn't look very hard.* He then began to ponder, but the moment was interrupted by Jess's voice.

"Something just doesn't feel right," Jess said as he returned to the bar.

"Take it easy. We have less than an hour to go. Anyway, what is the harm in waiting for a bit?"

Jess turned to him. "Because we're banking on *Heidi's* word."

January 8, 2045

Sunday, Late Morning

Mallard Island, New Jersey

Thirteen days after the event

General Eric Hyland stared out the sliding glass door on the top floor of the mermaid house. He could only keep watch with the aid of the naked eye since it was still too early in the day to use the telescope, but at the moment, it was enough. With his elevated view, he spotted the very top of three slow moving, gray-colored vessels over the low buildings on the island. He knew the ships would turn soon to moor off of Long Beach Island. The general picked up his walkie-talkie and reached out to his father in the bungalow, "All three ships are heading down the coast, and coming our way!"

"On my way over. I want to see this," Chris radioed back.

Barely a moment later, his father walked in the room.

"Did they anchor yet?" Chris asked as others filed in behind him.

"No, they are just pulling closer to shore now." Watching other survivors still walking into the room, Chris asked, "Did the whole group come over?"

"All except Karen and Drex. They're cooking so they stayed back. Everyone's abuzz about the ships moving down here and you can't see anything from the bungalow."

The group watched the creeping ships out the back door and from any available window.

"Any word from Kid and Jess?" Chris asked.

General Hyland shook his head. "No."

"Wait, one of the red trucks from the marina just pulled up in front of the other house. It must be them!" Wendy said as she peered out a side window. She looked relieved.

General Hyland turned his attention away from the ships.

Wendy stepped onto the balcony. "Kid! We're over here!" she yelled as she leaned over the rail and waved her hand.

As the general stepped to the threshold of the balcony sliding door, he saw Wendy's face. Her expression turned from relief to horror, and she screamed at the top of her lungs.

Inside the small house, Heidi was flustered. She finished tying Karen Stone's hands behind her back and demanded, "Where are they?"

"I have no idea," Karen answered. "Maybe they are over on the mainland."

"Then who is across the street?"

"Nobody I know of."

"Lying bitch," Heidi said and shoved Karen hard into the wall.

Karen gasped and tried to catch her breath as she fell to the ground next to Drex, who also had his hands bound.

"The rooms are all empty!" Elder-44 yelled as he walked back into the living room. "Other than these two," he pointed at Karen and Drex, "the bulk of the group is not in here, including Elder-41. We could only use the element of surprise once." His voice was gravelly as he snapped, "And it was wasted!"

"The vehicles outside this shithole are definitely theirs. Didn't you see the Vermont plate on the black SUV? How could we know they would not be in here?" Heidi knew her frustration was accentuating her Brooklyn accent, but she couldn't help it. She was too aggravated. Without sharing Kid and Jess's whereabouts, she spotted their truck parked near the restaurant, and it was her idea to take it. She now knew where the survivors were hiding, and by approaching with the familiar red marina truck, she thought she could hold the element of surprise a few moments longer.

Heidi's face was hot as she stared out the window. "The scream came from the third floor balcony of that tall house on the other side of the street and we saw people scurrying around. The rest of them must be there. And if they won't come out…" she pointed to Karen and Drex sitting on the floor, "…we have hostages to *draw* them out."

"That may be our only saving grace," Elder-44 responded and turned. "All eyes on that house across the street. Everyone open a window and be prepared to fire!" Doing a headcount, he muttered, "Only eight of us. We need the rest of our forces. That will triple our numbers." He proceeded to radio the other two vans waiting at the bridge to the island. He gave them quick directions and told them to get there immediately.

Heidi gazed at the tall house catty-corner across the street. She spotted a person on the top balcony and muttered, "It's that woman from Vermont. Wendy." She watched as Wendy stepped further outside and left herself completely exposed. Heidi hissed and pointed, "Up there!"

Elder-44 barked, "Top of target house! Fire!" Bolts erupted from the street and the living room windows.

The return fire was immediate as gun shots rang out from the tall house.

General Hyland was preparing to lead a final stand at the mermaid house. He and the others had spread out among the second and third levels and had taken up positions at windows and balcony doors. After the enemy launched a hail of bolts at them, he gave the command and everyone fired just one bullet at the bungalow. They had to use their ammunition sparingly as the general knew they would lose the battle of attrition in that regard. The enemy had the Medusa firearm, which had nearly unlimited ammunition, and the batteries inside would last for months. As an elder himself, the general had the lone Medusa firearm in his group. But he knew his weapon would not be enough, especially since all elders on such a mission, including Elder-44, would have three vials of the antidote.

The general still had three antidote vials from his last mission, when he was sent to eliminate the New Jersey and Vermont survivors. He touched the vials affixed to his belt to ensure they were still there. He prayed he would never need them, but a second later, that hope was dashed.

V:
REDEMPTION

CHAPTER 45

January 8, 2045
Sunday, Midday
Mallard Island, New Jersey
Thirteen days after the event

James screamed, "Mr. Hyland! Help! Wendy's been hit!"

That means the clock is ticking! The general hurried up to the third level. Sara and James were dragging Wendy's rigid body in from the balcony. She had a visible gash on the side of her head.

James was a bundle of nerves and couldn't stop talking. "She was shot in the chest and she fell straight into the balcony rail. She nearly tumbled over. If her center of gravity was a little higher she would have. . . ."

"James, get something to cover the wound on her head, a towel, shirt, anything," the general said as he uncapped one of his three antidote vials and stuck Wendy in the thigh. Gasping for breath, Wendy's hands trembled as she reached for her throat. "Easy, don't panic. Breath slow," the general coached.

When her heart came alive, the cut above her ear did as well and blood started pumping out. James balled up a pillowcase and held it to the wound.

As Wendy was recovering, Sara stepped out the balcony door and crouched down. She stuck the tip of her gun past the corner of the house and in an instant a bolt hit the balcony rail in front of her.

"Stay inside!" the general called as he stood.

Stepping back into the room, Sara muttered, "I wanted to see what was going on over at the bungalow. I hope Karen and Drex saw the soldiers coming and were able to hide away."

"Let's hope," her father said. "And where the hell are Kid and Jess?"

"I was just wondering the same thing," she replied.

"I'm heading back down." Turning to James, the general added, "Wendy will be fine, but stay with her. It will take a few minutes for her to fully recover."

He rushed downstairs to resume his position two floors below. He saw Melanie and her two daughters stepping into the kitchen pantry. Her girls appeared frightened and she was trying to calm them.

Melanie asked, "Is Wendy alright?"

"Yes, she'll recover." He reached into the pantry and grabbed a few packs of gum from an upper shelf. Bending down, he handed them to the girls. "This is special gum. As long as you chew it, you have special protection."

Katy looked excited, and then deflated. "My mom won't let us chew gum yet."

"Yeah, not even the sugar free kind!" her sister, Karly, chimed in.

"I'm old enough, but Karly, you're way too young to chew gum." Turning to the general, she clarified, "She's only five."

"So. You're only six!" her younger sister responded with puckered lips.

Reaching for the gum, Melanie seemed exasperated. "Today, and today only, you both can have gum."

Turning to the general, the girls said, "Thank you!"

"You are welcome. Now just sit tight for a little while." While walking away, the general felt a tug on the back of his coat. Turning, Katy Spatz stood behind him and held out a piece of gum. She smiled, displaying the gap where one of her front teeth had come out.

"Thanks, sweetheart." He took the stick of gum. "Now get back in the pantry with your mommy."

Running up to a front window next to his father, the general put the stick of gum in his mouth. "Any movement?"

"Not at the moment. Seems we're at a standstill," Chris answered.

"Wendy got hit and I had to revive her. I'm now down to two vials of antidote."

"Jesus. Lucky you were able to revive her. We need to be disciplined and maintain our cover. They're probably just waiting for us to get sloppy and impatient and step into the line of fire."

"Why don't they rush us? If they did, we might be able to pick some of them off," Dr. McDermott said with his Irish accent, while standing next to another window across the room.

"That's precisely why they are not," the general stated.

"Son, what would you do if you were them?" Chris asked as he contemplated. "I know what I would do." He seemed to be reflecting on his days as a military leader.

"Well, since we're trapped here, I would keep us at a standoff, while calling in heavy artillery," the general said.

"Did they have any heavy artillery on the ships?"

"No. It was never considered necessary. We always had enough to defend ourselves in case hostiles, like pirates, tried to take the ships, but that was primarily just shoulder-launched missiles and Medusa firearms."

"Alright, if not artillery, I would maintain the standoff and at least call in troop reinforcements," Chris concluded. Still pondering, he added, "Speaking of troops, since the ships are off of Long Beach Island now, I'm going upstairs to see if any are mobilizing over there."

"Elder-41!" called a voice from outside. The general remained silent, and seemed unsure as to who was calling his name. He was listening closely when he heard again, "Elder-41, acknowledge!" He groaned, now knowing the big mouth it came from.

"What do you want, Elder-44?" General Hyland yelled back from a window in the mermaid house.

"Before it is too late, end this defiance! Bring out your group and surrender. You cannot win this, and you know that." The voice was coming from an open window over at the bungalow.

"We'll see. It's not over yet!"

"It will be, you traitor! For the crimes you've committed against this project and the world, we will shoot you on sight!" Elder-44 shouted.

"We'll see about that too!"

Chris looked concerned as he came back downstairs. "They are mobilizing reinforcements which is probably why they aren't charging us yet. I watched a group march to the base of the Route 72 bridge and then I lost sight of them. I know they haven't crossed yet, but we better come up with something quick."

"Hey, everyone!" Dr. McDermott called out. "More vehicles just pulled up to the bungalow, but I don't think it is Kid and Jess!"

Heidi was watching out the window when the two vans pulled to a stop behind the red marina truck in front of the house. One was being driven by Elder-77 and the other by Sid Sherman. Elder-44 shouted instructions from a window. He advised them that cover fire would be provided while they exited the vehicle and crawled to the house. Elder-77 and the seven members in his van reached the house safely. The other van emptied and followed suit.

As soon as Sid came through the door, Karen burst into tears. He walked right over, crouched down, and licked her cheek. Rubbing his head, he said, "Trust me, you're going to pay for that pistol-whipping back at the lodge in Killington." He lifted his arm as if to backhand her.

Heidi grabbed his wrist. "We may still need her so keep your hands off."

"Yeah, we may still *need* her…again." Sid stood and grabbed his crotch. Karen pressed her legs together.

"Enough!" Elder-44 snapped. "Are these hostages still useful or not?"

"Yes, Sir," Heidi said. "We can use these hostages, especially this bitch, to draw out the one person in particular who she is close to. Her friend, Sara Hyland, is the real heart of their group. If we can kill Sara, then they lose the glue that holds them all together."

"Sara? You wouldn't," Karen uttered with an expression of disgust.

Heidi backhanded her hard across the face. "Shut your mouth! There's nothing special about her."

Karen's face was raw and red, and she appeared stunned.

"Hey, you said we may need her! We could have done that," Sid commented, which garnered a scowl from Heidi. He turned to Elder-44. "What about this old guy? Why are we keeping him alive? It just leaves us with someone else to worry about."

Elder-44 looked at Heidi. "We were told both of these hostages would be useful."

"It's only Karen you really need, right, Heidi?" Sid asked.

With her new, ever-present feelings of disgust and anger, Heidi walked back over to the front window and while peering out, she answered, "Of course it's Karen we need. She and Sara Hyland were really tight. With her as bait, we may be able to draw Sara out in the open."

Grabbing a fistful of Drex's coat, Sid asked, "So what about this old scumbag?"

She shrugged and said, "Not as useful, although he and Kid were getting kind of chummy."

"Kid's buddy huh?' Sid's face turned bright red as he pulled out his Medusa firearm. "Then this is for you, Kid, and for what you did to my bro!" he snapped as he stuck his weapon in Drex's gut.

"Wait…" Elder-44 started, then his walkie-talkie came to life. Elder-2 was calling from the base of the Route 72 bridge, and said she had a plan. Heidi overheard the entire conversation, and loved the idea. Something had to be done to take out Sara and the group across the street and end this. She noticed Elder-44 had a blood-thirsty smile as he crouched next to an open window and took aim at the roof of the mermaid house.

The general was perplexed. "What are they aiming at?"

From the window, Chris answered, "They appear to be firing at… our roof? And it can't be by accident, because they keep firing over and over."

"Then it's not by accident. But why would they do that?" A chill ran down the general's spine.

"Wait, they just stopped. Maybe they were firing warning shots," Chris said.

The general stared over at the bungalow. "What happened to the members they had positioned in the windows? The living room looks empty over there."

"Where did they go?" Chris asked.

"And just as importantly, why did they go?" The general's voice conveyed his sense of dread. He thought for a second and muttered, "It's like they're…" His eyes opened wide and he grabbed his father's arm and pulled him away from the windows, "…taking cover!"

Elder-2 stood at the top of the tallest arch of the Route 72 bridge. As she watched bolts hitting the roof of a tall house on the tiny island, she pointed. "We have our target. Are we locked?"

The member crouched next to her said, "Affirmative." He had a tube resting on his shoulder with the other half resting on top of the bridge's sidewall.

"Fire!"

Elder-2 heard a loud whooshing sound, and then followed the thin stream of smoke as the missile arced over the water toward the island. The missile dove at the last minute and exploded as it hit the bottom of the house. The structure began to topple over and Elder-2 felt a growing thrill. The action appeared to be happening in slow motion as the house fell on its side. With a bone-jarring crash, the roof and soffits of the house hit the ground and shattered on impact. It took a second for the sound of the crash to reach the bridge. The sound reverberated off the water in every direction, as if a multitude of crashes were happening in quick succession. Elder-2 could no longer see the house, which was a sign of success. She could not be more pleased with the result of the first strike.

CHAPTER 46

January 8, 2045
Sunday, Early Afternoon
Mallard Island, New Jersey
Thirteen days after the event

Inside the smoky and hazy collapsed house, the general checked himself for injuries. His body hurt everywhere and he had cuts and scrapes in too many places to count. But as he moved his arms and legs while sitting on the ground, he concluded he had no significant wounds. He was lucky. He was only able to take a few steps toward an interior hallway before the explosion, but those steps saved his life as he would have been crushed by a China Cabinet. Katherine Ryan next to him had not been so lucky. Rolling over and getting to a knee, the general met his father's eyes. "Are you alright?"

"Yeah, although my back is pulled," Chris groaned as his son helped him up.

"Dad!" Sara yelled.

"Sara? Thank God." The general felt overwhelming relief. He searched for his daughter, but was disoriented because the house was on its side. He spotted her peering down from the entrance to the stairwell ten feet above his head. The stairs used to end at the floor, but like rolling over a square box, that floor was now one of the side walls. He called up to her, "Gramps and I are alright down here. Where is your grandmother?"

"Gram is in the bathroom. She's catching her breath and is shaken up, but she seems alright."

"I will get her in a minute. You come down now. We need your help." The general walked over until he stood below her. "Lower yourself down and I will catch you."

With great agility, she did just that. Her father caught her and said, "Help get everyone out the back of the house. And be alert in case they attack from across the street."

Dr. McDermott was putting his cracked glasses in his shirt pocket and was standing next to 801.

"Doc! Help me lift this China Cabinet, and then we'll go find your family," the general instructed. Dr. McDermott and 801 lifted the heavy unit while the general pulled Katherine Ryan's body from underneath. "I've got it from here," the general said, but Dr. McDermott was already on his knees checking for a pulse. He shook his head.

Rick Ryan crawled over and screamed in agony as he pushed past Dr. McDermott. "Kat! Come on, Kat!" he yelled while shaking his wife's body.

"I'm sorry," the doctor said as he got to his feet. "I need to find my family," he added and took off.

"Where's my son!" Rick yelled.

"We'll find him," the general assured him.

Without hesitation, they began searching the rest of that level. Following Rick and stepping over piles of rubble, the general could see a large section of floor and one entire corner of the house on the other side of the room had been blown away by the impact of the missile. With the house tipped over, the floor was now a wall with a large hole in it. As the general approached the opening, the top edge was still aflame, but he could see the entire first level had been decimated. Splintered pieces of wood that were once part of the house frame smoldered on the ground. Visible were the pilings the house used to sit atop, two of which had been blown in half. Beyond, he saw glimpses of the bay and the northern end of Long Beach Island.

He did not see any members outside so he peered down at Rick, who was lifting an upside down desk. Crouching next to him, the general asked, "Do you see anything?"

Without answering, Rick rolled the desk over and revealed a body underneath. The general cringed upon seeing the face of 705, who appeared to be dead. Stepping around Rick to get a better view, he noticed one of 705's legs was a bloody, mangled stump ending just above the knee. The general turned away and just by chance his eyes caught something else. On the ground, although dirty and blending in with the surroundings, small fingertips could be seen sticking out from a pile of debris. He stepped over and moved some larger pieces of wood. "Dammit," he said as he hung his head.

Rick heard him and rushed over. Nothing could soften the blow that was about to come so the general just moved aside. On the ground was the lifeless body of 11-year-old Robert Ryan. As soon as Rick Ryan saw his son's body, he went wild with grief. It was tragic enough for him that he had lost his wife, but the double-loss proved to be too much. The general tried to console him, but it was no use. "Wait!" he called as Rick took off and jumped outside through the gaping hole in the wall. The general looked out the now-horizontal strip of transparent glass next to the front door and knocked out the few remaining shards. "He's storming the bungalow," he muttered, sounding forlorn.

Rick fired with every step until he was out of ammunition. He threw his empty gun at the door as he ran up the steps.

The general stuck the tip of his weapon through the narrow glass opening and fired at the open windows of the bungalow. He was helpless as he watched Rick take a shot to the chest from Elder-44, who appeared in one of the windows for just a second before ducking back. Rick's body fell forward and hit one of the columns holding up the front porch. His shoulder glanced off the pole, causing his form to spin and fall backward onto the steps. As the body turned, the general saw the expression frozen on Rick's face. It was a portrait of excruciating pain and torment, a snapshot taken at the peak of someone's grief. It was a visual the general would never be able to erase from his memory.

Turning away, he said in a solemn voice, "At least he's with his wife and child now." As he walked to the back of the house, the general muttered, "I can't say I wouldn't have done the same thing." Climbing outside, his foot crunched the balcony sliding door's broken glass and he saw the Moore's, 801, Sara, and Maria. He turned his head toward the sky, looking for another missile.

"Dad! James didn't make it, and Wendy won't leave!" Sara called over.

"We'll get her, but for now, watch out for an…"

He paused upon hearing Elder-44 yell from across the street, "Attack! Now!"

"Ambush!" the general finished as enemy members stormed around the corners of both sides of the house. "Fire!"

Fortunately, the group was prepared. Clarence and Marissa opened fire as a group of members emerged through the wisps of smoke from one side of the smoldering structure.

At the other end of the house, the general watched as Sara stood shoulder to shoulder with Maria and both started shooting. They quickly took out two of the approaching members but missed the third. The general started running in their direction as the third member raised his weapon, and it was aimed right at Sara.

January 8, 2045

Sunday, Early Afternoon

Toms River, New Jersey

Thirteen days after the event

It took much effort on Kid's part, but they stuck it out for the full two hours. Jess was like a caged animal, ready to spring free. Looking outside, they did not see any sign of vehicles coming to pick up the soldiers left at the restaurant. "Give it just a few minutes!" Kid said to Jess. "Once the soldiers are picked up, we have a clear run down to

Mallard Island. It's a better option than taking on four armed soldiers unnecessarily."

Five minutes later, Jess couldn't take it anymore. "We are getting out of here." Crawling out the narrow side opening of the bar, he stopped short. He pointed to the silhouette of a crouching soldier behind the drawn window blinds. "See, still there."

Kid checked his watch one more time. He hoped Heidi's group was just running late, but he started feeling an ache in his gut so he jumped to his feet. "We need to see where all four of those soldiers are posted. See where they are, and look for weapons and walkie-talkies."

For the next few minutes, the guys looked out the front door and every window. Reconvening in the dining room, they determined one soldier was posted on each side of the building. The one on the west side was sitting on a bench just outside the front door. He was much older and appeared to be one of their 'elders.'

"We have to get to the footbridge at Huddy Park so we can get back to our truck," Jess said. "I don't think we can get around them, so we need to take them out. But the first two should be easy because we have the element of surprise. Just open the front and back door at the same time and shoot them in the back. It is the other two we have to worry about."

"That could work, but we have to take out the elder at the front door right away. He's the only one with a walkie-talkie, and we can't let him radio out that we are here. I'll take him. You take the one at the back door," Kid said.

Jess nodded.

"Then close the door, and wait for another one to come see what is going on, and take him out too."

"If this actually works, we might be able to take out all four soldiers without even leaving the restaurant." Jess sounding encouraged.

"Then we can simply waltz down to our truck and drive away," Kid noted.

Following the plan, Kid headed for the front door. Pulling the tarp back enough to sneak past, Kid turned and signaled to Jess. Five second countdown. When he reached zero, Kid cracked open the front door slowly and stepped out. As the elder went to turn, Kid fired and hit him in the forehead. Simultaneously, he heard Jess's shot at the back of the restaurant. Closing the door, Kid left just a sliver so he could see any member that came over. He didn't have long to wait.

A soldier ran onto the porch and said to the elder, "Sir? What are our orders?"

Kid was concerned he would lose the draw as the soldier had a weapon in his hand. Recalling the word conditioning that triggered the soldiers slipping into a trance-like state, and had saved their lives once before, Kid stepped out and yelled, "*Ion!*" He knew his tone was wrong the moment the word left his lips, but for a second the soldier paused. That second was just enough. Kid fired as the soldier was raising his weapon. Despite being hit in the chest, the member started firing randomly as he fell backward on the porch. Kid dove in through the open door. He then heard Jess's second shot. Getting up, Kid ran into the dining room. "Mission accomplished?" Kid asked.

"Yes. Like a charm," Jess said as he took the two extra bullets from his coat pocket and stuck them in the cylinder of his revolver. "Might as well be fully loaded."

Kid followed suit, but after replacing the two bullets he had just used, he still had one bullet left in his pocket. Holstering his weapon, he said, "Let's get out of here."

The guys jogged across the footbridge in Huddy Park and headed south. Jess huffed, "I can't believe that went perfectly according to plan. We took out the four soldiers without leaving the restaurant, and were able to simply waltz down to our…" He stopped. "Where's our truck?"

"Dammit." Kid bent over and tried to catch his breath. "They must have taken it."

The guys continued jogging down the road. They came to an adult video shop with a few cars in the parking lot. The door wasn't locked, but the place smelled of death. Kid walked past a few peep show booths that were clearly occupied, creating a mess far more disgusting than the usual splatter of bodily fluid. Just inside the entrance of a booth, he found a pair of pants, and fortunately, a set of car keys.

As Jess drove a small grey sedan, he muttered, "We can't stop for anything until we get there, or we'll probably get stuck. No four-wheel drive."

Kid turned to him. "Keep your eyes open. That group has to be out here somewhere." He again checked his watch. "They might just be running late heading back to the ships."

"You still believe that?" Jess asked.

Hesitating, Kid said, "I'm not sure what I believe anymore."

While driving, Jess commented, "Jeez, how many laps did Drex do before coming down to Mallard Island?

"He was gone forever that day," Kid noted. "So I assume many."

"He certainly laid enough tracks."

A short while later, Kid repeated, "*Ion*!" He turned to his friend. "That's the tone."

Jess gazed at him with a combination of agitation and curiosity.

"I just needed to practice. I tried yelling the word back at Water Street and my tone was off. It almost cost me my life."

After a pause, Jess checked his watch and whistled. "Look at the time. They are probably wondering what is taking us so long."

Kid settled back in his seat and said, "I wouldn't worry about them missing us. I'm sure they are keeping busy."

January 8, 2045

Sunday, Early Afternoon

Mallard Island, New Jersey

Thirteen days after the event

"*Ion*!" the general yelled as the remaining member went to fire his weapon at Sara. The word made the member collapse, but not before pulling the trigger. Fortunately, the word also affected Sara. She wobbled and dropped to a knee and the shot went just over her shoulder.

"That was close," the general huffed. He grabbed his daughter's hand as she got to her feet.

"Help!" Clarence called out.

General Hyland snapped his head around to see Clarence holding 801's wrist, trying to push a pistol away. For the defense of the mermaid house, the general had decided 801 could also now have a firearm. *Damn! Why did I take that chance?* He sprinted across the back of the house. "*Ion*!" the general yelled again as 801 pulled the trigger.

Clarence saved his own life by pushing 801's arm as the shot was fired. The bullet went wide, nearly clipping the general, as 801 collapsed to the ground in a heap from the word conditioning.

Sara ran over and asked, "What happened with 801? He turned on us?"

"Yes. He tried to shoot Clarence. I had to intervene."

"Why would he do that? He's on our side now."

"It was Elder-44's attack order," the general said with assurance. "801's conditioning kicked in and he automatically complied with the order."

"He's still one of us. Even if we have to tie him up, can we save him?" she pleaded.

"If I hurry…" The general knelt next to 801, who was slipping further and further away, and he uttered the magic word that reversed the word conditioning, "*Fleson*." 801's trance was broken but he stayed on his back, panting. The general knew a prolonged trance would cancel any current orders and 801 was now unarmed, so he turned to check on Clarence. "Are you alright?"

"Yes. More shocked and saddened than anything else," he answered as he helped 801 into a sitting position

801's body was weak everywhere and he was tired. His breaths were heavy. As he looked into Clarence's eyes, he felt something he had never felt before and was having difficulty identifying. He felt a dull ache in his stomach, and it was not from hunger.

He had raised his weapon upon receiving an attack order. Clarence was the enemy. He had tried to eradicate him and could not stop himself, but for the first time in his life, he felt unsure about carrying out an order. This had never happened before and he did not know what it meant.

He knew he had interacted too often with Clarence individually over the past few days, which was simply not allowed. After feeling uncomfortable, he had tried to avoid individual interaction with him, but could not.

"I know he didn't really want to shoot me. It was the attack order that got to him. I could see the conflict in his eyes," Clarence said.

801 wanted to say something, but he could not find the words. This had never happened before either. This world was causing him to act in a strange manner. He finally said the only words he knew to convey what he was feeling. "We are glad you are alive."

"Yes, we are," Clarence repeated as he patted 801's shoulder.

801 felt better. The ache in his stomach was subsiding.

CHAPTER 47

January 8, 2045
Sunday, Early Afternoon
Mallard Island, New Jersey
Thirteen days after the event

"I'm fine," Clarence assured the general while making sure his weapon was fully loaded. "I'll keep guarding this side. But someone needs to cover the other side."

Turning to Sara and Maria, the general said, "You two go back over there and stand guard on that side of the house. I'm going in to get your grandparents and Wendy."

The general ran into the shattered house and called out, "Dad!"

"Over here!" Chris yelled back. "We need to get your mother down." He pointed up.

Evelyn peeked down over the edge. "Eric?"

"Mom!" She was ten feet off the ground, and couldn't just jump like Sara. "Let me find something to get you down." The general searched for anything that could be used as a ladder, and saw a bookcase laying on the ground. Wendy was on her knees next to it, and her hands were moving slow as she sifted through the debris on the floor.

Chris whispered, "Be gentle. James is underneath."

The general waded through broken pictures, a flat screen monitor, books, and pieces of furniture. As he reached down to lift the fallen bookcase, he said, "Wendy? You should go."

Wendy's voice sounded hollow. "Everything fell on him. Everything." She had multiple scrapes and contusions on her arms. The gash above her ear had reopened and a stream of blood ran down her face.

"We have to get out of here fast." The general strained to lift the bookcase. He stood it upright, revealing a battered body. James' eyes were open but unseeing and his skull was bloodied. Wendy crawled over and pulled James's limp body across her lap. She began crying while she rocked back and forth. The general crouched down and could see James was very much dead.

It was then he noticed Wendy's ankle was bent at an unnatural angle. "You're hurt." General Hyland pointed at her twisted foot. She did not respond so he touched her shoulder and said, "Take a moment with James while I get my mother."

He slid the bookcase over and stood it against the wall. It was four feet short, so the general used his elbow to make holes in the sheet-rock. Like a climbing wall, he used the holes to scale the last few feet. "Mom, are you alright?"

"Yes. I'm bruised but I survived because I was in the bathroom. If I was in my bed, I would've been crushed by the big dresser in there," she said. "I've seen a lot of things in my life, but never anything like this. Is everyone else alright?" she asked.

"Dad and Sara are fine, but some of the others are not. Some have perished."

"May they rest in peace," she whispered.

The general helped his mother climb slowly down to the ground. Chris hugged her and took her hand. "We need to move outside."

"Go ahead. I'll catch up in a minute," the general said as he turned around to get Wendy. She was still holding James and rocking. He grabbed her arm. "Come on, Wendy. We have to go." She did not flinch or respond. She was in shock. He took the opportunity to solve two problems at once. He reached down, grabbed her foot, and twisted hard. The sickening muffled pop made him cringe as he reset her ankle.

Wendy yelped and pulled back her foot, her face turning red. "Son of a bitch!" she yelled between shrieks of pain and agony. Reaching over James's body and squeezing her ankle, tears streamed from her eyes. With her face contorted from the pain, she screeched, "What the hell is wrong with you?"

The general carefully moved James's body and lifted Wendy over his shoulder. She struggled for a few seconds, but gave up and fell limp as he carried her outside. He lowered her down gently on the carpet of small rounded stones comprising the entirety of the tiny backyard. Next to her, a dazed but functioning Dylan McDermott held his semi-conscious sister while their mother Pamela tended to a wound on Megan's scalp.

Sara ran over and grabbed her father's arm. "Dad, where are Melanie and the girls?"

"They never came out of the house? They must still be in the pantry! Come on." The general started running and Sara followed.

As they re-entered the smoky and hazy mermaid house, they jumped up and crawled along the short, but now sideways, hallway toward the kitchen. The general stopped when the pantry door was right above his head. "Melanie? Girls?" he yelled up.

"Help!" he heard one of the little girls cry out.

Pointing up, the general whispered, "As soon as we turn the knob, the door is going to fall open." Sara nodded.

"We're going to open the door…" he called loudly.

"No! Don't! Mommy is sleeping on the door."

The general got in position, braced himself and said, "Open it."

Sara reached up and turned the knob. The latch released and her father flexed as the door pushed down on his shoulders. He grunted and let the door down slow.

The girls started screaming.

"It's alright girls! I've got your mommy," Sara said as a whole army of food cans rolled out. She dodged most of them and then her father snapped, "Watch it!" as she almost grabbed the jagged edge of a broken flower-patterned vase. She let it fall to the floor and pushed the heavy chunk of glass aside with her foot.

A red stream trickled off the edge of the door and the general's concern grew in proportion to the expanding puddle of blood at his daughter's feet.

"It's alright girls. We're here to help." Sara tried to sound calm and reassuring.

The girls' screams were reduced to whimpers.

"Now, I'm going to start by helping your mommy." She grabbed Melanie and laid her on the floor. "Dad, you can let it down."

Finally. I couldn't hold it much longer. The general moved back and let the door fall open.

Sara placed her foot over the puddle of blood, clearly trying to hide it. She then reached inside the pantry and helped Katy and Karly to the floor, which was actually the wall. The girls sat next to their mother.

Katy Spatz looked up at the general and waved him down. Cupping her hands, she whispered, "The special protection gum only works if you chew it. Mommy put it in her pocket."

The general was still panting as he put his arm around her and said, "I see. You're Mommy will be alright, but we need to get her outside."

The little girls followed them up the hall as the general and Sara carried Melanie's body. General Hyland was crouched over the whole way and his back was feeling it. Once they reached the end of short hall, the general took the limp body on his shoulders and headed outside.

Melanie's body was laid on the ground and Dr. McDermott ran over. Maintaining his doctor face, he checked her vital signs. "Still going." The general realized he was choosing his words carefully in front of the girls. Examining her body, the doctor found a cut and a lump on her head.

"What happened?" The doctor asked as he checked the girls for injuries.

"Something really big fell on us," Karly said.

Katy chimed in, "Yeah. Mom!"

The general and Dr. McDermott turned to each other and both pursed their lips. "She probably draped herself over her daughters to protect them," the general suggested.

"My presumption as well," the doctor agreed. "Wait, she's coming to," he added as Melanie moaned and reached for her head.

Thank God, General Hyland thought. *In a world like this, what would these poor girls do without their mother?*

Unable to eradicate the survivors, Elder-44's frustration continued to mount. In expecting the mission to now be a quick mop up, he wound up losing nearly half of his members in the attack on the fallen house across the street. He thought the screaming lunatic who charged over was representative of the mental state of the remaining survivors, if any were left at all. He had concluded they must be weak, injured, and disheveled. It was a big miscalculation on his part. Putting the walkie-talkie to his lips, he said, "Elder-2! Commence launch of second missile!"

"Elder-44, with the house toppled and with the smoke, we can't see its precise location," Elder-2 answered. "And we only have one missile left."

"We must continue the offensive. The enemy is still responsive and they have defenses."

"Then we should launch the last missile from in closer, where our strike can be more precise. We are coming down to finish this, but it will take us a few minutes to get there. With all of the marsh grass we see over there, they could easily sneak around you. Pull back and set up a position on the small bridge to that island, and maintain your containment of the enemy until we arrive. We are on the Route 72 bridge and will be there soon," Elder-2 said.

"Yes, Ma'am." As soon as Elder-44 released the talk button, he yelled, "Out the back! Run behind the houses and head for the small

ing desperate as the general uncapped a vial and stuck Karen in the thigh. Sara started chest compressions.

Feeling Karen's face, and then pushing up her pants and grabbing her ankle, the general said, "With how warm she is, she could not have been shot more than a couple of minutes ago."

Karen's mouth slowly closed and she muttered, "Oww," and grabbed the hand pushing on her chest. Her eyes blinked and she looked around.

Dr. McDermott ran into the room. Seeing Karen was revived, he went over to Drex's body.

The general came over and pulled out his last antidote vial, ready to administer it. After a quick evaluation, the doctor put up his hand and said with a somber voice, "Don't waste it. He's been gone too long. Way too long."

Still holding Drex's cold, dead hand, Maria began to cry.

CHAPTER 48

January 8, 2045
Sunday, Afternoon
Mallard Island, New Jersey
Thirteen days after the event

While driving south, Kid and Jess spotted an inverted cone of smoke rising in the distance. The closer they got to Mallard Island, the more queasy Kid's stomach became.

Finally, Jess stated the obvious. "That smoke is coming from our island."

"Which can't be good." Kid could not contain his blossoming feeling of dread. It seemed to almost hang in the air, thickening as they approached, and becoming increasingly palpable.

"Did they catch a house on fire?" Jess asked as he sped on Bay Avenue toward Heron Street.

"And if so, which one? Pull over and shut it down. We'll run the rest of the way," Kid said.

Jess turned to him. "Really? We're still so far away."

"I know, but until we know what is going on, I'd rather not announce our arrival."

They headed on foot to the bridge over to Mallard Island, only to find it fully blockaded. A large group of soldiers and elders stood atop the short span, including Heidi and Sid. They had a van parked at each end of the bridge, preventing anyone from getting on or off the island.

Hidden behind the corner of a restaurant, Jess conceded, "I'm glad I listened to you about approaching on foot. It probably saved our asses."

"But what are they all doing here? They were supposed to be going back to the ships!" he whispered with frustration.

"So Heidi said." Jess still sounded bitter.

"Even still, how could they find us this quickly?"

Kid and Jess both scanned the island, looking at the tops of the numerous houses standing above the fields of marsh grass. One structure was conspicuously missing and had been replaced by a steady plume of rising smoke.

"Oh, shit. I know where the smoke is coming from." Jess's voice sounded like it came through a tin can.

Having reached the same realization, Kid blurted out, "The mermaid house is gone! They must have taken it out."

Tapping Kid's arm, Jess pointed. "Look on the bridge. One of the soldiers is holding a missile launcher." A second later he said, "I just hope none of our group was at the mermaid house when they hit it."

If Kid let the possibilities and probabilities roam around his mind, he would have fallen to his knees in despair right then and there. He had to remain rational and keep his emotions in check. "Well, the fact they are blockading the bridge tells us there must still be people alive they are trying to keep from leaving. But I'll bet they don't know about the relief valve."

"What do you mean?" Jess asked.

"Our secondary means of escape, the footbridge at Bridge Street."

Kid froze while peering across the street. "Jesus. Come on!" He sprinted through the grass, trees, and frozen water behind the building until he reached Route 72. They ran east, cut back through the woods to Avenue D and headed up Bridge Street.

As they neared the footbridge, Jess grabbed Kid's arm. "What's going on?"

Slowing to a fast jog, Kid said, "The soldier back there with the missile launcher, and a couple of others, ran onto the island. They must be moving in for another attack."

Kid went across the footbridge and came upon a large patch of eight-foot high marsh grass. He knew they could use the cover of the grass field to reach the street up the block from the bungalow. "Move slowly and quietly," he whispered.

As they walked through the towering reeds, Kid looked up and was glad the sky had cleared. Using a trick he learned from Jess, he could now use the sun as a point of reference to ensure they were walking in the right direction as they made for the bungalow block. Now swallowed by the tall grass, he fully understood the basis for the old adage, 'getting lost in the weeds.' Fortunately, he had a bright and steady marker to follow.

Up the street from the bungalow, Kid came to the edge of the field of tall grass. He separated the final stalks and looked about. With the wind blowing in his direction, he could smell the smoke from the smoldering mermaid house. "Follow me, stay low," he whispered as he crouched and snuck up behind an old, weather-beaten sailboat. The vessel rested on concrete blocks and listed to one side. The green paint was faded and chipped, but the mast stood tall and defiant.

As Jess filed in beside him, Kid peered over the gunwale of the boat. His heart came up in his throat. His worst fears were coming true before his very eyes. Four enemies were hiding along the side of a house. One was Sid Sherman. Next to him, an Asian elder was inspecting the firing position of the missile tube as it rested on the shoulder of another soldier crouched at the front corner of the house. The soldier had his finger on the trigger and the missile was aimed at the bungalow.

"Shit! They're about to launch!" Kid uttered as he ran around the boat and started firing. His long distance shots missed the mark, but hit the side of the house the enemy was hiding behind. With the loud gunshots, the soldiers paused, long enough for Kid to fire again. His next bullet struck the soldier with the missile launcher and he crumbled. Before the elder could return fire a bullet from Jess hit him in the gut, and he fell face first to the ground. The other remaining soldier and Sid started returning fire, so Kid shot once, and then dropped and rolled.

Jess was already at the street, and dove behind a large rolling garbage can. He squeezed off a round and hit the soldier in the throat.

Now only Sid remained, but he kept pulling the trigger of his Medusa firearm without pause.

Kid crawled until he found cover behind a large anchor adorning the front yard of a house. He returned fire with a volley of shots, but missed as Sid grabbed the missile launcher from his fallen comrade and slipped behind a detached garage.

Kid's last pull of the trigger had resulted in a hollow click, as his gun was out of ammunition. He felt in his pocket and besides the spool of Zylon line he had taken from the marina truck while in Saratoga, he only had one more bullet. He put it in the cylinder and set the rotation so the final shot was cued up. Spotting a trampoline along the side of the detached garage, an idea came to him. It was a long shot, but they were out of time, just about out of ammunition, and Sid now had the missile launcher.

He signaled to Jess and told him to stay where he was and to fire on his count.

Jess pointed at his gun and signaled he was almost out of bullets.

"I know, I know!" Kid mouthed and waved his hand.

At that moment, Sid popped his head around the back corner of the garage and fired a barrage of bolts. Kid shot his last bullet to make the enemy take cover, and then took off at a sprint. He reached the side of the garage, took a leap onto the trampoline, and jumped as hard as he could. The metal springs creaked in protest at the interruption of their winter hibernation. On the third bounce, he flew up onto the gutter-less roof and was able to grab the only thing he could, the top of an exhaust vent pipe. He swung his feet up just as the couple-inch PVC pipe started to crack. He crawled to the edge of the garage's roof and made eye contact with Jess. Reaching into his pocket, Kid held up the roll of clear Zylon line and then started to unwrap it. He used hand signals to communicate his idea. After he unwound a healthy amount of line, he tied a noose-knot and crawled to the edge of the roof.

Peeking down, Sid was crouched as he slithered his way past the trampoline and along the side of the garage.

Kid tiptoed to the other side of the roof. He held a big wad of line and threw the spool of Zylon down to Jess, feeling it unwind as it traveled. Stepping back to the other side, Kid lowered the large noose and prepared to drop it over Sid's head. The clear line dangled behind the Sherman brother, who at one point turned and looked right through it. *Just don't look up*, Kid thought.

From his perch above, he watched as Sid peered around the front corner of the garage. At that exact moment, Jess popped his head out from behind the garbage can. Sid spotted him and sprinted toward the back of the structure to attack from the other side, but he ran into the Zylon loop. He pulled the string from under his chin and glared up before Kid could tighten the noose.

"You!" he bellowed.

With nowhere to hide, Kid jumped down from the roof. As he descended, he pulled the noose over Sid's head. At first, Sid grabbed for the Zylon around his neck, but with his target right in front of him, he raised his weapon.

Kid used the butt of his empty 38-caliber to slam Sid's wrist and knock the weapon away. Bending down to snag it, Kid took a foot straight to the face. His cheek was aflame, his teeth were rattling, and his one eye was squinted as he fell to a knee. Sid reared his leg back and swung it forward again, but Kid dodged and kicked his combatant's single leg out from under him.

Now on his rear end, Sid was still able to throw a wild backhand and catch Kid behind the ear. A high pitched whistle sounded. As the Sherman brother grabbed him by the hair, Kid threw a few wild punches. He was released after landing a fist squarely on Sid's chin.

Springing to his feet, Kid grabbed a hockey stick from the side of the garage and took a swing. Sid's arm took the brunt of it, but he was able to get to his feet and lunge for his weapon. Kid's experience playing street hockey saved him as he was able to poke-check the gun before his adversary could grab it. In one fluid motion, Kid drew the stick back and caught Sid's chin with the blade, and then he followed through with a slapshot that launched the weapon deep into the marsh grass.

"Jess, pull the…" Before Kid could finish, he was tackled and a fist was heading toward his mouth. Turning his head just in time, the fist glanced off his ear, which was still ringing. While Sid raised his hands to try and remove the Zylon noose from around his neck, Kid connected with a short-range jab to the midsection. His adversary dropped his hands over his stomach.

Getting to his feet, Kid yelled, "Jess, pull the line, now!"

Running along the side of garage, Kid jumped on the trampoline again. This time on the second bounce he was able to reach the vent pipe. He slid his hand down and held the cracked tubing close to the roof, which he assumed was its strongest point. Before he could pull his feet up, Sid grabbed them.

With the 5,000 pound test Zylon string strung across the peak of the roof, Jess began to pull. Sid grabbed for the noose tightening around his neck, so Kid kicked his feet free and scrambled up on the roof. He slid down the other side, jumped to the ground and pulled the line with Jess. Sid was as heavy as an ox. "Can you hold it yourself?" Kid asked.

"No!" Jess barked. "The line is cutting into my hands. Hold on, and pull with me." They backed up and circled twice around a hibernating dogwood tree. With the line taut, Jess held firm and braced his foot against the eight-inch trunk. "I got it. Go ahead."

Kid ran around to the other side of the garage and stopped.

Sid was struggling to free himself and was standing on the unstable trampoline surface. First he tried to move his feet to the sturdy trampoline frame, but he could not reach it without further strangling himself. He tried to bounce up enough to loosen the line around his neck, but when he jumped and grabbed the top of the PVC vent pipe, Jess pulled in the slack and the line tightened. The entire vent pipe broke free, causing Sid to plummet back down to the trampoline's surface. After he stopped bouncing, the Sherman brother stood on the tips of his toes. He seemed desperate to relieve the pressure constricting his windpipe, but there was nothing else to grab.

Reaching his belt, Sid pulled out a large hunting knife with a camouflage decorated handle and feverishly sawed the Zylon line.

CHAPTER 49

January 8, 2045
Sunday, Afternoon
Mallard Island, New Jersey
Thirteen days after the event

Sid was sawing at the Zylon line hard and fast, but was getting nowhere. It looked like he was trying to cut steel with a butter knife. Finally giving up, he threw his knife. Kid leaned to the side and the blade sailed harmlessly by.

General Hyland popped his head around the corner with his weapon raised. "Kid! We saw some of the battle from the porch of the bungalow. Is everything under control here?"

"Yes," Kid panted as he picked up his empty pistol from the ground and slid it in his coat pocket.

The general stepped back and waved to someone, and then he hobbled forward.

Turning to Sid, who was still trying to stay on the tips of his toes, Kid said, "It's over for you. You'll never lay your filthy hands on someone again like you did Karen Stone."

"She…was a whore…anyway," he spouted through a strangled airway. He tried to work his fingers under the strong Zylon line. He dug with his fingertips, but the noose was too tight and the line had already cut into the skin of his neck. "They…all are. We'll screw her…again…and again," he forced an airy, fake laugh, "when we get to Hell. She's already there…waiting for me." His reddened face broke into a menacing grin.

At that moment Kid heard someone coming around the corner. He braced, but then relief flooded though his body. "Sara!" She was alive and seemed fine. They made eye contact, and then she pointed behind her. Leaning back enough to see around the corner, Kid felt nothing short of blessed by good fortune.

He turned back to Sid. "I don't think so. First of all, Karen is not Hell material to begin with. Second, I think you're on your own down there." He turned his head.

Sara extended her hand and helped someone forward.

Karen limped around the corner. Although she was bruised and bloodied, she had survived. The girl was unbelievable, and Kid found himself inspired by her toughness. She put her arm around Sara's shoulder and glared up.

Sid's surprise was evident as he snarled, "That bitch…was supposed…to be dead!"

"Let her be the last thing you see on this planet, but look at her and look good. She made it, and you didn't," Kid stated. Despite his guilt at taking the life of another human being, he also felt a sense of relief, and maybe even vindication for those killed or harmed by the Sherman brother.

The general said, "Let's put him out of his misery and get back to the house. We're still in the middle of a war here." At that, he and Kid stepped forward.

"Wait!" Karen called out as she bent down and picked up Sid's knife. She crossed her other arm over her breast. "My blood is on this blade."

They all watched as Karen limped over to where Sid was hanging, trying to stay on the tips of his toes on the trampoline. He was struggling mightily. She glared up at him and said in her raspy voice, "I made a promise to my mother when she was dying."

"Who cares." Sid made a weak attempt to kick at her and the blade in her hand. But in doing so, he had to lift his foot, which put more pressure on his neck. He again tried to reestablish his footing.

She stuck the sharp tip of the knife against the surface of the trampoline. Her lips trembled as she fought back tears. "You can go to Hell knowing this…" Her voice was thick with pain but also strength and even defiance. "You may have violated me, you low-life scumbag, but you didn't break me."

Sid's eyes went wide as she pushed the tip of his knife through the surface. Using two hands, she sawed in a straight line until Sid's weight finally split the trampoline's taut cover. His feet fell through and he tried in vain to regain a foothold. After struggling for a long minute, his head hung limp and his feet swayed gently.

Breaking into tears, Karen turned away. Kid hugged her and whispered, "That nightmare is finally over."

Sara put Karen's arm around her neck and they walked away.

Kid bent over, and tried to catch his breath. A minute later, he called out, "Jess, you can let go. He's dead." Sid's body slumped down across the frame of the trampoline. With his eyes toward the back of the garage, Kid snapped his finger. "The missile launcher!" He ran around the corner and retrieved it.

The general took the launcher and inspected it. "This is loaded." He carefully twisted the missile head while depressing a button near the end of the tube. "There, it is no longer locked in."

"Would Sid have even known how to fire that?" Kid asked.

"Yes, it is easy. Once the missile is locked and loaded, you just aim and shoot."

As soon as Jess came around the corner they all started walking up the street. They were moving slower than usual given the general's noticeable limp.

"Where are we heading," Kid asked.

"The bungalow. We moved everyone over there since they took out the mermaid house with a shoulder launched missile, same as that," the general said and pointed at the tube Kid was carrying on his shoulder.

"Did we lose anybody?"

"The entire Ryan family, James Levy and 705. There are some injuries and some may be serious. It's amazing we lost so few of us since a missile hit the bottom of the mermaid house when we were all inside, except Karen and...Drex. They were still in the bungalow."

"Where is that old boy Drex?" With every passing second the general did not answer, the corners of Kid's mouth drooped a little more.

"I'm sorry, Kid. He also didn't make it."

Kid went to speak and the words were stuck in his throat. Drex's death hit him in the gut. In their brief time together, he had grown fond of his older friend. For a moment, he said nothing as he walked.

They reached the porch of the bungalow and Kid glanced up the road to ensure no soldiers were coming. He turned his head and stared at the fallen mermaid house. Wisps of dark smoke arose from the bottom of the still-smoldering structure.

Walking inside, Kid rested the missile launcher in the corner of the living room. As he reunited with the group, he found himself stunned at the condition of the survivors. They were all bruised or bleeding somewhere and their clothes were ripped and stained. Karen lay on a couch and appeared to be the most battered. He could not believe the girl was still functioning at all. Although she had a thick scarf wrapped around her neck, she was shivering.

"Kid, over here," Jess said from the kitchen. When he walked in, Jess slid over a box of shells for a 38-caliber and said, "Reload." After filling the cylinder and dumping a handful of extra shells in his pocket, Kid stepped back into the living room.

"It's still here. Thank God," the general said as he reached into a coat closet and grabbed his laptop computer bag. Turning, he said, "So Kid, how did you get here without running into the enemy group?"

"They have a blockade set up on the bridge to the island, so we had to go around them."

"How did y'all do that?" Sara asked.

"We took the alternate entrance." Kid turned to the general.

"Remember the footbridge at Bridge Street?"

The general nodded. "Then we should be able to get off the island the same way."

"I think it's the only option we have since they have the main bridge blockaded," Kid agreed. "The one good thing about them pulling back is we can just take the road over to the footbridge rather than having to take the group through a field of marsh grass."

"I remember the way over to the footbridge from when you took me there, but how far is that from the bridge where the enemy is entrenched?" the general asked.

"It has to be the equivalent of a few blocks?"

"That's too close for comfort," the general said. "Can we safely cross with a group this large?"

"I think it can be done if we distract the soldiers on the bridge," Kid answered.

"We can do more than just distract them." The general pointed to the missile launcher in the corner. "You all head for the footbridge and I'm going to launch that missile at them from in close."

"But you have a limp. How will you get there?" Kid asked.

The general shrugged. "I'll drive. There is a pickup truck up the street. I have to get in close enough to ensure an accurate shot."

"Who is going to fire the missile? With how many of them are on the bridge, you may not have enough time to drive *and* fire. I think it's too dangerous to do alone. How about I drive, and you can fire?" Kid offered.

"What he's saying makes sense, son," Chris chimed in.

Before the general could answer, Kid added, "But still, if we have to run or get out of there in a hurry, you have a limp. Maybe I should do it myself."

"Kid," the general started. "As you pointed out, it will be much more dangerous to do it alone."

Jess raised a hand in the air. "He won't be alone. Although it is probably against my better judgement, I'll go with him."

CHAPTER 50

January 8, 2045
Sunday, Afternoon
Mallard Island, New Jersey
Thirteen days after the event

The general exhaled and nodded his head. He turned to Kid. "You are sure you want to do this?"

"Yes. Me and Jess are in the best shape to do it. Can you just load and lock the missile? Then I just need to aim and shoot."

The general walked over to the launcher. He loaded and locked the missile, and then showed Kid the scope on the top of the tube. Pointing, he said, "Find the target in the scope, adjust for distance, and then pull the trigger right here."

Kid nodded, so the general rested the loaded launcher against the wall in the corner of the room.

Addressing the entire group assembled in the living room of the bungalow, Kid said, "Once you all cross the footbridge, head to the end of Avenue D. There is a large box truck parked outside a bait and tackle shop. It says 'Fresh Catch' on the side. I don't care how bad it smells in there, everyone should fit. Take Route 72 west, head away from Mallard Island, and wait for us a few miles down the road. Then we can all take shelter at the choice we didn't mark on any map."

"Where?" the general asked.

"RPH," Kid stated.

"We need to move out, but what is RPH?" the general asked.

"A large building north of here in Bayville," Kid answered. "It was being used as a health and rehabilitation center, but was closed for renovations, so it should not be full of dead bodies."

"Is it a secure location?"

"That place is like a fortress," Jess chimed in.

"Alright. You know your area." The general turned to the others. "Be on high alert. If the members scramble when Kid and Jess hit the bridge they may come our way."

"Let's get out of here before they send the next wave in here after us," the general stated. Shaking Kid's hand and surprising him with a man-hug, he said, "I have faith in you." General Hyland then slung his laptop bag over his shoulder and said, "Move out!"

"Why are you bothering with the computer?" Kid asked.

"I have a lot of files and information stored that we will need in the future. Not to mention, I didn't get a chance to ensure the last satellite is fully out of commission." He turned to the group. "Does everybody have everything they need? Including medications?"

Evelyn nodded.

Patting her coat pocket and creating a maraca-like sound, Maria said, "Still have my diabetes meds. I'm good."

Giving Kid a firm kiss and hug, Sara whispered in his ear, "Love you. Please, *please*, stay safe."

"You too, and I love you more."

Kid and Jess watched as General Hyland led the rag-tag group up the street. Kid hoped there would not be any confrontations. The group was not even close to battle-ready. Dr. McDermott had to carry his daughter, Megan, who was conscious but unable to walk by herself. Chris and his wife Evelyn had their arms intertwined, keeping each other steady. 801 helped Wendy, who could not put much weight on her dislocated ankle. Melanie was unsteady but capable of walking, and she held Katy and Karly by the hand. Sara assisted Karen, who was also barely able to walk.

Kid grabbed the missile launcher and went out the door. He tiptoed behind a row of houses as Jess followed. Shouldering open the back door of the residence where the pickup truck was parked, he was hoping the keys would be conveniently on the kitchen counter, but had no such luck. Breathing only out his mouth, he walked past a reclining chair occupied by a melted carcass facing a black, dead television screen. He ran into the bedroom, stepped over a small, hairy pile that was once the family pet, and found the keys on a bedroom dresser. He ran outside, in desperate need of fresh air.

Getting in the vehicle, he and Jess waited. Kid was nervous but remained patient. He handed Jess the car keys. "Let's give our group a few minutes to get over the footbridge."

The two groups of soldiers led by Elder-2 and Elder-44, having merged together at the Mallard Island Bridge, were alert as they waited between the vans parked at each end of the short span.

Elder-2 paced on the bridge and blurted out, "What is taking them so long? They should have fired the next missile by now. Why did we send a new junior elder in with them anyway?" She had not wanted the crazy kid from Vermont, Sid Sherman, going in. The guy was a head case.

While Elder-44 stood with his hands behind his back, he answered, "Because he is fearless, and more importantly, he is disposable. With any luck he will succeed and then perish."

"Maybe you should have disposed of him in Vermont after he served his purpose there, rather than bringing him back to the project," Elder-2 said as she turned to him. "His pattern of behavior is a perfect example of what we were trying to cure with the conditioning in the Utopia Project in the first place. He is a servant to his own rage and bloodlust, and not to society."

"True, but it will hopefully work to our advantage in this case."

Elder-2 turned to Heidi, "And we are sure there is no other way off of this island? Let me see that map."

Pulling a map from her pocket, Heidi opened it and spread it on the hood of a truck. "Look," Heidi pointed, "there is only one road on and off the island."

Peering closer, Elder-2 saw the one road, Heron Street. But then she noticed something odd. "Careless!" she hissed.

Stepping over, Elder-44 asked, "What is it?"

Slamming her knuckle hard against the map, she said, "Do you see that line over the water at Bridge Street? It is not a road, but it is a bridge! Likely a walking bridge." Pointing at Elder-44 and Heidi, she snapped, "You two, take a few members with you and get over to that walking bridge, now, before they escape!"

Tracing her finger quickly on the paper to plot their course, Heidi took the map and folded it as they hurried off.

After waiting a few moments, Kid's stomach was in knots. "Are we ready?"

"Hell no," Jess said. "But we're going in anyway."

Kid opened his door to get out. "As soon as I'm in the bed of the truck, hit it. Pull up next to the 'Welcome to Mallard Island' sign and stop. Keep your window up since their shots can't get through glass."

Jumping into the bed of the truck, Kid held the launcher in his already sweaty hands. He knocked on the back window. Jess turned on the truck and drove off. As soon as he turned a corner, Kid tensed upon seeing the bridge over to Mallard Island in the distance. The soldiers all turned their attention to the approaching vehicle. Raising their weapons, they fired.

Jess yelled as a bullet smashed through the windshield and hit the seat next to him. As the vehicle turned sharply, Kid slid across the bed and looked up in surprise. They did not consider the soldiers would have any conventional guns. A second later, a bullet shredded the driver-side front tire and the vehicle slid sideways.

Kid went airborne for a second as the back of the truck bounced over an uneven patch of grass hidden under the snow. He yelled, "Keep going and keep your head down!"

The back tire on the driver-side exploded as it was also ripped by bullet fire. The truck rims started digging down into snow and earth. As they approached the 'Welcome to Mallard Island' sign, Jess hit the brakes and turned the wheel. The sharp metal rims dug deep and caught, and the truck started to roll over. Kid was thrown in the air and landed hard on the ground next to the overturned vehicle. The soldiers continued firing, but he shook his head, grabbed the missile launcher, and crawled behind the welcome sign.

When he looked back, he could see his friend was now upside-down in the cab of the truck. Jess released his seat belt and eased himself down to the roof, which was now the floor.

Kid stayed crouched as bolts and bullets flew all around. A grouping of shots pulverized the brightly colored duck in the middle of the welcome sign above his head and shredded the electric meter affixed to the back. The hole blasted through the center of the welcome sign was gaping, so he stuck the end of the missile launcher tube through it. Kid had the bridge, a couple hundred feet away, in his sights. As he was aiming, he heard dull thuds as bullets pelted the body of the vehicle. With the precarious position of the truck, Kid had to hurry before a bullet found its mark and hit Jess, or the gas tank.

"One shot at this," Kid muttered as he locked onto the closest van blocking the bridge, and pulled the trigger.

The missile slid out of the tube with a pop and sped through the air. The head burst as it hit the ground just underneath the van. Debris flew in every direction with the blast launching the vehicle in the air. A section of the bridge was annihilated and a chunk of the road's asphalt cascaded over the side, falling to the partially frozen creek below. Kid watched as the mass of asphalt lodged in the ice and started slowly tipping over, like the head of a small garden shovel that had been whipped into a soft mound of topsoil. A second explosion followed as the gas tank of the thrown vehicle ignited, knocking the van at the other end of the span on its side.

Approaching the footbridge, Elder-44 stopped short. "There!" he snarled as he pointed at a group far in the distance walking up the road on the mainland. "The traitor, Elder-41!"

Suddenly, an explosion shook the ground. The sound was close enough that Heidi ducked down. Seeing a fireball rising in the sky, she uttered, "The bridge…" Turning, she asked, "Should we go back?"

With only a few seconds of contemplation as he watched the ball of fire, Elder-44 said, "We will take out the survivor group and circle back. We cannot lose them now that we have them in our sights. Come on."

CHAPTER 51

January 8, 2045
Sunday, Afternoon
Mallard Island, New Jersey
Thirteen days after the event

Throwing the missile tube to the ground, Kid ran over to the overturned truck. *Please tell me he wasn't hit!* His question was answered a second later as Jess kicked the driver side door open and crawled out. Despite bullets holes everywhere, none had hit him. Kid pulled out his pistol and ran toward the bridge, with his friend close at his heels.

One vehicle was on fire and they had to crouch to see through the smoke and flame. The soldiers on the short bridge were clearly obliterated by the missile blast. They never stood a chance.

Kid stared at the carnage with his mouth agape. Two soldiers, who he assumed were posted at the foot of the bridge, had been blown to the ground but were recovering and sitting upright. They both tried to grab their weapons. One of them almost succeeded before Kid plugged him with two bullets. The other soldier tried to reach down to his holster, but his arm had been neatly amputated at the elbow. As he looked up, Jess put him out of his misery with a quick bullet to the chest.

Peering into the creek, Kid winced as he saw the bloody face of Elder-2. She was sprawled out on her back, but her chest and midsection were torn to shreds and one hip bone was exposed. Elder-2's body was floating in the unfrozen center of the waterway and was being carried away by the current.

Jess said, "Let's go find the group."

With the bloodbath, the cratered road and the burning vehicle blocking the span, Kid said, "Forget crossing here. We'll make our way over to the footbridge and catch up to them that way before they take off in the box truck." He went to take off and paused. "We have to be cautious. There were no soldiers guarding the footbridge earlier, but is no way of knowing if all the soldiers were stationed on this bridge. Keep your eyes open and your guard up."

They ran along a road and then veered off and cut through the backyards of several homes. "Get down," Kid whispered as they arrived at the base of the footbridge. He pointed to the other side of the creek. An older elder and two younger soldiers had already crossed over and were hiding behind a house, stalking their prey. He was stunned upon recognizing the fourth person.

"Is that…" Jess started.

"Heidi," Kid finished for him. "Wait here." He crawled to the top of the small arch of the footbridge. "Damn!" he gasped as he got to his knees. General Hyland was leading the group, but they were walking up the middle of the narrow, one-lane, Avenue D. With so many injured in the group, their pace was slow, but what alarmed Kid even more was they were out in the open.

"What do you see?" Jess scrambled up next to him.

Focusing intently, Kid's feeling of dread doubled. The enemy appeared to be moving in for the kill as they stepped into the street behind the general's group. As Kid was about to yell and warn them, General Hyland fortunately glanced back and spotted the pursuers. The general reacted right away and ushered most of the group behind a vehicle parked on the street as the soldiers began firing.

Kid hushed Jess so he couldn't call out. "Shh! Mr. Hyland sees them and is taking cover. Don't give away our element of surprise!"

"Behind the car! Quickly!" the general yelled again.

Melanie wrapped her arms around her girls and took cover, but before they all could get out of harm's way, Clarence was hit by a bolt from Elder-44. He bounced off the side of the vehicle and hit the ground with a thud. Marissa screamed and draped herself over her husband's defenseless, stiff body.

As the general and his group returned fire, Elder-44 and his group ducked behind the corner of another house.

The general pulled out an antidote vial and stabbed Clarence in the thigh. "Marissa, CPR, quick," he said as they dragged the body behind the cover of the car. Within a minute, Clarence was breathing on his own. Marissa put her palms together and turned her eyes toward the sky.

"We can't take another Medusa hit," the general announced as he tossed away the tiny, spent tube. "That was my last vial of antidote."

Kid and Jess were about to run across the footbridge when they saw Elder-44 standing next to a shed with a rooster weathervane on top. The elder tugged at the front of his belt and threw three small objects into the tall marsh grass next to the structure.

"What did he just ditch?" Jess asked.

"I think they were his antidote vials," Kid whispered. "Remember Mr. Hyland had three on the front of his belt as well?"

"Why would he got rid of them?"

"I think he saw them revive Clarence." Kid paused as he felt a wave of discomfort. "I guess he wants to ensure nobody else gets revived, at least not at his expense."

Casing out the battlefield and the positioning of the combatants, Kid saw an opportunity and didn't hesitate to take it. "Follow me."

Tiptoeing over the footbridge and crossing the creek, Kid and Jess hid in the bushes behind a weather-beaten shanty. Elder-44, Heidi and the soldiers were taking cover along the side of the next house over.

From the bushes, Kid aimed his pistol. He said to Jess, "Open fire, and in the worst scenario, if we miss, hopefully we flush them out into the open. Mr. Hyland was leaning on a car in perfect shooting position to take them out. Ready?"

"Aim," Jess said and held his pistol with both hands.

"Fire!"

A bullet hit a younger soldier in the neck, and he collapsed in a heap like a ragdoll.

The enemy group seemed disoriented and did not know where the fire was coming from, so they bolted. Kid and Jess ran along the back of the next house and peeked around the corner to see Elder-44 running across the street. The elder kept the remaining soldier next to him, and seemed to be using him as a shield from the general's fire. Heidi followed behind.

Having practiced the proper tone that same day, Kid snapped, "*Ion*!"

The soldier stumbled and fell to the ground, leaving the elder exposed.

Elder-44 yelled, "*Fleson*," but kept moving. He headed for the cover of a house across the street, but it was to no avail as a bolt from General Hyland's weapon hit the elder in mid-stride. Elder-44's frozen body fell forward and the momentum made his head scrape along the slushy road.

Heidi had stumbled and slowed upon hearing the word command, but she made it across the street. She was followed by the last member who had quickly recovered. They both took refuge behind a house as Kid and Jess fired a few errant shots.

"We need to get to the other side of the street," Kid said. "That way we can sneak up on Heidi."

Gazing around, Jess said, "The only way we can do that without being spotted is to head back and army-crawl across the low-lying area at the base of the bridge."

"Let's do it," Kid said and tore off back through the backyards of a series of homes.

Heidi kept moving and ran behind the next house. She peeked around the corner and could see the car General Hyland and his group were hiding behind. She looked around, a bit frantic. Shots and words were coming at them from the side or the back. Hyland must have left a couple of his group behind, hidden, to serve as cowardly snipers. With Elder-44 and one of the members dead, she was left alone with just one member, and not many options. The attack plan on Mallard Island had been a miserable failure. Since there was still a sizeable group of survivors, Sid and the second wave had obviously failed to eliminate them with the last missile. If anything, it seemed the missile had found the area of the bridge, which made no sense. Then her group was too late in identifying the God-damned footbridge. She herself had missed it. "Fuck," she snapped.

With any luck, Kid and Jess were now captives, so she still had a chance. The plan would have to be modified, but all hope was not lost. She just had to survive. But, that bitch Sara Hyland was still alive, and still in the picture. That didn't just complicate plans, it ruined them, completely. That was the obstacle that had to be eliminated.

"Fuck, fuck, FUCK!" She spit the words so forcefully that she bit her lower lip and made it bleed. That is when an idea hit her. It was desperation for sure, but rather than just trying to escape, she would take one last shot at that bitch Sara. With any luck, she would remove her from the face of the planet, which would clear a path for her and Kid.

The member next to her stared with great curiosity as she bit her lower lip even harder until the blood was gushing. Heidi caught the red flow in a cupped palm and the pool quickly grew. Blood began to trickle through her fingers and drip on the ground. With her other hand, she unzipped the top of her uniform. She grabbed the necklace, lifted it over her head and opened the pendant.

When she was done, Heidi leaned around the corner and started firing repetitively. Return fire peppered the side of the house she was hiding behind as she balled up the piece of jewelry and packed it in the middle of a tight snowball.

As Kid and Jess reached the low-lying open area in front of the entrance to the footbridge, they got down and army-crawled to other side of the road. They had a clear view of Avenue D and watched as bolts streaked across the street, one after another. Reaching the other side, they ran behind the houses on the southern side of the road. They stopped and Kid looked for Heidi up ahead since they were now on the same side of the street she was, but she was nowhere to be found.

Need to stay down! Sara realized. Heidi's shots were coming at them head-high as the group hid behind the car. While her father and her grandfather returned fire, she grabbed Karen and pulled her down further. Her already-battered friend collapsed to the ground in a heap and moaned in pain. Sara caressed Karen's face. "I'm sorry!"

"Hey Sara," Heidi called out. "Why don't you come over and we'll talk it out. We will put our weapon down if you do."

While holding Karen's hand, Sara rose to a crouch and yelled across the street, "Heidi! Enough is enough. Stop trying to hurt us!"

"Why, Sara? Life *is* fucking hurt! That's all it is," Heidi yelled back.

"None of us deserve this!" Sara responded.

"Do you think you're the only one to get something you don't deserve? What would a spoiled bitch like you know about that anyway?" Heidi screeched.

Sara felt her face flush. "Spoiled bitch?"

Maria patted her arm and tried to calm her down while she called out, "Heidi, come on now! This madness has to stop!"

Ignoring the plea, Heidi continued, "Hey, I have a message for you, Sara. It is inside this piece of jewelry we found! You're not missing any jewelry, like maybe a necklace are you?"

Reflexively, Sara touched her neck, used to feeling the outline of her prized arrowhead locket.

Suddenly a large snowball was heaved in the air and was heading toward the car. It hit the ground a bit shy of the vehicle and exploded in a puff of powder. Clearly discernable in the scattered show was a gold piece of jewelry. Sara inhaled sharply and rose slightly to look closer. "Is that my locket..."

Her father grabbed her hard and pulled her down as a couple of bolts flew just past her face.

"There are now two things in there," Heidi yelled. "And I swear by Christ, I will have one or the other."

What is she talking about? Sara's frustration grew. She needed to know what Heidi did to her sacred locket.

"Go ahead and grab it," Heidi called out. "We won't shoot. I want you to open it while I'm here."

"Don't go anywhere," her father snapped.

For a minute there was only stillness and silence.

Heidi waited in a perfect shooting position. *Come on, bitch. Go out and grab it.* She knew how precious, if not downright sacred, the locket was to Sara. After they just missed her with the first shots, Heidi knew they were running out of chances. If Sara didn't come out in the open, Heidi had no choice but to try and slip away. Just her and one member could not win a battle against a survivor group this large. She would give it a few more seconds...

Sara snapped the slat of a four-foot white picket fence behind the car. She laid down and stretched as she tried to snag the familiar piece of jewelry. After struggling with it, she was finally able to drag it back behind the car.

Sara coddled the arrowhead locket and felt completely violated. It was special to her and was a powerful symbol of her and Kid's connection. When she flipped it open, she jumped back and yelped as blood splashed out and dripped on her leg. She was disgusted and held it away from her body as the remaining blood dripped out. Sara's teeth clenched as she looked inside and saw her special picture of Kid was soggy and starting to disintegrate. She recalled Heidi's message, 'There are now two things in there, and I swear by Christ, I will have one or the other!'

The locket contained blood, and Kid.

"Like hell!" Sara huffed and rose to her feet.

A split second later, Jess yelled, "Heidi's on the run!"

CHAPTER 52

January 8, 2045
Sunday, Afternoon
Mallard Island, New Jersey
Thirteen days after the event

Upon hearing Jess's loud voice, Heidi sprinted faster across the backyard of a house until she reached Avenue C. Pulling the map from her pocket, she stopped for a second and used a finger to trace a path back to Long Beach Island. "Follow me," she said to the lone member with her. She again took off in a sprint and headed toward East Bay Avenue.

Sara pulled out her weapon and tore off. Her father tried to grab her, but she slipped from his grip.

"Sara, no!" he called out.

"You want blood?" Sara yelled as she raced between two houses across the street and spotted Heidi in the distance.

Kid had taken off as soon as he saw Heidi dash from in between two houses. She was trying to escape. He was startled as Sara also popped out from in between houses right in front of him. His girlfriend was so focused on Heidi that she never even saw him. He was winded, making it nearly impossible to call out, and he could not slow down. He pushed his legs and hard as they would go and then tried to do the same with his lungs. He just needed enough air to call out once.

Heidi glanced over her shoulder. Sara was running after her. Realizing she had one last chance, Heidi stopped on Avenue C and turned. She tossed the map on the ground, dropped to a knee, and aimed her weapon with both hands. Someone was coming up behind Sara, but it was impossible to discern who. It was likely General Hyland, but from Heidi's angle, the person was largely blocked by Sara's body. It did not matter who it was. Heidi's eyes were laser-focused on one person. She held her breath and squeezed the trigger, launching a bright bolt at the bitch. Simultaneously, a sickeningly familiar voice yelled from behind her, "Sara!"

Heidi screamed, "No!"

Sara was jolted by Kid's voice, and tried to slide to a halt. He dove over her shoulder and reached out his hand. Kid caught the bolt in his palm when it was just a couple of inches from Sara's chest. She let out a shrill screech as his body hit the ground with a thud, and his outstretched hand, which was nearly curled into a fist, scraped along the ground.

"Duck!" Jess yelled behind her.

Sara jumped to the ground.

Jess fired his pistol at Heidi and her lone companion. General Hyland appeared, limping along, but blasting with his Medusa firearm all the while. The member was hit by a bolt and stood frozen. Heidi took off in a full sprint and turned onto East Bay Avenue. She was provided with some cover from the still-standing member until Jess fired an accurate shot and the body tipped over.

Turning to Kid, Sara inhaled loudly and scrambled on her knees to his prone body. As she turned him over, she yelped sharply and cringed. His body was rigid and his eyes were wide open. He was not breathing or moving, and his frozen face was a snapshot of desperation. She knew the stopwatch marking Kid's expiration was now ticking. "Dad! Antidote!"

"I'm out!" the general yelled.

"What! Oh God, no!" Sara was gripped by despair. There had to be more antidote. She blew a few quick breaths into Kid's mouth.

"Where can we get more?" Maria huffed as she approached with Marissa and Karen struggling to keep up behind her. Dropping to her knees, Maria immediately started doing chest compressions on Kid's now supine form.

"What about Elder-2 back at the bridge over to the island?" the general asked.

"She was blown apart by the missile, and it's too far from here!" Sara was beyond distraught and the clock was ticking louder and faster. She blew more air into Kid's lungs.

"And Elder-44 didn't have any more vials either." The general sounded despondent.

As Kid lay on the ground, he wanted to scream out, but could not. He felt the intense pain of his severely scraped knuckles and couldn't even yell or move to ease his suffering. He tried in vain to breathe and willed himself to suck in air, but his lungs would not expand, or move at all. It felt like a ten-ton plate was resting on his chest. Panic set in. He noticed the sky above him and people scampering around as they came into his fixed field of vision. He saw Sara and then Maria. They were so upset and frantic. Kid began to accept his fate as he heard the general say he had no more antidote, and neither did Elder-44. A sudden calm came over him. He was at peace knowing he had caught the bolt before it hit Sara. This time he had saved her, and it was the real her. But they still had so much life left to live and they had been through so much. Who would take care of Sara and protect her? His mind fought the overwhelming urge to stop fighting, and the panic and pain began to rise up again. Then it hit him. Elder-44 had the antidote but had thrown it in the marsh grass. He fought to tell them, but no words would come out. He could not even move his eyes and give them a hint or communicate in any way. Sara's desperate eyes met his. "There is antidote somewhere!" she screamed. "Where is it!!"

"Wait!" Jess yelled. "We saw the elder up the street throw his vials into the marsh grass on the other block! Keep doing CPR!" he blurted as he broke into a full-on sprint. Maria tore off behind him.

After blowing air into Kid's lungs, Sara again made eye contact and held it. "Don't you dare leave me, Kid," she said. "They are grabbing the antidote right now. Just hold on."

Running to the base of the footbridge at the creek, Jess tried to focus as he turned around and cased out the row of houses along the water. "Which one, which one," he said as Maria and the general came to his side.

The general checked his watch. "Over one and a half minutes already."

Jess spotted the rooster weathervane atop a shed. "This way!"

He dashed over to the field of marsh grass next to the shed, got on his knees and started searching. Maria and the general did the same. The task seemed impossible. At the ground level, the grass was intertwined and thick. Jess was looking for a needle, but in a marsh grass field rather than a haystack. Panic was setting in with every passing second.

"Come on," Jess snarled as he continued searching. Getting frustrated, he started swatting the stalks of grass.

"Wait! Don't move!" Maria yelled as she scrambled over.

She separated some intertwined reeds at the ground level and then screamed. She grabbed two vials lying side by side and handed them to Jess. He sprinted faster than he ever had in his life back to Kid's body. He slid on his knees, uncapped a vial, and stuck Kid in the thigh.

After Kid was given the antidote, Sara continued mouth-to-mouth while Marissa did chest compressions.

"Come on, Kid, please." As the seconds passed, Sara's anxiety increased. Between breaths, she fought breaking down in tears.

Her father approached and checked his watch. “Four minutes.”

“Please don’t leave me, Kid.” Sara turned, “Dad…we need to use a second vial!”

“Two vials would be deadly.”

“He’s already there!” she barked.

“Alright. Just a quick prick. Let me have it.” The general took the vial, uncapped it, and barely poked Kid’s leg. “Hopefully it didn’t unload the entire dose.”

While breathing into Kid’s lungs, Sara snapped her head up as his body jerked. She could not tell if he had taken a breath. With everything she had, she placed her lips against his and blew deeply. At that moment, she would have let her own life slip out of her mouth for him to live. A slight gasp escaped Kid’s throat.

“Come on,” the general urged.

Another gasp left Kid’s throat, this time stronger.

“It’s working!” Karen called out and put her hands together, as if praying.

“Come back, Kid. We need you. *I* need you,” Sara said and blew into his lungs. Her tears rolled down her cheek and onto his.

All of sudden, Kid’s arms shot up and shook spastically. He gasped like a person with food lodged in his throat. He brought his hands to his neck and his eyes went wide. He was trying to take in air, but was struggling mightily. Despite his wild movements, Sara locked her lips on his and blew warm breath down his throat. His arms flailed, but he did not push her away. As Kid began to breath on his own, Sara held his head and laid him down. The first word out of his mouth was, “Pain.”

Marissa stepped in and checked his vitals. “He’s not out of the woods yet. Not by a long shot. He needs oxygen. Is there a drug store close by? They usually have small oxygen canisters.”

“Just up the road on Route 72. I got it.” Jess took off in a sprint. A few seconds later he grunted when his foot slipped on something in the slushy road.

Sara looked up as Jess scooped a map off the ground. As he continued on, he shook the snow off the paper and stuck it in his back pocket.

"Careful. And watch out for Heidi or any members coming over the bridge," the general called after him. Jess waved his hand as he accelerated.

Heidi ran up the arch of the bridge. She had tears streaming down her face as she yelled, "No! No!!" She was aiming at Sara and the shot was dead on. That bitch was about to go down once and for all. What the hell was Kid doing there? He should have been captured up at Water Street restaurant. Heidi stopped as she saw Kid's body on the ground in the distance through a gap between houses. "We weren't aiming at you!" she screamed. Then Kid's arms shot up in the air and quickly dropped. Even though she was panting, Heidi's breathing stopped for a second and she grabbed the rail topping the sidewall of the bridge. She dropped to her knees and uttered, "He survived."

Hurry Jess! Sara begged.

Jess returned just in time with two small oxygen canisters, as Kid was still without the strength to breathe on his own and needed regular breaths of life from Sara. Marissa made quick work in opening the valve and putting the plastic oxygen mask over Kid's mouth. As his breaths became stronger, his body started shaking.

Sara caressed his face briskly.

"Feeling is coming back. We need to get him warm," Marissa said.

The general took off his coat and handed it down to her.

While draping it across his upper body and neck, Marissa asked Kid, "Can you move any of your extremities?"

He was only able to raise his hand a couple of inches off the ground and then it fell back down.

The general turned to Jess. "Where did Heidi go?"

“I saw her running over the Route 72 bridge toward Long Beach Island.”

“Before she comes back with reinforcements, we had better get out of here.”

“I’ll go get the box truck,” Jess said and took off again in a sprint.

The general turned to Maria. “Go back over to the next block and tell the others we’ll pick them up in a minute. And please grab my computer bag from behind the car.”

Maria nodded and also took off.

“Stay with me, Kid. I’m right here,” Sara said as she held the oxygen canister in place.

With his head resting in her lap, Kid made eye contact. He whispered as he strained to smile.

Sara leaned down. “What?”

He pushed the oxygen mask to the side and whispered again, “I caught it.”

“Caught what?”

“The shot that was going to hit you. This time I caught it.”

“Well, I guess we should be thankful you had a practice run with the other me.” She tried to laugh but began crying instead.

CHAPTER 53

January 9, 2045
Monday, Morning
Bayville, New Jersey
Fourteen days after the event

The next morning, Sara stood looking out a second-story window of the building Kid's group called simply, 'RPH.' Although the 'Fresh Catch' truck had wreaked of fish for the ride from Mallard Island, they had been able to secure fresh clothes, food and even another telescope after casing out several of the houses in the area. Given the RPH building was a convalescent center, they had a substantial supply of body wipes for patients who were bedridden, so Sara felt clean and refreshed. As she stared at a golf course in the distance, she caressed the now-sanitized and spotless arrowhead locket that dangled around her neck. The picture inside was damaged, but Kid's face was still recognizable. The photo, much like the subject, had barely survived. She peered back at Kid who was still in bed sleeping. She prayed he did not have any brain damage from his near-death experience. His body had been starved of oxygen for several minutes.

So many thoughts were running through Sara's mind at once. After all they had been through she had almost lost Kid, again, at Mallard Island. A shiver ran down her spine. She couldn't deny she still had some lingering resentment toward her father for putting Kid, as well as the others, at risk when escaping from the ships. She understood what her dad did and why, and that his priority was to save his daughter. But what her father did not understand was Kid was truly her soulmate, and she would have rather died with him then live without him.

And how much of what had gone on was premeditated on her father's part, and in accordance with a plan of which she was completely unaware?

Kid woke up groggy, sore, and disoriented. For a moment he did not know where he was but saw Sara standing by a window. The sun bathed the room in bright light, so he went to cover his eyes and noticed his hand was wrapped with a bandage. He tried to sit up in bed and as soon as he moved he knew he was going to vomit. He groaned as his stomach contracted. He tried to roll over, but could only turn his head. "Sara?" he whispered.

She turned upon hearing him and rushed over. She seemed ready for this as she grabbed a waste basket from next to the bed and held it to his face. Sara braced him by holding his shoulder. "I'm sorry. Let loose. Marissa said this might happen."

With his head in the bucket, Kid tried to heave. He wanted to let it out and push the wave of nausea along, but it was tough going. Every time he got a small burst of energy to allow for a good launch, he would seize up from the pain. He hurt everywhere. Besides one good splattering expulsion, for the most part he wound up spitting and drooling into the bucket. After a few minutes, and sick of smelling his own vomit, he said, "I'm done."

Running out of the room with the bucket, Sara came back with a clean waste basket and antibacterial body wipes. She cleaned Kid's face and repositioned his pillow. She held a bottle of water to his mouth. "Rest, you need it. Do you know where you are? Do you recall anything?"

He had a faint recollection of the group heading to the gothic eight-story convalescent center in Bayville. He remembered the truck smelling like a fish factory and changing into new clothes when they got to RPH, but after that, exhaustion had knocked him out. "I know where we are. Was the building empty like it was supposed to be?"

"Yes. Jess thinks if the destruction had happened a week later, the building would have been full of patients."

"It would have been a mess. What floor are we on?" he asked.

"Second floor. We are all staying on this floor, but the rooms throughout the building have new beds, with sheets and blankets still unopened in the packaging."

Kid repositioned himself and Sara reached for the bucket. "No, I'm fine. The wave passed," he assured her. "Who is keeping watch or standing guard?" His first concern was for the safety of the group.

"We've got it covered. Clarence is guarding the front door, which is securely locked, and Jess is on the eighth floor keeping watch. Jess said that from the roof, he could actually see all the way to the ocean with a telescope. Now stay still, please, and just rest." She walked across the room and looked closely at the fancy engraved lettering on the back of the doorknob.

Kid gritted his teeth and propped himself so he was sitting up in bed. He succeeded in doing so without groaning from the pain that came with every move he made. His movement still made him dizzy, but not nauseous. Lucky for him. He would never be able to reach the bucket in time.

He felt awful, but he was thankful to be alive. When he was lying on the ground after being shot, the fuzzy edges had started to close in, but his focus would not leave the point of light in the middle. He was ready to fight to the end until the darkness overcame him. Sara's voice was a distant echo, but through that point of light, he could see her face. He struggled with every last ounce of his will to maintain the connection to her. The point of light started to open wider. Her voice was closer and clearer. 'We need you. *I* need you…' He couldn't let her down. He had fought, and survived, for the both of them. He shuddered as he realized he had placed one foot inside the threshold of death's door, but was somehow able to pull it back. Most people could not.

As Sara turned and saw him sitting up in bed, she cocked an eyebrow in disapproval. "Comfortable?"

"Yes, much better." He tried to grin, but it hurt. "How long was I frozen?"

"Over four minutes, but thankfully I'm not seeing any signs of permanent damage. You are pretty banged up, but your mind seems with it so far. I was so worried that last night I prayed for you for hours." She pointed at the three letters engraved in script on the brass doorknob. "RPH. That's your nickname for this place. What does that mean?"

"Royal Pines Hotel," Kid responded.

"This building was a hotel?"

"Yes, originally, and an upscale one."

"That explains the fancy floor in the lobby area and the decorative ceiling and chandeliers in the dining hall, and of course," she tapped the doorknob with her finger, "the incredible brass finishes. Not what you would expect to see in a 'health and rehabilitation center.' I could see it as a hotel, given the architecture and sheer size, but the building stands out in this part of New Jersey. When was it built?"

"In the 1920's, as part of the Pinewald Project, which went bankrupt around the time of the Great Depression. It was part of a luxury resort. There was a 36-hole golf course and…a manmade lake out back behind the separate boathouse," Kid huffed, as if he had just run up a flight of stairs.

"I saw a sign on the outside designating the building as a bomb shelter. It must be well-built," she noted as she walked over.

"That's because it is a brick building, built with walls within walls. That's why it's still solid enough to be a bomb shelter more than 100 years later."

"Walls within walls? And it was built around the time of prohibition? Are there hidden passages in here?" Sara asked. "I saw a television show once about some building with double walls and there were secret passages everywhere."

“The story is that this was originally built as a mobster hotel, and one of the safety features for high-profile guests were the escape passages within the walls and through the tunnels under the hotel. They say Al Capone stayed here.” Kid took a few breaths.

“There are tunnels under this building?”

“So they say. And under the boathouse and the lake as well, heading east and south away from the building. They had found some evidence to support that claim.”

“Under the lake? That seems precarious.”

“I know, and that is where all the tunnels supposedly met, like a central hub.”

“Interesting.” She sat on the bed next to him. “You’re getting winded, but your brain seems as sharp as ever.”

“That’s not a real high bar,” he said.

“And you haven’t lost your sarcasm either. That’s a good sign.”

Kid felt like he was being studied. “I have a headache, but I’m thinking straight. Is this history lesson a test for me?”

“Maybe. I don’t know the history, so you could be talking complete nonsense for all I know.”

“Jess could confirm,” he noted.

“No need.”

“So, I passed?”

She kissed his forehead and smiled. “With flying colors.”

After helping Kid down the stairs to the first floor, one step at a time, Sara eased him into a wheelchair. She pushed him to the large, ornate dining room, where the group was having breakfast. She kissed Kid on the cheek and turned through the doorway. His eyes gravitated upward as the first thing he noticed were the exposed heavy wood rafters and the rows of gothic-looking, tarnished metal chandeliers.

“It lives!” Jess called out as he raised a hand.

Everyone stopped and turned. Suddenly, the entire room broke into applause.

Kid was stunned as he glanced around. He felt like a celebrity for a moment as he waved. "Why are you clapping?" He was a little embarrassed by the attention.

"Just the fact you have to ask shows you are too humble," Evelyn stated.

General Hyland added, "Besides the fact you out Elder-2 and the entire group of members at the bridge, you helped eliminate Elder-44, and you gave your own life to save my daughter, I guess you didn't do much." In a rare moment, the general displayed an unguarded smile as he came over and shook Kid's hand.

"And you were instrumental in erasing Karen's living nightmare, Sid Sherman, from this planet," Chris said.

Wendy tacked on, "And his brother, Scott."

"I didn't do any of that alone. Everyone helped." For a second, Kid felt like he was 16-years-old again at the scout summer camp where the two derelicts had gone on a rampage with hunting knives. He had the same feeling of discomfort and conflict now, but wasn't sure why. "Trust me, I'm no hero," he said, with almost too much assurance. "Anyway, enough of the pomp and circumstance. Please, eat."

Maria came over and rubbed his shoulders. "Hey Mr. Walking-Dead, are you up for some food? You're not craving human flesh now are you?"

"Give me your hand to nibble on and we'll find out."

Bending down, she whispered, "Listen Zombie-Boy, how about you start with my ass, and we'll go from there?"

A smile came to his face.

Maria gave his shoulder a gentle squeeze. "You sure seem like your usual smartass self. We were worried after how long your heart had stopped. Let's get you some food."

"What is on the menu?" he asked.

"Oatmeal. 801 cooked it by himself. He's starting to have a mind of his own, especially when it comes to food."

"Well, it's progress." Kid's nostrils flared. "What do I smell? Is that…maple?"

"Yes," Maria started. "We are adding it to our oatmeal. I'm glad we did. I could tell my blood sugar was getting low. But I'll tell you, these people from Vermont love their maple syrup," she said and they both chuckled. Her smile disappeared and her expression turned serious. "Real maple syrup…" They both knew whose words she was repeating.

Drex.

CHAPTER 54

January 9, 2045
Monday, Morning
Bayville, New Jersey
Fourteen days after the event

Kid exhaled and looked down for a moment. "Did you bring Drex's body back so we could have a funeral for him?"

"We couldn't. We had to get out of there before more soldiers came." She lowered her voice to a whisper. "We had to leave James's body too."

At that moment, although Kid did not have the strength to yell, he waved his hands and got everyone's attention. The room went silent.

"We unfortunately lost some great people yesterday, and I'm sorry. James. Mr. Drexer. The Ryan family. Can we honor them with a moment of silence?"

Everyone bowed their head and remained silent for more than a minute.

Kid raised his head and brought the moment to a close. "They will always be with us."

"Thanks for doing that, Kid. I'll go get you some food," Maria said she wiped the tears from her cheek.

A minute later, Maria came back holding a steaming bowl of oatmeal with warm maple syrup drizzled across the top. Kid inhaled and took in the sweet smell. As he started eating, he turned to the general. "So, what did I miss? What is the plan?"

"For now, our only plan is to rest and recover for a few days," the general responded. "I don't know if everyone realizes how close to extinction humanity was back at Mallard Island. The battle was all but over until you and Jess came and turned the tide."

"Maybe now we'll get a reprieve and they will leave us be and focus on their base camp," Dr. McDermott said in his Irish accent while adjusting his glued and repaired octagonal glasses. Seeing the look on the general's face, the doctor added, "Maybe not, based on your expression?"

"I'm afraid not. I think we're safe for a few days, but with Elder-2 now gone, that leaves Elder-3, in charge. Since the very beginning of the project he has been the most hostile member of the Board of Elders. But his true colors really showed in the week leading up to the destruction, and even after. Most of the other board members accepted and supported what needed to be done, but Elder-3 actually seemed to enjoy all of the death and destruction. And he was beside himself as to how a small group of survivors could win battles against trained and physically superior members. They will continue setting up the base camp, but trust me when I tell you, with him in charge, killing off any and all survivors will remain a primary mission."

"Dad, speaking of the beginning of the project, when I was on the ships, Elder-1 told me the Utopia Project really started as a continuation of that old CCP program…" Sara said. Dr. McDermott cast a questioning glance, so she clarified, "the Child Conditioning Program, that was shut down in 2025?"

The doctor said, "After the death of Anna Delilah and the birth of the CCP's Baby Doe?"

Sara nodded.

"I've heard the story more times than I can count."

The general exhaled. "Yes, it is true the Utopia Project was born from the ashes of the CCP."

Sara sat in silence contemplating. Kid wondered what she was thinking.

The general continued, “So Elder-3 will be a problem. The only good news is Elder-1 and Elder-2 are out of the picture now. If we can take out Elder-3 and some more key elders, I think the core power of their group will be seriously weakened. I think they will begin to come undone and will become quickly fragmented, which could work to our advantage.”

“I guess we need an attack strategy?” Kid asked. “We’ve been on the defensive the whole time. When are we going on the offensive? We have a society to infiltrate.”

“I don’t think you’re in any position to attack anything.”

“Except that oatmeal,” Maria interjected. “Don’t make me come over there and force-feed you.”

“But we’re working on it,” the general finished and then stood to speak to the whole group. “Before we make any plans, we should give everyone the opportunity to leave if you want to. Remember, I knocked out the satellites. Without eyes in the sky, it would make hiding out easy. You could go anywhere in the world you want to go. So, if anyone here wants to take off, we would not look down upon you.”

He peered around the room. Everyone murmured to the negative, but his eyes settled on Melanie, who was wearing a headband to hold a bandage over the cut on her head. She did not hesitate to answer. “Me and my girls are not going anywhere. With the satellite system eliminated, we’ve overcome what you said was the most major hurdle, right?”

“That is true,” the general agreed.

“Anyway, we’re in this together now. We are like a family here. Not to mention, you have a great doctor and a great nurse in the group, which comes in handy, especially after you get clocked by a heavy vase.” Melanie nodded to Dr. McDermott and Marissa. “So, no, we are not leaving. I just hope we can protect ourselves.”

“We need more weapons and ammo,” Jess noted.

“We definitely need to restock.” The general leaned back in his chair. “That brings us to our next hurdle anyway, the Joint Base. For a few reasons, we need to get over there before they do. First, to get more weapons and ammunition. Second, I want to secure an M3 Transport. And third, so we can disable or destroy any weapons and transports we don't take so they can't be used against us."

Chris turned to his son. "An M3? Can you pilot one?"

"I know most of the controls. Anyway, I understand we have a licensed pilot in our midst."

They all again turned to Melanie. After coaxing Katy and Karly to eat their oatmeal, she looked up and shook her head. "Listen, I'm happy to be with you all, but I don't think so. I learned to fly small planes, not high-tech military aircraft."

"The principles of flight are fairly universal," the general offered. "But we can cross that bridge when we get there."

Now done with his food, Kid glanced around the table. Seeing Karen, he smiled and waved. She was sitting in a chair with her face black and blue, but she was alive. Kid felt relief, and even hope. She was an inspiration to them all. "Can we go over by Karen and see how she's making out?"

Sara wheeled Kid over and despite the protests from his aching body, he leaned over and kissed Karen on the cheek. "You may be the only person here in worse shape than me."

"I'll survive," Karen responded.

"I have to say, you are one seriously tough girl," Kid added, and he meant it. He then noticed a patch of her hair was missing and her scalp looked raw.

Sara kissed her other cheek. She gently brushed the purple highlighted hair from Karen's face and made eye contact. "We know you will survive, sis. We'll make sure of it."

Karen's lips pursed and she waved her hand. "Thanks, but stop before this 'tough girl' starts crying."

Kid gently touched her arm. "So how bad do you feel this morning?"

"I feel rough, but it could be worse, much worse. I don't know where I'd be without Doc McDermott and Marissa either," Karen acknowledged. "They had a busy evening tending to the wounded, between me, you and Melanie."

"And I don't know where we would be if we didn't find that tunnel in the basement, which led to a storage building full of medical supplies," Dr. McDermott chimed in.

Kid and Sara's eyes met.

Turning to the doctor, Kid asked, "You found an old tunnel?"

"Yes. It runs underground to that building across the entrance road, which they are using for storage. Jess said it used to be a boathouse. But the tunnel didn't seem old. Actually, the concrete looked fresh."

"The tunnels have supposedly been there since the building was constructed in the 1920's. I guess they refurbished that one," Kid speculated.

"Tunnels? Plural?" Dr. Mc Dermott raised his eyebrows.

"Doc, ask Kid later about the history of this building. It is pretty interesting," Sara noted.

"801, can you pass me the syrup?" Jess was focused on his bowl of oatmeal.

"Can we give him a real name instead of calling him by a number?" Maria asked. "It's no wonder he slipped back at the mermaid house. We still treat him like he is one of them."

The general sat forward at the table. "There may be some truth in that."

"So," Jess started as he turned to 801, "we want to call you by a name, not a number. What name do you want? The choice is yours."

After contemplating for a second, 801 made his choice. "Romeo."

Everyone burst out laughing. Jess walked over and put his arm around his shoulder and shook him a little. "Perfect."

801 sat stone-faced, unsure why everyone was laughing. Maria told him it was humor.

This is, 'humor,' 801 thought as the others laughed. He did not understand what the name Romeo had to do with humor. Maria had said the real Romeo touched many women. 801 had touched many women, so the name Romeo made sense.

Jess smiled as 801 said, "The name Romeo now brings humor and makes you happy. When you first called me Romeo, the name brought…anger."

Maria smirked. "Yeah, he didn't see the humor at that moment, but he's over it now."

"We do not fully understand how this humor works."

"Don't worry about it. You'll make a good Romeo," Maria concluded. "Unlike my heathen," She made a face at Jess, who had returned to his seat and was sticking an overflowing spoonful of oatmeal into his mouth. "But I can't help but love him."

Jess groaned.

Becoming more serious, the general said, "With how quickly 801, Romeo, relapsed, it reminded me just how effective and deeply rooted their conditioning really is."

"How do we fix that?" Kid asked.

"We need to develop a program to extricate the deepest part of the conditioning, especially if we are able to capture some or all of the members. I am hoping to soon have with us the foremost expert in conditioning, someone who can help reverse its effects. She was the lead project psychologist, responsible for the conditioning on the ships," the general stated.

Kid looked curious. "So she is on the ships?"

"No, she escaped before the destruction, and she is supposed to be in the third area left unscathed by the satellites." Off the cuff, he added, "Assuming she survived."

"Where is the third area?"

A silence fell about the room and everyone turned to the general.

"Italy," he finally responded. "Off of the Sorrento Peninsula."

"How are we going to get somebody from overseas?" Kid asked.

The general answered, "If we can get to the Joint Base and secure an M3 Transport, we could be over and back in just a few hours."

Sara seemed confounded. "Dad, you were behind the 'malfunctions,' and you used the third and last one to save a...project psychologist in Italy?"

"Not just a project psychologist. She was *the* Utopia Project psychologist in charge for more than 15 years, but she is more than that." The general stood.

Cocking an eyebrow, Sara seemed to be onto something. "So what is this woman's name?"

"Dr. Carmelo."

With a knowing look, Sara shook her head.

Putting his hand on his daughter's shoulder, he added, "Yes. Your Aunt Adele. She is known professionally as Dr. Carmelo."

Sara appeared both relieved and disturbed. "Don't take me wrong, I would be so thankful if she survived, but I'm just in a bit of shock. First I find out you were involved with the Utopia Project for years, and now Aunt Adele? Who next, Gram and Gramps?"

Kid could tell Sara was less than pleased.

The general tried to laugh it off, but Sara's eyebrows were pinched and her gaze was steadfast. She was not laughing as she got up and walked away.

CHAPTER 55

January 9, 2045
Monday, Evening
Bayville, New Jersey
Fourteen days after the event

Throughout the day Monday, Kid's strength picked up. He was determined to recover quickly. By midmorning, he was out of his wheelchair and walking on his own. After a short early-afternoon nap, he jogged up and down the hall and ran some stairs to regain his stamina. He tired quicker than usual and every single muscle in his body was sore, but he felt like he was well on the road to recovery. It was a miracle he had no apparent lasting effects, physical or mental, from his heart not beating for more than four minutes.

As night fell so did the temperature. Kid and Sara used a flashlight and took a slow walk up the chilly stairwell. They wanted to check on Maria and Jess, who were keeping watch on the eighth floor. They reached the door of the lookout room, which was about halfway up the hall, and Sara said, "Knock, knock. Are you two decent?"

"For a change?" Kid added.

"We're dressed. I don't know about the *decent* part," Maria quipped. She and Jess were sitting on a couch together, with it angled so they could watch southeast out the window. They were both sharing a blanket and were basking in the reddish glow of the propane heater sitting in front of them.

"Kid, if you can withstand the cold and wind, you should check out the roof of this place," Jess suggested. "It's like being up in the battlements of a castle from the Middle Ages. The view is unbelievable. And I have a telescope up there so we can keep an eye on the ships in the distance. I found it last night when we cased out the houses up the road, and it's better than the one we had at the mermaid house."

"Maybe later," Kid said.

"Then grab a seat," Maria offered as she nudged Jess. "If couch-hog here would move over."

"I'm moving, I'm moving," Jess mumbled.

Sara sat. "What was going on down here in the woods of central New Jersey that inspired them to build a fortress like this building?"

Kid squeezed next to her. "Prohibition? Organized crime?"

Maria threw the blanket across their guests. "If they thought this area was desolate then, they should see it now," she noted.

Sara nestled against Kid's chest and peered out the window. "The stars and the moon seem so…bright."

Kid responded, "That's because, for a change, there is no competing light."

They all sat entranced for several minutes. Kid absorbed the stillness. He needed it to refresh himself and regain his mental strength. It was also a time of reflection. He had endured a vicious emotional roller coaster ride over the past several days. He felt sadness at the loss of Drex, James and the Ryans; and although she wasn't dead, Heidi as well.

But he was also thankful. Sara was very much alive and he no longer felt the sickening emptiness that had plagued him from the moment he thought she was gone. He was also grateful most of his friends had survived despite nearly insurmountable odds at every juncture. It was nothing short of miraculous.

It struck Kid that he and his friends had lived several lifetimes in the span of mere weeks. This was not the typical life of young adults. At the same time, he knew their lives would now be anything but typical. The world they knew was gone and every day would have its own risks, struggles, stresses, and accomplishments. Kid, and most of the others, used to struggle for prosperity because the basics were always covered. Now, they struggled for survival each and every day. The bar had moved.

Kid finally broke the silence. "You know, I can't figure out how the soldiers and Heidi found the group on Mallard Island."

Jess looked over at Sara. "You didn't tell him, did you?"

"Not yet," she answered. "I was going to tonight."

"Tell me what?" Kid asked.

"Move over Maria, so I can reach my back pocket." Jess said and struggled to pull something out.

In the darkness, Kid heard a familiar crinkling sound. His body tensed and his eyes opened wide. "What is that sound? I've heard it before."

"It is our lost map," Jess said and handed it over to him.

"Where did you get it?" Kid asked.

"Heidi had it. When she made a break for the Route 72 bridge she left it on the ground. You would have seen it, but you were kicking back, taking a rest."

Maria smacked Jess's arm.

Kid did not smile, as he felt a growing sense of dread.

Maria added, "Open it up. Mallard Island is circled, so they knew exactly where we were and that's how they were able to ambush us. I guess Heidi must have taken the map when she stormed out on us at Water Street."

Unfolding the map and hearing the same crinkling sound, Kid had a sudden and painful realization. He knew why it was ringing a bell and he cringed. "Son of a bitch," he muttered.

"What is it?" Sara asked.

"Heidi didn't take the map when she stormed out on us. She found it behind the bar at Water Street. Actually, she went right to the bar, like she knew it was there. Remember that Jess?"

"I remember her running over there, yes."

"I heard her folding something, but didn't know what it was," Kid said. He cursed himself for not watching Heidi close enough, or following up on the odd crinkling noise he had heard. He should have known something was up, especially when she was crouched behind the bar forever looking for a glass when there were glasses galore.

"Heidi went to the Water Street Grill yesterday?" Sara looked surprised. "Before they attacked us down here?"

Kid stared at her. "Jess didn't fill you in on everything that happened?"

They both turned to Jess, who said, "No." After Maria smacked Jess's arm, he said, "Sorry. Maybe I wanted to forget."

"Does anyone communicate around here?" Maria sounded exasperated.

In a somber voice, Kid shook his head and explained. "Yesterday morning, Heidi and the group of soldiers came to search Water Street. Jess and I were inside the restaurant when they showed up, so we hid."

Maria then had a realization herself. "Wait a minute. It all makes sense now. When the soldiers came down to Mallard Island, one of their vehicles was yours!"

"Yes, they stole it from us," Jess acknowledged.

Maria sat forward on the couch. "You guys knew Heidi and the soldiers were searching the mainland? Why didn't you radio down and warn us?" she asked. "Or hustle back to Mallard Island before they got there?"

Jess cleared his throat. "Let's just say we were stone-walled and deceived big-time and leave it at that." Kid knew that despite the fact Jess could have stood and screamed, 'I told him so,' he was making a noble effort to protect his longtime friend.

"We're not going to leave it at that," Maria said definitively. "You guys better fill in the blanks and quick."

Kid could see by the cocked eyebrows that Sara and Maria were eager to pepper him with questions. He loved them both, but knew they would not let up until it all made sense. There were still missing pieces of the puzzle, pieces that were necessary for the picture to come into focus.

It was time for Kid to put the cards on the table. He started, "None of this was Jess's doing. It was mine. Here's what happened. Heidi must have found the map behind the bar..."

"The one place we never thought to look," Jess grumbled.

"...and after grabbing it, she took our walkie-talkies and our vehicle, and then lied to delay us by two hours before we came down south," he stated. "That's how we were stone-walled and deceived."

"I thought you said y'all were hidden?" Sara asked. "Heidi found you?"

Pausing, Kid said resignedly, "No."

Jess exhaled and let out a slow rolling groan. "Game over," he mumbled into his hands.

Kid continued, "I came out of hiding to confront her when the soldiers left for a few minutes and she was alone."

Sara's gaze hardened. "So you left the safety of a hiding spot, putting yourself at risk, to talk to her?" Her next question sent a chill up his spine. He could hear the words before they even left her mouth, knowing the conversational path had become a slippery slope toward the fiery pits of Hell. Sara's tone had an undercurrent of incredulousness, and the question was simple, but heavy. "Why?"

Kid stood and put his hands on his hips. Sara had zeroed in on the heart, or rather, the crux, of the issue. The question of why Kid had confronted Heidi hung in the air until he answered, "Why? For what I thought, at the time, were the right reasons. I was trying to get her to come back."

Sara seemed to be contemplating as she leaned on the arm of the couch.

"Come back?" Maria sounded flustered. "You couldn't see she had fallen off the deep end? That she had lost it? Everyone could see the girl had completely given herself to the side of evil and was already gone. Were you that oblivious?"

"In fairness," Jess chimed in, "it wasn't until that day we saw just how evil she really was, and…" Turning toward Maria, the fire in her eyes silenced him in an instant.

Kid felt awash with agony. "How could I know what she was pulling?"

Maria moved to the edge of the couch and snapped, "You would've noticed if you had taken the blinders off!"

The revelation was disconcerting. With all of the drama the past day, and with him being shot dead and then being brought back to life, Kid had yet to connect all of the dots. He knew a part of him did not want to. It was such a wild sequence of events, but he knew the connected dots were not going to present a pretty picture.

Sara seemed exasperated. "Kid, she took advantage of your conscience and of the fact you always try to see the good in people. And look at what it led to. After finding the map she distracted you so they could ambush us on that island." Standing up, she added bluntly, "And she didn't drag you into her evil world. You stepped into it of your own volition. I'm still not sure why."

He knew that was the moment it all went wrong, the moment he decided to step out of hiding and try to convince Heidi to come back. His soft spot for her and his misplaced trust had caused a significant loss of life. He shuddered as he thought of the risk to his entire group. He never imagined Heidi could be so malicious. "It was an error in judgment on my part. Trust me, it would never happen that way again." His voice was sullen.

At that moment he understood the greater implication. He had not only put his group at risk, he had put the last remnants of humanity at risk. He lost his breath and had to steady himself by grabbing the doorway molding. He then felt hot with anger. *What the hell were you thinking?* he reprimanded himself. "I told you I was no hero," he said, repeating his words from breakfast that day.

Sara seemed lost in thought as she sat back down. He feared she was writing him off. Her fist rested in front of her mouth as she sat with her elbow on the arm of the couch. She would not even look at Kid.

He turned and walked toward the exit. He stopped at the doorway, which was a dark outline on a gray background, like an entranceway to the underworld. Lowering his head, he choose not to leave, but rather leaned against the door frame and faced the others. It was as if time was standing still as several minutes passed.

Sara was caressing the gold locket around her neck when she finally stood and walked over to him.

"I can explain why…" he started. As she gazed into his eyes, she seemed to be reading him, but not listening to him. He knew what she needed to see, and feel, that in reaching out for Heidi, his conscience was more his master than his heart.

"No need," Sara said as a gentle hush.

Like flicking a switch, he was suddenly sure she knew this. He felt it deep inside. Any concern he had about Sara misreading his intentions in reaching out to Heidi evaporated.

Sara took his hand. "I know whatever choices you made were for what you thought were the right reasons. You were trying to save her because you thought it was you who killed her spirit and her soul. The truth is, it was terminally cancerous before she ever turned her eyes your way." Pulling him closer and taking his other hand, she looked him straight in the eye and said with conviction, "Not to mention you have put yourself in harm's way so many times to save people. I don't know where we would be without you, so the word 'hero' certainly fits."

Jess added, "Sara's right. I mean, I know you screwed up, but she is right."

"Without you, we would be dead," Maria agreed. "See, now I feel bad. Sorry for getting so hostile with you, Kid."

He was touched by their faith in him. "It's alright. Thanks guys." Feeling a need for some mental closure, Kid stood. "On second thought I think I will go check out the view from the roof."

On top of the building Kid was numb to the cold and the beautiful sky that was open above his head. The constellations were clear, but just not registering. At that moment, surrounded by roof battlements, he was staring southeast toward Long Beach Island and the ships beyond. He swore Heidi would pay for the harm she had brought upon them all, and for using him to do it. He shuddered as he imagined how much more harm would have been done if Heidi had succeeded. He had given her the benefit of the doubt, and in return she had played him every step of the way. It was the ultimate betrayal. He now knew she was evil to the core and her soul was a well of pure poison.

He shivered as he also realized she would not rest until she had her revenge against him and Sara. He had never wished someone literally dead in his life like he did now with Heidi. Although he was still focused on their mission to take control of the 20,000 Utopia Project members and save what was left of humanity, taking out Heidi had become a priority mission for him on a very personal level. He would not live in fear for Sara and himself every day for the rest of his life.

Right then he sensed Sara was with him. He did not even flinch when she put her arm around his and stared up at the starry sky. Somehow he knew she understood exactly what he was tormenting about.

Sara said simply, "She will be back."

Kid put his arms around her and said with assurance, "But next time, I will be ready for her."

For several minutes they shared a firm embrace. While holding hands, he extended both of their arms toward the ground. Somewhere deep inside, his conscience bowed and conceded. "And I know she cannot be saved," he whispered as he extricated the malignant cancer-like soft spot he had for Heidi Leer.

Together they cast it out of his heart and soul and sent it back to Hell. There it would be reunited with the darkness from whence it came. He trembled and exhaled a heavy breath. As they lowered their arms, Kid's eyes met Sara's. Not another word needed to be said as they both looked up at the Orion star constellation in the sky.

The die was cast.

The collision course was set in stone harder and colder than an unnamed tombstone.

EPILOGUE

January 9, 2045
Monday, Evening
New Jersey coast, Utopia Project Ship Number One
Fourteen days after the event

Leaning on the deck rail of Utopia Project Ship Number One, Heidi Leer stared up at the Orion constellation. She tried to focus on the darkness between the stars comprising Orion's Belt, but her vision was clouded. Tears ran down her cheeks and the torrents were uncontrollable. The breeze slapped at her wet face, but the frigid air was counteracted by the burning of her anger.

Her plan was perfect. Kid was to stay at Water Street for two hours. The map she found behind the bar, the one she herself had crumbled and tossed there, had the location of the survivor's home base circled. She thought it would be a quick and deadly ambush. After, she would have gone back with the group who were rounding up the four members they left behind at Water Street. She would kill them all and save Kid, and maybe Jess. She would've cried to Kid that she was really working for the survivors all the while, and she tried to prevent the massacre at Mallard Island, but failed. And then she would've taken Kid to Mallard Island to see the carnage for himself, which hopefully would include Sara's dead body. And then Heidi could have spent the rest of her life together with Kid. The plan was perfect; absolutely fucking perfect. Where did it go wrong?

First, the survivors withstood the ambush far better than they should have. Second, the members left at Water Street did not do their job and capture Kid and Jess, and it was those two who turned the tide and saved the entire survivor group at Mallard Island. Figures.

And just her luck, Kid miraculously appears right as Heidi is about to kill Sara. Of course he saves her, and survives, making their bond even more unbreakable. Despite the sharp sting, she bit down on her swollen lower lip.

She felt a desperate and uncontrollable urge to slay Sara for owning Kid's heart. The bitch needed to feel Heidi's wrath, and her pain. Kid was the one man who had reciprocated and showed Heidi true, unconditional love. She had given all of herself, without holding anything back. She knew somewhere inside Kid was a place that was hers. Even if just a part of him, it represented all of her. She could not bear the thought that her part would be smothered and snuffed out by the love he had for Sara. And to think she actually knelt at, what she thought was, that bitch's grave! If only the real Sara had been the one buried in the ground at Ironside cabin!

Heidi's last chance was the possibility that Kid's seed would find a waiting egg. She desperately hoped their one night in Vermont would be the first non-Utopia Project pregnancy of this new world. If she was Eve, Kid could not deny being Adam. Kid would have no choice but to take Heidi, but only if Sara was no longer in the picture. That is why eliminating Sara and the survivors needed to remain a top and immediate priority.

Heidi exhaled and closed her eyes for a few seconds. She so desperately wanted to be pregnant, and needed to be pregnant, that despite being due for her period, she could not bring herself to use any feminine hygiene products or protections whatsoever. Her last hope would bleed out and die with the rest of her, or would be fulfilled in one word.

Conception.

AUTHOR'S NOTES:

First and foremost, thank you for reading this book and for sharing in the Utopia Project series journey! As always, I am humbled and beyond appreciative.

Stay tuned! The story continues in the soon-to-be-released third and final book in the trilogy: **Utopia Project - The Arrow of Time**. After the hunt becomes even more intense, the small group of survivors will have no choice but to fight back. They will put their lives and humanity on the line in a winner-take-all, life or death offensive against the merciless Utopia Project forces. All the while, mysteries will unfold, secrets will be revealed, and the fate of humanity will be tied back to one incident from the past that altered the course of history.

To stay abreast of the release of the next installment, please check the utopiaproject.com website, follow us on Instagram (utopiaprojectseries) or Facebook (Utopia Project by Billy Dering).

Please, also consider posting a review of this second book: **Utopia Project - The Frayed Threads of Hope**. Such reviews provide invaluable feedback for the author as well as other potential readers! Thank you.

Made in United States
North Haven, CT
10 May 2023